A LITTLE HEATSTROKE

"Howdy, ma'am," the man said with a smile that practically obliterated the sunset. "I'm Will Haskins."

She knew he was real, but no man could look like that. It simply wasn't possible.

"I'm here to see about buying your bull," he said when she didn't respond.

How could she think about anything as mundane as selling a bull when she couldn't breathe?

"You did get my letter, didn't you? Did I get the day wrong? Isabelle says I never can keep things straight."

She had to think, to speak, to do something besides stand there staring at him like she was a stuffed dummy.

"Are you alright?" he asked. "I saw you out next to the hog pen when I rode up. Maybe you were in the heat too long."

"I am feeling a little dizzy." She was feeling so weak she was about to faint.

"Maybe you'd better sit down," he said, eying their small parlor. "Would you like some water?"

She had to get control of herself. She wasn't a silly girl who would fall speechless at the sight of a handsome man. Instead she was twenty, a woman of experience. There was no reason for her to act like a brainless ninny just because this man was twice as good looking as she'd ever thought possible.

Other books by Leigh Greenwood:

THE RELUCTANT BRIDE
THE INDEPENDENT BRIDE
COLORADO BRIDE
REBEL ENCHANTRESS
SCARLET SUNSET, SILVER NIGHTS
THE CAPTAIN'S CARESS
ARIZONA EMBRACE
SEDUCTIVE WAGER
SWEET TEMPTATION
WICKED WYOMING NIGHTS
WYOMING WILDFIRE

The Night Riders series:

TEXAS HOMECOMING
TEXAS BRIDE
BORN TO LOVE

The Cowboys series:

JAKE
WARD
BUCK
DREW
SEAN
CHET
MATT
PETE
LUKE
THE MAVERICKS
A TEXAN'S HONOR

The Seven Brides series:

ROSE
FERN
IRIS
LAUREL
DAISY

CRITICS ARE RAVING ABOUT LEIGH GREENWOOD!

"Leigh Greenwood continues to be a shining star of the genre!"

The Literary Times

"Leigh Greenwood remains one of the forces to be reckoned with in the Americana romance subgenre."

—Affaire de Coeur

"Greenwood's books are bound to become classics."

—Rendezvous

"Leigh Greenwood NEVER disappoints. The characters are finely drawn...always, always, a guaranteed good read!"

—Heartland Critiques

A TEXAN'S HONOR

"A delightful addition to the Cowboys series... Greenwood brings readers straight into the heart of the west and into his likable characters' lives with a charming, fast-paced and enjoyable read."

—RT BOOKreviews

THE MAVERICKS

"Fans of Greenwood's Cowboys series will be delighted with this latest installment. He delivers an action-packed story filled with tender moments."

—Fresh Fiction

THE RELUCTANT BRIDE

"Leigh Greenwood always provides one of the year's best Western romances, but his latest tale may be the best in an illustrious career. ...Once again Mr. Greenwood will have one of the subgenre top guns of 2005."

—Harriet Klausner

THE INDEPENDENT BRIDE

"Leigh Greenwood unfolds his Westerns like an artist.... Like his other books, *The Independent Bride* should be placed among the Western classics."

—Rendezvous

LEIGH GREENWOOD

Texas Tender

LEISURE BOOKS NEW YORK CITY

A LEISURE BOOK®

January 2007

Published by

Dorchester Publishing Co., Inc.
200 Madison Avenue
New York, NY 10016

ISBN 0-8439-5685-2

The name "Leisure Books" and the stylized "L" with design are
trademarks of Dorchester Publishing Co., Inc.

Printed in the United States of America.

Visit us on the web at www.dorchesterpub.com.

Texas Tender

Chapter One

Central Texas, 1886

Will Haskins slowed his mount to a walk as he approached the town of Dunmore. Most people would have said the small cluster of buildings bunched close together on the flat Texas plain was a poor excuse for a town. But to a man familiar with the tiny communities that dotted the Hill Country, it was just the right size—big enough to offer a choice of places to eat, drink, and entertain himself, but not so big he'd get lost on his way back to his hotel.

The grass-covered prairie soon changed to soft ground cut up by the hooves of hundreds of horses and the wheels of dozens of wagons and buggies. Will headed his horse toward the main street that bisected the town in a clean, straight line. Flies buzzed around horse droppings, a yellow dog lounging in the shade under a porch yawned sluggishly, and the few people out and about moved slowly because of the heat. Summer in central Texas could be downright brutal. Will was looking forward to finding a saloon or gambling establishment. Not that he gambled. Everyone agreed he wasn't stupid. Unfortunately, they all thought he was as shiftless as that yellow dog.

There was a reason he'd allowed himself to be saddled with such a reputation, but Will hadn't successfully explained it to anyone yet, not even his brother. His feelings of frustration, however, had continued to climb. Hell, he was twenty-eight. He might be the baby of the family, but he had been a grown man for ten years.

A young mother and her son caught his attention. While the young woman walked sedately along the edge of the beaten path, her son and his small dog dashed from one side of the street to the other—the boy throwing a stick, the dog catching it, and the boy chasing the dog to pry the stick away so he could throw it again. Will was so caught up in watching the play that he nearly didn't notice the sound of a horse approaching at a gallop. The boy ran to the protection of his mother, but the little brown-haired mongrel dog—thinking he was finally going to be allowed to keep the stick he'd chased so often—gamboled down the middle of the street, directly into the path of the horse and rider.

With no time to shout a warning or an explanation, Will dug his heels into his mount's sides. The powerful quarter horse was in a full gallop three jumps later. Despite being headed for a collision with the oncoming rider, Will didn't alter his course. Knowing he couldn't scoop up the dog without falling out of the saddle, he planned to put himself between the dog and the oncoming rider before the rider reached the dog, which had crouched down, frozen in fright at the sight of two horses hurtling toward him.

The two riders came together with the grunt of colliding horses, the squeak of leather, and curses from the other man, but Will's powerful quarter horse held his own against the tall, leggy bay gelding.

"What the hell do you mean by riding into me?" the other rider shouted. "Are you blind or just stupid?"

"Only a fool gallops a horse in town. Didn't you see that dog?" The little dog had recovered its courage and was scampering toward its owner.

"Nobody calls me a fool and gets away with it!" The man struggled to get his horse under control so he could draw his gun. By the time he had a hand free, Will was sitting calmly on his obedient mount, his rifle pointed at the man's belly.

"I don't think you want to do that," Will said quietly. "You might hit somebody by mistake."

The young man clearly hadn't bothered to notice that the woman and her son were in the direct line of fire. He stared at the rifle, rage twisting his handsome face into an ugly mask. "Get out of town," he growled. "If I find you in my way again, you might not be so lucky."

Uncowed by the young man's threat, Will replied, "I doubt there'll be any need to depend on luck."

Losing the struggle to control his horse, the man put him into a canter and headed toward the center of town. Will sheathed his rifle and rode over to the woman and her son.

Still in shock, the woman finally managed to pull herself together with a visible effort. "Thank you for saving Pepper," she said. "Lonnie would have been heartbroken if he had been killed."

Will dismounted and held out his hand to the little dog, who looked like a scruffy mongrel cross between a terrier and some kind of hound. Pepper dropped his stick and crawled over to Will, his tail wagging feverishly.

"You need to teach him to stay out of the way of horses," Will said to Lonnie.

"I shouldn't have let him play in the road." His mother still looked stunned.

"The young man shouldn't have been riding so fast in town."

"Van does what he wants. Nobody can stop him."

"Who is this Van, and why doesn't anyone stop him?"

"His father, Frank Sonnenberg, owns the second largest ranch in this area. Van thinks he can do anything he wants, and we don't have a sheriff to tell him different."

The little boy looked up at Will. "Who are you?"

"Lonnie, that's rude!" his mother said.

Will smiled as he mussed the boy's hair. Who *was* he? Hell, he didn't know. "My name is Will Haskins. I guess you could say I'm a cowboy."

"Mama says cowboys are mean."

His mother blushed, and Will couldn't repress a smile. "If Van is the only example you have, I can see why she thinks so."

"You're nice. You didn't let Van hurt Pepper."

"Just make sure he stays out of the road. Now, ma'am," he said turning to the woman, "where can I find a place to get out of the sun and have a drink?"

"We only have one respectable saloon," she said, frowning in disapproval. "The Swinging Door is just past the Gaiety Theater on the right. Come on, Lonnie. We ought to be getting home."

"Sorry, but I didn't catch your name," Will said.

She blushed again. "I don't know what happened to my manners. My name is Dorabelle Severns. My husband, Lloyd, is president of the bank."

"Nice to meet you, Mrs. Severns," Will said. "I

hope every lady in Dunmore is as nice and pretty as you are."

Dorabelle turned pink with pleasure. She turned crimson when Lonnie announced, "My daddy says Mama is beautiful."

"Your daddy is right," Will said as he mounted up. "And you're a handsome young man. I hope to see you again."

He tipped his hat and headed toward the center of town. He was less than pleased when he saw Van's bay gelding hitched in front of the Swinging Door. He'd had more than enough of that young man. He wanted to relax a bit before heading out to Idalou Ellsworth's ranch to buy the bull she had for sale.

He pulled up in front of the saloon, dismounted, hitched his horse, and walked through the swinging doors.

After squinting against the blazing sun for the last two hours, he felt as if he were entering a cave. By the time his eyes had adjusted, everybody in the saloon was staring at him. He guessed they didn't get many strangers in Dunmore. The saloon was large, roomy, and busy for so early in the afternoon. At least a dozen men had bellied up to the polished walnut bar, each with one foot resting on the brass foot rail. Three large mirrors set in a heavily carved walnut frame backed the bar and reflected the dim light from six kerosene lamps hanging from the ceiling. Will stepped up to the bar. "I'll have a beer if you don't mind," he told the bartender.

"You're new in town," the bartender said as he drew a beer from a keg behind the bar.

"Just rode in," Will said. "Glad to get out of the sun."

"Been hotter than hell all week," the bartender said.

Will slapped his money down, picked up his beer,

and was about to take a sip when a hand clamped down on his shoulder and spun him around.

His beer went sailing off between two tables to splash against the pant legs of the men sitting there. Will's right arm blocked the punch aimed at his jaw, while his left connected solidly with Van Sonnenberg's angry face. Before the young man could recover, Will landed a punch in his midriff and an uppercut to the jaw that lifted Van off the floor. Staggering back, Van fell into the table behind him.

Will straightened his vest and readjusted his coat. "Never try to sneak up on a man who's looking in a mirror." He turned back to the bartender. "I guess I need another beer. I'll pay for the first."

"Forget it," the bartender said, grinning at Van, who was having trouble finding his feet. "It was worth it to see somebody stand up to that brat."

"I guess his mama didn't teach him manners."

"His mama died when he was a little kid, and his daddy thinks he can do no wrong."

"I never met his daddy, but running down little dogs is wrong in my book."

"He kill somebody's dog?" One of the men at the table asked as he pushed Van away and got to his feet.

"He would have if I hadn't gotten in his way. Didn't apologize to Lonnie or his mother, either."

"You tried to run over Pepper?" the man demanded, turning to Van.

"How am I supposed to see anything that small?" Losing a fight he'd started hadn't improved Van's mood. "I'd be ashamed to have a dog that looked like that." He directed a hate-filled glare at Will. "I'm not done with you."

Will looked him straight in the eye. "Didn't I hit you hard enough?"

The laughter and grins all around made Van so mad

Will thought for a moment he might go for his gun. Instead, he turned and stormed out of the saloon.

"Watch your back," the bartender said to Will as he handed him his second beer. One of the customers handed him the unbroken glass. The spilled beer had already begun to soak into the soft wood of the floor.

"I'm Andy Davis," the man said to Will. "I own the mercantile here in Dunmore."

"Will Haskins. Glad to meet you."

"You passing through or planning to settle?" Andy asked.

"Just here to do a little business." Will took a swallow of beer. It wasn't too bad, but he'd certainly had better.

"Do you mind if I ask you what business that is?"

Just about anybody else in the Maxwell clan would have minded a lot, but Will figured everybody would soon know what he was doing here.

"I'm on my way to the Double-L ranch to talk to Miss Idalou Ellsworth about buying her bull."

Andy grinned broadly. "You better give him straight whiskey," he said turning to the bartender. "He's going to need something stronger than beer if he means to tangle with Idalou."

"What do you mean, you can't find the bull?" Idalou demanded of her brother. "Mr. Haskins is coming to look at him today."

"I mean I can't find him," Carl Ellsworth said. "We should have penned him up."

"He can't impregnate cows locked in a pen."

"Well, we can't sell a bull we don't have."

"We own him no matter where he is. We just have to locate him before Mr. Haskins gets here."

Idalou was six inches shorter than her brother's

even six feet, but that in no way affected her position as the older of the two and the one responsible for him as well as the ranch. Having the body of a man hadn't given Carl the emotions or reasoning ability of a man. If it had, he wouldn't have fallen in love with the only daughter of the man who was determined to destroy them.

"Do you have any suggestions?" Carl demanded angrily.

"Ride over to Jordan McGloughlin's place and tell him to show you where he hid our bull."

Carl's exasperation nearly got the best of him. "I know you don't like me having anything to do with Mara, but that's no reason to think her father has our bull."

"My thinking Jordan McGloughlin has the bull has nothing to do with you liking Mara, though I've got plenty to say on that score."

"I've already heard it," Carl snapped.

"It has to do with Jordan doing everything he can to force us to sell this ranch," Idalou said, ignoring her brother's comment. "He knows the money from the bull will tide us over for the next two or three years."

She had tried to talk her father out of mortgaging everything he owned to buy an expensive bull to upgrade his stock, but her father had decided it was the only way he could compete with the larger ranchers on either side of him, McGloughlin to the east and north and Sonnenberg to the west and south. His plan might have worked if Idalou's father and mother hadn't died three years ago.

"I want to keep the ranch as much as you do," Carl said, "but it doesn't help to have you accusing Mara's dad of everything bad that happens."

"I wouldn't blame him for trying to buy our ranch

if he weren't so underhanded about it," Idalou snapped. "I don't know how you can have anything to do with Mara. She's likely to turn out just like her father."

Carl grabbed his hat and jammed it on his head. "If you weren't blind when it comes to anybody named McGloughlin, you'd know Mara is the sweetest girl on the face of the earth," he shouted. "I can't help it if you were in love with Webb before he went and got himself killed."

Idalou bit her tongue to keep from saying something she'd have to apologize for later. "I've told you a hundred times I wasn't in love with Webb."

"You sure as hell acted like it until he took up with Junie Mae Winslow."

Webb had taken pride in being able to ride the toughest horses anyone could find. A fall from a rogue horse had ended up being fatal when his head hit a rock and he was knocked unconscious. He died a week later without ever waking up. His father hadn't been the same since.

"Try sweetening that temper of yours so you won't run Mr. Haskins off before I can get back," Carl said. "You don't have to tell me again how hard things have been since Mom and Dad died. I know all that. I also know you took it real hard when Webb turned his back on you. I know you're worried about the ranch, and you're worried about me falling in love with a girl who may never marry me. But," he added after taking a big breath, "you're never going to get a man to look at you twice if you don't stop treating them all like they're out to steal our last nickel." His frown eased and he smiled. "You're a great gal, Idalou. You'd make some man a wonderful wife if you'd give yourself a chance."

Carl took advantage of Idalou's momentary silence

to leave the house before she could launch her rebuttal. Jordan McGloughlin's cows had been straying onto their land, eating their grass, mating with their bull, drinking their water. Everybody knew longhorns were wild creatures that didn't understand the concept of ranch boundaries. However, Idalou was certain Jordan had instructed his hands to *encourage* his cows to wander onto Double-L land. It was all part of his campaign to force her to sell.

Idalou walked to the doorway of their small house and watched as her brother mounted up and rode off on his favorite pinto mare. He had the height and strength of a man, but she supposed she'd never stop thinking of him as a younger brother she needed to take care of. She didn't want to do anything to discourage him from growing into a confident adult, but he was too emotional, too willing to see good in others without noticing the bad as well. He worked as hard as she did to hold things together, but they both knew it would be a tough fight even with the money they'd get for the bull.

Their father had been a dreamer, and having his own ranch had always been his ambition. He'd gambled with the future of the family when he'd mortgaged the ranch to buy that bull. Idalou had thought it was too much of a gamble and had tried to talk him out of it, but her mother had sided with her husband.

"It's been his dream since before we got married," she'd told her daughter. "How could I possibly ask him to set it aside?"

Now Carl was gambling with his own future by falling in love with Mara McGloughlin. Everybody knew her father would never allow them to marry. Jordan McGloughlin had made it plain he wanted Mara to marry Van Sonnenberg. Combining the two spreads would create one of the biggest ranches in Texas. The Double-L ranch stood in the way of that ambition, just as Carl stood in the way of Mara's marriage to Van.

Idalou turned back inside, the enforced idleness irritating her. If she hadn't had to wait for Will Haskins, she would have been out searching for the bull herself. She'd already straightened up their small sitting room and made her preparations for supper. Her bedroom was always neat, and she didn't bother with Carl's room regardless of the chaos. The washing was done, the chickens fed, and the eggs gathered. She'd have to milk the cow and pen the chickens before nightfall, but she would do that after Mr. Haskins left.

She couldn't help wondering what he was like. It was rumored the Maxwell family owned half the Hill Country. She hoped it was true. She wanted them to be rich enough to pay a lot for the bull. The decision to sell had been agonizing. The calves the animal fathered had been intended to be the future of the ranch. But there wouldn't be any future for the ranch if they didn't sell him. Ironic.

Unable to stand the inactivity any longer, Idalou took the slop bucket from the kitchen, left the house through the back door, and headed toward the hog pen where a sow nursed half a dozen piglets. At least they'd have meat for the winter. If either she or Carl had the time to gather berries and wild grapes, she'd make jam. Their father had planned to plant fruit trees, but had never gotten around to it.

She had just emptied the slop bucket into the feed trough and turned back toward the house when she saw a rider approaching the house. It was impossible to tell anything about him with the sun in her eyes, but it had to be Mr. Haskins. Just her luck. She'd waited inside like a proper lady for the last hour only to have him arrive when she was slopping the hogs. Why didn't men get anything right? She couldn't decide whether to stay where she was, go to meet him, or return to the house and wait until he knocked on the door.

Deciding to meet him in the house, she hurried inside, washed her hands, checked to make sure she hadn't dirtied her dress, then made last-minute adjustments to her hair in a small mirror on her bedside table. By then she heard his boots on the front porch. She opened the door and completely lost her ability to move or speak.

"Howdy, ma'am," the man said with a smile that practically obliterated the sunset. "I'm Will Haskins."

She knew he was real, but no man could look like that. It simply wasn't possible.

"I'm here to see about buying your bull," he said when she didn't respond.

How could she think about anything as mundane as selling a bull when she couldn't breathe?

"You did get my letter, didn't you? Did I get the day wrong? Isabelle says I never can keep things straight."

She had to think, to speak, to do something besides stand there staring at him like she was a stuffed dummy.

"Are you all right?" he asked. "I saw you out next to the hog pen when I rode up. Maybe you were in the heat too long."

"I am feeling a little dizzy." She was feeling so weak she was about to faint.

"Maybe you'd better sit down," he said, eyeing their small parlor. "Would you like some water?"

She had to get control of herself. She wasn't a silly girl who would fall speechless at the sight of a handsome man. Instead, she was twenty, a woman of experience. There was no reason for her to act like a brainless ninny just because this man was twice as good looking as she'd ever thought possible.

She allowed Mr. Haskins to lead her into the parlor and persuade her to take a seat on a small sofa. "I would appreciate some water if you don't mind," she said.

"I'll be back in two shakes of a coyote's tail."

She didn't take her first full breath until he'd left the room. It wasn't his clothes, even though the tan shirt, off-white vest, and faded pants were clean and neat. It wasn't his hat, which was almost new, or his boots, which had obviously been cleaned that morning. Nor was it the way those clothes fit his tall, muscular body. It was his face that had brought her nervous system to the edge of breakdown. If any man could be considered absolutely perfect, maybe even beautiful, it was Will Haskins.

How was a woman supposed to think straight around him? She was only human. Men like him shouldn't be allowed. She wouldn't be surprised to wake up tomorrow and find she'd offered to give him the bull.

"Here we are," he announced as he returned to the parlor, a glass of water in hand.

"Thank you," she said, taking the glass with an unsteady hand. "I'm sorry to make such a pitiful appearance. I assure you I don't usually act like . . . feel this way." *Drink. If you're swallowing, you can't talk.*

"Don't worry your head about it." He settled into a chair directly across from her. "Isabelle says if God had been thinking about a woman's comfort, he'd never have created Texas."

He grinned, and she choked on her water.

"She also says no man who loves his wife would force her to stay in Texas, but you couldn't drag her out of the Hill Country with a double team of oxen. She just likes teasing Jake."

Idalou couldn't follow his conversation, but she didn't care how much he rambled as long as it kept her from having to speak.

"I'm glad we don't have this kind of heat in the Hill Country. It's hard to think when it's this hot."

It was impossible to think when he smiled at her, his eyes more blue than the summer sky, his smile dazzling in its brilliance. What right did a man have to look like this? How many women were homely because God had used so much beauty to make this one face?

"You get used to the heat after a while," she managed to say.

Mr. Haskins made himself comfortable. Considering how easily she'd been overpowered by his looks, it was a good thing he wasn't a demanding guest.

"I expect so."

Idalou took another swallow of water. The very ordinariness of the process of swallowing seemed to help her regain her balance, her sense of being in control of her mind and body. "I should have been the one to ask if *you* wanted anything to drink."

"Thanks, but I stopped off at the Swinging Door to cool off and ask directions. I had a beer while I was there. I can't say I care for all the company, but it seems like a nice place."

She wondered who had failed to meet his approval and why.

"Would you like some coffee instead?"

His laugh was easy, invited her to laugh with him. "I know it'll make you doubt I'm a true Texan, but I can't drink coffee in this weather."

"I can drink it in any weather."

14

"So can Isabelle. I don't think Jake could function with it."

"Are they your parents?"

"Yep."

"Forgive me if I'm being rude, but why do you call them by their first names?" If he didn't stop smiling at her, she was going to have a relapse.

"My real parents died when I was very small. I'd been calling Jake and Isabelle by their first names before they adopted me and my brother. It was easiest to keep doing it."

Idalou couldn't believe she was sitting here making small talk with a stranger. She *never* did that, not even with other women. She'd been accused of being too direct, too businesslike, even unfeminine.

"I'm sure you're wondering why I haven't gotten down to business," she said.

"No hurry," he said. "It's a short ride back to town, so we've got plenty of time."

Well, she didn't have plenty of time. She didn't have a father who practically owned a whole county. She couldn't afford to hire dozens of men to help with her work. She could barely pay their two cowhands. "You'll probably learn before long that I have a reputation for being impatient."

"I'm sure it's undeserved."

"No. It's well deserved."

"Then I'm sure you're impatient in a very nice way."

"Are you always like this?"

"Like what?"

"Relaxed. Accommodating. Uncritical."

"It's much easier than getting my stomach in a knot."

"Don't people get irritated with you?"

"All the time, but I don't let it bother me."

"Why not?"

"Because I don't want it to."

He said that like it was the most logical thing in the world.

"Besides, my brother gets agitated enough for both of us."

"I'd like to talk about the bull."

"I'd better see it first."

"That's impossible."

His startled look took more energy than anything he'd done so far. "Surely you don't expect me to talk about price without even looking at the animal."

She didn't like having to tell him she didn't have the bull. It embarrassed her, made her feel less in control, less competent. She unclenched her hands in her lap. "Of course not, but he's not here."

"That's okay. We can ride out to see him."

"I don't know where he is right now."

Mr. Haskins's gaze narrowed. "Do you mean he's wandered off and you'll find him in a little bit, or you've lost him and have no idea where he is?"

"I know where he is, but not where to find him."

His brow knitted. "I know I'm not very smart, but that doesn't make sense. You'd better explain it."

"Our neighbor Jordan McGloughlin took the bull. He's trying to force me to sell him my ranch. He knows I need the money from the sale of the bull to keep going until the first calves can go to market. My brother is out looking right now, but he's mooning over McGloughlin's daughter and refuses to believe our neighbor would do anything like that."

Mr. Haskins got to his feet. "That's no problem, ma'am. I'll just ride back to town and wait until your brother finds the bull. Or until you and Mr. Mc-Gloughlin come to an understanding. I think I can give you at least a week to work things out."

"I don't want you to go back to town," Idalou said,

getting to her feet as well. "I want you to ride over to McGloughlin's place with me and force him to tell me what he's done with the bull."

He looked at her as if she'd just asked him to steal the gold candlesticks from the church altar. "Sorry, ma'am, but I can't do that."

Chapter Two

His answer was so unequivocal, so unexpected, Idalou could only stare. After he'd been so concerned about her momentary weakness, even thoughtful enough to bring her water, it had never occurred to her that he would refuse to help her. "Why? Are you afraid of him?"

"Why should I be afraid of a man I've never met?" His lazy smile had reappeared. "He could be old and crippled, even blind."

"He's in excellent health, not yet fifty, and likes nothing better than spending his day in the saddle riding herd on his crew."

"Sounds a lot like Jake, and I have great admiration for Jake."

"I should hope Jake wouldn't steal his neighbor's bull."

"No, ma'am. If he had, I wouldn't be here looking to buy yours. I probably shouldn't tell you this, but Jake had his eye on that bull when your father slipped in and bought it right out from under him. He had a lot of things to say about your father's character."

Idalou took immediate offense. "My father was an honest and respected man."

"That's what Isabelle said, but Jake needed to work out his frustration on somebody. Since he didn't know your father, it seemed harmless enough to say a few mean things about him. He wasn't happy to have to buy a bull he didn't like as much."

Idalou was beginning to question whether Mr. Haskins had traded sanity for good looks. She was also starting to wonder about Jake and Isabelle. She was gradually recovering from her stupefaction over Will Haskins's looks. It was a lot easier to cope with overwhelming handsomeness when the person's character was flawed, and Idalou suspected this man's character was in need of serious rehabilitation.

"We really can't conduct any business until we recover the bull," Idalou said.

His lazy smile didn't change. "You're right, ma'am." He turned toward the door. "Since you've got things to do, I'll get out of your way." He stood, settled his hat on his head, and started for the door.

"You really aren't going to help me, are you?"

He turned back. "I'd be in a heap of trouble if I made a habit of sticking my nose in things that were none of my business."

"I would think seeing that the people with power don't take advantage of those without it would be the responsibility of every respectable man."

"It is, ma'am."

"Would you stop calling me 'ma'am'? You make me sound like somebody's grandmother. My name is Idalou."

"And my name is Will. Calling me Mr. Haskins

makes me feel like I ought to be responsible for something."

She had followed him outside, but she couldn't see his face in the glare of the sun. "Apparently, you don't feel you're responsible for anything."

"Begging your pardon, ma'am—I mean Idalou— but I've only heard your side of the story. For all I know, you could have sold the bull to Mr. Mc-Gloughlin and now you're trying to hornswaggle me into helping you steal it back so you can sell it to me."

"I'd never do anything as despicable as that!" Idalou exclaimed. "I can't believe you'd even think it."

"I don't," he said, with a smile Idalou now thought was evil rather than dazzling. "I'm just trying to make the point that I can't go busting into situations when I don't know any of the facts or the people in- volved. Hell, I'd have to be a better shot than Luke if I was to do that and come out with a whole skin."

"Who's Luke?"

"One of my adopted brothers. He's a hired gun- slinger. His brother Chet used to be one, too, but he quit when he got married."

Idalou was losing her grip on the makeup of the Maxwell family. "You're welcome to look into the facts as much as you wish while you hang out in the Swing- ing Door—that is, if you're sober enough or can sum- mon the energy—but you'll find the facts are exactly as I've stated them."

"I'm sure they are, and I'll be happy to speak to the sheriff on your behalf."

"I can speak to the sheriff on my own behalf," Idalou said between gritted teeth.

"I have no doubt you'd do so very eloquently," Will said, "but I was assuming you'd already done so without the desired results."

She wasn't about to tell him that the sheriff—when last they'd had one—had basically ignored her complaints about McGloughlin. "Jordan McGloughlin is a very clever man as well as a very powerful one. Even if I had absolute proof of everything he's done, I'm not sure the men who've been our sheriff would have done anything about it. It's very difficult for a woman to be taken seriously when she goes up against a man with money and influence."

"I understand, and I'm really sorry there's nothing I can do."

She got the feeling he was holding back, that he wanted to help but wouldn't let himself. The change was subtle, but she had the sense he had dropped his facade and was actually speaking to her instead of acting a role.

"You have to understand I have no standing in this situation," he continued. "But that's not the most important reason. In a few days, I won't be here to protect you. If I intervene, it'll leave you vulnerable between two very powerful neighbors."

Idalou knew he was right, but that didn't keep her from being angry at him. "You might as well head back to town. My brother will let you know when he gets the bull back."

"I hope it's soon," he said, falling back into his glib role. "I know you want to get the sale completed as soon as possible."

She *had* to get the sale completed soon. The bank loan was coming due and she didn't have the money for the next installment. If she couldn't pay it, the bank would auction off their property. McGloughlin would get her ranch at a low price, and she and her brother would be practically destitute.

"Since neither finding the bull nor completing the sale quickly is important to you, I won't keep you any longer." Idalou tried to inject every bit of disdain possible into her tone of voice. "I'm sure you'll find more convivial company at the Swinging Door."

"Maybe more welcoming, but certainly not more attractive," Will said.

She felt her cheeks grow warm, but she quickly recovered. "I don't like flattery." Idalou was certain Will believed fancy words would solve any problem. With a face like his, he was probably right. She had to keep reminding herself she was furious at him, that he was a graceless scamp. She probably ought to thank McGloughlin for making it impossible for her to close the sale today. She had gone so weak in the knees when she'd set eyes on Will, he could probably have talked her into selling the bull for any price he named.

"Neither do I," Will said, his eyes surprisingly hard. "I've experienced it often enough. But I've also seen enough women to know there aren't many more attractive and spirited than you. If you think that's flattery, you need a better mirror."

Now Idalou was angry at herself for letting her temper get the better of her. "There's more to me than a face."

Will leaned against the porch rail, a quirky smile causing his eyes to gleam with amusement. "I was warned I'd need plenty of liquid courage if I had to tangle with you."

Idalou knew people talked about her temper. Considering how she'd behaved toward him during the last twenty minutes, he probably believed the talk was justified. "It makes me angry that people don't take me seriously just because I'm a woman."

"You ought to meet up with Isabelle. The two of you probably wouldn't stop talking for weeks."

Even if they did share an idea or two, Idalou

thought it was probably better that she kept a safe distance from Will's peculiar family. "I really have to go help Carl look for the bull. You may be in no hurry, but I am."

Will walked down from the porch and unhitched his horse, a sleek quarter horse of good breeding. "I'll get out of your way. I hope you find him soon."

As she watched Will mount up and ride off, she was irritated that she'd gone and done just what the men in town had said she would. They said she was too temperamental, but she was temperamental because they ignored her efforts to be taken seriously. She'd been foolish to let Will Haskins's handsome face make her think he would be different. Webb Mc-Gloughlin had been unfaithful as well as reckless. Van Sonnenberg was the worst of the bunch. Was it possible to find a man who was honest as well as hardworking and dependable? A man who believed a woman was worth paying attention to at other places, besides the table or the bed?

A tremor shook her. The thought of sharing a bed with Will Haskins was like being struck by lightning. If she had any sense, she'd put him out of her mind. It wasn't any consolation to know he was so handsome that any woman would be overwhelmed just by meeting him. She couldn't afford to act like *any woman*. Her father had never listened to her, and now the ranch was in trouble. Webb hadn't listened to her when she'd begged him not to ride the rogue horse that killed him. Carl wouldn't listen to her because he was in love with Mara. Idalou refused to let Will ignore her. She had a ranch to save, a brother to protect, and a lot of men to teach that they couldn't disregard her just because she was a woman. She couldn't do all that if she was mooning over Will Haskins.

Yet somehow Idalou wasn't able to convince herself that she wasn't just a little bit in danger of liking Will Haskins, and not just because of his looks.

As he rode away from the Double-L ranch, Will had reason to be glad all over again that he'd talked Jake out of coming with him. All a woman like Idalou had to do was tear up, and Jake would have been on his way to demand why Jordan McGloughlin would do anything as dastardly as steal a poor young woman's bull. Will wasn't immune to women, even when they weren't as attractive as Idalou Ellsworth, but he was averse to sticking his neck out when he was certain that things would be worse for her after he left.

He hoped his presence wasn't going to complicate the situation. He'd been trying to convince Jake and Isabelle that though he was the youngest of the orphans they'd adopted, he was too old for them to keep looking over his shoulder. Jake didn't hesitate to assign him the most difficult jobs on the ranch, but he always kept an eye on him. Jake insisted he was just making sure Will's work was up to standard, but Will knew he was watching to make sure nothing happened to him. He was the only one left at home, so all the attention that had previously been divided among twelve was focused on him alone. It had gotten so bad, Will had threatened to move away.

The look on Isabelle's face when he'd stated that intention had caused him to spend the next couple of days convincing her he was just kidding, but she and Jake both knew he wasn't. Six of the orphans were married and raising their own families. Pete, Luke, Hawk, and Zeke were somewhere out West, and Eden was off at school. Though his parents would never have admitted it, they had been holding on to him because he was the only one left. And he had stayed for the same reason.

Up until three years ago, he also stayed because he couldn't leave his brother Matt, who was a moody recluse determined to take in any boy who needed a home or protection. Though Will was five years younger than Matt, he had always stood between Matt and the outside world. But three years ago Matt had gotten married and adopted three kids to go with the two he already had. With his wife soon to give birth to their second child, Matt was finally settled and happy. Most important, he had a wife who loved him despite his past and knew what to do when the ghosts threatened to descend on him.

Now Will had a chance to build a life of his own, but it hadn't turned out to be as easy as he'd thought. Though six of his adopted brothers and sisters lived within riding distance of Jake and Isabelle, they'd insisted that one of them ought to live at home. Despite his protests that Jake and Isabelle were too young and healthy to need anyone to watch over them—especially not someone *they* were watching over—Will had been elected. Deciding to buy this bull was Will's desperate effort to establish some sort of independence without alienating half his family.

He paused to wipe the perspiration out of his eyes and from his forehead. He didn't know why anyone would want to live in central Texas. It was hot as hell, flat as a plate, and as close to a desert as Will hoped to see. He loved his own home, with its rugged hills, cool breezes, and shaded valleys. It could get a little dicey when it rained too much and flood waters came roaring through the valleys, but that added a bit of excitement. What could be exciting about a flat terrain that stretched the same for miles in every direction?

He wondered if Idalou would move away when she got the money for her bull. She gave every indication of being determined to stay where she was, but surely she could see that she and her brother would have a better chance of making a go of it if they weren't sandwiched in between two larger ranchers who wanted her land and water. Her father had had the good sense to homestead both sides of the creek, but her water rights made her a target. Idalou wasn't in a position to compete with Mc-Gloughlin or Sonnenberg.

As much as he sympathized with her, Will knew better than to get involved in a local dispute. Despite what the men had told him, he really didn't know the facts behind the situation. And he wasn't going to be around long enough to handle any repercussions. It wasn't right to come in, disturb the balance of things, then disappear, leaving Idalou vulnerable and possibly unable to defend herself.

Besides, he wasn't the kind of guy to go looking for trouble. He'd had more than his share of it when his parents died and he and Matt were thrown out of the orphanage and left to fend for themselves. If Isabelle hadn't come along, he didn't know what might have happened to them.

Drops of sweat rolled down his back between his shoulder blades. How did people stand this country? Why did Idalou want to save her miserable little ranch when she would have enough money to buy land someplace that hadn't been cursed by the devil?

Because she was a stubborn female in the same mold as Isabelle. Though he adored Isabelle and would have fought any man who disparaged her, she was something of a tyrant. Idalou had all the makings of a second Isabelle—beauty, intelligence, and iron determination. Jake seemed to like being led a merry dance, but Will was just as happy to observe from the sidelines. There were ways to solve life's problems without butting heads. Life was too short to spend it perpetually in a lather.

Still, guilt nibbled at the sensitive edges of his conscience. He couldn't keep from thinking he ought to have found a way to help Idalou. He *had* considered offering to help her find the bull. That wouldn't have looked like he was interfering and taking sides. But Idalou wanted him to ride over to McGloughlin's place to confront him. That would definitely have put a coyote in the chicken house. Though Isabelle would take him to task for not helping any woman in need, no one would thank him for stirring up trouble.

His musings were interrupted when he saw a rider heading toward him. He didn't know the boy, but it was polite to stop and greet a stranger. "I'm Will Haskins," he said by way of introduction.

"Carl Ellsworth," the boy replied. "My sister and I own the Double-L ranch."

Will could see a strong resemblance between the brother and sister. Both had rich brown hair and luminous big, brown eyes. Carl kept his hair cut short, while Idalou had tied her luxuriant tresses up in a ponytail. Carl was tall with a body that had yet to fill out the promise of his broad chest and wide shoulders. Idalou was slim, but her body had reached its full glory of womanhood. Both had the same smooth skin, but Carl's was deeply tanned from being in the sun. Though Idalou's eyes could bore a hole through you, Carl's gaze was curious and inviting.

"I've just come from there," Will said. "I gather you still haven't found the bull."

Carl knitted his brow. "I expect he'll turn up in a day or two. I've tried to make Idalou understand that bulls don't stay in one place unless you put them in a pen, but she's determined he'll impregnate every cow possible before you take him away."

Will hesitated a minute before telling Carl that Idalou had asked him to help her find the bull.

"Idalou thinks Jordan is behind everything that happens to us. The bull's just wandered away looking for more cows."

It was obvious that Carl was trying to keep his emotions in check. Will suspected he was angry his sister had asked a stranger for help. It didn't reflect well on him. At Carl's age, self-image was very important and extremely fragile. Even though his own brother was now happily married and a successful and respected member of the community, Will knew Matt still struggled to respect himself after what had happened to him.

"I don't have to get back to town right away," Will said. "If you'd like me to—"

"I don't need anybody's help," Carl replied a little too readily for politeness. "I'll find him."

"I'm sure you will," Will said. "I'll be putting up at the hotel. Just let me know when he turns up. I'm anxious to put him to work." But first he needed to buy some cows and convince his family he wasn't being an unappreciative siphon just because he wanted a place of his own before he turned thirty.

"He's a willing breeder," Carl said, some of the tension in his expression easing. "We don't have enough cows to keep him busy, so he's been sneaking over to Jordan's land. Idalou is really steamed that he's servicing some of Jordan's cows without Jordan having to pay for it."

"Did Jordan offer to pay for the bull's services?"

Carl looked surprised. "Why should he?"

"Because those calves will bring a better price

when he sells them. It's only fair that he offer to pay you something."

Carl was looking uneasy again. "That's what Idalou said, but Jordan said he didn't ask us to have our bull service his cows."

"Then he ought to have offered to sell you the calves."

"We don't have money to buy stock," Carl said, anger in his eyes. "If we did, we wouldn't be selling the bull."

"Still, Jordan ought to..." Will broke off. He shouldn't start putting ideas in Carl's head. The last thing he needed was the boy doing something rash and saying it was Will's idea.

"Maybe he will when he sells them," Carl said, looking uncomfortable with the turn in the conversation.

"I'm holding you up," Will said. "I'm sure you want your supper."

"I've been out looking for the damned bull all day," Carl said, his handsome face relaxing. "I haven't eaten anything since breakfast."

"Then I won't keep you," Will said. A young man Carl's age wouldn't want to miss any meals. "I'll look forward to hearing from you."

Carl nodded and rode off. Will noticed that the horse he was riding didn't seem to be of top quality. He wondered if Carl and his sister were so strapped for cash they couldn't afford decent horses. He nudged his own horse's flanks, and headed toward town. He'd do well to think less about Idalou and her brother and more about how to get the bull for the best price.

Still, he sympathized with Carl. Will had nine big brothers and one big sister. He knew what it was like to have people always telling him what to do and never being satisfied with what he did or how he did it. It would be a lot worse when he announced he intended to set up his own ranch.

Will felt so much better after an afternoon rain shower caused the temperature to drop, he decided to take a walk around town before supper. He was used to being more active than he'd been today. He had some surplus energy he needed to work off. A light breeze stirred the stagnant air. He pulled off his hat and ran his fingers through his hair, massaging his scalp, which made it feel better. He settled his hat back on his head and headed west along the boardwalk, reading the names of the stores and other businesses he passed.

He nodded to people as he walked by, inwardly amused when they did a double take. He'd gotten used to people being startled by his looks, but he wasn't greatly impressed because he'd grown up being compared to his brother Matt and to Luke and Chet Attmore. And though he might be the best looking of the four, one of the others was always bigger, stronger, better with a rope, faster with a gun, more charming—no, he guessed not more charming. Isabelle always said he had more charm than a snake-oil salesman. She never said that about the others. But since she didn't say it in a good way, he didn't take the remark as a compliment. When it was coupled with what she said about his being too lazy to get out of his own way—well, good looks weren't enough to overcome all of that.

Having reached the north end of town, Will crossed the street and turned south. It was actually rather nice to have something to do on his walk besides look at the stars or wonder if the clouds would bring rain. Back at the ranch there were no lights to compete with the star-filled sky, but light came from several sources along the main street of Dunmore. And the sound of people laughing, talking, even singing, drowned out all other sounds of the night.

Not quite. Will heard a woman's voice raised in alarm not far ahead. He couldn't tell what she was saying, but it was clear she was frightened. He was reluctant to get involved with something that wasn't his business, but he couldn't ignore a woman in danger. He'd never be able to face Isabelle if he did.

He wondered why no one responded to the girl's distress. There were other men closer to her, but no one stopped. In fact, they seemed to make a point of looking the other way. That intrigued Will as well as angering him, and he picked up his pace. The sounds were coming from an alley between two large buildings that were dark and silent. Will turned into the alley to see that a man had backed a young girl up against a building. He wasn't touching her, but it was clear he wouldn't let her go.

"All I want is a little kiss," the man was saying. "You're free enough with that Ellsworth boy."

If the rumor that Carl was sweet on Jordan McGloughlin's daughter was true, then the girl must be Mara McGloughlin. She couldn't be more than eighteen, and the man had to be over thirty.

"Let me go," the girl said.

"Not until I get my kiss."

Will could tell from the man's slurred words that he was drunk, or very nearly so, but that didn't excuse his mistreating the girl. What Will didn't understand was why a second man was standing only a few feet away and doing nothing.

"One little kiss won't hurt," the man said.

"Maybe not if the young lady wanted to kiss you," Will said. "Since she clearly doesn't, I think you ought to let her leave now."

All three people turned to stare at him, the two men in surprise, the girl with relief.

"Get out of here," the man growled.

"I'll be more than happy to leave as soon as you release Miss McGloughlin and allow her to go on her way."

"I said get out!" the man shouted.

"I heard you," Will said calmly as he moved closer. "I'm not deaf."

Mara tried to escape by slipping under the man's arms, but he caught her around the waist and pulled her against him.

"You really have to let her go now." Will stopped just a few feet from the man. "This behavior is unacceptable."

"You talk like a damned dude," the man said.

"Thank you," Will replied with a forced smile. "My mother wants me to act like a gentleman." Will reached out to Mara. "Come with me. I'll help you find your father."

The drunk man pushed the girl in the direction of the other man. "Hold her while I teach this fool not to mess with Newt Mandrin."

"I think you're the fool for being too drunk to know it would be dangerous to trifle with the daughter of Jordan McGloughlin."

"I'm about to teach you what everybody, including Jordan, already knows," Newt bellowed as he charged Will.

Chapter Three

Newt plunged forward, but Will sidestepped him and landed a fist to his jaw. Newt spun around as if to see if an unknown attacker had materialized, but Will hit him so hard in the throat, he was left gasping for breath. His body drained of all strength, he sank to his knees, his hands clawing at his spasming throat.

"It would have been a lot easier if you'd just let Miss McGloughlin go on her way." Will flexed his fist and grimaced.

"Watch out!"

Mara's warning was unnecessary. Will had already relieved Newt of his gun and spun around. He aimed Newt's gun at the other man's belly before he could draw his gun.

"Go ahead. I don't know who you are, but I won't mind ridding Dunmore of a piece of trash who did nothing while Newt assaulted Miss McGloughlin."

The man's eyes blazed with fury, but his hand fell away from his gun.

"He's Isaiah Thomas," Mara said, scorn dripping

from her lips. "He hangs around with Newt because he's too much of a coward to do anything without somebody to back him up."

"Not too much of a coward to pull a gun on a man he thinks is unarmed," Will noted.

The moment Newt had turned on Will, Mara had darted away from him. Instead of leaving the alley, she had stopped just a little behind Will.

"Get out of here," Will said to Isaiah. "If I have to look at your face a minute longer, I'll drag you to jail with your friend."

"Newt will kill you for this," Isaiah threatened. "He's the fastest draw in three counties."

"I guess he'll have to wait until he's feeling a bit better to prove it." Will grabbed Newt's collar and jerked him to his feet. "Meanwhile, he can wait in jail. Now, if you'll show me the way," Will said to Mara, "I'd like to get shut of this piece of filth."

Weakened by his continuing struggle for breath, Newt didn't resist when Will dragged him into the street and directed him toward the jail.

"How're you going to keep him in jail?" Isaiah asked. "Dunmore ain't got no sheriff."

"Hang around and you'll find out from the inside of a cell." Will was relieved to see Isaiah fall back, then turn and walk away.

Their little three-person procession attracted immediate attention, aided considerably by Mara's telling everyone she met that Will had defended her from Newt and Isaiah simultaneously, having beaten Newt to a bloody pulp and scared Isaiah so badly he'd slunk off to hide in the night.

"Newt is the fastest draw around," one man said.

"And the best fighter."

"Not anymore. Mister . . . you saved my life, and I don't even know your name," Mara exclaimed.

"It's Will Haskins, and I don't think Newt meant to hurt you."

"You don't know Newt," Mara declared. "He's mean as the devil. He killed the last sheriff."

"And a cowhand over in San Angelo in a bar fight over a woman," a man added.

"Well, he's going to jail. Does this town still have a deputy?"

"You'd better ask Andy Davis," one man said. "I expect you'll find him at the saloon."

"Lloyd Severns, too," another voice added. "He owns the bank."

"My daddy, too," Mara said.

"Why don't you people round them up and have them meet me at the jail."

Several men immediately headed off in different directions.

"Anybody know their way around the jail?"

"I do." A short, tubby man stepped forward. "I'm Bud Fox. I clean the jail and feed the prisoners when we got any."

"Lead the way," Will said. "I want to get rid of this man."

The news that a stranger had beaten Newt Mandrin in a fight and was taking him to jail spread through town faster than a plague of locusts. By the time Will reached the jailhouse, half the population of Dunmore was on the street—including every boy over six and under sixteen. Will ignored all requests to describe the fight until Mara's description so far outstripped reality, he had to intervene.

"Newt was so drunk he could hardly stand up," he snapped. "One punch to the windpipe, and he was down for the count."

As brief as it was, that description excited the boys more than Mara's more extravagant version. In seconds they were pantomiming hitting each other in the throat and falling on the ground, noisily gasping for breath. Will was relieved to reach the jail and be able to close the door on the crowd. Bud Fox retrieved the keys from the desk. Will propelled Newt into one of the two jail cells, and Bud locked the door behind him.

"What's going on here?"

Will turned to see Andy Davis enter the jail followed by a man he didn't know.

"I found Mr. Mandrin trying to force Miss McGloughlin to kiss him," Will said before Mara could launch into what he was certain would be a version of the evening's events with only tenuous connections to the truth. "He was drunk, so I thought it would be better if he sobered up in jail."

"He knocked him down with just two punches," Mara informed the two men, her bright eyes looking at Will with utter adoration. "He drew his gun on Isaiah so fast I couldn't see his hand move."

"That's because I wasn't wearing a gun," Will explained. "I had to borrow Newt's."

"You *borrowed* his gun to draw on Isaiah?" Andy asked in disbelief.

"Actually, I took it," Will said, "but he was in no condition to object."

"He was on the ground gasping for breath." Mara dropped to her knees and gave a performance that equaled that of any of the boys outside.

Will wondered if the extreme heat could account for the behavior of these people. All this excitement didn't seem normal. Hell, any one of his brothers could have done what he did.

Two more men entered. Before they could introduce themselves to Will, a tall, handsome man who appeared to be about fifty burst into the jail.

"Daddy!" Mara cried and threw herself at him.

Nobody made a move until Mara had finished sobbing and spinning a tale that made Will blush.

"It really wasn't that dangerous," he insisted. "Newt is drunk. It didn't take much—"

"You saved my daughter from the shame of having that man touch her," Jordan McGloughlin declared.

"Isn't he wonderful, Daddy?" Mara practically swooned, and Will started looking for a way out before things got too ridiculous.

"I don't know anybody else who'd have had the courage to tackle Newt and Isaiah at the same time," Andy Davis said. "Newt's killed two men. Everybody tries to stay out of his way."

"I'm Lloyd Severns," said the man who'd entered with Andy Davis. "My wife told me how you stopped Van Sonnenberg from running down Pepper."

"He very neatly disposed of Van when Van tried to attack him from behind in the Swinging Door this morning," Andy added.

The three men looked at each other. "I think he's the very man we need," Lloyd said.

Jordan and Andy agreed. All three men turned to Will.

"We want to offer you the job of sheriff," Andy said.

Just the idea of his being sheriff of any town, regardless of how small, was absurd. His whole family would laugh themselves silly if they ever got wind of it. If he weren't so shocked, he'd probably laugh, too.

"That's impossible," he said.

"Why?" Jordan McGloughlin asked. "You've already handled two of the most dangerous men in Dunmore."

"It was luck," Will insisted. "Besides, I'm only here as long as it takes to buy the Ellsworths' bull."

"We don't need you to take the job permanently,"

Lloyd said, "just while we look for a man we can hire full-time."

"I don't like fighting," Will protested. "I don't wear a gun, and I like to sleep late." Not that Isabelle would let him, but they didn't need to know that.

"That doesn't matter," Lloyd said. "We just need somebody to wear the badge."

"And be a target," Will guessed.

"Nobody'll bother you once they hear how you handled Van and Newt on the same day."

"You've got to do it, Mr. Haskins," Mara said. "You're practically a hero."

Will choked. About the last thing he wanted to be—behind a husband and father—was a hero. It was an exhausting job. And any hothead looking to make a reputation would head straight in his direction. Luke Attmore always said he was more worried about crazy kids hunting a reputation than honest-to-goodness gunmen. Kids didn't think they could die. Gunmen knew better.

"I haven't got time—" Will started to say.

"We'll get you a couple of deputies to do most of the work," Andy said.

"What have you got to do besides wait for Carl to find that bull?" Lloyd asked.

"We just need someone behind the badge," McGloughlin said. "You'll hardly have to do anything."

Will was about to refuse point-blank when it occurred to him that as sheriff, he would have a legitimate reason to look into what had happened to Idalou's bull. It didn't seem like enough reason to do something as foolhardy as be sheriff of this half-crazy town, but he had felt guilty about not being able to help Idalou. He didn't know why he should like such a prickly woman, but life was full of little mysteries.

What else could account for the fact that he was even considering this crazy proposition?

"Please," Mara pleaded, looking up at Will with wide, imploring eyes. "All the other young ladies of Dunmore need someone to protect them just like you protected me."

Will had a nearly uncontrollable urge to tell this foolish girl she ought to spend a few months living with Drew so she could learn how a female with a backbone and a few grains of sense ought to act, but he figured she wouldn't appreciate being told she was a silly twit.

"I don't imagine money is an issue for you," Mc-Gloughlin said, "but after what you did for my daughter, I'd double your wages."

Any successful businessman knew money always mattered, but getting out of Dunmore with a whole skin mattered more. Still . . .

"What would it take to convince you?" Lloyd asked.

Will thought of how little he was looking forward to eating his meals at the unappetizing little restaurant in town and decided he could put up with a bit of danger as long as he had decent food. Isabelle was a tyrant, but she had turned into a fabulous cook.

"Food," Will said.

"What?" three male voices asked in unison.

"If you can arrange for somebody to provide me with three meals a day—cooked at home and served at a table with clean linens—I'll be your sheriff until I buy the bull."

"You mean you want a table set up in the jail?" Andy asked.

"I'll be happy to eat with the family. I just don't want to be poisoned before I can get out of here."

The men looked at each other. "Do you think we can do that?" Jordan asked.

"After what he did for Pepper, Dorabelle would cook for him every day," Lloyd said. "I wouldn't be surprised if we have women lining up to cook for him."

"Of course they will. He's gorgeous," Mara gushed.

Sometimes Will got impatient with people's reaction to his looks. After all, he could have been as evil as he was attractive, but occasionally his looks came in handy. Besides, with two deputies, he wouldn't have much to do. Getting to meet a different family every time he sat down to eat might be an interesting way to pass the week.

"Is it a deal?" Will asked.

"It sure is," Lloyd said. "And to prove it, you're coming home with me for supper. Andy can arrange for breakfast tomorrow and Jordan for supper. By then we ought to have the rest of the week taken care of."

Will could practically hear Jake laughing at the mess he'd gotten himself into. At least he'd have something decent to eat. And as soon as he got a chance, he'd look into what had happened to Idalou's bull.

"My first act as sheriff will be to make it a rule that no young woman is to be out alone after dark," he said, directing his remark to Mara. "There are too many drunks wandering around for that to be safe."

"I already have that rule," McGloughlin said, giving his daughter a severe look.

"Then I'll leave it up to you to enforce it," Will said.

"Anything else?" Lloyd asked.

"Yes. My stomach thinks my throat has been cut."

Lloyd laughed. "Come on. If we don't hurry, we'll be late for supper."

* * *

Being sheriff had its advantages. Will had gotten up
from Dorabelle Severns's table the previous evening
feeling in charity with the world. A good wine and a
stout brandy had topped off a very satisfying meal.
Mrs. Davis's breakfast this morning hadn't been as
spectacular, but he'd had to push back from the table
while he was still able to stand. He seated himself at
his desk, opened a drawer, and idly surveyed its con-
tents. "How's the prisoner this morning?" he asked
Emmett, one of his two deputies.

"Mad as hell and threatening to plant you in the
ground next to our last sheriff."

"Since I have no desire to be planted in the ground,
regardless of whom I'm next to, maybe we ought to
let him spend a little more time in his cell."

"We never keep drunks longer than overnight."

"So?"

"So there has to be some reason you want to keep
him locked up."

"You think I'm afraid of him?"

"Everybody else is. He's the fastest draw in three
counties."

"I keep hearing that," Will said as he got to his feet.
"I think I'd like to see for myself."

Emmett blanched. "You going to face him in a
gunfight?"

Will opened drawers in the desk until he found one
with a pair of guns. "How else am I going to find out?"

"It won't do you no good iffen you're dead."

"I don't plan to die." He checked each gun for bullets. Both were empty. He held up one to show Emmett. "I don't plan to use bullets."

Emmett followed Will back to the jail cells, shaking
his head as he went. Newt sprang to his feet.

"Let me out," he shouted. "I ain't done nothing
wrong."

"I suppose you consider it perfectly okay to force an unwilling young woman to let you kiss her."

"I didn't mean no harm," Newt said.

"I'm not interested in that just now," Will said. "I want to see if you're as fast as everybody thinks."

A calculating expression claimed Newt's face. "How do you aim to prove that?"

"I'll give you a gun. On Emmett's signal we'll both draw. He decides which one is the fastest."

"The bullet will do that," Newt said with a grin.

"It might if the guns were loaded, but they won't be." Newt turned angry. "Okay, let me out."

"Not yet. You might decide to run away before we find out who's faster."

Newt's expression turned contemptuous. "I'm not afraid to try this with bullets."

"I am. I wouldn't want you to have a second sheriff's scalp to add to your gun belt." Will handed a gun and holster through the bars to Newt and waited while he strapped it on. "We'll both nod when we're ready." Will removed his coat, hung it on a nail in the wall, and strapped on his own gun. "Then we wait for Emmett's signal."

Newt's confidence was so high, he was practically dancing in his cell. "You going to let me out if I prove I can kill you in a fair fight?"

"I've asked Mara McGloughlin to stop by this morning. I'll let you out after you apologize to her."

Newt stopped dancing and scowled at Emmett. "Hurry up, then. I want to get out of here."

Emmett took a deep breath, held it for a second, then said, "Now!"

Two hands flew to the holsters. Two guns were drawn and two clicks sounded loud in the limited confines of the jail.

"He beat you!"

All three men turned to see a dazed Mara Mc-Gloughlin standing in the doorway.

"He sure did," Emmett said, looking at Will in shocked disbelief. "I wouldn't have believed it if I hadn't seen it with my own eyes."

"You can't tell which gun would have fired first," Newt protested.

"It was the sheriff's," Emmett insisted.

"How did you do that?" Mara asked. "Nobody's ever beat Newt."

"Have you ever heard of Luke Attmore?" Will asked.

Mara shook her head, but Newt said, "He's the most famous gunman in three states. Don't try to tell me you beat him."

"I never could, though I tried hundreds of times."

Newt laughed. "Nobody's lasted more than one gunfight with him."

Will unbuckled his holster. "We didn't have real fights. He's my brother. He taught me how to draw." He was confronted by three disbelieving faces. "My adopted brother," Will clarified.

"You going to let me out?" Newt growled.

"As soon as you hand over the gun and apologize to Miss McGloughlin."

Newt unbuckled the holster and pushed it through the bars, letting it fall on the floor.

Will stopped Emmett from picking them up. "That doesn't demonstrate good manners," he said to Newt, "and throws doubt on whether your apology to Miss McGloughlin would be sincere."

Mara and Emmett looked at Will as if he were insane. Newt glared at him through rage-filled eyes.

"I'm going to kill you."

"I expect you'll try," Will said calmly, "but you can't do it from jail. And you won't get out unless you pick up that gun, hand it to Emmett, and apologize to Miss McGloughlin. If you can't manage to apologize in the next few minutes, I'll give you another day in jail to think about it."

Newt turned so red in the face, Will thought he was going to start screaming at him. Instead, he collected himself, reached through the bars, picked up the gun and holster, and handed it to Emmett. The deputy handled it like a hot coal.

"I'm sorry I bothered you," Newt said to Mara. "I was too drunk to know what I was doing."

Mara nodded her acceptance of his apology.

"Let him out," Will said to Emmett before turning back to Newt. "Next time you drink too much, have one of your friends get you out of town before you land in trouble."

"I'm not done with you," he said to Will when Emmett stepped back and let him leave the jail cell.

"Then don't let the grass grow under your feet," Will said. "I won't be here long."

Newt muttered a threat and stormed out of the jail.

"You're so brave," Mara said with a sigh.

Emmett left to make his rounds, and Mara followed Will back to his office.

"Mama said supper would be ready at six, but you could come anytime before that. She says she's got to thank the man who saved her little girl's honor."

"I'll be sure to be there on time." Will sat down at his desk, dropped the two guns into their drawer, and closed it.

"I hope you do come early," Mara said. "There are lots of things I want to know about you."

"Like what?" Will asked, suddenly aware of the true nature of Mara's expression and beginning to feel like a fly cornered by a spider.

"Are you married?"

"No."

"You sweet on anybody?"

He should have answered yes to both questions, but he'd learned long ago that although telling lies might help at a given moment, in the long run they caused even more trouble.

"No, but I'm not the marrying type."

"Why? You're not very old."

"I'm twenty-eight."

"I like older men. They're more mature."

"You're too young for someone my age," Will said. "You need a husband who won't be old when you're still young."

"I'm eighteen," Mara said.

"See, that's ten years. Practically a lifetime."

Mara laughed. "You're funny."

Will wasn't feeling the least bit amused. He realized that saving Mara had turned him into a hero in her eyes. From there it was only a short leap to husband material. He hadn't been avoiding the clutches of females for more than ten years to fall victim to some young woman who couldn't see reality because of the shining armor blinding her.

"You shouldn't be thinking of marriage yet. You have years and years to enjoy having men adore you."

Mara frowned. "Mama says I should be married already. She was a mama when she was my age."

"Do you want to be a mama?"

Mara looked besotted. "If I can have your babies."

Will nearly choked. "You don't even know me. I could be a murderer, for all you know. You should marry some nice young man you've known all your life."

Mara frowned again. "Papa wants me to marry Van, but I used to be sweet on Carl Ellsworth."

"Used to be?"

"Until I met you."

Now he was in for it. All he wanted to do was buy a bull. How complicated could that be? Instead, the damned bull was missing, he'd let Lloyd Severns talk him into being sheriff, and now the daughter of the richest man in town was infatuated with him and wanted to have his babies. He could barely resist the temptation to toss his badge on the desk and hop on a fast horse out of town.

"Stick with Carl. He's a nice fella."

"Papa says I can't marry a poor man."

"What makes you think I'm not poor?"

"You're buying that bull."

"Maybe I'm not buying it. Maybe my father is."

"If your father is rich, you are, too."

Boy, did this girl have a lot to learn. "Jake adopted eleven kids, then had one of his own. Even if he wanted to give me money, it wouldn't be much. I'm probably no richer than Carl."

"Papa said everybody knows that Jake Maxwell owns practically a whole county. He thinks you'll make a fine husband."

"You mentioned this to your father!"

"To Mama, too. She can't wait to meet you. That's why she wants you to come early to supper. They won't let me marry Carl, and I don't want to marry Van, but they said I could marry you."

Chapter Four

Will felt the noose tightening around his neck. All he'd done was protect a young woman from abuse, and now she wanted to marry him. What was wrong with women that once they got a look at his face, nothing else seemed to matter? Everybody knew the best-looking horse rarely had the most stamina, coordination, intelligence, or a decent disposition. Didn't they understand it could be the same with people? Especially men.

"Choosing a husband is much too important to compromise on," he said. "If you don't really love him—"

"I love you." Mara assured him.

Unfortunately, she spoke just as Carl walked through the door. For a moment he looked devastated. In an instant his expression changed to anger. He turned his blazing gaze on Mara, but Will was certain it would find him soon enough.

"Just yesterday you said you loved me," Carl said. "Seems all it took was a pretty face and you forgot all about that."

"He saved me from Newt," Mara said.

"I'd have saved you if I'd been there," Carl insisted.

"But you weren't there," Mara pointed out. "Besides, everybody in Dunmore is afraid of Newt." She favored Will with a brilliant smile. "Will's not. And he can draw faster than Newt. I saw it."

"I don't believe you."

"Emmett saw it, too," Mara said, drawing herself up to confront Carl. "I can't love anybody who doesn't believe me."

"Mara, everybody knows you make up things."

"I do not. I only exaggerate sometimes."

"I think you're straying from the point here," Will said. "You two are in love with each other. You need to be talking about how to convince your parents that you're perfect for each other."

"How can he be perfect for me when he can't stop his sister from accusing Papa of trying to ruin them?" Mara demanded of Will.

"How can she be perfect for me when she thinks she's in love with you just because you kept a drunk from kissing her?" Carl countered.

Will thought he'd done a little more than that, but his reputation wasn't the issue here. "I only stepped in because no one else was helping her."

"Van would have stopped Newt," Mara said. "He's not afraid of anybody."

"Van is a spoiled, selfish brute who's not smart enough to know when he's in danger," Carl said. "He'll get himself killed just like Webb did."

"How dare you say that about my brother!" Mara said and burst into tears.

Will looked at Carl for an explanation. "Webb thought he could ride anything with hair," Carl said, then turned to Mara. "He wouldn't have been on that horse if he hadn't been showing off for his new girl-friend after he'd ditched Idalou."

"He wouldn't have ditched her if she'd stopped accusing my father of being behind everything bad that happens on your ranch."

Remembering his own desolation when Jake had nearly died from a gunshot wound, Will felt some empathy for Mara. Still, he was horrified to find himself in the middle of a squabble that was dragging up family skeletons faster than a grave robber. He didn't know what to do to calm these tempestuous waters—Isabelle was the peacemaker in the family, even if she had to use a big stick to do it, but Isabelle was far away.

"Look, kids—"

"We're not kids." Mara and Carl turned in unison and glared at him. "We're eighteen."

"Then stop acting like you're eighteen *months*," Will shot back. "You're not going to solve anything by dragging up things to blame on each other."

"I don't have to drag up things." Mara eyed Carl angrily even though she was speaking to Will. "He and his sister keep handing them to me." When she spun around to face Will, all traces of anger had vanished. "Don't forget to come early to supper. Mama's had me tell her at least half a dozen times how you saved me. She can't wait to thank you in person." She flashed a brilliant smile filled with defiance at Carl. "I have something special for you," she said, speaking to Will again.

"You're a low-down, rotten sneak," Carl fired at Will the moment Mara went through the office door. "You're a belly-crawling snake, a yella coyote, a—"

"Hold on before you run out of interesting things to call me," Will said, relieved to have just an irate young man to deal with. "I'm none of those things and wouldn't be if I had the chance."

"What do you call a *skunk* who makes up to another man's girl by having dinner with her parents?"

"Dinner is part of my payment for being sheriff. I wasn't going to set myself up to get shot at and have to eat bad food in the bargain."

"Don't go," Carl said.

"Are you going to cook supper for me?"

Carl looked stunned that the idea would even occur to Will.

"I didn't think so. And you can get shut of the idea that Mara's in love with me."

"I wouldn't have to *get shut of it*," Carl snapped, "if you'd minded your own business."

"So you think I should have let Newt have his way with Mara."

"Of course not, but—"

"There's no *but* about it," Will snapped impatiently. "Besides, how was I to know you and Mara were having a fight and she'd turn to me as the answer to her prayers?"

"She's just bowled over by your looks," Carl said, scowling. "Every female in Dunmore is. Even my sister."

That stopped Will in his tracks. He hadn't gotten off to a very good start with Idalou, but that hadn't affected his eyesight. Idalou was a damned fine-looking woman. A little too spirited, mind you, but he'd entertained thoughts of a few strolls in the moonlight. Just because he didn't want to get married didn't mean he wanted to turn in his tickets to the dance. "Your sister thinks I'm nice-looking?"

"No guy has a chance with you parading around looking like some fancy actor in one of them shows I saw in Fort Worth. You wouldn't be so popular if you had my face."

Carl still looked like a teenager, but he had muscles on those broad shoulders and a tan from working in the sun. He'd soon develop into a man women would definitely give a second glance. "There's nothing wrong with your looks," Will said.

"Yes, there is. I don't look like you."

"If you looked like me, you'd have to *be* like me, and that would get you in all kinds of trouble. Would you have let yourself be talked into being sheriff of a town you'd never seen the day before?"

"Hell, no. That's stupid."

Will shrugged. "There you go. You wouldn't want to be stupid. Mara wouldn't like that. Idalou wouldn't like it, either."

"I wouldn't care if I was stupid if Mara would marry me."

Will hadn't grown up with nine older brothers without recognizing the signs of a lovesick kid. Left alone, Carl would probably just make things worse. "Sit down," Will said. "Being angry with me isn't going to solve anything."

"Nothing can fix things," Carl moaned, charging across the small office. "Mara hates me, and we'll lose the ranch because I can't find the bull."

"Sit down," Will said. "I can't think with all this activity."

Carl threw himself into a chair next to Will's desk and dropped his head in his hands.

"Women are a peculiar breed," Will said. "They have this way of making a man think his life isn't worth a bent horseshoe unless he can corral one for himself, but they don't make it easy. They don't mean to be so contrary, but they can't help themselves."

"What are you talking about?" Carl demanded without looking up.

"Women want to get married, but it goes against their nature to make it easy for you. Chances are, Mara decided you were the one the moment she set eyes on you, but did she let you know that?"

"No. I was mooning after her for months before she'd even talk to me."

"Exactly." Will came around the desk and leaned against it with arms crossed. "They set it up so you have to do all the work. Then if anything goes wrong, it's your fault because you were pursuing them, not the other way around."

"But men are supposed to pursue women. Any woman who went after a man would be considered loose."

"And who made up that rule?"

Carl looked blank.

"Women. You won't see a man objecting if a loose woman takes a shine to him. No sirree. He'll consider himself a lucky devil and dive right in."

"I don't want a loose woman," Carl protested. "I just want Mara."

Will decided this wasn't the time to describe some of the attractions of loose women. "And she wants you," Will said. "I'm sure of it."

"She sure has a funny way of showing it."

"I know this is hard for you, but try looking at it from her viewpoint."

"You don't have to tell me I'm not rich like Van or handsome like you."

"That's not what I was going to say," Will said, restraining his impatience. "Now, here's an attractive young woman caught between two handsome men. She likes you very much and wants to marry you, but you're not rich and her parents disapprove. Van, however, is rich and her parents do want her to marry him. She doesn't, so she's at an impasse."

"I tried to get her to run away, but she won't."

"Of course she won't. She'd miss out on all the drama and on a bang-up wedding. Now, imagine this impressionable young woman is suddenly rescued by a handsome stranger who just happens to be the son of a rich man. Naturally, she'll think she's fallen in love with him. She wouldn't be a woman if she didn't."

"I don't see how any of this is going to help me," Carl moaned. "If she wants to marry you, and her parents want her to marry you, I don't have a chance."

A shiver of fear ran down Will's spine. If he left town now, he'd miss dinner but be spared a wife. But he wanted to buy the bull, so he'd better get things straightened out first.

"Mara doesn't want to marry me. Do you think she'd have gotten so mad at you if she did? She over-reacted and is probably now wishing she hadn't said anything to her parents about marrying me. She's in a quandary. How can she marry you and save face doing it?"

"She can't," Carl moaned.

"Certainly she can."

"How?" Carl asked, hopeful.

"That's what you have to figure out."

Carl looked deflated. "I thought you had an answer."

"Hell, I don't understand females. They scare me to death. We'll have to put our heads together to figure out something. And while we're doing it, we have to find that bull."

"I've looked everywhere," Carl said.

"Well, there's one place you haven't looked."

"Where is that?"

"Where he is. Once you figure that out, you'll have the money to keep your ranch, I'll take the bull and leave town, Mara will marry you, and everybody will live happily ever after."

Carl didn't look convinced.

"Come on," Will said. "I need to work off some of Mrs. Davis's breakfast. You can show me what's so wonderful about this hot-as-hell part of Texas that makes everybody determined to stay here."

"I need to know what will happen if I'm late with the next payment on Dad's loan," Idalou said to Lloyd Severns. She hated having to admit to anyone that she couldn't meet the loan payment on time, but it was better to know what she was up against than to find out when it was too late to do anything about it.

"Why will you be late?" Lloyd looked like a banker. Married at twenty-five, he wore a black suit, kept a punctual schedule, and was unflappable.

"I can't find the bull."

"When do you expect to find him?"

"Any minute. Carl is out looking for him now."

Lloyd opened a drawer, looked for and found a folder, which he laid open on his desk. "You haven't been very regular with your payments in the past."

"You know how much trouble we've had since Mom and Dad died. It seems like everything that happens around Dunmore hits us worse than anybody else."

"That's because your place is so small you don't have any margin for safety," Lloyd pointed out. "You ought to sell the ranch and move into town."

"And let Jordan McGloughlin win?"

Lloyd sighed and closed the folder. "I know there are bad feelings between you and Jordan, Idalou, but it doesn't help to blame everything on him."

"Everybody knows he's trying to get me to sell him my ranch."

"What everybody *doesn't* know is that he'd do anything underhanded to force you to sell." Lloyd leaned forward. "You and Carl have worked hard to make the place pay off, but I told your father I didn't think it would work even before he mortgaged the ranch to buy that bull. I'm sympathetic to you, but I have a duty to my investors. I can't keep their money tied up in loans that don't pay. And as much as I like and admire you—"

"You don't have to say the rest," Idalou said. "Even though I am only a woman, I understand business as well as you do."

"I never disputed that."

"You're about the only one who hasn't." She heaved a deep sigh. "I'll have the money on time, but just in case I can't, what will happen?"

"I'll have to foreclose on the loan and put the ranch up for sale."

"Which would mean Jordan would get it for a fraction of what it's worth."

"Frank Sonnenberg is just as anxious to have control of Dunmore Creek as Jordan. If you were to put the place up for sale yourself, you could find yourself the beneficiary of a bidding war."

Her father had been farsighted enough to homestead the only year-long source of water. McGloughlin and Sonnenberg had offered to buy her father's ranch several times, but he'd always refused. What he hadn't understood was that controlling the water didn't necessarily mean he controlled the land on either side of it, especially when his neighbors were rich, powerful, and had a bunkhouse full of cowhands.

"I don't want a bidding war," Idalou said. "I just want to keep our ranch."

Lloyd leaned back in his chair. "I'm sorry, but I can't give you any extra time."

"I wouldn't need it if we had a sheriff who could force Jordan to keep his cows off my land."

"You know as well as I do that grazing land belongs to the man, or woman, who can control it."

"My father established the boundaries before either Jordan or Frank Sonnenberg came here. They honored them until Dad died."

"That's out of my control. Why don't you discuss it with the new sheriff?"

"What new sheriff? Who is he?"

"Go see for yourself. He stopped Van Sonnenberg from running down Pepper and stopped Newt Mandrin from forcing his attentions on Mara. He might be interested in helping you find your bull."

"Is he a gunslinger?"

Lloyd laughed. "Not at all. He appears to be an easygoing man with a way of handling guys other men can't."

Idalou left the bank and headed toward the sheriff's office without much hope of finding a quick solution to her difficulties. She didn't like the way Lloyd had grinned at her when he'd said the sheriff might be interested in helping her find the bull. Lloyd was usually pretty serious, but occasionally he found humor in things that other people didn't think funny.

Still, it was good to have a sheriff. After Newt killed the last one in a fair fight, she had given up on anyone ever taking the job as long as Newt stayed in the area. And as long as Frank Sonnenberg gave him work, Newt would stay.

Idalou looked up at the sound of her name to see Mara waving at her and preparing to cross the street. Idalou didn't want to speak to anyone whose name was McGloughlin, but she couldn't very well ignore

Mara. Dunmore was a small town. It would be uncomfortable not to be on speaking terms with people she met nearly every day.

"Have you heard about the new sheriff?" Mara asked. She had dashed across the street oblivious to the two horses, a buckboard, and a wagon that could have run her down if the various men in charge hadn't scrambled to avoid her.

"I'm headed to meet him now." Idalou didn't slow her pace.

"He saved my life," Mara announced breathlessly. "Papa says I can marry him if I want."

Idalou had often thought Mara was too immature to be a wife. But occasionally batting her eyes at Van Sonnenberg was a far cry from wanting to marry a man she'd just met. "I thought you were in love with Carl."

Mara compressed her mouth and looked very much like a little girl about to throw a tantrum. "We had a fight. Besides, Papa says he'll never allow me to marry a poor man."

"Carl wouldn't be so poor if your father wasn't trying to destroy us."

"That's another thing," Mara said, firing up. "I'm sick of you always blaming Papa for everything that happens. Even Carl doesn't think that."

"That's because Carl is so much in love with you he can't see what's in front of him."

Mara tossed her head. "Well, I don't think he's all that in love with me now. But it doesn't matter. I'm in love with the sheriff. Did I tell you he saved my life?"

"This makes the second time."

"You should have seen him," Mara continued, undaunted. "He knocked Newt down just like it was nothing. And he can draw faster than Newt."

"Nobody can draw faster than Newt."

"Will can. I saw him do it."

"Will! Do you mean the sheriff's name is Will?"

"It's Will Haskins." Mara sighed. "He's the most gorgeous man I've ever seen."

"Lloyd Severns made Will Haskins sheriff?" Idalou was aghast. She couldn't imagine what had possessed him to do such a thing.

"Daddy and Mr. Davis did it, too. Daddy thinks he's the perfect man for me to marry."

"He's just here to buy our bull." Idalou was convinced somebody was playing a joke on her. No one would hire a man who just rode into town to be their sheriff, especially since Will wasn't going to be here more than a few days.

"I don't know anything about that," Mara announced. "I just know he's coming to dinner tonight. After what I've told her, Mama can hardly wait to meet him."

Idalou had no doubt Will would make a complete slave of Alma McGloughlin. Idalou had been so stunned by his looks, she could hardly talk. Why should Alma be any different?

"I'd love to stay and talk, but I have to see the sheriff," Idalou said.

Mara went all stiff and prim. "If Carl's still there, tell him it's no use dropping by the house this afternoon. I'll be helping Mama get ready for Mr. Haskins."

Idalou thought if Mara said one more word about Will, she'd scream, but fortunately, the girl said she had to buy some new ribbons for her hair. And look for a new bonnet. And her mother thought it would be nice to have something special for dessert, so Mara had been instructed to pick up some extra sugar and dried fruit. She hoped there'd be enough eggs for baked meringues.

"Then you'd better make your purchases and hurry home."

Idalou was relieved when Mara rushed off to Andy Davis's mercantile. She headed toward the sheriff's office, her thoughts in turmoil. It was hard to believe Will Haskins was Dunmore's sheriff. Even if it was true that he'd outfought and outdrawn Newt, why would he want to be sheriff when he was going to be here for such a short time? She didn't have much respect for the good sense of most of the men she knew, but she had thought Andy Davis and Lloyd Severns were at least halfway intelligent.

Maybe it was the way her fast, energetic stride caused her heels to pound on the boardwalk or the frown on her face which she noticed when she passed the bakery window, but no one stopped to speak to her. It was just as well. She was in no mood for idle chitchat. She entered the sheriff's office to find Carl and Will getting ready to leave. The sheriff's badge gleamed on the latter's vest like the afternoon sun on the Texas horizon. It was impossible to miss.

"Lou, did you hear—"

"Lloyd couldn't wait to tell me," Idalou said, cutting her brother off. "I think he actually enjoyed it."

"Will's going to help me look for the bull."

"I thought you couldn't interfere in local situations," Idalou challenged Will.

"That was before I was sheriff. Now it's my duty to look into complaints."

"I've got a long list. I doubt you'll be here long enough to get through it."

"Lay off, Lou," her brother said. "He hasn't been here long enough for you to get mad at him."

"I made her angry in our first meeting," Will volunteered.

"Damn, Lou, can't you meet any man without making him your enemy?" Carl asked, apparently completely out of patience with his sister.

"I'm not her enemy," Will said. "She just didn't like something I said."

"She doesn't like anything anybody says. Let's get out of here before she makes you so mad you won't help look for the bull."

Idalou didn't know how the tables had been turned so quickly, but her own brother had done it. "I'd like to talk with the *sheriff* alone for a moment," she said.

"Not on your life," Carl stated flatly. "I'm gonna stand right here and listen to every word you say."

It was probably best that Carl didn't leave. She was so incensed that Will was sheriff, convinced he'd done something underhanded to make Mara tumble in love with him, she would most certainly have said something imprudent. Still, she had a lot of questions, and she meant to get answers. Before she could ask even one of them, an altercation outside the office door drew their attention. Two girls were arguing over which one should open the door for the other.

"I've got the hot coffeepot," one said. "I can't open the door without setting it down."

"Well, I've got a plate of bread and butter as well as a cup," said the other.

Carl got up, walked over, and pulled the door open. Two surprised young girls—Andy Davis's daughters Louise and Sarah—stood frozen, caught in mid-argument. Recovering quickly, both tried to pass through the doorway at the same time. Carl rescued the plate of bread and butter before it slid from Louise's grasp. Taking advantage of her sister's barely averted disaster, Sarah scurried forward, bearing the coffeepot like a symbol of victory. She sailed by Idalou without being aware of her existence.

"Mama sent you some fresh coffee," she said in a voice that practically wilted from the brightness of the smile she bestowed on Will. "She made it black and strong just the way you like it." The child stood there, holding the hot coffeepot out to Will just as if she expected him to take it from her with his bare hands.

"Set it down on the desk," Will said. "And tell your mother I think she's wonderful to go to so much trouble for me."

"It was no trouble at all," insisted Louise, recovered from her momentary setback and pushing her sister aside. "She sent some hot bread and butter. She said you'd probably be hungry for a snack by now." She preened and looked down on her younger and shorter sister. "I helped Mama make the bread."

"I ground the coffee beans," Sarah said, attempting without success to elbow her older sister aside.

"Mama said she'd send more coffee at lunchtime," Louise informed Will. "She said Mrs. Wentlock can't make decent coffee to save her life."

"Please thank your mother for me, but tell her I won't be in the office for the rest of the day, so I don't need any more coffee."

"Where will you be?" the two girls asked in unison, dismay in their voices as well as their expressions.

"I've promised to help Miss Ellsworth and her brother see if we can find their bull."

"Don't you want the coffee?" Louise asked.

"Don't you want the bread and butter?" Sarah echoed.

"I most certainly do. I'm sure Miss Ellsworth and her brother will enjoy it as much as I will."

Neither girl appeared to like the idea of their offering being shared with anyone else. "Mama has already put her name down for supper tomorrow night," Louise said.

"She said breakfast wasn't nothing compared to the supper she would cook for you," Sara added.

Idalou didn't know whether to be angry at Mrs. Davis, her daughters, Will, or just be disgusted with every female who couldn't wait to make a fool of herself over Will. The man was incredibly good-looking, but that didn't make him the best catch in Texas any more than it made Junie Mae Winslow the most desirable female in Texas. Idalou metaphorically kicked herself for thinking of the woman Webb had been seeing when he died. She'd intended to put that woman out of her mind for good.

"You'd better be getting home before she starts to worry about you," Will said. "Pretty girls like you are liable to get some young man so distracted he'd ride his horse right into the saloon."

The girls, only average in looks, giggled delightedly. Rather than leave, they stood there, waiting expectantly. Understanding what they were waiting for, Will poured himself a cup of coffee, offered the cup to Idalou and Carl, who refused, then took a swallow himself.

"Perfect," he announced. "Just how I like it."

Meanwhile, Sarah buttered pieces of bread, which she offered to Will. He directed her offering to Idalou first. She declined, but Carl took a piece and so did Will. Both men declared it was the best bread they'd ever eaten. Pleased, the girls took their leave. Idalou was certain they'd carry the praise straight to their mother, who'd spend every minute between now and next evening planning a supper that would eclipse anything Dorabelle Severns had made. She was irritated all over again.

"That was disgusting," Idalou announced as soon as the door closed behind the girls. "And you goaded them on with ludicrous compliments."

"I thought it was funny," Carl said, laughing. "Besides, the bread was really good."

"I couldn't very well send it back or tell them I didn't like it," Will said.

Idalou knew that, but it made her even madder that she cared what Will said or did. This fawning acceptance of a virtual stranger was in sharp contrast to the way the townspeople treated her and Carl, people they'd known for years, people who shared common interests, common dangers. "Why did you decide to be sheriff when you'll only be here a short time?"

"Lloyd and the others seemed desperate to have somebody fill in while they look for someone to take the job full-time."

"What's the story about beating up Newt and outdrawing him?"

"He was too drunk to put up much of a fight," Will said.

"He wasn't too drunk to draw his gun this morning," Carl said. "Emmett saw the sheriff beat Newt. So did Mara. He did it right here in the jail."

"With guns?" Not even an idiot would have a shootout in the jail, and she was certain Will Haskins was not an idiot.

"They weren't loaded," Will explained.

"Do you know Mara thinks she's in love with you, that she's going to marry you? Don't you know how impressionable she is?"

"You didn't fall over yourself when you met me. Why should I think Mara would?"

"Because she thinks you saved her life."

"The sheriff thinks she's momentarily bowled over by his looks," Carl explained. "He says girls get really excited about something romantic, like a man saving them from danger. He says they turn the man into a hero and want to marry him."

"He said all of that, did he?" Idalou asked before turning a menacing eye on the squirming sheriff.

"It didn't sound quite like that when I said it," Will offered.

"I'm sure the gist was the same," Idalou said.

"Probably," Will admitted. "I'm sure you'd like to talk some more, but I promised Carl I'd help him look for your bull. I expect you have things to do."

"Nothing as pressing as finding that bull. Lloyd says if I don't make the loan payment on time, he'll put the ranch up for auction."

"Damn!" Carl said. "Why won't he give you more time?"

"He said he's done that too many times before, that it's not fair to his investors." Idalou didn't like sharing this information with Will, but if he understood the urgency of the situation, maybe he would talk to Jordan.

"Give me time to get my horse," she said. "I'm coming with you."

Chapter Five

Will supposed it was good that Carl could ignore the tension that practically vibrated in the air between him and Idalou. He chattered away with the simple pleasure of a young man who takes pride in his accomplishments. He had a love for the land that his sister didn't appear to share. Whereas Carl could be excited at the shape of a ridge or the sweep of open prairie, Idalou was more likely to point out that the land had been overgrazed.

"We're lucky to be on the edge where the soil changes from limestone clay to red or brown clay," Carl was saying. "Because we have the darker clay, we have more substantial soil, which gives us better grass."

"Little good it does when McGloughlin's cows come over and eat it up before our own cows can," Idalou commented.

"We have the only dependable water, too."

"At least McGloughlin's stock hasn't been able to drink it all up," Idalou said.

They'd been following a beautifully clear creek whose pure spring waters sparkled brilliantly in the sunlight. Tiny fish darted to safety among the large stones that caused the water to rush and tumble with a satisfying murmur. A scattering of mature trees—pecan, ash, oak, and cottonwood—shaded the banks and created thickets along with mesquite, hackberry, and black willow that provided food and shelter for a wide variety of birds and small rodents. A cowbird strutted nonchalantly in the open, ignoring a hawk that circled overhead, depending on the large body of a three-year-old steer for protection while it fed on weed seeds or insects stirred up by the steer's hooves as he searched for grass among the cactus, sage, and various thorny bushes.

"We get most of our rain in the fall," Carl was saying, "so we have a dam that helps us through spring and early summer."

"What about the other ranches?" Will asked.

"McGloughlin and Sonnenberg have water of their own, but we never cut off the flow," Idalou said. "Dad said that would be unfair and certain to cause trouble."

They had passed two dry streambeds that joined the creek, one from each of the neighboring ranches.

"The late summer rains will start soon," Carl said. "Until then, the other ranchers depend on wells."

Will was getting a much better picture of the basis for the Double-L's trouble with its neighbors. Better grass, better soil, and the only dependable water.

"Has Frank Sonnenberg put any pressure on you to sell to him?" Will asked. They had stopped under the widespread limbs of a live oak to give their horses a breather.

"He offered us more than McGloughlin for the land, but he didn't get angry when I told him we didn't want to sell," Idalou said. "Van helped Carl repair the corral fence. He even told us how to make the dam stronger."

"He's always been nice to you," Carl said to his sister, "but I don't like him. I think he wants to marry you."

"His father intends for him to marry Mara. Joining their two ranches would make the combined spread one of the largest in Texas. That's another reason they're so anxious to buy our ranch. They want to get rid of me so Van won't be tempted to marry me, and get rid of Carl so Mara can't marry him."

"If you were good enough for Webb, you're certainly good enough for Van," Carl put in.

"Who's Webb?" Will asked, struggling to keep up with this complex weaving of interests and motivations.

"Mara's brother," Carl said. "He and Idalou were sweet on each other until he got himself killed."

Idalou blushed slightly and looked away. Did that mean she was still carrying a torch for this dead guy? Will wondered. If he was as handsome as Mara was pretty, Will wouldn't be surprised. Handsome, rich, and probably nice was a powerful combination. A woman could be forgiven for still thinking about a man like that. Will was able to attribute his irritation at Van's interest in Idalou to thinking the man was basically unworthy to marry any decent woman, but why should he be jealous of a dead man?

"Nothing was ever put into words," Idalou said. "Being neighbors, it was natural we'd see a lot of each other."

"It was more than that, and you know it," Carl insisted. "At least it was until Junie Mae came to town and Webb got a good look at her."

"Well, he did meet Junie Mae," Idalou said, not

looking away this time. "We've gotten completely off the subject. We ought to show Will the dam."

The dam—constructed in a narrow neck where the stream passed between two rocky outcroppings before tumbling noisily down a boulder-strewn slope—was a wooden structure ten feet high. It looked like at least five feet of water was backed up behind it in a lake that filled a wide depression.

"We'll leave the chutes open until the rains start and all the dry creeks begin to flow again," Carl said.

Will wondered why McGloughlin was the only one to put any real pressure on Idalou and her brother to sell. If Van was any indication of what his father was like, Frank Sonnenberg would be more likely than McGloughlin to use underhanded methods to drive Idalou and her brother off their land. The men he'd met in the saloon didn't much like Sonnenberg or his son. At the same time, everybody liked McGloughlin. Will found that curious.

"Do you have anyone to keep watch on the dam?" Will asked.

"We only have two hands," Carl said. "We can't afford to put someone on it all the time."

"It's not far from the house," Idalou added. "I check it every day after breakfast. If anything is threatening to break, I want to know about it as soon as possible. If the dam broke, it could threaten the house."

Thinking back on yesterday, Will remembered that the creek ran close by the ranch house. While they were talking, several cows came up to the lake behind the dam to drink.

"Dammit!" Idalou said. "Jordan promised to keep his cows off our range."

"Lou, you can't tell from here whose cows those are. Besides, you know he can't watch every cow."

Ignoring her brother, Idalou drove her horse through the stream and along the bluff.

"Where's she going?" Will asked.

"To a break in the bluff," Carl said. "That's the fastest way to get up to the lake on the far side."

The two men turned their horses and followed. By the time they reached Idalou, she was sitting on her horse about twenty feet from two cows with their calves.

"Those cows have bred with our bull," Idalou fumed. She pointed at two calves that clearly showed different breeding from their longhorn mothers. "Jordan will get twice as much for these when he sells them, without ever having to buy his own bull. Now do you understand why I'm so angry at him?" she demanded of Will.

Will could understand quite well. "What did he say when you talked to him?"

"What he says every time," Idalou answered. "That he can't keep his cows from wandering onto our land any more than we can keep our bull from wandering onto his."

"He does send his men after them every time you complain," Carl said to Idalou.

"And they're back within the week." She turned to Will. "*Now* will you go with me to confront Jordan?"

Will didn't believe in confrontation except as a last resort. It was the same as cornering a wild animal. Jordan would turn and fight regardless of the circumstances that had led to the problem. "I'm going there for supper," he said. "It may be better if I try to see what I can find out on my own."

"Are you afraid of Jordan, or have you gone over to the side of the rich?"

"Lou!" Carl exclaimed. "That's not fair."

"He has visible proof that Jordan's cows are on my

land, but he won't do anything about it," his sister responded, not backing down.

"The cows are on *our* land," Carl pointed out.

Will wasn't angry, just disappointed. He liked Idalou. He thought she'd been handed a rough deal, but she wouldn't back off long enough to let anybody help her. "As long as you're certain you have all the answers, you'll never know any more than you do now. I'll head back to town."

"She didn't mean it," Carl said, following Will. "She just gets riled and says the first thing that comes into her head."

"People can't know when she means something and when she doesn't, so we have to assume she means everything she says," Will said. "If you'll come by the office tomorrow, I'll let you know what Jordan says."

"Our house is on your way back to town."

"I think the less your sister sees of me, the better."

Will thought he was merely disappointed, but as he put more distance between himself and Idalou, he realized he was angry as well. He didn't like to be judged, especially when it was unfair. He knew he was spoiled, that he'd had things easy most of his life. Between his looks and good manners, he got along famously with women as long as they didn't try to marry him. He wasn't used to being shoved in the corner with the bad guys.

There was one thing that pleased him, though. Idalou might have judged him prematurely, but she hadn't fallen into a stupor because of his looks. He couldn't tell what most women thought about him— the *real* him—because they never looked past his face.

When Idalou had opened the door and first seen him, he'd thought she was going to be just as bad as Mara, but she'd recovered quickly. Any lingering effects she might have suffered had disappeared when he'd refused to go with her to confront Jordan. Given time, maybe she'd get to know what he was really like.

It surprised him that he cared what she thought. He'd never been this interested in any one woman. He'd watched his brothers get married, wondering what it was that suddenly made it imperative that they have one particular woman and no other would do. Maybe his interest in Idalou stemmed from the fact that she had misjudged him and he was determined to prove her wrong. Maybe it was that she was mostly unimpressed by his looks. Maybe he just wanted to help a woman who found herself in trouble without a way out. He didn't know, but he did know he had several questions for Jordan McGloughlin, and he didn't mean to leave the man's house this evening until he had answers to some of them.

"I hope you're satisfied with yourself," Carl raged. "This was our only chance to get the sheriff to help us find out what happened to that damned bull, and you ruined it. Why don't you wear a sign that says *I hate men!* and save everybody a lot of time."

"I don't hate men," Idalou said. "I don't even hate the sheriff."

"I'm not sure I believe you. I know he doesn't."

Idalou knew she had let her temper get away from her, but she was operating under tremendous pressure. Jordan was responsible for the disappearance of their bull, but she couldn't get anyone to believe her, not even her brother. They had to sell the bull to keep their home, but she couldn't do that as long as she couldn't find the beast. And if she didn't make the next payment on time, Lloyd was going to auction the ranch off to the highest bidder. On top of that, the girl Carl loved was now in love with Will.

"I'll apologize to him next time I see him."

"Stay away from him before you have him hoping Lloyd does sell the ranch out from under us," Carl snapped.

"I said I'd apologize."

"You might, but I expect you'd find something else to get upset about immediately afterwards." He slapped his hat against his leg. The sound startled his horse. "You can't hold it against every man that Webb is dead or that he broke up with you."

"I don't—"

"He might not have if you hadn't torn into him every time you got mad at his father."

"How dare you—"

"Get mad at me, too, if that'll make you feel any better. Maybe that's the only way you can relate to people. I love you, Lou, but sometimes it's hard to like you. I'm going to look for the bull. I'll see you back at the house."

Idalou was stunned. She'd loved Carl from the time he was born. She'd looked after him when he was growing up. The deaths of her parents had been hard on her, but she'd struggled to be father, mother, and sister to him. She'd fought to keep the ranch because it was his only inheritance. She knew they disagreed over Mara, but she couldn't understand why he'd condemned her.

Jordan's cows looked just like every other longhorn she'd ever seen, tall and skinny with mottled hides and horns that spanned nearly six feet, but their calves were a solid rust-brown, shorter in stature and broader in build. They'd grow up to have fifty more pounds of meat than a longhorn. They were meant to be the future of the Double-L, not a windfall for Jordan McGloughlin. It infuriated her that everyone knew what he was doing and no one would take action about it. How could Carl expect her to hold her tongue when Will was just as bad?

She liked Will, and not just because of his looks. He'd barely laid eyes on her before insisting she sit down and bringing her a glass of water. Not even Webb had been so kind and thoughtful. It seemed she'd finally found a man who would treat her like a real person, yet everything he'd done after that made him appear to be just like every other man she'd ever known—thinking that just because she was a woman, she was automatically an inferior being.

Maybe she hadn't given herself a chance to get to know him, but her whole world was falling apart. In a few days she and Carl could be without a place to live or a way to support themselves. How was she supposed to—

"Are you out here all by yourself?"

The sound of Van Sonnenberg's voice yanked Idalou out of her abstraction. She turned around to see his handsome face smiling at her, but she wasn't tempted to think his expression betokened anything beyond friendship.

"My brother and I were looking for our bull. Carl's gone off to search in one direction. I was about to head off in the other."

"It's a shame you have to sell him," Van commiserated. "Dad says your father put all his hopes on that animal." Van pointed to Jordan's cows. "From the looks of those calves, in a few years you could have made more money than either Dad or McGloughlin."

"Those aren't our cows. They're McGloughlin's."

"Son of a bitch!" Van cursed. "Is he still pushing his cows onto your land?"

Idalou wasn't sure she liked Van Sonnenberg. Though he'd always been nice to her, she knew his bad reputation was well earned. Still, it was nice to have someone who felt the same way she did about McGloughlin. She'd be curious to see how he'd get around that dislike when he decided to start courting Mara. She figured the only reason Van had waited this long was because at twenty-one he wasn't ready to settle down. "I don't know how they got here. I just know I'm sick of chasing them back."

"I'll do it for you," Van said, grinning. "It'll give me a reason to needle his cowhands for sloppy work."

"I'd rather you didn't give Jordan any more reason to dislike me."

"You want me to help you look for your bull?" Van's trademark grin appeared. He wasn't anywhere near as handsome as Will Haskins, but he'd been setting young hearts aflutter since he'd turned fourteen. And breaking a few, if rumor could be trusted.

"Go chase the cows away. That'll cause less trouble," Idalou said.

Van laughed as he turned his horse. She watched as he rode off, yelling and fanning the air with his hat to get the cows moving. He was filled with high spirits and a love of life that came from the belief he could have anything he wanted—but why should that make her think of Will Haskins? She was certain Will's looks had gotten him virtually anything he wanted, but he had a settled air about him. If everybody could be believed, he'd handled both Van and Newt with ease, yet he'd refused to confront Jordan for her. If Van had been in his place, he'd be heading for Jordan's ranch right now, fire in his eyes.

So why was she relieved that Will *didn't* act like Van?

She didn't know why she felt that way any more than why she seemed to lose her temper with Will every time they met. Something about him set her off. Maybe it was because he seemed to have had better luck than her family had. Because his life seemed so golden, when hers was badly tarnished. What was wrong with her?

Probably too much pressure. From the time her father had purchased that bull, nothing had gone right, and she'd been helpless to fix any of it.

And she wouldn't fix anything by sitting here like a mindless idiot. She had to find that bull. Until she did that, nothing else mattered.

"I can't tell you how grateful I am for what you did for my daughter," Mrs. McGloughlin said to Will for what had to be the fifth or sixth time in the last hour. "Since Webb's death, I've been petrified that something might happen to her. Mara's my only child now."

Will could sympathize with a mother's concern for her daughter. He wasn't an anxious person, but he was beginning to feel the need for a long walk in the wide-open spaces.

"I think you've convinced him of that, Alma," Jordan McGloughlin said to his wife. "Let the man relax, or he won't be able to enjoy his supper."

"I'm just so thankful, I don't know what to do," his wife said.

Will was tempted to suggest she begin by keeping her daughter home after dark, but he took a swallow of his whiskey and said nothing. "Do you mind showing me around before supper?" Will asked.

"Not a bit," Jordan said, getting to his feet. "We can saddle up a couple of horses."

"Maybe just walk out in the yard," Will said, standing and following Jordan outside. "I don't want to get too far from the wonderful smells coming from the kitchen."

Like many men who grew up in the East, Jordan had planted trees to shade his ranch house, but they were a far cry from the towering oaks, maples, cypresses, and cedars of the Hill Country that some-times formed a dense canopy that even the most bril-liant sun couldn't penetrate, allowing mosses and ferns to grow in the cool, moist soil.

"Your daughter is a lovely young woman," Will said. "I'm sure you and your wife are very proud of her."

"We are," Jordan said, beaming with fatherly pride, "but she's a bit headstrong. That can be a worry."

"Like when she decides she's in love with a man she barely knows."

"Better you than Carl Ellsworth," Jordan said. "He's hardly more than a boy."

They had wandered over to the edge of the low rise on which Jordan had built his ranch house. A few cows grazed on the treeless prairie stretched out be-fore them. A bell rang somewhere on the far side of the ranch house, signaling it was time for the cowhands to eat supper.

"I was told you were hoping she'd marry Van Sonnenberg in order to join the two ranches," Will said.

Jordan shrugged and pressed his lips together in apparent frustration. "At one time I thought Webb would marry Idalou and Mara would marry Van. All the ranches would have been connected by family, and all of this tension would disappear. After Webb died, it seemed the only logical thing was for Mara to marry Van, but she *said* she'd fallen in love with Carl Ellsworth. I told her I would never let her marry a man who was too poor and too young to provide for her. At the same time, I wasn't too happy with the way Van was developing. He's become so self-centered, he doesn't care how he affects others. Sometimes I think he doesn't even realize it. So you understand why I was pleased when she said she'd fallen in love with you. You've got all the good qualities of Carl without the bad qualities of Van. Plus you've got maturity. You know how to handle yourself, how to deal well with people."

This wasn't what Will had been hoping to hear. "I wouldn't depend on her interest in me lasting more than a few days."

"With your looks, you could make sure it does."

His looks again. Didn't people ever think there was anything to him other than his face? "I'm not in the marrying mood right now." And if he had been, he wouldn't have been interested in a young woman who changed her mind every few days. "Besides, I'm going back home after I find the bull. You wouldn't want your only child that far away."

"Her mother would be terribly upset."

"You ought to reconsider Carl Ellsworth. I know he's young, but he has the makings of a solid, dependable man. And I think he'll make a fine rancher. He likes the Double-L far more than his sister does."

"You'd never know it from the way she tears into me every time she thinks I've somehow taken advantage of her."

"Why shouldn't she feel like that, when you've got ten times as much land as she does but your cows spill over onto her land?"

"That hasn't happened in a long time."

"Two of them were at the dam this afternoon. They had calves that had been sired by her bull. What kind of stud fees do you pay her?"

Faint color rose out of Jordan's collar. "I don't pay her anything. I can't help it if her bull wanders onto my land and impregnates my cows."

"What if those cows had been on *her* land when the bull serviced them?"

"They weren't."

"How do you know?"

Jordan was looking decidedly uncomfortable. "My problems with Idalou aren't your concern."

"That's not quite true. You're one of the men who wanted me to be the sheriff. Since Idalou has asked *the sheriff* to look into the problem, she's put it squarely in my lap."

"What are you planning to do?" Jordan had gotten his back up. He looked angry, even belligerent.

"I'm not planning to do anything. I'm hoping you and Idalou can sit down and work this out between you. You ought to include Carl in the discussion. I think you'll be surprised at how reasonable you find him."

"Which is more than I can say for his sister," Jordan said, appearing to calm down. "I've tried to talk to her."

"I'm sure you have. But as long as your cows keep wandering onto her property and breeding with her bull, you can understand why she might think that you don't mean what you say."

"Dammit!" Jordan's voice had risen in volume. "I don't need the use of her bull to make a profit. I've got good longhorn bulls of my own."

"I don't doubt you," Will said, "but Idalou is the one you have to convince. I'd give some thought to paying her something for all those calves her bull sired. It would go a long way toward helping her believe you are serious."

"I don't care what Idalou thinks. She's a stubborn, fractious woman."

"Who just might one day be your daughter's sister-in-law. It's always helpful to think ahead. Children have a bad habit of having ambitions that don't agree with those of their parents. Besides, you're the richest man in this area. It's up to you to set the tone of the community."

Fortunately, before Jordan could become incensed at Will's intrusion into his personal affairs, Mrs. Mc-Gloughlin signaled that it was time for dinner. Now Will had to find a way to turn Mara's thoughts back in Carl's direction.

Chapter Six

Will couldn't think of anything more likely to give Mara the wrong impression about his feelings for her than being alone with her in the moonlight. To make matters worse, Alma McGloughlin had spent the entire evening staring at him with a dazed look that had the power to instill terror in his heart. He'd seen that look before. It was the *I'm going to be your mother-in-law* look that had been fatal to so many incautious young men. But Will wasn't incautious. Despite his rather easygoing attitude, he had a highly developed sense of self-preservation. He and Mara were now sitting in the yard facing away from the house. They were close enough to the house to cause no anxiety to her parents but far enough away to be able to talk quietly without being overheard.

"You won't have to buy a ranch or cows for your bull," Mara was saying. "Daddy has everything you need right here."

What was it about women that took them from seeing a man they liked straight to planning the wedding and the next twenty years, all in less than twenty-four hours? Mara had never even asked if he was single. No one had. It was time he shifted the focus of the conversation. "What was it you saw in Carl that made you fall in love with him?"

Mara's blissful expression turned to confusion, tinged by melancholy.

"Carl is a sweet boy, but he's so immature."

She was trying to sound grown-up but only succeeded in sounding insincere.

"Maybe, but what was it you liked about him originally? You can't have forgotten it already."

Mara's lips pushed forward in a pout. Before she could make the expected objection, her expression changed. She took her lower lip between her teeth, dropped her gaze to her hands, which had begun to twist in her lap.

"I don't know. I just liked him," she said.

"Did you look forward to being with him?"

"Yes."

"Why?"

She looked away. "He was always doing sweet things."

"Like what?"

"Like telling me how pretty I was, how he dreamed about me, how he couldn't imagine spending the rest of his life with anyone except me."

"Is that important?"

"Yes, but—"

"What did you like to do when you were together?"

"We'd take rides. Sometimes we'd find a place to sit and talk."

"What did you talk about?"

She blushed. "He'd talk about the flowers he'd bring me, or the pretty dresses he'd buy for me. You probably think that's silly."

"Why would I think that?"

"Daddy and Webb said real men didn't talk about flowers and women's clothes."

"Is that what you think?"

"I don't know." She looked confused. "Van says the same thing." She looked embarrassed. "He laughed at me when I asked him what kind of flowers he'd give a girl."

"Do you like Van?" The quiet of the evening seemed to be affecting Mara. She became more contemplative as the sun sank out of sight and the sky turned orange shot through with blood red.

"He's okay."

"But you feel more comfortable with Carl?"

Mara nodded.

"Why?"

"Van makes me feel like a little girl. He thinks all the things I say or do are silly. He says I'll think differently when I'm a woman."

Will had a poor opinion of Van, but now he added stupidity to his list of shortcomings. He didn't know if Van didn't want to marry Mara or if he was just after her father's ranch and considered her a necessary part of the bargain.

"Everybody's ideas change a little as they grow older, but there's nothing wrong with what you feel now," Will said. "It certainly doesn't mean you're silly."

"Daddy says I'll understand when I get to be Van's age."

"I'm older than Van, and I don't think a man giving a woman flowers or buying her pretty dresses is silly. Women like things like that, and I think it's important for a man to want to make his wife happy."

Mara's face lit up like lightning against a black sky. "That's why I love you. You understand all about women."

Will could see he wasn't getting anywhere trying to convince Mara that she liked Carl better than him. She was confused by thinking he was a hero and having her parents enthusiastically support her choice. This wasn't something he was going to fix in one night. It might be a good idea to get a woman's perspective on the situation. Maybe he'd ask Idalou. She wasn't too happy with him, but surely she'd be eager to see Carl and Mara back together.

"No man understands everything about women," Will said. "The best we can do is hope to keep from getting in so much trouble that some woman starts dreaming about our being trampled by a loco steer."

"Well, I think you're perfect," Mara stated. "And so does Mama. Even Daddy says he can't find anything wrong with you, and he finds something wrong with everybody."

Will decided it was time to admit defeat and head home. "We'd better go in. I have to get up early in the morning, and your parents are probably starting to worry."

"They'll never worry as long as I'm with you," Mara said in a hopelessly romantic way. Will was thankful that none of his brothers had witnessed this scene. They'd taunt him for the rest of his life. He stood and helped Mara to her feet.

"They ought to worry," he said. "There's something wrong with any man who's completely trustworthy when he's with a girl as pretty as you."

Mara blushed and looked so discomposed by the compliment, Will decided he couldn't allow her father to force her to marry Van Sonnenberg. A man like him would crush the life out of her, or make her despairingly unhappy.

"You talk like Carl," Mara said.

"I knew there was a reason I liked that boy."

"Because he talks like you?"

Will's poor effort at humor was obviously a little beyond Mara, but he didn't hold that against her. She'd been sheltered by overly protective parents.

"I like him because he's a nice young man who hasn't let adversity make him angry or spiteful. I'm certain he'd be unspoiled by success, too."

"Daddy says he'll never be successful on that little bit of land he and his sister have."

"I think your daddy may have underestimated Carl and his sister. And if you married him, your ranches would be joined. I've got some things to take care of, so I'd better say good night to your parents."

He could have told her he was riding over to tell Idalou and Carl that Jordan had agreed to meet with them to work out their differences. He had no intention of telling her he wanted Idalou's advice on how to make a young girl fall out of love with him.

After what she'd said that afternoon, Will was the last person Idalou had expected to see riding up to their ranch. She'd been sitting on the porch trying to decide if Carl was right in saying she'd misjudged him. Everyone else seemed to think he was wonderful, but everyone else was overwhelmed by his looks. Until Will rode into Dunmore, Van and Webb had been the two best-looking men she'd ever known. Both had grown into selfish young men. How was it possible that Will, who was twice as good-looking as either of them, wouldn't have done the same? She got up as he brought his horse to a stop at the foot of the porch steps.

"I was hoping you'd still be up," Will said as he dismounted.

"I was enjoying the cool of the evening." It had

clouded up. She hoped they'd get a little rain. "Did you have a nice supper?"

Will smiled up at her, and she had trouble remembering she was angry with him. It wasn't fair for a man to look that good. He dismounted. His horse blew though his nostrils as Will tied him to the hitching post.

"I ate too much."

"Mara said her mother was planning to go all out tonight."

"Getting the women of Dunmore to feed me was one of the conditions I laid out when I took the sheriff job, but I had no idea they'd try to fatten me up like a hog for the slaughter." He walked up to the steps but didn't mount them.

Idalou laughed, though she didn't feel like it. "Women can't resist feeding a handsome man. The more you eat, the better we think you like us."

"In that case, there are three nervous husbands in Dunmore. I've eaten enough to make them think I want to run off with their wives."

Idalou thought there were probably more than three women in Dunmore who would have dreams that would embarrass them come morning. She hoped she wouldn't be one of them. Carl came around the corner of the house from where he'd been talking to their two hands.

"What brings you over this way at night?" he asked Will.

"I had a few minutes alone with Jordan before supper, so I mentioned the cows I saw at your dam this morning. He seemed genuinely surprised. He said he'd given his hands orders to make sure his cows stayed on his land."

"And you believed him?" Idalou asked.

"Why shouldn't I?" Will asked.

"Because he's a liar who'll do anything he can to drive us off our land." She'd never forgiven Jordan for trying to have a judge invalidate her father's homestead along the creek.

"Have you talked with him?" Will asked.

"A dozen times. All he ever does is deny that he's done anything wrong."

"I wasn't talking about accusing him. I meant *talking* to him." Will turned to Carl, then back to Idalou. "He is your neighbor. You've got to learn to live with him."

Idalou didn't know whether Will believed what he said or if he was just trying to get her to shut up and go away, but she decided she'd judged him accurately, after all. Too agitated to sit still any longer, she got up and walked to the top of the steps where she could look down at Will.

"I thought a sheriff was supposed to investigate the complaints of every citizen. I don't call having dinner with Jordan, then telling me I ought to *talk* with him so he can spin more lies, much of an investigation. It looks to me like you've sold out, Sheriff."

"Lou, I don't think—"

"I'm sure you've had a rough time of it," Will said so calmly it was infuriating. "Jordan and others may have taken advantage of you, but there's nothing I can do about that. I'm only going to be here a few more days." Will included Carl in his glance. "You're the only ones who can do anything that will make a lasting difference."

"I've tried, but no one will listen to me," Idalou said.

"You're older now. So is Carl. It's time to make people start treating you like adults."

Idalou walked to the end of the porch, looked out over the yard of the ranch that had cast a shadow upon her life. She found little to admire in the buildings, the small house, even the tall trees along the creek. Carl loved it, but to her it was just an unending burden. "They'll never do that, because they can't stop seeing me as a woman."

"Take Carl along when you talk with Jordan, Lloyd, or anybody else. I think Jordan knows his cows were on your property when they mated with your bull. I can't tell you what he'll do, but I think he wants to work something out."

"When does he want to meet with us?" Carl asked.

"Tomorrow. If you'll take my suggestion, you and Carl will talk over what you want to say and what you want Jordan to do. You'll have a better chance of convincing him if you're in agreement. If you're going to argue with each other, you might as well save everybody time and stay home."

"I appreciate you talking to him for us," Carl said. "We'll do what you suggest."

Will turned to his horse. "One other thing. I haven't been here long, but I'm usually a pretty decent judge of people. It might be a good idea if you don't assume Jordan is lying about everything." He mounted up. "Come by tomorrow, Carl, and let me know how things go."

"Why didn't he ask *me* to let him know how things went?" Idalou asked after Will rode off.

"Probably because he expects you'll get mad at him again. Just for once, Lou, could you give somebody the benefit of the doubt?"

"How can you do that when he's trying to steal Mara away from you?"

"He's not in love with Mara. Hell, he'd be interested in you if you didn't tear in to him every time you set eyes on him."

Idalou was so shocked, she hardly knew what to think. She was attractive, but Will could have virtually any woman he wanted. She hadn't even been nice to him. "He couldn't possibly be interested in me."

"Why not?" Carl climbed the steps, pulled a chair over, and sat down. "You're a damned fine-looking woman. You just get your back up and don't give a man a chance. Now we've got to decide what we want Jordan to do. I think we ought to consider that he might be telling the truth."

"But he's not!"

"Nothing we've done so far has worked. I'm willing to give this a try. Will you?"

Idalou was in a quandary. They were on the verge of losing the ranch. Even if she didn't believe Will's plan would work, she was desperate enough to try anything once. But no matter what agreement they reached with Jordan, it had to include getting the bull back. Its sale was the only thing that would save them.

If she did what Carl wanted, it would mean she believed that Will knew more about how to solve her problems than she did. Of course, men always stood together, even when they were strangers, but there was something different about Will. He was the most easygoing man she'd ever met, yet he was capable of handling himself with his fists or with a gun. From all she could gather, he knew his way around a ranch. And through some mysterious method she had yet to begin to understand, he'd inspired a town of strangers with enough confidence to make him their sheriff.

There was clearly more to this man than met the eye. Well, more than met *her* eye. Everybody else seemed to think he'd hung the moon.

Funny, but until this evening she hadn't realized how bone tired she was. She couldn't remember a time over the last five years when she hadn't been struggling against something. The harder she worked, the worse things got. The more desperate she became, the more impossible the situation. It would be wonderful to share some of the load. If Carl wanted it, he could have it. After all, he was the one who really loved the ranch.

As for Will Haskins, he had gotten Jordan to agree to sit down and talk with them. That was more than she'd ever managed.

"I'll give it a try," she told her brother. "Will Haskins has more tricks up his sleeve than I suspected."

Idalou was determined not to lose her temper, but remembering his past duplicity made it hard to endure Jordan McGloughlin's air of self-importance. She couldn't hold him personally responsible for all the circumstances that made selling their bull necessary, but if he'd been a good neighbor, he'd have helped her out when they were having trouble. Completely ignoring her because she was a woman was his worst sin.

"The sheriff told me you found some of my cows on your land yesterday," Jordan said as soon as Idalou and Carl were seated in his office. Alma McGloughlin had provided coffee. Idalou had declined, but Jordan and Carl had poured cups for themselves while discussing whether the cooler weather would bring the possibility of rain.

The office had been furnished with deep leather chairs and a desk featuring a dozen pigeonholes stuffed with pieces of paper. The walls were covered with mounted heads of deer and buffalo, a style of decoration Idalou found tasteless and a bit gruesome. The dominating presence of so many shades of brown gave the room a somber, almost depressing feeling. Idalou itched to add a little color to alleviate the heaviness of the room.

"Two cows with their calves," Carl said. "They're

the first I've seen in a couple of weeks. And I've been over every inch of our land searching for the bull."

"You still haven't found him?" Jordan asked.

It was all Idalou could do to keep her lips pressed together and her hands clenched in her lap. *Everybody* knew they couldn't find their bull. How was she supposed to believe in Jordan's goodwill when he said things like that?

"No, but I will."

Carl seemed to have no trouble acting as though he and Jordan were on good terms. They were sitting back in their chairs acting as if they weren't talking about anything of greater importance than whether to go into town for a beer or stick with coffee. Idalou decided she simply didn't understand men.

"We should be looking for him right now," she said with as much control as she could muster. "Our loan payment is due soon." Everybody knew that, too.

"I'd appreciate it if you could ask your men to be on the lookout for him," Carl said.

"I want you to know I have given my men orders to keep my cows off your land," Jordan said.

She'd heard this before, yet the cows still came on her land.

"I expect a few will wander off, no matter how carefully you watch them," Carl said.

Idalou couldn't stand it any longer. "Both of the cows we saw yesterday had calves sired by our bull."

"I've got my own bulls. I paid good money for them." Jordan's response to her showed none of the calm that had been in evidence when he addressed Carl. "If it comes to that, some of *your* cows have bred to my bulls."

"We know that," Carl said, flashing his sister a look that said *leave this to me.* "It's just that you've got so many more by our bull than we have by yours. I was hoping that when you came to sell them, you could give us a little something in the way of a stud fee—if they sell real good, that is. It would help us a lot."

Idalou bit her tongue to keep from speaking. Carl was practically begging for what should have been theirs by right. She knew Jordan would never give them a single dime, so it was useless to ask.

"I'll have to wait until I see what kind of price they bring," Jordan said after a pause, "but I'll see what I can do. It may not be much," he hastened to add, "but it ought to be something."

Idalou was too surprised to speak. Jordan had always denied any responsibility for his cows being on their range or breeding with their bull. What could account for the change in his attitude? Could it have been Will?

"We'd sure appreciate that," Carl said. "Your cows wandering on our land isn't such a problem as long as we can get a little compensation."

"I told your father not to spend so much money buying that bull," Jordan said. "It's too much of a risk with a small operation like yours."

"Lou felt the same way," Carl said, "but it was Dad's dream."

"And now you're left trying to get out of the hole he dug. You shouldn't feel guilty about what's happened. If he'd been alive, he wouldn't have made it, either."

It made Idalou angry to have Jordan speak that way about her father, but she'd said the same thing herself.

She was glad she hadn't said anything about the stud fee, because now she'd have to take it back. She still didn't know if she could believe him. She just hoped they could hold on long enough to put him to the test.

One thing she did know: None of this change in Jordan would have happened without Will Haskins. She had no idea what Will had said or how he'd said it, but he'd managed to do in one evening what she'd been unable to do in three years—get Jordan to admit he'd taken advantage of them. She didn't entirely trust Will. After her father's bad judgment had gotten them into debt, Jordan's sharp dealing had made it worse. Webb's jilting her had so devastated her self-confidence, she wasn't sure she could trust any man, but she had to thank Will. Now, before she said something to ruin the whole morning, she'd better leave. She stood.

"Thank you for seeing us." She was unable to make herself thank him for doing what he should have done without Will's prodding. "Carl and I had better be going if we expect to find that bull before the loan payment is due."

"I really appreciate what you've done," Carl said, shaking hands with Jordan. "I'd like to talk with you again soon."

"Anytime."

The look in Jordan's eyes didn't match his words. Idalou was certain he thought Carl wanted to talk about marrying Mara. He didn't know her brother if he thought Carl would try to marry a woman who professed to love another man. Carl loved Mara, but he had his pride.

Idalou stopped by the kitchen to thank Alma McGloughlin for the coffee. She was relieved that Mara wasn't around.

"I hope Jordan means what he says," she said to Carl once they were in the saddle and away from the house. "Of course, if we don't find that bull, he won't have to back up any of his promises."

"I'm sure he means it, and I'm sure we'll find the bull," Carl said. "Now stop trying to find something to complain about, and be glad the sheriff is better at talking to Jordan than you are."

"Than either of us."

"I've never talked with him before, but that was probably a good thing. He doesn't like it that Mara's sweet on me."

"She says she's in love with Will."

"I told you Will explained all that."

"Then he needs to explain it to Mara's mother. I went to thank her for the coffee, and she couldn't stop telling me how wonderful Will is. If she has her way, your precious Mara will be married to him before the summer's out."

"Will says he's too old for Mara. He's probably too old for you, too."

Idalou didn't believe Will could ever be interested in her, but compared to Van, he was practically perfect. Even if he did have a way of making her lose her temper. She promised herself she'd be very careful how she behaved around him in the future. At the very least, she owed him a lot for bringing Jordan to a sense of his duty.

"I came to invite you for breakfast tomorrow," Idalou said to Will. "I was going to invite you for supper, but it seems the ladies of Dunmore have already lined you up for lunch and supper for the next two weeks."

Will's morning had been filled with a string of visits from at least half the female population of Dunmore. He'd had enough coffee for a roundup crew, enough sweet breads and cookies to hold a party for all the children in town, and enough invitations to *drop in* whenever he was in their direction to fill his social calendar for weeks to come. He was regretting having asked that the town provide his meals. What had seemed like a harmless way to meet people and fill in the extra hours had turned into a nightmare.

"I could skip breakfast for the rest of my time in Dunmore and still have too much to eat," Will said, pushing aside a plate of doughnuts. "Do I look underfed? Why is everyone trying to force-feed me?"

"Because you're male, single, attractive, and apparently rich," said Idalou.

When she stopped and looked thoughtful, Will prepared himself for another devastating truth.

"Do you mind if I take some of that food with me?" she asked.

Will knew things weren't going well for her and Carl, but he'd had no idea they had to go hungry. "Take all of it if you want. I won't eat it."

He didn't understand how she could laugh so easily if she was hungry enough to ask for food. "I'd never be able to eat a tenth of this," she said.

"I'm sure Carl would enjoy the rest," he suggested.

"Carl never eats sweets."

Will was confused. "If you don't want it and Carl won't eat it, why . . ." He let the sentence trail off when Idalou blushed.

"I don't want it for us. There are some families in town that don't have much money. Their children never have anything like this. It would be a treat for them."

Will felt relieved as well as embarrassed. "Send over all the hungry urchins you can find. I'll be happy to watch them devour every crumb."

"Thanks," Idalou said. "That's very generous of you. Now I have to thank you for talking to Jordan. I don't know what you said, but he's never been so agreeable."

"I just reminded him that, as the richest and most powerful man in Dunmore, people would look to him to show them how they should behave. He's really a decent man. You just have to know how to talk to him." He didn't expect Idalou to believe that, but he hoped Jordan wouldn't give her any more reason to disbelieve it.

"I'll take your word for it," Idalou said. "Can you come at seven o'clock? Carl and I need to spend as much time as we can looking for that bull if he's still missing."

Will was beginning to believe that somebody had taken the bull. He didn't know whether the bull had been stolen or someone was just hiding it until Idalou and Carl lost the ranch. With an animal that valuable, it was never wise to discount theft.

"As long as Jordan insists he doesn't have the bull, I can't go searching his property looking for it. If you want to swear out a complaint—"

"If he has the bull—and I'm certain he does—he would move it before you got there. All the same, I do appreciate what you did for us. And I apologize for saying you'd gone over to his side because you wanted to marry Mara. Whom you marry is none of my business."

"Unless I wanted to marry you."

Chapter Seven

"What?"

Idalou forgot to look furious, forgot that men ignored her because she was a woman, forgot she was about to lose her ranch. She looked confused, vulnerable, human. And prettier than ever.

"I just agreed with you. It wouldn't be your business unless I wanted to marry you."

"But you don't."

"I probably shouldn't marry anybody. I have it on good authority that I'm too spoiled to make a good husband."

"I didn't say that."

"No. My mother did, and she ought to know because she spoiled me." Maybe spoiled wasn't the right word. She'd smothered him with all the love she'd once lavished on twelve children. It didn't matter that she now had more than a dozen grandchildren running about the Hill Country. Being under her roof, Will was closer.

"I'm sure she didn't mean it," Idalou said.

"I'm sure she did. She rattled off a long list of examples to support her statement." Will looked at all the food scattered around the office. "And this is proof she's right."

He felt a little disgusted with the way things were going. He'd intended to come to Dunmore, buy the bull, then inform Jake and Isabelle he planned to move out and set up his own ranch. Now he couldn't leave town because nobody could find the damned bull, he was a sheriff with virtually nothing to do, the women of Dunmore were trying to kill him by force-feeding him, and every female over the age of eight found a reason to come by the office to gape at him at least once a day. If he had to listen to any more stories about cats and dogs that could have used rescuing in the past and might need it again—the story about Pepper had made the rounds the first night—he was going to swear off pets forever.

"People are just trying to be nice," Idalou said. "Everybody likes you."

"Everybody except you."

She reacted with shock. "I like you."

He hoped his smile was sympathetic, not accusatory. "You don't have to pretend. I dislike lots of people, and I don't intend to apologize for it."

"I don't dislike you," she stated firmly. "I don't understand you, but I don't dislike you."

"What's so hard to understand? Isabelle says I'm so simple she sometimes worries that I might be stupid."

Idalou's body lost some of its rigidity. "I think you're rather complex, and a lot smarter than anybody thinks."

Will's eyes blinked in amazement. That was just about the nicest thing anybody had ever said to him. The fact that Idalou had been the one to say it was even more amazing.

"The only problem," Idalou added, "is that you're too good-looking. People take one glance at you and their brains stop functioning."

"And your brain doesn't stop functioning when you look at me?"

"Absolutely not. I'm not such a poor female as that!"

Will couldn't stop the smile. "I never thought you were a poor female. I'd say you were a rather splendid example of one." It pleased him to see Idalou become confused and fidgety. Apparently, she wasn't the wildcat people made her out to be. Rather, she was a woman with sufficient spirit to fight back when people tried to ignore her or take advantage of her. Yet there was a soft side to her that responded to gentleness as well as compliments.

"I think somebody has been slipping something into your coffee," Idalou said with a nervous laugh. "I'd throw out the rest of it if I were you."

Aha! She was uncomfortable enough around him that she had to make an excuse for his having said something nice about her. She wasn't used to it, she didn't trust it, but she liked it nonetheless. She grew more interesting by the minute. He wondered if she'd have been more trusting and accepting if her parents had lived. He barely remembered his own parents. He didn't even remember the uncle who'd taken him in very well. For all practical purposes, Jake and Isabelle were the only parents he'd ever had. Life with them had been safe and secure with more than enough love for any orphan boy. They'd expected him to work hard, but they'd also spoiled him. He had a feeling that Idalou had had to be responsible long before her parents died.

"I don't think another cup or two will do me any

harm. It'll give me something to compare your coffee to when I have breakfast with you tomorrow."

"I can promise my coffee won't affect your brain."

"My brother says my brain is already too small to be found," he said.

"If he did say such a thing—which I tend to doubt—it was probably because you'd been practicing your *I'm-too-bone-idle-to-do-anything* act."

Will hoped he didn't show just how startled he was. No one had ever caught on to him so fast. When you combined the fact that she was pretty and feminine with her willingness to tackle anything in pants, this woman could be dangerous.

"Not idle. Just unwilling to do things the hard way unless I'm forced."

She studied him with an unwavering stare.

To break the tension, he said, "I'm headed over to Sonnenberg's place. Since he doesn't have a wife, I'm not in danger of being forced to eat anything."

Idalou looked him over. "You don't look overfed to me."

"I would be if I ate all this. Don't forget to round up your urchins." He looked at the food and shook his head. "I doubt there's a pound of sugar or a spoonful of honey in all of Dunmore that hasn't been wrestled into some sweet intended for my consumption."

Idalou choked. At least that was what it sounded like until she started laughing.

"I always thought a sheriff was supposed to protect the townspeople from thieves, murderers, and the occasional drunk," she said when she managed to regain control of her voice. "It never occurred to me that we'd have to protect you from the wives and young women."

"That's because you haven't been saddled with this face," Will said pointing at himself.

"I'd never considered good looks a handicap before. I'll have to tell Carl. He's been making faces at himself in the mirror because he's angry he'll never look half as good as you."

"Tell him to throw away his damned mirror. Mara fell in love with him just the way he is. She'll love him the same way once she gets over the excitement of my having saved her from Newt's attentions."

"You tell him when you come to breakfast. He doesn't believe me."

Will started putting the goodies in a paper sack. "Moderation in all things," he muttered to himself as his fingers grew sticky with sugar. "Too much of anything is a pain in the neck."

Will had about decided that being sheriff was a cushy job. Okay, you probably had to handle a fight once in a while, but for the most part it consisted of walking around town, talking to people, and listening to their complaints about their lives . . . and sometimes about their neighbors.

He had expected that being followed by a posse of little boys who copied his every move would get tiresome, but so far it had given him an opportunity to get to know every urchin in town. If adults had any idea what their kids knew about them and didn't hesitate to tell anyone who'd listen, they'd lock their children up and never speak above a whisper. He could blackmail half the town if he wanted.

Doing rounds in the evening was different. The kids were home in bed, but the men were out getting drunk. Given his choice, Will would have stuck with the kids.

"Evening, Sheriff."

Will greeted two men who hurried past him to one of the buildings, where beams of light and the sounds of music and laughter beckoned. Women rarely ventured out after dark even when accompanied by their husbands, so the men felt relaxed enough to be themselves. Which pretty much meant they got stumbling drunk and began arguments. Will was considering a law that required wives and other female relatives, especially grandmothers and old-maid aunts, to roam the streets until the saloons closed. Few things could sober up a man faster than the sight of his mother or older sister approaching, encumbered with a load of wrath and indignation she was eager to pour over his head.

"Howdy, Sheriff. Quiet night so far."

"It's early yet, Andy," Will said to the owner of the mercantile. "Plenty of time for trouble."

"Drop by the Swinging Door before you go to bed, and I'll stand you a whiskey if you have any trouble with anybody."

"I'll take you up on that."

Andy laughed and headed for the saloon while Will continued his rounds. Clouds had come in late in the afternoon to obscure the moon, plunging the streets into darkness. Will had just told himself it was the perfect kind of night for trouble when he heard the sounds of a scuffle. He could tell the sounds were coming from deep in the alley between the lawyer's office and the barbershop. Feeling for his gun, he charged into the alley.

The sounds were actually coming from behind the lawyer's office. Newt was in a fistfight with Mort, one of Idalou's cowhands.

"Break it up, Newt," Will shouted, "or I'll put a bullet into you." Newt hit Mort one last time, then stepped back.

"Remember what I said," he growled at Mort.

"What's this all about?" Will asked as he drew

closer. It was dark behind the law office, but he could tell that Mort had come off a lot worse than Newt.

"Just a personal disagreement," Newt said.

Mort had a bloody nose, a busted lip, and a torn shirt. Newt, much bigger than the wiry cowhand, hardly looked as if he'd been in a fight.

"It looks like more than that to me," Will said.

"You calling me a liar?" Newt asked, his hands balled into tight fists.

"I'm not sure yet," Will said. "Give me a minute, and I'll let you know. What's this all about?" he asked Mort.

"A difference of opinion," Mort said without looking Will in the eye.

"You're both liars," Will said. Newt didn't seem to mind. He just grinned.

"You want me for anything else, Sheriff?" His tone was insolent.

"If I do, I'll find you. Come with me to my office," he said to Mort as Newt turned and left. "You need to clean up before you go back to the ranch."

"I'm fine," Mort said.

"You're not fine."

Mort searched for and found his hat. "I'd better be getting back. Miss Idalou likes us to be in the saddle by seven." He punched his hat back into shape and settled it on his head.

"Newt jumped you before you could get to the saloon, didn't he?"

Mort nodded.

"Will you tell me what this is really about?"

"Like Newt said, it's personal."

"His fist in your face is personal. It's the reason behind it that I doubt."

"You'll be gone in a few days, Sheriff, so it's best if you just leave this alone."

"The town will have a new sheriff."

"No, it won't," Mort said. "What fool will take the job once they know Newt killed the last one?"

"*I* took it," Will said.

"For a week. Miss Idalou told me how long you agreed to wait for her to find that bull. Well, she's not going to find it, and you'll be gone. Don't mess with things you won't be around long enough to fix."

Mort brushed some dirt off the knees of his pants and walked away, leaving Will angry and helpless. He had taken this job to bridge the gap until the town could hire a new sheriff, but now he found himself in the middle of a tangled web of potential alliances and conflicting ambitions. He was certain the fight between Newt and Mort factored into the conflict over the Ellsworth ranch and the missing bull. He just couldn't figure out Newt's role. He lived in a run-down cabin on a dry creek and picked up odd jobs from time to time. He'd tried to assault Mara and now had attacked Idalou's cowhand. Newt was a bully and a brute, but he wasn't irrational, so what reason did he have for these attacks? Because he could? Because no one except Will would try to stop him?

Will didn't believe so, but he was up against a problem Mort had stated with perfect clarity. Did he have a right to mess with things he wouldn't be around long enough to fix?

Will knew something was wrong as soon as he saw Idalou's face. "Has something happened to Carl?" he asked as he stepped inside.

The aromas of bacon, coffee, and hot bread reached out to him from the kitchen, causing his stomach to rumble ominously. Idalou turned and headed back toward the kitchen.

"Carl's fine. It's Mort and Henry. They've quit.

Carl's in the bunkhouse right now trying to change their minds, but they say they're riding out this morning."

"Did they give a reason?" Will asked.

"No, but it must have something to do with the fight."

"Do you know why Mort would be fighting with Newt?"

"No. As far as I know, he has never had anything to do with Newt."

"Mort wouldn't tell me what was going on last night, but maybe he will now."

Idalou moved the bacon to the side of the stove, took the bread out of the oven, and covered it with a towel. "I'm coming with you."

"Have either Mort or Henry tangled with Newt before?" Will asked as they covered the short distance between the house and the bunkhouse.

"As far as I know, they've had nothing to do with each other."

A heavy overnight rain had left the ground soggy. The air was still cool, but it would be hot and humid by afternoon. Two saddled horses stood outside the bunkhouse, one already burdened with bedroll, stuffed saddlebags, a canteen, and a rifle. Before they reached the bunkhouse, the door opened and Henry stepped out, loaded down with his bedroll and saddlebags. Carl and Mort followed.

"You know we can't find anybody else this time of year," Carl was saying. "Can't you at least wait until fall?"

"We gotta go now," Mort said.

"Why?" Will said. "Is there a family emergency?"

Swollen and badly bruised, Mort's face looked worse than it had last night.

"You might look at it that way," Mort said.

"Newt's suddenly decided to take a dislike to Mort and Henry," Carl explained. "He doesn't like their looks, so he says. If they stay around, he's going to make sure they look a whole lot worse. We can't let him run people off just because he doesn't like them."

"What are you going to do to stop him?" Mort asked.

"That's the sheriff's job."

"It would be if he was going to stay here," Mort said, "but he ain't, so whose job is it going to be then?"

"It'll be mine," Carl said.

"You can't do nothing," Mort said as he tossed his saddlebags across his horse's back. "Newt's bigger than you and me put together. And he's faster with a gun."

"There's no reason for this to become a gun issue," Idalou said.

"I expect that's what the last sheriff thought." Mort finished securing his saddlebags, then turned to face Idalou. "Look where that got him."

"Is this the first time Newt has threatened you?" Will asked.

"No," Mort said. "He's done it a couple other times. Only this time he said I wouldn't see him next time. That means I'll get a bullet in the back and no one will ever know who did it. Look, I don't want to leave, but Henry and me are just cowhands. I didn't hire on for a range war, but it looks like that's what you got." Mort tightened the rawhide strips holding his bedroll in place. "If you're going to keep this place," he said to Carl, "you need a gunfighter."

"Do you know something you're not telling us?" Will asked.

"McGloughlin's cows don't wander onto our land," Henry said. "Somebody pushes them this way. That bull doesn't wander off by himself, neither."

"Do you know who's doing it?" Will asked.

"Neither of us knows," Mort said. "If I hadn't seen hoofprints, I wouldn't be sure myself. This place is too big for three men to watch everything."

"Then how do you expect one to do it?" Carl asked.

"That's not my problem." Mort swung into the saddle. Henry was already mounted and waiting. "All I want is a place where I won't get shot for doing my job."

Will couldn't think much of two men who would cut and run when things got tough, but it was hard to expect a man to risk his life for twenty-five dollars a month.

"Can't you put Newt in jail?" Idalou asked Will. "He has no right to beat up people and threaten their lives."

"As long as Mort isn't willing to tell a judge what he just told us, all I can do is let Newt know I'm watching him and will jail him the next time he puts his toe over the line."

"What I don't understand is why Newt gives a damn about Mort or Henry," Carl said. "He's never had anything to do with them."

"Could be somebody's paying him to cause trouble," Will said. "According to what I hear, he doesn't have a steady income but always has enough money for beer."

"It's got to be Jordan," Idalou said. "Newt's worked for him lots of times."

"That doesn't make sense," Carl said. "Why would he try to kiss Mara if he was working for her father? I think he hasn't gotten over the sheriff knocking him down or outdrawing him. I think he's trying to do everything he can to rile Will without doing enough to get himself thrown in jail."

"That sounds like something Newt would do," Idalou admitted.

"That still leaves Henry's assertion that someone is behind the movement of stock from Jordan's land to yours and from yours to Jordan's. Do you think Newt could be doing it for somebody else?"

"He could do anything," Carl said.

Will hoped Andy and Lloyd found a new sheriff soon. Things could get completely out of control if he had to leave and Dunmore still had no sheriff.

Breakfast was a very solemn meal. Convinced that Jordan was behind everything, Idalou didn't bother to comment on her brother's probable or improbable solutions. Will's thoughts were divided between the perilous situation and Idalou. It worried him that he was becoming more and more attracted to her. Not the physical part—the rest of it. His admiration of her fierce loyalty to Carl and the ranch even when it caused people to dislike her. His desire to stay around long enough to help her out. The thought of spending time with her talking about something other than bulls, ranches, and the perfidy of Jordan McGloughlin. His constant comparisons of her to Isabelle.

Isabelle was one of the most uncompromising women alive. She never stopped going, doing, thinking, and she couldn't understand anyone who did. Nevertheless, Will adored her. Comparing anyone to Isabelle was a danger sign. Doing so favorably was an indication it was time to cut and run. The fact that he didn't want to run should have thrown him into a panic. So why hadn't it?

Seeing Idalou look as if she carried the weight of the world on her shoulders made him want to shoulder that weight himself. She was too young to have been thrust into the role of responsible adult and parent. She should have been going to parties, flirting with the best-looking men in Dunmore, spending more time thinking about her clothes than the whereabouts of a bull. She should be looking forward to each day, rather than gearing up for another struggle she had little chance of winning. Men should be willing to take risks for her, not run the other way when they saw her coming.

If he knew what was good for him, he'd run away, too. Hers wasn't the only bull in Texas, even though he thought it was the best. He should concentrate on setting up his ranch, buying breeding stock. He could use Jake's bulls or the fancy critter Chet had bought in Dallas last year. But Chet's bull had to be pasture bred. The animal would breed meatier calves, but Will wanted a bull who could be master of his range, ruler of his universe. So he had to stay here if he wanted this bull. He also had a job to do, whether he wanted it or not.

Then there was the problem of Mara. He didn't believe for a minute that Mara was in love with him. She was simply infatuated. If he left before she recovered, she just might set him up as the love of her life who'd gotten away. She'd still probably marry Carl, but she wouldn't give him the love he deserved because she'd have built a shrine around Will. He owed it to both of them to get the matter straightened out before he left.

So, having decided that he had to stick around for a while, he wondered what Idalou would say if he asked her to go walking in the moonlight.

"I heard your hands rode out this morning," Van said to Idalou.

"How do you know? They've only been gone since breakfast." Idalou was supposed to be looking for the bull, but she couldn't concentrate. She hadn't been able to think straight since Will had asked her if she'd walk with him on his rounds some evening after supper. It had to be boring to walk around the same street for hours, but she couldn't understand why he'd asked her to walk with him. If any other man had asked her, she'd have thought he was interested in her. She was certain Will wasn't.

"They rode through town to buy supplies," Van said. "I was in getting some stuff for the ranch."

Idalou couldn't imagine Van lowering himself to buy supplies for the ranch, but she had little inclination to think about Van. Her loan payment was due in two days, and she still hadn't found the bull. She and Carl had spent every hour of daylight for the last two days looking for him without success.

"What are you going to do for help?" Van asked.

"Unless we find the bull by tomorrow, it won't matter. Lloyd will put our ranch up for sale, and we won't have any place to keep the bull once we do find it."

"You think it could have wandered onto our land?"

"It could have gone anywhere."

"You want to look?"

Idalou couldn't hide her surprise. It was well known that Van's father didn't like anybody riding across his range. Even though Van had always been friendly with her, even stopping to help out on occasion, he and Carl were competing for Mara's affections. "What would your father say?"

"Why should he say anything? We didn't take your bull, so he can't have any objection to your looking anywhere you want. I'll ride with you if it'll make you feel more comfortable."

"I wouldn't feel so much like I'm trespassing."

Idalou didn't like Frank Sonnenberg. He wasn't a pleasant man, but she didn't hold that against him.

Losing his wife and daughter to an infectious fever shortly after they moved to Dunmore was enough to sour any man on life. He stayed pretty much to himself.

"If you'd like, I can lend you a couple of men," Van said. "You and Carl can't cover all the ground by yourselves."

"You don't need to do that."

"I want to," Van said with the trademark smile that had caused so many female hearts to flutter. "If we do end up with your ranch, I don't want to feel like we were responsible for your losing it."

Idalou was finding it hard to be thankful for Van's offer of help when he kept referring to the impending loss of the ranch. The possibility—the near certainty—was all too real. She didn't want to think of the consequences. They were too dire. "It's very good of you to offer, Van. I really appreciate it."

"It's not a problem. Let's go round up a couple of hands. Then you can look anywhere you think the bull might have gone."

Idalou tried not to let her hopes get too high. Sonnenberg controlled more range than Jordan, but his grass wasn't as good. It didn't make sense for the bull to have wandered from good graze to poor. But it was always possible he'd gone in search of cows.

If she had to lose her ranch, she just might sell it to Sonnenberg before Lloyd Severns could put it up for auction. At least that way, Jordan wouldn't get it, and she and Carl would get some cash out of the sale.

But even as she swung her mare alongside Van's gelding, she couldn't stop wondering why Will had invited her to walk with him. She wished she had a close friend she could talk to. Except for Webb, she'd never been interested in a man, nor had any man been seriously interested in her. She was certain Will *wasn't* seriously interested in her, but if he wasn't, why had he asked her to walk with him? Surely he would realize that in a town like Dunmore a walk in the moonlight practically meant they were seeing each other.

But what concerned her even more was her own re-action to the invitation. Shock, she'd expected. Disbe-lief, even thinking he was playing some trick on her. Yet in spite of all that, she had definitely felt excite-ment. Lots of excitement. She *wanted* to walk with him. More importantly, she wanted him to *want* to walk with her. And not to discuss the ranch or the bull or what she was going to do if they lost the ranch. It was stupid, even more stupid than being up-set after Webb turned his attention to Junie Mae. Even though she'd suspected Webb wasn't in love with her, that had hurt far more than she could have antic-ipated. Will had no reason to be interested in her ex-cept in his capacity as sheriff. She certainly had no reason to be interested in him. He was too handsome, too sure of himself, too willing to take the word of the rich and powerful. She supposed that was natural when he was one of the rich and powerful himself. Which was still more reason to be certain his interest wasn't romantic.

But what upset Idalou the most was that she hoped it was.

Chapter Eight

Idalou told herself there was no point in dragging her feet. They were going to lose the ranch whether she went to see Lloyd Severns in person or whether he sent the sheriff out with a notice of foreclosure. She'd known this day was coming. She had accepted it, even if Carl hadn't. Still, it was like dirt in her mouth. She'd failed her brother, her father, even herself. How could she expect the men of Dunmore to respect her if she couldn't hold on to her own property?

She hadn't found the bull on Sonnenberg's property. Nor had the two cowhands Van had lent her been any more successful. Carl was out looking even now, but it was time to turn her mind to what to do next. They wouldn't get much for the ranch unless Sonnenberg and Jordan got in a bidding war, but she doubted that would happen. Both men wanted Mara and Van to marry. No matter who got the ranch, it would end up in the same place eventually.

She had never liked entering the bank. Nothing good had ever come of it for her or her father. Its cool, dark interior seemed ominous rather than welcoming. "I want to see Mr. Severns," she told the teller. "I'm sure he's expecting me."

"I'll see if he's free," Austin Ledbetter said. He was a nice young man even if he did look like a beaver.

"He'll see you now," Austin said when he came back. "You're looking a little down this morning." His smile was sympathetic.

"We haven't been able to find the bull. I'm sure everybody knows what that means."

"I'm sorry," Austin said as he opened the gate and allowed her to pass. "I wish there was something I could do to help."

"Thanks. Just keep speaking to me when I have to start cleaning rooms to keep from starving."

"I'm sure it won't come to that."

She hoped not, but right now she didn't have any idea what she was going to do. Lloyd smiled and rose to meet her. She thought it was particularly unkind of him to be so cheerful when he knew why she was here. She chewed the inside of her mouth, determined she wouldn't become emotional.

"I'm sure you're feeling a lot better today," Lloyd said as he pulled a chair up and waited for her to be seated.

"Why should I feel any better?" she demanded, struggling to hold her temper in check. "I'm tired of the endless struggle, but I'm not glad my struggle has ended because we've lost the ranch."

"What are you talking about?" Lloyd asked as he seated himself. "You haven't lost the ranch."

"We haven't found the bull, so we can't sell it to Mr. Haskins. Consequently, we don't have the money to pay the loan installment."

"There is no installment," Lloyd said. "There is no loan. Mr. Haskins has paid off the whole thing."

Idalou sat there unable to move, to speak, barely able to breathe. She heard the words. She even understood them, but they didn't make sense. Will had no reason to do anything so thoughtful, so kind, so incredibly generous as to cover her loan payment, much less pay off the entire loan. She had struggled all her life, yet none of the people who called themselves her friends had offered to do anything like this. This was something she'd never be able to forget . . . or repay.

"You seem surprised," Lloyd said. "I assumed you'd made some arrangement with him for the delivery of the bull when you finally found it."

"We talked about the financial arrangements," Idalou said, fighting for words to keep from showing her complete ignorance, "but I didn't think we'd reached a final decision."

Lloyd laughed easily. "It looks like Mr. Haskins thought you had, or he'd never have laid out so much money."

"It does seem so." Idalou wasn't sure whether she wanted to kiss Will's feet or take him to task for not speaking to her first. "I guess I'd better talk to him."

"He's ridden out to help one of the smaller ranchers with his branding. It seems he's quite an accomplished cowhand."

"Mr. Haskins has a great number of talents," Idalou said. "I don't think anybody in Dunmore has any idea just how many."

"I think you're right," Lloyd said. "I wish we could persuade him to stay. We could use a man like him in this town." His gaze narrowed and favored Idalou with a cautious glance. "Do you think you might be able to do that?"

If Idalou had been stunned when Will asked her to walk with him, she was flabbergasted that Lloyd should think she had that kind of influence over him. "I don't know what you mean."

"Well," Lloyd said, his gaze never wavering, "It's not every day a man plunks down several thousand dollars to pay off a loan. I figured he must have a reason." Lloyd allowed himself a half grin. "He seems to spend a lot of time with you."

"With me *and* Carl. And in case you've forgotten, Mara has declared to anyone who will listen that she's in love with him."

Lloyd laughed at her. "I'm sure she thinks he'd make a perfect husband, but I don't see him as a man to be attracted to a flighty female. I'd think *you* were much more his style."

"I have yet to hear that Mr. Haskins came to Dunmore seeking anything more than a bull."

"But he took the job of sheriff and paid off your loan. It looks to me like his plans may have changed."

Idalou was certain something had changed. Realizing she wasn't going to be able to change Lloyd's mind or stop his speculations, she got to her feet. "Thank you for being so understanding in the past."

"I was glad to do it. Now you can relax."

No, she couldn't. Whatever Will's reason for paying off her loan, she was positive it was contingent on their finding the bull. Until then, nothing had really changed.

No, something *had* changed. She just didn't know exactly what or why.

"You look like a man who's spent the morning working hard," the hostler said when Will rode into the livery stable.

"Branding is always hard work," Will said.

"How's Clarence's boy doing?"

"I think his arm will be good as new in a couple of

months." Will dismounted and turned his mount over to the hostler. "Right now he can't do much."

"It was good of you to offer to help."

"I didn't mind. I needed to work off some of this food I've been eating." He bent down to scrape some mud and manure off his boots.

"The ladies are having a high old time trying to outdo each other feeding you," the hostler said with a laugh. "If it goes on much longer, some long-standing friendships will be a bit strained."

"Then I'd better wind up my business and head home. Make sure to give my horse a good rubdown and some oats along with his hay. I want him in good shape in case I have to make a run for it."

"Why don't you consider staying? You've handled Newt better than anybody."

Will was flattered, but as much as he'd like to have a reason to lock Newt up and throw away the key, he couldn't.

"I've got things to do back home." He brushed some dust off his shirt with his hands, off his pants with his hat. "I've already been gone longer than I'd planned."

He squinted as he stepped out of the livery stable into the sun. Settling his hat on his head and pulling it low over his eyes, he headed toward his office along the alley that ran behind the buildings fronting the Main Street. He'd gone only a short way when he became aware of voices. He looked up to see Van Sonnenberg and a young woman he didn't know having a heated discussion. Van was waving his hands in the air at the young woman, who was looking at the ground. Will was about to turn down an alley when Van stormed off and the young woman sank to her knees crying.

Will paused, hoping someone from inside the dress

shop behind her would come out and see to her. When no one did, he had no choice but to step forward. The young woman was so distraught, she didn't hear him come up.

"Can I help you?" he asked.

The young woman's sobs stopped abruptly, and she looked up with panic in her eyes.

"You don't have to be afraid. I'm the sheriff," Will said, pointing to his badge.

"I'm fine," the young woman said, struggling to compose herself. "You don't have to bother with me."

"You're not fine. Besides, my mother would hit me with a log if she heard I turned my back on a woman in distress."

"You can't help me," the young woman said, struggling to regain control. "Nobody can."

"Is that what Van Sonnenberg told you?"

With that, she broke down again.

"You can't sit here crying," Will said, wondering why one of the dozens of females who regularly found their way into his office didn't come to take this young woman off his hands. "Come along to my office. I'll get you some coffee and you can have some time to compose yourself."

"You don't want to have anything to do with me," she said. "I'm disgraced."

"My mother says the same thing about me, so I guess we'll get along just fine."

"You don't understand," the woman said. "I—"

"You can tell me once you're comfortable." Will helped her to her feet. "Come along out of the sun. Your face is much too pretty to ruin it with a sunburn."

"I wish I weren't pretty," the woman said. "Then I might not be in trouble."

Will felt the same way. He had women trying to stuff him like a pig for the slaughter, an impressionable teenager convinced she was in love with him, and Idalou convinced he believed his face could get him anything he wanted.

By the time Will had the woman settled in his office, watched her drink half a cup of coffee and nibble on one of the sweet muffins Mrs. Olah had sent, Will thought she had calmed down enough that he could ask her name.

"I'm Junie Mae Winslow. After my parents died, Aunt Ella and Uncle Tuley invited me to come live here with them. They don't have any children."

Will had met Tuley Hoffman. He owned the saddle shop. He and his wife were an older couple, conservative and very religious, he'd been told.

"I'm sure they'd be more than glad to help you with what's troubling you."

Junie Mae burst into tears. "I've disgraced them. They'll turn me out, and I'll have no place to go."

"I'm sure you'd never do anything that would cause your aunt to do that," Will said.

"I'm pregnant," Junie Mae said. "And I'm not married."

Nice going, Haskins. Just the sort of confession to make your day. "Is Van Sonnenberg the father?"

Unable to speak through a renewed burst of tears, Junie Mae nodded. In Will's experience, when a young man got a girl in trouble, he married her. From what he'd seen, he gathered that Van had told Junie Mae he wasn't going to do any such thing. That didn't surprise him. As lovely as Junie Mae was, an inheritance of a saddle shop didn't stack up well against Mara's ranch.

"Have you talked to his father?"

She shook her head.

"Are you going to?"

She shook it even more vigorously. It was probably

just as well. Will didn't think Frank Sonnenberg would believe that Junie Mae hadn't set out to seduce Van.

"Want to tell me about it?"

Junie Mae dried her tears, took a couple swallows of coffee, and faced him.

"My father left us when I was very small, so I came to Dunmore straight from my mother's funeral. I was very lonely, and it was nice when Webb McGloughlin started paying attention to me. I hadn't had time to decide if he really liked me or was just flirting when he died."

Will kicked himself for not having made the connection before. This was the young woman Webb had become interested in after he broke up with Idalou. Though Junie Mae was certainly very pretty, he thought Webb showed very poor taste.

"It was stupid of me to believe all the things Van said, but after losing my mother and Webb, I was desperate for someone to lean on." She focused her clear blue eyes on Will. "Aunt Ella makes me feel like it's a character flaw not to be stoic in the face of any kind of misfortune, no matter how devastating. Van would hold me when I was lonely and let me cry on his shoulder when I was sad. I see now that it was very foolish of me to think he loved me, but I was desperate to feel close to someone."

"Did you see him more than once?" Will asked.

"Whenever I could," Junie Mae said. "He would get a room in the hotel and I would meet him. We were very careful to make sure no one saw us."

Will was certain that in a town this size, quite a few people knew something had been going on between them.

"Did he know you were in the family way before today?" Will asked.

Junie Mae buried her face in her hands and shook her head.

"What did he say?"

"He doesn't believe it's his baby; he said that I can't prove we've been together."

Will thought that might be relatively easy to establish, but he had no intention of doing anything to force Van to marry Junie Mae. A marriage to Van under those circumstances would be a living hell. Yet something had to be done.

"I think you ought to tell your aunt and uncle."

Junie Mae looked up. "I could never do that. I'd rather kill myself." She uttered a hysterical laugh. "I might as well kill myself anyway. They'll turn me out when they learn the truth. I'll die on the street."

As attractive as she was, Will considered that highly unlikely, but she looked frightened enough to do something crazy. "I'm sure things look desperate to you right now, but this has come as a shock to both you and Van. I think you both need some time to get used to it. Having a baby is a wonderful thing. Why don't you go home and get some rest? It takes most men a little time to get used to the idea of being a father, but they generally come around."

Junie Mae threw herself at Will, gripped his vest in both hands, and starting crying. His arms felt awkward hanging at his sides so he reluctantly put them around Junie Mae.

"You don't have to cry anymore." He patted her on the back, but that only made her cry harder. "If you don't get control of yourself, everybody in town will know something is wrong. And if I know women— and I *do* know women—they'll have the secret out of you before nightfall."

Junie Mae lifted her head and released his vest.

"I'm sorry. I'm just so relieved to have someone I can depend on."

Will wished Isabelle could hear that. Maybe then her criticisms wouldn't be so stringent. "Just dry your eyes and pull yourself together. I promise I'll think of something."

Junie Mae looked up at him with adoring eyes, and Will felt his heart sink. *Not again!*

"I think you're the most wonderful man in the world."

With that, she threw her arms around his neck and kissed him. Will had been on the receiving end of such emotional displays too often to be thrown completely off his stride. That lasted just until he looked up to see Idalou staring at them with a look that had trouble written all over it.

Idalou had told herself not to be a fool so many times the words played over and over in her head like a litany. That was partly because her brain was too paralyzed to function. If her horse hadn't known the way home by himself, she could have ended up in West Texas. As it was, she arrived at the house without any conscious memory of how she got there.

She took longer than usual to unsaddle her horse and rub him down before turning him out in the corral. Then, instead of going inside to change her clothes and begin preparations for supper, she leaned on the corral fence and watched her horse roll in the dust. She studied the way his steel-gray coat wasn't a solid color but was composed of swirls of dark hair against a background of silvery white. She wondered why she'd never noticed that he was lop-eared. Actually, he was a really ugly horse.

Bored with watching him stand in the shade of a

cottonwood, his left rear leg drawn up beneath him and his head hanging down, she turned toward the creek that ran some distance from the house. The day was relatively cool for late July, but it felt good to settle in the shade of the cottonwoods, oaks, and pecan trees that bordered the stream. A cardinal flew in and out of a tangle of grapevines, willows, and hackberry bushes, squawking loudly at a jay trying to feed in the same area. Nearby a towhee scratched vigorously in the leaves for seeds and insects. All in all, it was a lovely summer day, one that reminded people of why they chose to live on the prairie of central Texas.

But Idalou couldn't get the image of Junie Mae kissing Will out of her mind. Junie Mae Winslow! The woman who'd stolen Webb from her. Now Junie Mae had set her sights on Will, and the spineless man hadn't been putting up a fight. There was no use denying that Junie Mae was a pretty woman, but Will already had Mara declaring she was in love with him. What was Will doing asking Idalou to walk with him when he was playing fast and loose with any female who was willing?

Idalou had been flattered that he'd asked her. If she hadn't had to search for the bull, she'd have accepted. After her run-in with Newt, Jordan had forbidden Mara to leave the house after dark unless Will was with her. Now, probably Junie Mae would be walking with him, too. Will probably thought it was perfectly normal to have several women running after him at the same time. She didn't know a single man who could turn down a pretty woman. There was no reason to expect Will to be the exception.

The problem, though, wasn't Will or Mara or Junie Mae. It was herself.

She could still recall the weakness that had gone all through her when she'd opened the door and found herself face-to-face with the most incredibly hand-some man she'd even seen, but Will had restored her to normal by refusing to help find her bull. She'd been irritated when he'd put on the sheriff's badge, and had gotten really angry when Mara became infatuated with him.

But sometime during all of this her feelings had changed. When had that happened, and why?

It had been before she found out he'd paid off her loan. She was glad he'd been able to talk Jordan into meeting with her and Carl, but that wasn't any reason to become infatuated with him. It had been kind of him to explain to Carl that Mara's thinking she was in love with Will was just a phase. Okay, he'd kept Van from running over Pepper, and stopped Newt from kissing Mara. So he was a decent man, but that wasn't reason to think he was somebody special. He was only going to be in Dunmore long enough to get his bull.

Feeling frustrated with herself and the situation, she walked over to the grapevine to see if any of the grapes were ripe, even though she knew they wouldn't be ready to pick until just before frost. The cardinal took exception to her interest. She responded by shaking the vines until the bird gave vent to an angry squawk before flying off. The blue jay watched silently from a willow limb.

She could find only one reason for these unexpected feelings. Just like every other female in Dunmore, she'd fallen in love with Will's looks. How could she have done anything so stupid? She'd thought she was in love with Webb, and look how that had turned out. She'd had reason to think Webb was partial to her; absolutely no reason to think Will considered her anything other than a pain in his side. And she'd done everything she could to reinforce that opinion.

The sound of an approaching horse was a welcome distraction. When she saw Carl riding toward her, looking tired and downcast, she was relieved. She was anxious to tell him that they didn't have to worry about losing the ranch just yet.

"Are you sure you don't know why he paid off the loan?"

Idalou had insisted that she and Carl thank Will together and do so at once. Carl must have asked her the same question a dozen times while they rode to town.

"I was sure he disliked me. After the way he let Mara attach herself to him, I wasn't sure he liked you any better," she responded.

"He's been real decent about it," Carl said, "but he's such a gentleman Mara is more in love with him than ever. I know her mother is. When I rode over the other day, that's all she could talk about."

"What were you doing at Jordan's ranch?"

"I went to let him know I hadn't seen any of his cows on our range. After the way he behaved when we talked, I figured I ought to do something to let him know I believed he was trying."

Idalou wasn't convinced that Jordan was innocent, but she didn't say anything. They'd reached town. She hoped Will hadn't left for one of the sumptuous dinners that were quickly becoming a source of conflict among Dunmore's matrons.

The streets were surprisingly quiet for late afternoon. They didn't meet anyone they knew well enough to call out a greeting before they reached the sheriff's office. They dismounted and tethered their horses at the hitching post.

"Let me speak first," Idalou said. "I'm the one who's been most critical of him."

"That's a good reason why *I* should speak to him

first." Carl didn't offer to help his sister dismount. She'd been doing it unassisted for so long, the thought never occurred to either of them.

"Let me give it a try," Idalou said as she self-consciously brushed dust from her skirt. "If I make a mess of it, you can take over."

When Idalou opened the door and stepped into the sheriff's office, she could just as easily have thought she'd stepped into the middle of a quilting bee. Close to a dozen women filled the room, all talking at once and passing two pieces of paper back and forth, which they regarded with unhappy expressions.

"You can't sign up for breakfast or supper until everyone has had a turn," Andy Davis's wife informed Idalou. She was backed by her daughters, Louise and Sarah, who regarded Idalou in a manner that made it clear the girls saw her as a rival.

"Carl and I just stopped by to thank the sheriff for a kindness. Do you know where he is?" She'd noticed almost immediately that Will was absent.

"He's back at the jail cells," Mrs. Davis said. "He said it was an unsuitable place for ladies."

"Is anybody in jail?"

"He had two drunk cowboys," Louise Davis said with a superior smirk only a thirteen-year-old could achieve, "but he let them go before we got here."

"Then I guess it's okay for me and Carl to go find him." The shocked expressions on several faces amused Idalou, because she knew that some of the women thought her working on the ranch alongside her brother was very unladylike. Idalou moved quickly among the throng and passed through the door separating the office from the part of the building that housed the two jail cells. She found Will sitting in the farther cell, chewing on a straw, and looking out the small window with a pensive expression.

Chapter Nine

"Have you behaved so badly that the women have put you in jail?"

Will turned away from the window when he heard Idalou's voice and smiled when he saw her and Carl. "It's the only place I'm safe. They're in there deciding who can feed me when, and what each of them can cook. I thought they'd come to blows when two women wanted to use the same prairie chicken recipe. One finally settled on goose. I hate goose."

"It's your own fault," Idalou said, unable to repress a smile. "You shouldn't be so charming. You could be as crabby as a bear."

"Not when I grew up with Isabelle and Drew both lecturing me on how to behave, and Jake and nine older brothers ready to break my head if I upset either of them."

Idalou doubted that was true. Will seemed to be a basically nice man, but it was obvious that everyone in his life had spoiled him. Being the youngest and the best-looking in his family had probably made that inevitable.

"I wish you'd tell me how you do it," Carl said. "I don't want every woman in Dunmore swooning over me. Just Mara."

"You're fine as you are," Will said, coming out of the cell. "Looks can be a curse."

"Please curse me," Carl said with a laugh. "I never had a female fight to feed me."

"Count yourself lucky. They load my plate with enough food for two people," Will said. "Then they expect me to come back for seconds. And that's before they bring out the dessert. If I don't want seconds of something, they demand to know why I didn't like it, if they used too much pepper, not enough salt, maybe more butter or cream would make it richer. By the time it's all over, I'd rather have gone hungry."

Idalou was surprised to find herself feeling sorry for Will. It was her fault in a way. If she hadn't lost the bull, he wouldn't have had to stay in Dunmore and no one would have asked him to be sheriff.

An uncomfortable fluttering in her stomach made Idalou edgy. If they never found the bull, their only other option would be to hand the ranch over to Will. Would he let her stay at the ranch to cook and take care of the house and the animals, the chickens, the milk cow, and the pigs? Would he let Carl work for him? Would he share a room with Carl? Would he move Carl to the bunkhouse and stay in the house alone with her?

The fluttering turned to a sinking feeling. Will had no reason to stay in Dunmore when his family had huge holdings in the Hill Country. The sensible thing would be to sell the ranch.

"I can't sympathize with you about the food," Carl said, "but I can about an office full of bickering women." He nodded his head in the direction of the female voices coming through the closed door.

"All of them arrived with food," Will said. "Fortunately, they were so anxious to make sure theirs was the best, they kept tasting until most of it was gone."

"The kids are going to be disappointed," Idalou said. Will's snack breaks were famous among the kids below the age of ten.

"They've already promised to send more for the afternoon," Will said with a groan. "I'm thinking of inviting all the teenage boys to stop by."

"We didn't come to add to your troubles," Idalou said. "In fact, we came to thank you for relieving us of ours, at least temporarily." Having struggled for so long, her first feeling had been relief, followed by extreme gratitude. But close on its heels she realized that she'd only gained time. She now had a new and greater obligation which she had to repay. It brought all sorts of new uncertainties.

"Why did you pay off the whole loan?" Carl asked. "All you had to do was make the quarterly payment."

"It seemed pointless to have to go through this again in three months when I could put an end to it altogether."

"But you haven't put an end to it," Idalou said. "Now we have to pay you."

"You'll find the bull."

"What if we don't?" Carl asked. "I'm starting to think someone's stolen it."

"Then pay me when you can." Will paused, apparently turning over a thought in his mind. "McGloughlin and Sonnenberg have too many cowhands in the saddle for anyone to steal an animal like that and not be seen. Animals don't usually wander far from their range, so I expect he's holed up in a ravine or wash somewhere with good grass and enough cows to keep him contented. I've known bulls to get so shy of people, they actually hide from them."

"You seem to know a lot about cows," Carl said.

"I've lived on a ranch most of my life. I don't know much about anything else."

"We really do need to talk about how we can repay you," Idalou said. "It makes me uncomfortable to owe you money. You still haven't told us why you did it."

"A couple of reasons. I don't like to see anybody forced off their land, especially not when something as simple as finding a bull can fix everything. It didn't seem fair."

"But it wasn't your worry."

"As sheriff, I didn't like seeing what was shaping up to be a fight over your land. This way all the pressure is off and everybody can go back to things as they were."

Idalou knew things would never go back to the way they were. McGloughlin was too determined to have their land. If Mara married Van, Carl would leave Dunmore, and there wouldn't be any reason for her to stay either.

But she didn't want to think that far ahead.

"We still need to talk about it," Idalou said.

Will seemed to brighten. "Why don't you accompany me on my rounds tonight? We'd have plenty of time to discuss everything that concerns you."

"Carl should be present when we talk."

"He could come, too." Will didn't seem as enthusiastic.

"I'd rather discuss things in a more businesslike environment," Idalou said. "If you want company, ask Junie Mae to walk with you."

Idalou was sorry for the words as soon as they

were out of her mouth. Saying something like that was spiteful and jealous. Will looked as if she'd flung something unpleasant in his face.

"If Junie Mae's not feeling up to it, there are lots of other young women who'd be delighted to keep you company," she added in hopes of making her words sound less rude. Junie Mae hadn't been looking her best recently, but she was still a very beautiful woman.

"I have to be careful not to foster unfounded expectations," Will said. "I can walk with you because everybody knows you dislike me."

"I don't dislike you," Idalou blurted out. "I've never disliked you."

Will didn't look convinced. "Let's just say that no one would believe you're likely to become infatuated with me."

"I wouldn't allow myself to become infatuated with anyone," she declared.

"That's a wise decision," Will said. "Now, I'd better get busy and do something to earn my pay. I doubt hiding from a bunch of women qualifies."

"I haven't thanked you yet," Carl said.

"Your sister thanked me enough for both of you."

"I want to speak for myself," Carl stated. "I don't know why you decided to pay off the loan, but it was a damned decent thing to do. After the way Idalou and I have been plaguing you, I'm surprised you'd want to have anything to do with us, but I'm glad you did. You've got to let me know if there's ever anything I can do for you."

"Clear all those women out of my office," Will said in a joking manner.

"You got it." Without waiting, Carl turned and opened the door to the office. The sound of voices poured out like an avalanche, but was cut off when he closed the door behind him.

"How does he intend to get rid of those women?" Will asked Idalou.

"I don't know." She was feeling like a louse. What was it about this man that made her act so ungraciously? Carl had made her look like an ill-mannered ingrate, even though he was male, and younger to boot! What kind of woman was she turning into? She hadn't always been like this, snapping at anyone who tried to help her or offered a little kindness. She used to be cheerful, friendly, to enjoy being around people. When had she turned into a disgruntled shrew?

When her parents died. When her brother and the ranch both became her responsibility. When it became clear she couldn't keep the bull and the ranch, too. When she became convinced that Jordan was trying to ruin her and no one would listen.

But Will had listened. He'd taken the extraordinary step of paying off the loan. Why couldn't she be nice, say something grateful? Why wasn't she feeling enormously relieved instead more insecure than ever?

"Your brother has grown up," Will said. "You can stop worrying about him."

"I'll probably never stop worrying about him."

"Then don't let it show so much. It makes him feel like you don't have faith in him."

What made Will think he knew more about Carl than she did?

"I've been a younger brother all my life," Will said as though reading her thoughts. "Somebody has always been trying to take care of me. They do it because they love me, but they don't know how to stop. One day it'll become too much, and Carl will break away regardless of how much it might hurt you.

You're the only one who can make sure that doesn't have to happen."

Idalou resented Will's interference in her relationship with her brother yet she realized he was right. In a way, she even resented his paying off the loan—it made her feel a deeper obligation to him—at the same time as she breathed a sigh of relief. She resented his being sheriff, though he'd surprised her at how much everybody in town liked and admired him. She resented that every female in town was falling over herself to impress him, and that he was accepting all the adulation gracefully.

She'd just made a list that would have made any other man a saint in her eyes, and all she could do was feel resentful toward him. What was wrong with her?

She was upset that somehow she felt outside the circle. He didn't treat her with the exaggerated politeness he reserved for other women, or hold her in his arms while she cried, or let her kiss him in thankfulness. He treated her like an equal. That was what she wanted, but she hadn't expected equality to feel so rotten.

The door to Will's office opened and Carl stood in the opening. "They're gone," he said.

The silence from the room backed up his words.

"How did you get them to leave?" Idalou asked.

"I told them if they didn't leave the sheriff alone when he was working, he'd have to stop coming to their houses for meals."

Will laughed. "A dose of truth that came better from you than from me."

"Certainly not from me," Idalou said. "They'd have been certain I was trying to keep you for myself."

"Instead of turning me down at every opportunity," Will said.

Idalou didn't know whether to blush or return a sharp remark.

"Lou doesn't mean to be rude," Carl said, "but she hasn't stopped being angry at men since Webb threw her over for Junie Mae."

"Junie Mae is a beautiful woman." Idalou managed to get the words out despite her embarrassment. Will's laughter startled her.

"You ought to hear what my mother says about the value of looks," Will said, "especially when she's talking about me. It's character that counts, and I'm sure Webb would soon have realized you have an ample supply of that."

"More than enough," Carl said with a sigh that made all of them laugh.

"We'd better be going," Idalou said, "but we do need to sit down soon and decide how to pay you back."

"Find that bull," Will said. "In the meantime, I'll keep on being sheriff. I'm enjoying sticking my nose in other people's business without getting a lecture for it."

"Why do you always have to be so mean to the sheriff?" Carl asked when he and Idalou were mounted up and riding out of town.

"I wasn't mean."

"You probably didn't notice, because it's the way you always act with him. And why did you have to tell him to ask Junie Mae to walk with him? Hell, Lou, the man was asking *you* to walk with him. That's the same as saying *I* like you and want to spend some time with you. If you don't like him, fine, but you had no call to mention Junie Mae."

"You didn't walk in on Junie Mae kissing him,"

Idalou said, too angry at Carl's unjustified charges to keep that piece of information to herself.

He was so shocked he pulled his horse up. "Why was she doing that?"

"I don't know. I didn't stop to ask her."

"Then you shouldn't jump to conclusions."

Idalou knew that men stuck together through thick and thin, but she hadn't realized until now that her brother had joined their ranks. "What would *you* have thought if you'd been in my shoes?"

"I don't know, but if he'd asked me to walk with him, I'd assume he did it because he liked me and wanted to get to know more about me. That wouldn't mean he couldn't like somebody else, too."

"You don't understand. You're not a woman."

"I'm glad I'm not if it's going to keep you as ill-tempered as a dog with a sore tooth."

"I'm not ill-tempered—am I?"

Carl shook his head in disbelief. "Lou, half the town warns the other half against having anything to do with you. Not because they don't admire you, not because they don't like you, but because nobody can get along with you. I know you've felt weighed down ever since Dad died, but you don't have to worry about me, and you don't have to worry about the ranch anymore."

"Yes, I do. If we can't find that bull—"

"We'll give the ranch to the sheriff and do something else."

"What?"

"I don't know, but the ranch isn't worth what it's doing to you."

"You love this place. You love being a rancher."

"I love you even more. I'd give it to Mr. Haskins right now if I thought it would turn you back into the girl you used to be five years ago."

Five years ago she'd been fifteen, her parents were alive and healthy, and Webb McGloughlin was beginning to show an interest in her. Jordan McGloughlin was friendly, Mara was too young to have become interested in boys. Idalou had had plenty of duties, but the responsibility for the success of the ranch didn't weigh on her shoulders.

Everything had seemed perfect.

Then her father had mortgaged the ranch to buy the bull he was certain would save it, both parents had died of a virulent fever, and she was left to take care of her brother and the ranch. After that, everything seemed to go wrong. Webb jilting her, then dying, McGloughlin poaching her grass and her bull, no one in Dunmore treating her with respect, and the constant struggle to make the payments on the mortgage. Then Carl fell in love with Mara, when everybody knew Jordan intended her to marry Van. Finally, after they'd reached the agonizing decision to sell the bull, the damned animal had disappeared.

She had every right to be ill-tempered. If there ever was a female Job, she was it.

"I'm sorry if I've been sullen, ill-tempered, and argumentative. I didn't mean to be. It's just that everything keeps piling up. Nothing seems to get better."

"Have you ever asked yourself what *you* want?"

They were riding across a flat stretch of prairie between their ranch and town. Despite the recent rain, the grass was brown and skimpy. No trees blocked the horizon, just flat ground for five miles until they reached their ranch and the section of rolling hills and rich soil that made theirs the best grazing land in the area. Half a dozen grazing cows with calves were scattered over the prairie. They saw an occasional white-tailed deer on their land but rarely on the open prairie. A cowbird walked alongside a cow and her calf, foraging for weed seeds and grasshoppers and other insects stirred up by the cow's hooves. A meadowlark kept its distance even though it was looking for much the same food.

There were times when this homespun scene would calm her, provide balm to her soul and salve to her scoured nerves. Other times, like now, it struck her as barren and unproductive, sapping the life out of anyone foolish enough to depend upon it for a living. She didn't understand what it was that drove men to want their own land—any land—regardless of the price.

"Yes, and I don't have an answer," she replied. "But I know what I *don't* want. I don't want to be weighed down by anything that sucks the life out of me or turns me into a shrew no one likes having around. And I don't like being ignored just because I'm a woman."

Carl chuckled. "Believe me, Lou, *no one* ignores you."

"You know what I mean," she responded, irritated. "They listen very politely, pat me on the head, then go right on doing the same thing."

"Then you ought to make up to the sheriff." Carl's grin was sly. "Nobody ignores him."

That was something Idalou couldn't understand. The women she could understand, but what excuse did the men have? Okay, he'd apparently handled Van and Newt, but what else had he done? *Be realistic*, she told herself. If he can handle those two, he doesn't need to do anything else. And he'd brought Jordan around. The trouble was, she hadn't *seen* any of this.

"I'm not going to *make up* to anybody," Idalou told her brother.

"You don't have to," Carl said with a grin she'd like to wipe off his face. "I think the sheriff is sweet on you. All you have to do is stop scratching him every time he puts a hand in your direction."

"It's not what you're thinking," Idalou snapped.

A cow not too far away lifted her head to watch them pass, the ends of the grass she was chewing sticking out of both sides of her mouth. She was one of Jordan's longhorn cows, but her calf obviously had been fathered by their bull. It seemed no matter where she looked, something reminded her of all that had gone wrong.

"If you could do anything you wanted," Carl asked his sister, "what would you do?"

"First, I'd forget that I ever knew anything about our ranch or that bull. Then I'd get married and move as far away from here as I could."

The words were out of her mouth before she even thought them. But once spoken, she knew they were the truth. Only there was no chance it would ever happen.

"Riding out in the heat of the day?" the hostler at the livery stable asked Will.

"It can't be helped," Will replied. "I have something I need to do, but I have to be back in town for supper."

The hostler laughed. "You sure got every woman in Dunmore flapping her wings over you. I never saw such a fuss."

Will waited patiently while the old man saddled his horse. He'd have been happier to do it himself—no one back at the Broken Circle ever offered to do it for him—but it was clear the old man considered it a privilege. Whether Will liked to admit it or not, he was something of a celebrity in Dunmore. It was easier to keep from hurting people's feelings if he just went along with them.

"I won't be here long," Will said. "Then everything will go back to normal."

"There's lots of people hoping you'll stay." The man checked the cinch to make sure it was tight, then stepped back to hold the horse while Will mounted. "Nobody's ever seen Newt quiet for so long."

Considering that Newt had assaulted Mara and had attacked one of Idalou's cowhands in little more than a week, Will didn't want to know what he was normally like. Will gathered the reins and swung into the saddle. "I'm sure they'll find someone who will do a much better job than I have. I don't know when I'll be back, so don't wait around for me."

"I'll be here," the hostler said. "I don't have no place else to go."

That had been Will for the last several years—all grown up and no place to go. And try as he might, he really couldn't blame his predicament on anyone but himself.

Rather than ride down the main street of Dunmore and have to stop and talk to nearly every person he passed, Will rode down the alley. Junie Mae came out of her aunt's store to throw something into a trash barrel. She didn't look happy.

"How's it going?" Will asked.

"My aunt is getting suspicious." Junie Mae looked like a hunted animal. "I don't know what I'm going to do when she figures it out."

"Come to me. We'll think of something."

"I don't know how I can thank you for what you've done."

"I haven't done anything yet. Now smile. When you do, you look so pretty nobody can think of anything else."

Junie Mae smiled, but it was obviously an effort.

"I'll try," she said before turning around and going back into the store.

Will would have liked to force Van to face up to his responsibilities, but Junie Mae wanted Van to have nothing to do with her baby. That was probably best for the baby, but it would be hard on Junie Mae. For the moment, everything hinged on the response of her aunt and uncle.

But another woman monopolized Will's thoughts. He was headed out to Idalou's ranch to talk to her even though he wasn't sure what he wanted to say.

Despite being warned, he'd been attracted to Idalou from the moment he'd first seen her. He could still remember her standing in the doorway, staring at him as if he were an apparition. He'd prepared himself to deal with another woman who couldn't see anything beyond his looks, but it wasn't long before she was treating him like anybody else. It was such a pleasant surprise, he hadn't been really upset when she got angry that he wouldn't go with her to confront Jordan. She had proved she was an intelligent woman, so he was certain she'd feel differently after she had time to recover from her disappointment.

But things hadn't worked out as he'd expected. No matter what he did, she found a way to see it in a different light, one that didn't flatter him. What he didn't understand was that this only made her more attractive to him. He'd gone through most of his life working hard at just one thing—keeping out of trouble. So why should he be attracted to one of the most troublesome females he'd ever met?

It was Isabelle's fault. She loved her husband and children with a fierceness that was almost scary, but that didn't stop her from arguing with them or delivering devastating criticisms of their characters, their actions, or anything else that fell short of her expectations. She did that because she wanted them to be their best and wouldn't accept anything less. She was the most difficult female he'd ever known, yet he adored her. After living under her benevolent dictatorship for twenty years, he'd sworn he wanted a wife who was exactly the opposite. Yet no easygoing woman had ever held his interest. Instead, he was intrigued by Idalou, who was blind to his looks but not to his perceived faults and shortcomings.

Was that why he'd paid off the loan in full rather than simply making the next payment? He had no idea how he was going to explain his action to Jake and Isabelle especially since he couldn't really explain it to himself. Idalou and Carl might never find that bull. Then he'd be stuck with a ranch he didn't want, and without the cash to buy another bull.

He scanned the land on all sides and found nothing to appeal to him. It was as flat as the top of a table, with no trees to break the monotony. Approaching a prairie dog town, he couldn't help grinning when the little animals sat up straight at the sound of an approaching horseman. All but one scurried to their mounds, ready to dive into their burrows at the slightest threat of danger. Seeing a hawk circling overhead, he decided they were probably more afraid of it than of him. As far as he knew, people didn't eat prairie dogs.

There must have been fifty little animals in this colony. Thinking of it as the prairie dog equivalent of Dunmore, he laughed aloud. That stubborn little critter that hadn't run for cover made him think of Idalou, undaunted by danger, determined to protect what was hers. The prairie dog chattered at Will as he rode past, as though remonstrating with him for needlessly upsetting their little community.

"At least I kept the hawk from attacking you," Will said, then laughed at himself for talking to a prairie dog. He was beginning to act a little weird. And it was all Idalou's fault.

As the miles rolled by—and the uninteresting prairie passed largely unnoticed—Will tried to figure out the nature of his feelings for Idalou. He didn't think it was simple curiosity. He certainly hoped he didn't just feel challenged because she was immune to his looks.

He finally came to the conclusion that Idalou had awakened emotions or feelings he'd never experienced, which explained why he didn't know exactly what they were. This was exciting, but he didn't like uncertainty. He'd had more than enough of both in the years between his parents' deaths and being adopted by Jake and Isabelle. He liked things to be well organized, his plans well thought out, his—

His horse threw up its head and stopped abruptly. The creek, which had been a trickle no more than a foot deep, had turned into a tumultuous watercourse that spilled out of its banks and carried debris from trees and bushes ripped up from its banks. There could be only one explanation. Idalou's dam had burst.

Chapter Ten

Idalou clung to the corral post, wondering if she could hold on until all the water had drained from the dam. Or if the post would be uprooted and carried along with the other debris that swirled past her. Or if the branches of an uprooted tree would tear her loose and plunge her into the floodwaters.

Several minutes earlier an explosion that sounded like a distant clap of thunder had been the first indication something was wrong. Almost immediately the chickens started clucking and jumping around frantically. The pigs started to squeal. Idalou's horse ran back and forth along the corral fence.

That was when she heard the sound of rushing water and knew that someone had blown up the dam.

She didn't know how many minutes it would take before the water reached her, but she had to free the animals. The chickens were first. They came fluttering and squawking out of their pen. She hoped they could find safety in the trees. Next she went to the pigpen and opened the gate. She had to push the reluctant sow out while trying to keep from stepping on the pigs that ran around their mother's legs.

She saw the first of the water about the same time she got the sow out of the pen. The water crashed over rocks and around the trunks of trees and was rapidly spilling over the banks, but it was only about two feet deep. She breathed a sigh of relief that part of the dam still held. No sooner did that thought go through her head than she heard what sounded like the cracking and shattering of large pieces of wood.

The entire dam must have given way. Moments later, a wall of water strong enough to destroy anything in its path was rushing toward her.

The corral was far enough from the creek that it wasn't in the direct path of the water, but the horse could be pinned against the rails and drowned or badly injured by floating debris. She grabbed at the poles to the corral. Ignoring the splinters in her fingers, she pulled the poles back and tossed them aside. Panicked by the sounds of rushing water, her horse leaped the last rail before she could remove it.

By now the water had risen high enough to soak the bottom of her dress. She looked back at the house, but it was impossible to cross the turbulent water to reach it. She tried to decide if she could climb one of the trees along the creek. Before she could calculate the risk, the wall of water came rushing down the creek. In seconds a lake of water filled the space taken up by the ranch and all its outlying structures.

The water rose so rapidly, Idalou knew she wouldn't be able to outrun it. Her best hope would be to climb up on the corral rails and pray the water didn't rise high enough to wash her away.

In no time the pigpen was flooded and the chicken coop swept away. She climbed up on the corral fence, but the water covered first the bottom rail, then the middle rail. Wrapping her arms around the top rail with her feet on the bottom, she managed to stand even as the water reached her thighs.

The sound of wood screaming, of joints being torn apart, caused her to look up to see their house being wrenched from its foundation. Before her stunned and horrified gaze, the front porch disintegrated and fell away as the flood waters lifted the house and carried it toward the towering cottonwoods that lined the creek bank. The water hurled the house against the tree trunks, some measuring more than four feet in diameter. The house shuddered, spun around, and was slammed into a tree a little further along. Flanked by eddies on either side, the floodwater thundered down the main channel, ripping up shrubs and small trees, and tossing the foot-thick beams from the dam around like toothpicks. The current battered the house against the trees before lifting it and flinging it toward the main channel.

A beam as large as a tree struck the house broadside. It shuddered, hung for a moment, then simply came apart. Seconds later all that remained of Idalou's home was floating downstream or sinking to the bottom of the creek.

She was in shock. Everything they had was gone, including her grandmother's prized set of china, destroyed beyond reclamation in a matter of minutes. Not even Will's money could save the ranch now. There was nothing to save.

She clung to the fence as the water rose higher and higher, swirling around her thighs, her waist, and then just under her breasts. There was nowhere for her to go, no way to climb higher. She was stranded with the deadly floodwater swirling around her. She had to do something before the water swept her away and the weight of her clothes pulled her under. She couldn't shed her clothes and keep her hold on the corral fence. As much as the thought of being found naked appalled her, drowning appealed to her even less.

Seeing a horseman riding toward her increased her sense of helplessness. No one could reach her through the swirling water. As he drew closer, she recognized Will. She called out to him, but her voice couldn't be heard above the roar of the water. But he could see her, and as she watched, he uncoiled the rope attached to his saddle. Going upstream, he rode his horse knee deep into the water. Then he made a lasso, whirled it over his head, and threw it far out into the water.

The current brought the rope toward her, but it passed well out of her reach. Will retrieved the rope, re-coiled it, and prepared to throw it again. It took two more tosses before the rope came close enough for Idalou to grab hold of it. But having done so, she didn't know how she could use it to reach the shore. She wasn't strong enough to stand up against the current. Will was motioning her to hook the lasso over the corral post. When she had done that, he secured the other end to his pommel and backed his horse until the rope was taut. Next he took off his hat and tossed it aside. That was followed by his vest, shirt, and boots, leaving him naked to the waist. Then, using the rope to hold him, Will waded into the water.

Idalou's heart nearly stopped when she realized what he intended. She gestured frantically to him to go back. It would be better to wait and hope the water went down instead of continuing to rise. The muscles in her arms screamed from the strain of holding onto the fence, but she was young and strong.

Will ignored her warning and continued coming toward her. A tree or a stray log could strike the rope, ripping it out of Will's hands. Idalou watched helplessly as he was repeatedly thrown against the rope and had to struggle to hold on. Still he waded on with the water now up to his waist. Once, he had to lift the rope high over his head to keep it from getting tangled in the branches of a small tree. The current knocked him off his feet. Idalou held her breath until he regained his footing and once again was headed toward her.

The man was crazy. What good would it do anybody if they both drowned? Carl was the only one who would miss her. The entire town of Dunmore would go into mourning if anything happened to Will. She was tempted to yell at him to go back, but he had already come more than halfway. Besides, even though she didn't know how they could possibly make it to safety, she wanted the chance to try. Anything was better than a lonely death marooned atop a corral fence.

"How is the fence holding up?" Will called when he got close enough to be heard over the noise of the water.

"I think it'll be okay as long as nothing hits it." Fortunately, the corral wasn't close to the center of the floodwaters and most of the debris from the dam had already floated downstream.

"Take off your skirt," he called. "It'll catch the current. It's like an umbrella catching the wind."

She knew what he said was true, but the thought of coming out of the water with nothing to preserve her modesty but a thin chemise made transparent by the water was paralyzing.

"Your blouse, too."

When Will finally covered the last few feet and

grabbed for the fence only inches away from her, it didn't matter that his hair was in his face or that bits of leaves and other detritus stuck to his shoulders. He was the most beautiful sight she'd ever seen. That he was insane enough to take such a risk for her made him that much more beautiful.

"I'll hold you while you take off your clothes," Will said.

Without waiting for her assent, Will wedged himself between two poles leaving his arms free to encircle her waist. Idalou knew this was no time to be thinking of such things, but she was acutely aware of his arms pushing up against her breasts. Forcing herself to concentrate, she struggled to unfasten her skirt and pass it under her feet. Much to her shock, she lost it altogether and it floated away in the swirling waters. Her blouse followed.

Idalou was suddenly acutely aware that she was nearly naked in the arms of a man who was practically a stranger, but who in a few short days had become a major factor in her life. There was no way to shield the fullness of her breasts or the shape of her lower limbs from his gaze or from contact with his body. Yet the enforced intimacy of this moment seemed to bring them closer, to remove some of the needless restraint between them.

At the same time, she had a lump in her throat that Will hadn't hesitated to risk his life to rescue her. No one had ever risked half as much for her.

"I'm going to turn my back to the current." Will appeared to be far more in control of himself than she was. "Stay behind me with your arms locked around my waist. The current will push you up against me. You'll be safe as long as you don't let go."

Idalou had to force herself to leave the safety of the fence. Will didn't move until she passed her arms around his chest. She could barely reach around him to lock her fingers together. She'd had no idea Will's chest was so large. Even though she was fighting for her life, Idalou couldn't be completely oblivious to the fact that she had her arms around a man. She'd seen a man bare to the waist only a few times and then only at a distance. She was equally aware that only a thin piece of fabric separated her from him. Just thinking about it made her dangerously weak.

Forcing all thoughts of Will's nearness out of her mind, she concentrated on keeping her footing. The water was still rising, and the current was getting more turbulent as debris from upstream caught and lodged in the trees, creating swirling currents that more than once swept her off her feet. She was certain that if Will hadn't been upstream from the rope and therefore leaning into it, he'd have lost his hold and they'd both have been swept away.

As it was, their lives depended on the staunchness of a fence post and the strength of Will's horse. She cast more than one apprehensive glance toward shore, but the horse held steady against the fearsome pull of the current. She was relieved when she saw Carl ride up. He attached a rope between his saddle and the saddle on Will's horse. Then he backed his horse up until the strain on the rope was shared between the two horses.

Idalou had hardly taken a deep breath when she felt the rope jerk so violently, Will nearly lost his hold on it.

"Something has hit the corral fence and knocked it loose," Will said. "It's pulling us downstream."

The current that had been pressing them against the rope now pushed them hard downstream. Pulled off her feet, Idalou clung desperately to Will. She knew she'd be swept to her death if she lost her hold on him. Miraculously, Will had managed to keep his balance despite being whipped about by the current, but she wasn't sure how long he could stay upright.

"Back the horses!" Will shouted and gestured.

Carl understood despite the roar of the water, and they were gradually pulled away from the most dangerous current. If they could just hold on to the rope, they would be pulled to safety. Even though her feet could now reach bottom, she could only stumble along behind Will, her feet bumping into his. The muscles in her arms and fingers screamed from the strain of holding on to Will, but she blocked out the pain and concentrated on trying to get her feet under her. Her weight pulling on him made it even more difficult for Will to stay upright.

Finally, Carl had backed the horses up so far that the outward lip of an eddy swept Will and Idalou toward the edge of the flood. The water swirled so rapidly, Idalou found herself running to keep from falling down. Suddenly the water was only up to her knees. Though her legs were shaky, she managed to stand. Carl left the horses and rushed forward to take her hand as she and Will staggered out of the water and stumbled onto dry ground.

Will dropped to his knees, then fell forward on the ground, his chest heaving, his limbs shaking. Only Carl's support kept Idalou from falling. Giving in, she sank down, then flopped back against the earth.

She lay still, her eyes closed and her mind blank, as her body labored to recover from its exhaustion. The heat of the sun pierced her soaked clothes to warm her body and gradually help release the tension in her arms and shoulders. Gradually the pain eased and she began to breathe more deeply. Opening her eyes, she was struck by the irony of a sunny, nearly cloudless day serving as the backdrop of a flood that had destroyed her ranch and nearly taken her life. The noise of the torrent began to abate. The water behind the dam was nearly gone. In a short while the stream would be back within its normal banks.

Left behind would be the destruction of everything her family had worked to build since they'd come to Texas.

"When the tree hit the corral fence, I thought you were goners," Carl said.

He had finished pulling Will's rope out of the water and laid it on the ground to dry. Idalou could only imagine his horror at seeing his sister in the middle of floodwaters and being afraid she was about to die. If their roles had been reversed, she wasn't sure she would have been able to act as quickly and intelligently as Carl. Will was right. Carl had grown up.

"What caused the dam to break?" Carl asked.

"It didn't break." Idalou sat up and shaded her eyes so she could see her brother. "Somebody blew it up."

"That's impossible," Carl said.

"I heard the explosion," Idalou said.

Will sat up. "I thought the dam looked too well built to collapse on its own."

"Why would anybody do that?" Carl asked.

"Jordan wants our ranch," Idalou said. "Now that Will has paid off the loan, he has to think of another way to drive us out."

"I know what you think of him, and I know he's taken advantage of us in the past, but he wouldn't do anything like that," Carl declared. "You could have been killed."

"We both could have been killed," Idalou pointed out.

"Weren't you both supposed to be out looking for the bull?" Will asked Idalou.

"Yes, but spending every minute in the saddle had

put me way behind in my chores. I hadn't even taken up the eggs in two days."

Carl looked toward where the chicken coop had been. "You won't have to worry about that any longer."

"I expect whoever blew up the dam chose this time because he believed both of you would be away from the ranch," Will said. "He wanted to destroy the ranch but not hurt either of you."

"In that case, I'm certain Jordan is behind it," Idalou said.

"I don't believe he did it," Carl insisted.

"Then who else could it have been?" his sister asked.

"Frank Sonnenberg wants the Double-L, too," Carl reminded her.

"He hasn't put any pressure on me," Idalou said. "He just said he'd top Jordan's offer and left it at that."

"He's not rich enough to do that," Carl said.

"Is there anything you can do to stop Jordan?" Idalou asked Will.

"Not unless I can prove he's responsible for blowing up the dam."

"He's a hard businessman, but he's not evil," Carl insisted.

Idalou hadn't thought so either, but there was no getting around the fact that someone had blown up the dam.

"I'll question both men," Will said. "In the meantime, we have to find a place for you and your sister to stay."

"I'm not leaving the ranch," Carl said. "The moment rustlers hear there's nobody here, they'll clean us out."

"Where will you sleep?" Idalou asked.

"I've got my bedroll," Carl said.

"But you don't have any food or clothes. Everything we owned was in the house."

The tops of the stones that had served as the foundation for their house were barely visible above the receding water. One of the joists had been shattered, the twisted pieces protruding from the water. Everything else had vanished.

"I can buy food."

"With what? The little money we had was in the house."

"You don't have any money in the bank?" Will asked.

Idalou shook her head.

"That's not a problem. I'll lend you what you need."

"I can't accept that," Idalou said.

"Since I paid off the loan, you can think of me as owning the ranch," Will said. "If that's the case, you're working for me. That means I have to pay you wages."

Idalou knew this was all wrong, but she was too tired and too upset to think. Once she had time to recover from the shock of what had happened, she'd figure out something.

"None of us will own anything if the cows disappear," Carl pointed out.

Will got to his feet. "Then we'd better be going. The sooner we get your sister settled, the sooner we can decide what to do about the ranch."

Idalou stared at the area that had once contained the buildings making up their home. Everything was gone, swept away by the flood. They might not be ready to admit it, but there was no ranch to save. Will held out his hand. She took it and got to her feet. Only then did she remember she'd lost her clothes, that she was standing up in her chemise.

"I can't go into town like this," she said, more horrified at being exposed to Will than that anyone in town would see her.

Will picked up his shirt from where he'd dropped it and handed it to her. "Put this on. It's not much, but it'll protect your modesty."

"What about you?" she asked as she reached gratefully for the shirt.

"I still have my vest," Will said with a sly grin. "That ought to keep me from completely scandalizing the women of Dunmore."

"It's more likely to give them dreams that'll have them groaning in their sleep," Carl said, unable to contain a laugh.

"You're disgraceful," Idalou said, caught between her own embarrassment and being forced to acknowledge the incredible sight that was Will's bare chest. It was impossible to believe that a man as lazy as Will claimed to be would have a chest and shoulders like that. No wonder he'd been able to hold on to the rope despite the force of the current. His chest and shoulders jutted from a narrow waist. His skin was alive with the movement of powerful muscles whenever he lifted his arms or twisted his body. The muscles in his abdomen rippled. Idalou had never guessed that his loose clothes concealed a body that had the power to ignite such heat in her.

"Just willing to face the truth." Carl's grin disappeared, to be replaced by an angry scowl. "When I find out who blew up that dam, I'm going to break his neck."

"That's my job," Will said. "You might as well give me a chance to earn my salary."

* * *

Idalou had been certain that by the time she'd traveled the five miles to town, she would have a solution to all the difficulties facing her. She was wrong. The closer they came to Dunmore, the more divergent her thoughts became, until she couldn't make any decisions at all. Fortunately, Will and Carl made them for her. Every time she attempted to insert her opinion into the discussion, she'd remember that her modesty was protected only by Will's shirt. That realization so unnerved her that she was incapable of doing anything beyond trying to come up with a way to get herself inside the hotel without a single citizen in Dunmore seeing her.

Of course that was impossible. At first, people would be too shocked at the news about the dam to comment on her mode of dress. But after the excitement of the destruction of the dam began to subside, they would remember that she'd been only half dressed. That she'd been wearing Will's shirt would make the incident memorable and the subject of gossip for as long as either of them stayed in Dunmore.

"I don't mean to desert you," Carl said to his sister, "but I want to get to the store and back to the ranch as fast as possible."

"I can take care of your sister," Will said. "Just tell Andy to charge everything to me."

"I can take care of myself," Idalou insisted.

"Don't be a dope," Carl said to his sister. "You don't have any clothes, any money, or any place to stay. Let Will take care of all that. We can figure out how to repay him later."

Idalou had already reached that conclusion, but she didn't like hearing it stated. She agreed that the hotel was the logical choice, but staying there meant she'd have no privacy at all.

"Once you have a room, I'll see about getting you some clothes. What shops do you like?" Will asked.

"Ella Huffman's store is the only one with made-up clothes," Idalou said, "but I can't afford anything she has."

"We can afford at least one dress," Will said. "That will give you time to get something made."

Will clearly didn't have any idea how long it took to put together a woman's dress, but maybe she could get one of the housewives to run up something quick and simple that she could afford.

As they approached town, Will and Carl rode close on either side of her. Still, she knew that wouldn't be an effective shield once they reached Main Street.

"Let's ride down the alley," Will said. "Idalou can stay in my office until I make arrangements for her room in the hotel. Then we can take her there."

"I'd prefer to wait until after dark," Idalou said.

"Once people hear that your home was destroyed, they'll be too sympathetic to worry about what you're wearing."

Will didn't understand that to be seen in his company was the same as shouting to every female in town that something was going on between them.

"Maybe we ought to go to the dress shop first," Will said. "That way no one will have any reason to comment on what you're wearing."

Idalou would have suggested the same thing, but she couldn't bring herself to ask Will to spend money buying her clothes.

Maybe it was the heat or the fact that it was mid-afternoon and everyone was a little sleepy after lunch, but they passed only three people as they rode down the alley. None of the three gave them more than a glance or spoke except to greet the sheriff. They arrived at the back of the dress shop and dismounted.

"Wait here while I go inside," Will said.

"I can't go in there," Idalou said when Will was out of earshot.

"Why not?" Carl asked.

"I forgot that Junie Mae works with her aunt."

"For God's sake, Lou, can't you forget that Webb was sweet on her?"

"How would you feel if Mara was sweet on Van?"

"She's sweet on Will, and I get along just fine with him."

"That's because *he* isn't sweet on *her*."

"For all you know, Webb wasn't sweet on Junie Mae, just tired of you blaming his father for everything. Everybody knows she turned to Van soon enough after Webb died."

That had made Idalou even more angry at Junie Mae. It was bad enough that she'd stolen Webb from her. It was unforgivable that she couldn't stay faithful to his memory for even a week. "I don't care. I don't want to—"

The back door to the store opened and Will stepped out. "Ella Huffman is at lunch, but Junie Mae says she'll be glad to take care of you."

If she had had any place to go, Idalou would have turned and ridden away. The idea of letting Junie Mae help her choose a dress while Will watched was almost more than she could contemplate.

"Come on, Lou," Carl said as he dismounted. "You've got plenty of class. Now's the time to show it."

That was the trouble with having class. You had to do all sorts of things you didn't want to do and pretend you liked them. You had to be nice to people when you were aching to scratch their eyes out. You had to be thankful for things you'd rather throw on the ground and grind under your feet.

"Let me help you down," Will said.

Before she could object, he put his hands around her waist, lifted her from the saddle, and set her gently on the ground. The sound of her feet squishing against the wet socks inside her boots made her feel even more like running away. Could she be more humiliated?

Junie Mae was waiting just inside. The back room of the store was the workroom where dresses were cut out and sewn together. Bolts of material were stacked on shelves lining one wall. One table was covered with material being cut out for a dress while patterns lay scattered over another. Pieces of dresses lay across two sewing tables. Cards of ribbon, lace, and various trims rested in a specially built case along with dozens of spools of thread.

"You poor thing," Junie Mae cooed. "How awful."

Idalou wanted to tell her it was no such thing, but it *was* awful and she did feel like a poor thing.

"We need a dress for her to wear," Will said. "All her clothes got lost in the flood."

"I'm sure we have something in your size," Junie Mae said.

"Nothing expensive," Idalou said. "I can't afford to stay in the hotel and buy fancy clothes."

"I won't hear of you staying in the hotel," Junie Mae said. "You can stay with me."

Chapter Eleven

Idalou was certain it was impossible to be more humiliated. She didn't want to stay in the hotel because of the lack of privacy and Will's having to pay for it, but how could she share a room with the woman who'd stolen the only man she'd ever thought she wanted to marry?

"That's awfully kind of you, Junie Mae," Will said, "but it is your aunt's house."

"That's right," Idalou said, grasping at the straw Will had handed her, however unintentionally. "I couldn't even consider it without your aunt's consent."

"She won't mind," Junie Mae insisted.

"Still, it might be better if Idalou could choose a dress so we can head to the hotel," Will said.

Before Idalou had time to look at any of the dresses, Junie Mae's aunt returned from lunch.

"Somebody blew up Idalou's dam and the water washed the house away," Junie Mae said to her aunt. "She was going to stay in the hotel, but I invited her to share my room. Is that all right with you?"

Before Idalou could think of an excuse, Ella Huffman had gripped both of Idalou's hands in her firm grasp.

"You poor child," she said. "What kind of horrible person would do something like that?"

"I don't know," Idalou said, "but you don't have to—"

"I didn't hesitate to give my sister's child a permanent home when she died," Ella said, cutting off Idalou's protest. "Of course you'll stay with us."

"The hotel is really quite comfortable," Idalou said.

"But it's filled with men, isn't it?" Ella asked.

"Yes, I suppose." She didn't recall a woman ever staying there.

"That's all the more reason for you to stay with me."

"That's very kind of you, but I can't—"

"I won't hear a word of protest," Ella said. "I'm sorry I can't offer to let your brother stay, but it wouldn't be right to have a young man who's not a blood relative in the house with Junie Mae."

Idalou came to the conclusion that unless she was willing to appear ungrateful, even rude, there was nothing she could do to keep from sharing a room with Junie Mae. However, she intended to do everything she could to make her stay as short as possible.

"It's very kind of you," Idalou said, giving in. "Carl's staying at the ranch to keep an eye on our cows."

"Where will he sleep?" Ella asked.

"He has his bedroll," Will said.

"Men do all sorts of things a woman would never do," Ella said with a wink, as though she and Idalou were sharing a secret.

"I'll check on Carl to make sure he's okay," Will said.

Ella beamed at Will. "So kind. Dunmore is very fortunate to have you with us, even for a short while."

Idalou wasn't surprised at Ella's almost fawning attitude toward Will, but she was surprised to see Junie Mae looking acutely uncomfortable and staring at her feet.

"Idalou is looking for a dress," Junie Mae told her aunt. "Everything she had was washed away in the flood."

Apparently, Ella hadn't noticed that Idalou was wearing only a shirt. Once she did, however, it didn't matter that Will had pulled her bodily from the water or had ridden next to her for five miles through open country. The rules of propriety had to be strictly observed. She bundled Will out the door with assurances he could, at a suitable time, come see for himself that Idalou was being properly cared for. It would have been funny if Idalou wasn't afraid that Will was secretly relieved to have her taken off his hands.

"Is she really going to share a room with Junie Mae?" Carl asked Will, caught between surprise and amusement. "I'm surprised she didn't bolt."

"If she'd had anything to wear, I think she would have."

"Idalou is a great gal, but sometimes she needs taking down a peg," Carl said with a boyish grin. "I could never do it."

"I wouldn't even try."

"You could." Carl's expression turned serious. "She complains about you all the time, but she listens to what you say."

Will would have placed a substantial bet that the only reason Idalou would ever listen to him would be to take the opposite position. They were in the jail, and Carl was carefully packing all the provisions he'd bought into two saddlebags. He'd told Will he didn't intend to come back to town for at least a week.

"Everybody listens to you," Carl said. "Now that they know you saved Idalou, you'll be even more of a hero."

After leaving Ella's store, Will had headed to the Swinging Door. There he'd found Carl regaling more than twenty men with his account of Will fighting his way through the floodwaters with Idalou on his back. Apparently, Carl had told Andy Davis about it while buying his supplies, and Andy had insisted that he go to the saloon and tell everybody else. All the men expressed proper indignation over the destruction of the dam and promised to do anything they could to bring the culprit to justice.

"If anyone does listen to me—and I'm not sure they do—it's only because I was fool enough to take this job when nobody else would."

"You stopped Van from running over Pepper, you put Newt in jail, and you convinced Jordan he ought to pay us for using our bull. Nobody else has ever come close to doing that."

Will figured they hadn't tried very hard. Any one of his brothers—Luke, Zeke, or Hawk—would have had this town buttoned up tight in less than twenty-four hours.

"I haven't figured out who took the bull, I don't know who blew up the dam, and I don't know who's behind all the trouble on your range. That doesn't make me sound too all-fired great."

"You'll figure it out."

Will wondered why Carl had more confidence in him than he himself had. "Then there's Mara thinking she's in love with me, your sister disliking me, and Junie Mae . . ." He fell silent.

Carl looked up from his packing. "Mara would get over you if her ma wasn't drumming it into her head that you'd make the perfect husband. Idalou doesn't dislike you. She's just real aggravated by the trouble we've been having. I didn't know anything was wrong with Junie Mae, but come to think of it, she has been looking a little peaked lately."

"I think she may have been disappointed in love," Will said, kicking himself for mentioning Junie Mae.

Carl turned back to his packing. "I used to think Van and Webb were both sweet on Idalou, but after Webb died, Van's pa made it clear he wanted Van to marry Mara. Van can be a real bastard, but he'd never go against his pa. Junie Mae never had a chance."

If a boy as oblivious as Carl could tell that Junie Mae was looking off-color, it was a surefire bet every woman in town had noticed and was speculating as to the reason. It looked as though things would be coming to a head sooner than Will had thought. He was glad he'd already written Isabelle.

"I'll come check on you in a couple of days," Will said, hoping to get off the subject of Junie Mae.

"You don't have to check on me." Carl seemed offended. "I can take care of myself."

"I'm sure you can," Will assured him, "but if I don't check on you, your sister *will* be mad at me. What's more, she'll check on you herself. You get your choice, her or me."

"You," Carl said with a defeated sigh. "I've got to be the only eighteen-year-old boy in Texas whose sister checks on everything he does."

"I'm twenty-eight and my mother still checks on me," Will said. "My father, too. And that doesn't count two sisters and nine brothers. Fortunately, they're not all home at the same time. Want to trade places?"

"No," Carl said with a grin. "I'm surprised you didn't run away."

"I sort of did."

Carl's eyes grew wide. "Men your age don't *run away*. They just leave."

Will didn't know what had gotten into him. He'd nearly given away Junie Mae's secret, and now he was trying to do the same with his. As for leaving, Carl didn't understand. No one *left* Isabelle. Even when she was a thousand miles away, she was with you, looking over your shoulder, whispering in your ear, reminding you of the lessons you'd forgotten. Luke said she followed him like his personal rain cloud.

"We're a very close family, and I'm the youngest male."

"I feel sorry for you," Carl said. "I've only got a sister."

"Don't get me wrong," Will said, remembering the sweetness of Isabelle's smile and the comfort of Jake's presence when he was a kid. "I love my family. I even love the little brats they keep having, but I had to get away. They wouldn't let me breathe."

That sounded silly even to himself, but it was true. He could still remember the feeling of relief when he rode out of the Hill County. And the guilt for feeling relieved. The desperate need to leave, and the feeling of loss once he had. What did you do when the thing you wanted to get away from most was the thing you loved the best? You established the sort of independence Buck, Drew, Sean, Chet, Matt, and Bret had. And you didn't do it by running away like Pete, Luke, Zeke, and Hawk. He had run away, but it was just temporary.

"Sometimes I don't want to come home because Lou makes me feel like such a baby," Carl said. "Even

Jordan treats me more like a man, though he told Mara she couldn't marry me because I'm too green." He looked up at Will and grinned. "Maybe we ought to make a pact to help each other out."

"If you want to help me, find that bull."

Carl's grin faded. "I guess I have to face the fact that somebody stole that bull. We've looked everywhere. Even Sonnenberg's hands couldn't find it."

The mention of Sonnenberg caught Will's attention. "Sonnenberg had his hands search his land for the bull?"

"No. Van let Idalou search his land. His hands searched *our* land in case we'd missed something, but I've gone over every inch of our place. Let's face it. The bull's gone."

Will didn't trust Van and had no reason to trust his father. He could see why Van might invite Idalou to search his ranch, but he didn't see why Van's men should search Idalou's property. According to what he'd learned since he'd been in Dunmore, Frank Sonnenberg wanted Idalou and Carl's ranch as much as Jordan McGloughlin did. If Van was anything to go by, Frank would be more willing than Jordan to use any method he thought would work.

But would he go so far as to blow up the dam? Will didn't know anybody in Dunmore terribly well, but he didn't believe Jordan would do that. In all fairness, he had to say he didn't have any reason to believe Sonnenberg would, either.

Carl looked up. "What will you do if we don't find the bull? You must have considered that possibility when you paid the loan. You don't strike me as a man to do anything without thinking it through first."

Will wished his family could hear that. "I've got a feeling that bull is still here, but if he's gone, I'll pay you to run the ranch for me."

"You wouldn't stay in Dunmore?"

Will had never considered leaving his family. His parents and siblings were all too much a part of him. He was relieved to be away, but he missed them, too. "I've got some land already set aside for my ranch. As soon as I get the bull, I'll buy some cows and set up my own operation."

"There's plenty of land around here."

"It's not the land, it's my family. I don't want them looking over my shoulder all the time, but I do want them close by."

"I guess I feel the same way about Lou."

"Of course you do. Now tell me where you'll set up your camp. I don't have time to go looking all over for you."

Idalou hated to admit it, but Junie Mae's clothes looked better on her than her own. "I'll only take one dress," she told Junie Mae. She couldn't deny being pleased that the dress made her look so attractive, but she felt uncomfortable in clothes that weren't her own.

"I have more clothes than I need," Junie Mae said, pulling two more dresses out of the closet and laying them on the bed. "Besides, that dress looks better on you than it does on me. You can keep it."

"I can't do that."

"I'm blond and pale. You're a brunette and your skin has real color. I'm going to go through my clothes and give you everything that makes me look washed out. Look," Junie Mae said when Idalou started to protest, "my aunt says the clothes she and I wear are her best advertisement. Nobody asked about that dress when I wore it, but you'll get plenty of notice. Aunt Ella will probably give you more dresses to wear."

Idalou didn't know what to do. She couldn't go

around wearing one dress every day, but she didn't see how she could accept so many. And try as she might, she couldn't forget that Junie Mae had stolen Webb from her. His jilting her without warning and without a reason had been a terrible shock. It had hurt her deeply to know how little she meant to him.

Yet there was something about Junie Mae that puzzled her, that made her feel Junie Mae was clinging to her, that as incredible as it seemed, she needed her. It wasn't just the lost color or the gauntness in Junie Mae's face. There was fear in her eyes. Idalou doubted her impressions at first, but changed her mind when she noticed how nervous Junie Mae was around her aunt, how she did little things to keep out of Ella's range of vision. The whole time her aunt was with her in the store, Junie Mae had fiddled with a couple of dresses, holding first one and then the other in front of her to show Idalou why it would look good on her.

"I'll move back to the ranch as soon as everything dries out," Idalou said to Junie Mae.

"You said the water washed everything away. Where will you stay?"

"I plan to buy a tent."

"Why would you want to go back?"

"It's my home," Idalou said. "Besides, I have animals to care for."

"Won't they have drowned?"

"I let them out before the floodwaters reached us. I'm hoping they survived."

The two of them were in Junie Mae's room with dresses spread over the bed they would be sharing, over two chairs, and hanging on the door. Idalou had never had a mirror larger than six inches high, but Junie Mae had a mirror on the back of the door that was so big Idalou could see almost her whole reflection.

As much as she castigated herself for her vanity, she couldn't stop looking at herself in the mirror. It was wonderful to feel attractive.

"I'm sure the animals can take care of themselves," Junie Mae said.

Junie Mae's bedroom was bigger than the little parlor in Idalou's ranch house. The walls were covered with a cream-colored wallpaper decorated with bunches of blue and red flowers tied with pink ribbon. The two windows had shades to keep out the sun and gauzy white curtains embroidered with dozens of blue forget-me-nots. The big four-poster bed had been fashioned out of a dark wood and was piled high with comfortable mattresses. A white bedspread covered with white tufts reached down to the floor on each side of the bed. A chest of drawers filled with underclothes was flanked by a dressing table covered with combs, brushes, ointments, rouge . . . more things to make a woman beautiful than Idalou had ever seen.

"The chickens provide eggs as well as meat," Idalou told Junie Mae. "The pigs will be slaughtered in the fall, and we need the cow for milk and butter. I had a garden, too, but I'm sure there's nothing left of it."

Junie Mae laid aside the dress she'd been holding and sank into the chair at the dressing table. "Do you like living on a ranch? It sounds awfully hard to me."

Idalou used to believe that living on a ranch was what she wanted because it would be the only thing she could have. Unbidden, Will's image popped into her mind. He was a rancher, but he didn't look or act like McGloughlin or Sonnenberg. He obviously had money, but he didn't use it as an excuse to grow soft. He was as comfortable in a hotel or at a supper table as he was in the saddle or fighting floodwaters. Somehow he had made being a rancher fit him, not the other way around.

"I don't like having to struggle to keep from losing the ranch or having people cheat me."

"Van used to say he was afraid McGloughlin would get tired of waiting for you to fail and run off your herd."

"Nobody would try that now, not with Will . . . I mean the sheriff around."

Some of the strain disappeared from Junie Mae's eyes. "He's the most wonderful man. I don't know what I would have done without him." She seemed stricken by what she'd said. She jumped up, went to her closet, and began looking through her clothes.

"What did he do?" Idalou asked, fighting down a demon of jealousy.

"Nothing, really. I was just feeling really down and he made me feel better."

Idalou didn't believe that for a minute. Whatever the problem, it had been serious enough to make Junie Mae unwilling to face her. Now that she thought of it, Junie Mae didn't look good. Idalou didn't want to become enmeshed in Junie Mae's problems, but she couldn't ignore them after Junie Mae had offered to let her share her room.

"I don't want to pry," Idalou said, "but if I can help, just let me know."

"Thanks," Junie Mae said, her eyes swimming with tears, "but it's nothing serious."

Will surveyed what had once been the Ellsworth ranch with a sinking feeling. There was nothing to rebuild. He even questioned whether it was worthwhile trying. It wasn't simply that the ranch buildings were gone. The landscape itself had been scoured by the floodwaters and the debris it carried. Mud was everywhere, sticky, viscous, and deep, making it impossible to walk over much of the area, but in a few days it would dry to rock hardness or become powdery and blow away in the wind.

"I don't know where to begin," Idalou said.

Will could hear the defeat in her voice. They were sitting their horses, not an easy position from whence to dispense comfort, but Will reached out to take Idalou's hand.

"You don't have to worry about that for a few days yet."

She tried to pull her hand away, but he held on. Giving up, she gripped his hand hard.

"I can't *not* worry about it. Carl's out there with no one to help him or even know if he gets in trouble. Suppose the person who blew up the dam comes back. What about whoever took our bull?"

Will gave her hand a squeeze. "Carl is capable of taking care of himself. Besides, his horse is a better watchdog than any man would be."

"I can't stay with Junie Mae forever."

Idalou turned big brown eyes up at Will, and he felt something turn over inside. It was a little bit like nausea, but today that didn't seem like such a bad thing. He had an ominous feeling he was making a mistake, but he didn't care about that either. He had the sinking feeling he was about to become more than slightly interested in a young woman. A week ago that would have sent him running for his horse. Now he just squeezed Idalou's hand a little harder and stared back at her with what he feared was a really stupid look on his face.

"You can move to the hotel anytime you want, but I think Junie Mae likes your company."

Idalou's eyes narrowed. "Something's wrong with her, and you know what it is, don't you?"

"Why do you think that?"

Idalou pulled her hand from Will's grasp but held

his gaze. "She's as nervous as a cat around her aunt, which I don't understand because Ella dotes on her. Only last night she was saying she thought Junie Mae had been working too hard. She's always encouraging her to eat more. Ella said she was glad I was staying there, that Junie Mae had been acting depressed for a while and that she hoped having someone her own age to talk to would cheer her up."

"It might," Will said, hoping Idalou wouldn't dig any deeper.

"It might if she'd talk to me," Idalou said, not letting up. "I've told her several times I'd be happy to help her, but she assures me it's just delayed grief over her mother's death."

"She's probably right."

"Then why does she look at you like you're her savior?"

Will should have known that Idalou wouldn't give up so easily. He didn't see what he could do except tell her as much of the truth as he felt he could. "Junie Mae does have a problem, but it's confidential. I found out about it by accident. She only looks at me like that because I agreed to help her if I could."

"If it's so serious, why hasn't she told her aunt?"

"That was her decision, not mine."

Idalou studied him for a moment. "What is it about you that makes women depend on you?"

"I don't know. Maybe I look harmless."

"That's not why they're falling over themselves to feed you."

Will's shoulders slumped. "Don't start with my looks again."

"I can't help it. Everybody's mesmerized by them. And you're mesmerized by people in trouble. One look at Junie Mae with tears in her eyes, and you rush to help her like a knight in shining armor."

Will frowned angrily. He'd spent his whole life hearing about his looks. Okay, so he'd taken advantage of them on occasion, but he had no intention of leaning on them for the rest of his life. It seemed impossible for people to understand that he wanted to be seen as something more than a face that earned him privileges for no other reason than that people liked to look at him. His brother Pete had once told him that he ought to be an actor, that women would pay a fortune just to look at him.

What Pete didn't understand, because he was a pinch-faced little brat who was constantly in trouble, was that people didn't see Will at all. They couldn't get past his face. It had taken him many years to figure that out. The adulation was nice at first, but after a while it started to go sour. Everybody assumed he was going to use his looks and charm to ease his way through life, so they started expecting less of him. He'd been having an argument with Matt over how Matt was dealing with the orphans he'd adopted when Matt had flung that at him. Will had denied it at first. Later, when he was calm enough to think rationally, he'd realized it was true.

"Let me tell you what my looks have brought me," he said to Idalou.

Chapter Twelve

"My parents died when I was four and my brother was nine," Will said. "An aunt with five children wanted to take us in, but my uncle insisted she had enough children already. He was single and had a farm in Texas he said was perfect for two boys. For a while I thought things *were* perfect. He made sure we had plenty to eat, never worked us too hard, and always gave us a hug before we went to bed. He told us how special we were, and how fortunate he was to have two such handsome nephews. What I didn't know was that he'd started sexually abusing my brother almost from the day we arrived in Texas."

"My God!" Idalou's hand covered her mouth; her eyes were wide with shock.

"I was too young to understand. When he started telling me how beautiful I was, putting his hands all over me, even kissing me when he put me to bed, I didn't realize that his interest had turned to me. I was just seven. Several times I overheard my brother shouting at my uncle, but I didn't know what it was about until he took me out behind the smokehouse, pulled my pants down, and bent me over. He was taking down his own pants when Matt found us."

Will had to stop speaking. Twenty-one years later the events of that afternoon still had the power to make his blood run cold.

"He killed my uncle with a butcher knife and buried his body in the pigpen. He turned himself into a murderer to protect me."

Overcome with emotion once more, Will turned away to stare at the scarred trunks of the cottonwood and pecan trees along the creek. They'd withstood the fury of the floodwaters, emerging with their roots still firmly planted in the ground, but they bore the scars of that conflict. That made Will think of Matt, standing tall for all the boys he'd adopted, yet bearing scars that could never be erased.

"It was this face," Will said, turning toward Idalou with sudden anger, "that drew my uncle's attention. It was this face that forced Matt to kill for me."

"It wasn't your fault," Idalou said. "You were only a child. There was nothing you could do."

"We endured two years of being shuffled from one foster home to another because Matt wouldn't talk, of being thrown out of the orphanage and into the streets because he attacked anybody who looked at me too long or touched me by accident. Before my parents died, Matt was the kindest, gentlest person in the world. Most of the time, he still is. But there's another part that is hard and unforgiving, and it was all because of my face."

"I don't know what to say. I never would have guessed."

Will could see the tenderness, the compassion she felt for him, but he feared there might be pity, too, and that was something he couldn't accept.

"But you can believe I like having women fighting over feeding me, I like having a silly little girl believe she's in love with me. Now you think I'm helping Junie Mae because I'm bedazzled by her face. Nobody knows better than I how little can be behind a pretty face. And no one knows better than I do how few people can see beyond that face . . . or even try."

Now that he'd relieved himself of the burden of his built-up frustration, he felt guilty for dumping it all on Idalou.

"I shouldn't be saying any of this to you, but you're the only woman in Dunmore who doesn't give a damn about my looks."

No sound disturbed the silence beyond the chink of metal whenever one of their horses shook its head to drive off flies or stamped a hoof into the soft ground. Even the birds had deserted the area.

"I'm not unaffected by your face," Idalou said, "but we got started off on the wrong foot. I saw everything going your way, when nothing was going mine. I saw no reason for your good fortune and no honest reason for my misfortune. You were a double villain because you were not only buying the bull, you refused to help me find it. You defended Jordan, Mara fell in love with you, and I saw you kissing Junie Mae. I admit I was angry, and a little jealous."

"You were jealous of me?" Considering how she'd acted toward him, he found that hard to believe.

Idalou looked down at her pommel. "Carl and Lloyd said you were interested in me. After you asked me to go walking with you, I decided they might be right. You can understand why I was so upset when I saw you kissing Junie Mae."

"Junie Mae kissing me," Will corrected automatically, his mind quickly processing what Idalou had just said. He'd assumed that the warming of Idalou's attitude toward him was the result of his pulling her from the floodwaters. But if she'd been interested in him *before* her dam was blown up, then maybe she really did like him. At least a little. Now the question became, how much did he like her?

He had been attracted to several women over the years, but none seriously enough to ask himself that question. It wasn't just a question of *if* he liked her. More important was *how* he liked her. As a friend, as a business partner, as a woman whose company he enjoyed on occasion, or was it more serious than that?

Did serious mean willing to risk his life to pull her from the floodwaters? Maybe, but he'd have done the same for anybody else. Even Van. *Ugh.* He hated that thought. Serious enough to pay off the loan? Now he was getting somewhere. No woman had cost him money before. Well, not much money. Isabelle said it was good he was a skinflint since he was so lazy. Hell, he couldn't be all that lazy. He'd been busting his butt since he got to Dunmore, and all for some suppers that were getting to be more trouble than his job.

"I don't know how women do things in Dunmore," he said, "but if you want a fella to know you like him, you kinda have to give him a hint. And telling him to go walking with another woman isn't going to do it."

"I don't know how to talk to a man," Idalou said, still not willing to meet his gaze.

"You didn't seem to have any problem with Webb or Van."

She looked up. "I've known them for years. Besides, they didn't leave me speechless when I first set eyes on them. Then you were concerned that I might have become overheated. You even brought me water."

"I couldn't ignore the fact that you looked about ready to faint."

"Then you refused to help me look for the bull."

"I refused to go with you to accuse Jordan of stealing the bull," Will corrected.

"It didn't matter. I was too angry to notice the difference. Then they made you sheriff, and I was sure they'd made a huge mistake. Even though I was mad, I began to notice you got things done in a quiet way."

"Are you trying to say you don't think I'm an incompetent idiot?"

Idalou laughed. "I guess so. Was I doing such a bad job?"

The tension in Will's stomach relaxed, and he smiled. "Women have a way of talking about a thing without ever using the word. 'You're an idiot.' 'You're *not* an idiot.' That a man can understand. All this other stuff leaves too much room for misunderstanding. And if there's one thing that makes a woman mad, it's a man misunderstanding her, even if what she said didn't make a lick of sense."

"Are women really that hard to understand?"

"Sometimes I think they feel they're required to use up a certain number of words every day. Hell, I've got two brothers who can go for days without saying a word, and they understand each other perfectly."

Idalou laughed so cheerfully Will couldn't help laughing, too. "I like you, Will Haskins. I don't understand you, but I like you. Is that clear enough for you?"

"I like you, too. I don't know why, but I guess I'll figure it out soon enough."

Idalou looked at him with a kind of confused amazement. "Are you always like this?"

"Like what?" That didn't sound good. It was the kind of question that could be followed by either a kiss on the cheek or a knockout punch.

"Open. Without guile. Saying what's on your mind without worrying about how it sounds."

"Isabelle says—"

"I'm sure your mother is a remarkable woman, but I want to know what *you* think."

It wasn't often that anyone wanted to know what Will thought about anything. The notion was kind of unsettling when he came to think of it.

"It's a whole lot easier on everybody if they know exactly where you stand right from the get-go," he said. "Beating around the bush just confuses people. As for saying what's on my mind, it's just easier to go on and get it out of the way. People are going to have to hear it sooner or later. Honesty saves a lot of time."

He wasn't sure he liked the way Idalou was staring at him. He had enough sisters-in-law to know how women looked at the men they loved, and this wasn't it. There was an element of fondness there, as if for a child or a small dog, but not the *I'm crazy about you* expression that made a man feel like he was king of the world. This was closer to the kind of look that made you want to slink away and think about a complete change of wardrobe. He decided to change the subject instead.

"You're going to have to stay with Junie Mae longer than you thought," he said. "You won't be able to set up a tent here for at least a week."

"What about the animals?" Idalou appeared surprised by the change of subject.

"If they survived, they can take care of themselves for a while. I could get some wire to pen up the chickens, but you'll have to feed them. The ground has been swept clean of anything they could eat." He supposed coyotes would get most of the chickens if they weren't rounded up soon. "You could take any we find to Alma McGloughlin."

"Will you help me?"

If he was willing to go tramping through mud looking for chickens not to mention catching the flapping, squawking, pecking things—he supposed he had to be serious about Idalou. But catching chickens didn't seem much like courting to him.

"I think my aunt knows," Junie Mae said tearfully to Will, "or at least suspects. "She's been looking at me very closely these last two days."

Junie Mae was crying on his shoulder again. It made him very uncomfortable, but he didn't have the heart to deny her. The poor woman had no one else she could talk to. "Has anything changed?" Will wasn't conversant with the details of pregnancy, but he had too many sisters-in-law not to know about morning sickness.

"I've lost my appetite."

That didn't sound too terrible. It could be blamed on a lot of things.

"This morning the smell of bacon nearly made me sick."

Morning sickness in its infancy. Another day or two and she'd have to confess or claim she had influenza. But even that would only postpone the inevitable. He needed to hear back from Isabelle soon.

"Well, there's no point in worrying until we know what she's going to do." Junie Mae pulled away from Will, and he had to struggle not to heave a sigh of relief.

"She'll throw me out."

"I'll make sure you have a place to stay until you have a chance to decide what to do about your future. Has Van spoken to you since you told him?"

Junie Mae wiped her eyes and sniffed. "Not a word. The other day he crossed the street when he saw me coming. What did he think I was going to do, proclaim my shame before half the town?"

Men who found themselves the fathers of babies

they didn't want weren't liable to think too clearly, if at all. Most took the first opportunity to get out of town. Since Van didn't have that option, he probably hoped that if he stayed as far away from Junie Mae as possible the whole thing would go away.

"Then all we have to do is decide what to do about your future."

His remark brought on another bout of tears that wet the few places on his shirt that weren't already damp. By the time Junie Mae had stopped crying, dried her eyes, and slipped out the back door, Will was ready to jump on his horse and go chase a few steers. He hadn't had time to reach for his hat before Mara stormed in.

"What was that man-stealing Junie Mae Winslow doing in here?" she demanded. Her color was high, and her breasts were heaving.

"We were discussing a problem that has come up," Will said, hoping that explanation would stall her curiosity.

"I was looking through the crack in the door," Mara informed him. "She was crying, and you were hugging her."

"Well, if you saw what happened, why did you ask?" Will demanded, feeling aggrieved. "It would have been a fine thing if I'd lied with you knowing the truth the whole time."

"I was giving you a chance to tell the truth."

"No, you weren't. You were hoping to catch me in a lie so you could blame me for breaking your heart."

"Well, you have," she said, big tears beginning to roll down her cheeks. "I thought you loved me, and all the while you were seeing Junie Mae."

"You never thought I loved you, because I told you I didn't," Will stated.

"Well, I love you."

"Well you shouldn't. I'm leaving as soon as Carl finds my bull."

Mara threw herself at Will. "Take me with you!" she exclaimed in a dramatic fashion which would have been overdone even in a stage melodrama. "I don't want to stay in this horrible town any longer."

Will pried Mara's arms from around his neck. Taking her by the wrists, he held her away from him. "You should stop trying to convince yourself you're in love with me and go back to Carl. He's a fine young man who'd make you a wonderful husband."

Mara pulled away from Will. "Daddy won't let me marry him. He says I ought to marry Van." Mara pulled a face. "I don't like Van."

"That's the most intelligent thing I've heard you say in a long while. Just keep telling your father that, and before long he'll give in and let you marry Carl."

Will wasn't entirely sure of that, but he didn't think Jordan would force Mara to marry Van against her will.

Mara pouted. "Don't you like me a little?"

"Sure, I like you, but Carl loves you. He'd do anything to make you happy."

Mara puckered her lips like she was on the verge of a temper tantrum. "Carl wants to be a rancher. I don't want to live on a ranch. I want to live in a city and have some fun."

"I want to be a rancher, too. Besides, I've been to enough cities to know they'll drive a sane person crazy. You'll be much happier here in Dunmore. Your parents and all your friends are here."

"That's why I want to get away. I want to meet people I've never met before, see places I've never seen, do things I've never done."

Like act mature enough to be considered ready for marriage. But he didn't say that, because he could understand the lure of the unknown, the excitement of imagined adventure. But he had the advantage of having looked behind the facade of the glamorous and exciting city life to see its sordid and dishonest side.

"Have you told Carl that?"

"I've tried, but all he can think about is finding that bull."

It was hard to underestimate the gulf between one person who'd had too little of everything and another who'd had too much. He didn't know if love was enough to bridge the gap. He wondered if the same could apply to him and Idalou. She seemed to think he was a rich, spoiled brat who just happened to be able to take care of himself occasionally.

"You have to try to understand the things that are important to Carl, just as he should try to understand what's important to you."

"He says I'm too young and too pampered to know what life is really like."

Carl needed to learn that there were times when the truth, especially the unvarnished variety, should be kept strictly out of sight. "What does Van say?"

"He's even worse. He says a wife should do what her husband says and never question him."

That sounded like Van all over. "Have you told your father what Van said?"

"It wouldn't help. Daddy's the same way. Mama never questions him."

Will could see that Mara was getting dangerously wrought up. "I'll talk to your father and to Carl. I know they both love you and wouldn't want to see you so unhappy."

"I wish I were like Idalou," Mara said. "She does exactly what she wants and doesn't care what anybody says."

Will was glad that Idalou was intelligent, dependable, and able to take care of herself, but it wouldn't hurt if she'd be a little romantic. Even after he'd risked his life to pull her from the floodwaters, she still looked at him with clear, cool eyes. He wouldn't have minded if she'd been so thankful she'd thrown her arms around him and kissed him like Junie Mae had. If one of the three women had to think she'd fallen desperately in love with him, why couldn't it be Idalou?

Love! Where had that come from? He couldn't even decide how much he liked Idalou, and she had barely stopped treating him like a bad rash. It was time to put a halter on his galloping imagination before it infected his tongue.

"Idalou is a long way from doing exactly what she wants," he said to Mara, "but she agrees with you that men don't pay nearly enough attention to women. You ought to talk to her sometime."

Mara looked away. "She doesn't want Carl to marry me."

"Idalou loves her brother deeply and wants him to be happy. If that means marrying you, then she'll be the best sister-in-law in the world. She'd take on your father if necessary."

"Would she really do that?"

"Mara, she's already taken him on over that bull. How much more important do you think her brother's happiness is to her?"

Idalou returned to Junie Mae's bedroom to find her roommate throwing up into the washbasin. "Why didn't you tell me you were sick? I'll get your aunt."

"No!" Junie Mae managed to say before another spasm wracked her.

Caught between what she felt she ought to do and what Junie Mae clearly didn't want, Idalou decided the most immediate need was to help Junie Mae. Supporting her until the spasms stopped, she helped clean up. "I'm going to throw this away. I'll be back in a moment."

Idalou was relieved to hear Ella talking with her husband in their bedroom. She cleaned the washbasin and hurried back to Junie Mae, who was sitting on the edge of the bed looking as if she were about to pass out. "Have you seen the doctor?"

Junie Mae shook her head. "I'll be fine in a little while."

Idalou sat down on the bed next to her. "You don't look fine. You look like you've seen a ghost."

"I wouldn't mind a ghost," Junie Mae said without humor.

"You've been looking bad all week. Now I find you throwing up. You've got to see the doctor before you get worse."

Her laugh was bitter. "The doctor can't fix what's wrong, and he can't keep it from getting a lot worse." Junie Mae grabbed Idalou's wrist in a vise-like grip. "You can't tell Aunt Ella. No matter what happens, you can't tell her."

"She's your aunt. She has a right to know."

"She'll find out soon enough." Junie Mae released Idalou's wrist.

Idalou wondered if Junie Mae had some wasting disease. Not even sickness could erase her beauty, but her features seemed gaunt, her skin without color or luster. Even her luxuriant blond hair seemed dry and frizzy. Her lips were a pale slash across her face. Her blue eyes looked huge.

"I'm not sick," Junie Mae said. "I'm just going to have a baby."

In that instant Idalou had the horrible fear that Junie Mae was about to tell her she was carrying Will's child. Junie Mae had said he was helping her, and she'd seen them kissing. It was a logical assumption. However, once she got over the initial shock, she refused to believe Will was the father. Besides, right now she needed to put her confusion aside and concentrate on Junie Mae. Regardless of who the father might be, her condition couldn't be hidden for long.

"Now you understand why I can't tell my aunt," Junie Mae said. "She'll figure it out on her own before long. Then she'll throw me out of the house."

"I'm sure she won't," Idalou said, barely able to control her voice. "You're her niece."

"I'll be disgraced. She won't want anything to do with me."

"What are you going to do?"

"I don't know."

"You should tell the father. This is as much his responsibility as it is yours."

For a moment Idalou thought Junie Mae was going to break down. Idalou put her arm around Junie Mae's shoulder, and in a few minutes she managed to get herself under control.

"He doesn't want anything to do with me. He says this can't possibly be his baby, though he knows it can't be anyone else's."

Idalou was ashamed for feeling relieved. Whatever Will might have done in an unguarded moment of passion, she was absolutely certain he'd never turn his back on his own child. "Are you absolutely sure it's his?"

Junie Mae spun around toward Idalou, angry sparks flashing from her eyes. "I know that having a baby without a husband makes me a loose woman, but I swear I've only been with one man."

Idalou hardly knew what to say. Whether or not it was fair, she'd always held Junie Mae responsible for

Webb's defection. To know that she'd been intimate with another man was a shock. She really didn't know much about Junie Mae, and this whole situation had taken her by surprise. She truly didn't know what to think.

"What do you plan to do?"

Junie Mae's face fell, and tears rolled down her cheeks. "I don't know."

"I think you ought to talk to the father again. I'll go with you if you want."

"No."

"Junie Mae, you can't protect him forever. Your aunt and uncle are going to demand to know who he is."

"He's not going to marry me no matter what anyone says. I can't prove he's the father. Unless it's a boy who grows up to be the spitting image of his father, nobody will ever know."

"You don't have to give up so easily," Idalou said. "People in Dunmore won't like seeing a man refuse to take responsibility for his child. He may not marry you, but he'll have to help you support the child."

"He doesn't want me or the baby," Junie Mae said. "That's just as well, because I don't want him to have anything to do with my child."

"You must have loved him."

"I thought I did, but I guess I was wrong. In any case, it doesn't matter, because he doesn't love me and he doesn't want to marry me."

A sliver of doubt reared its head. Will had told Idalou that Junie Mae had kissed him but that he had no feelings for her. That was exactly what the baby's father had said.

Idalou told herself to stop thinking like a jealous woman. Just because Webb had turned his back on her for Junie Mae didn't mean Will had or would. She couldn't go around believing the worst of people all the time. She had to learn to trust, and who better to start with than Will. She wanted to believe him, especially when he said he liked her, but it was hard. She had to be fair to Will. Virtually anyone could be the father. Right now she had to stop being so concerned about herself and more concerned about Junie Mae. "What are you going to do?" she asked.

Junie Mae squared her shoulders and smiled for the first time. "Talking to you has cleared up a few things in my mind. I've decided to talk to the sheriff."

Chapter Thirteen

If Idalou hadn't been sitting down, her legs would have gone out from under her. Why would Junie Mae say that if it wasn't Will's baby? She told herself to stop leaping to conclusions, that she'd always been wrong about Will. She knew he was a sucker for a woman in trouble. Hadn't he said he'd become sheriff so he'd have a legitimate reason to help her? Hadn't he paid off her loan? Hadn't he put up with Mara's infatuation? Why was it so hard to believe that he would help Junie Mae in her time of need? Marry her, even if he wasn't the father! The horrible image of Will marrying Junie Mae to save her reputation exploded in Idalou's mind with the force of a shock wave. She'd seen Junie Mae kissing Will. Will had thought of Junie Mae right off when Idalou needed a place to stay. Now that she thought of it, Junie Mae looked at Will as if he were a knight on a big white horse. Having Will to turn to must have seemed like the answer to a prayer.

"What is he going to do?" Idalou gripped her hands

together, hoping Junie Mae wouldn't say the words Idalou dreaded to hear.

"I don't know," Junie Mae answered. "I told him about my situation the day you found me kissing him." She blushed. "I shouldn't have done that, but I was so desperate, his offering to help me seemed like the answer to my prayers."

"Do you love him?" Idalou asked. She felt crushed, her secret hope of being with Will gone.

Junie Mae looked surprised. "Why would you think that? I hardly know him."

"That didn't stop you with Webb." Idalou was mortified the moment the words were out of her mouth. Junie Mae was the one in trouble. The ending of Idalou's romance with Webb didn't begin to compare with having a baby out of wedlock.

"I didn't know you were sweet on him until he'd asked me out a couple of times," Junie Mae said. "I was new in town and didn't know anybody. Besides, I was only seventeen and still so upset over my mother's death, I would have gone out with almost anybody to have something else to think about."

"I'm sorry," Idalou said. "I shouldn't have said anything."

"I'm glad you did. I always wanted us to be friends, but I knew that Webb stood between us. He really didn't like me the way he liked you. He just wanted someone to have fun with, and I was desperate for the same thing."

Idalou didn't know if Webb had ever really loved her, but it was time she stopped holding Junie Mae responsible for what he had done. She had to accept that her own actions had in all probability been a more important factor. Carl had warned her that her accusations would drive Webb away.

"You weren't to blame for Webb losing interest in

me. But that's neither here nor there. You and your baby are all that's important now. Are you sure your aunt will throw you out once she knows?"

Junie Mae nodded. "Mama told me that Emma turned her back on her best friend years ago when she had a baby by a married man."

"Is your baby's father married?"

"No."

"Good. We can bring pressure on him to marry you. Who is he?"

"I don't want anything to do with him."

"You've got to have someone to help you."

"The sheriff said he would figure something out. I trust him."

Idalou was beginning to have a good deal of respect for Will's abilities, but this wasn't the same as breaking up a fight or rescuing her from a flood. This meant rescuing a woman from social ruin and providing for her and her child. The only way Idalou could see for him to guarantee that was to marry her. The only good thing about this whole mess was that if the real father had refused to marry Junie Mae, Will couldn't be the man.

"Are you sure you don't want to marry him?" Idalou asked.

Junie Mae's gaze locked with Idalou's. "I would if he asked."

"You've got a cozy little hideout here," Will said to Carl.

"It won't keep me dry, but it'll keep me out of sight."

Carl had built his camp in the midst of a thicket of hackberry, willow, and soapberry made nearly impenetrable by vines that provided a barrier between him and any passing rider. Water was only a few steps away.

"Have you had any trouble?" Will asked.

"No."

"How about the bull?"

"I've about given up on him."

Will ground-hitched his horse and followed Carl into his camp. They talked about odds and ends while Carl boiled water. When they had settled back with cups of coffee, Will brought up an idea that had been knocking around in the back of his head for some time.

"I don't think you ought to give up on that bull," he said. "I've got a feeling he's still here."

"He can't be," Carl said. "Everybody has looked for days."

"But not everybody wants to find it."

Carl stopped blowing on his hot coffee and looked up at Will. "What do you mean?"

"I've been thinking about the situation with your ranch," Will said, "and the two men who want it."

Carl sipped his coffee and burned his tongue.

"Neither man would hesitate to apply a little pressure, but I think what each man is likely to do is different. I don't see McGloughlin intentionally driving his cows onto your property. It's too obvious."

"Then how do you explain so many of them being here and breeding with our bull?"

"They were driven here, but I don't think Jordan's men did it."

"That doesn't make any sense."

"I've had a chance to spend some time with Jordan, even talk to a few of his men. He's sharp, but not dishonest."

Carl had lost interest in his coffee. "What are you saying?"

"I think Jordan has hidden your bull somewhere on his property. He's not using it to build his herd, just keeping it out of sight until you have to sell your ranch. Then he'll let it go."

"You don't call that dishonest?" Carl asked, disgust in his tone and a question in his eyes.

"I do, but Jordan doesn't. Look, you're on good terms with him now. He probably wouldn't object if you were to ride over to his place every day or so. It would give you a chance to spend some time with Mara. I know she's been acting a little silly, but she really loves you."

"I'm not going to beg any woman to marry me," Carl said, but his anger didn't sound as if it went very deep.

"Mara's seventeen and full of romantic ideas. She wants to know that you think she's wonderful, that you can't get her out of your mind, that you think she's beautiful, that—"

"I've told her all that." Carl sounded impatient, frustrated.

"Telling her once about your future plans for the ranch is enough. Telling her a hundred times you think she's beautiful and can't stop thinking about her is just a start."

"Is that what you'd say to Idalou?"

Will had never been particularly good at keeping things to himself, but it was disconcerting to realize that people he'd only known a few days could read him like a book. "I'm not so sure how to talk to your sister, but if I was thinking about marrying her, that's what I'd want her to know."

Was he thinking about marrying her? Was that the reason he'd spent so much time thinking about her problems? He suddenly chuckled. "Idalou would probably want to talk about cows. I'd be the romantic who wanted to know if she'd missed me while I was in town."

He'd said that partly as a joke, but he knew as soon as he heard himself speak that he was right.

Carl appeared to be thinking hard. "I keep telling Idalou I'm old enough to take care of myself, but she wants to know everything I do."

"For a woman, no man is ever old enough to take care of himself. That's her job, and she'll be real put out if you don't let her do it."

"Mara never worried about me."

"I expect she did. You just didn't know it. Now, before we get so far off the track I forget it, I think you ought to take every opportunity you can to nose about Jordan's place. I think he's got your bull in some arroyo or thicket where nobody can see him without knowing where to look. I also think he's got one cowhand who's supposed to make sure nobody finds that bull until Jordan gets his hands on your ranch."

"You really believe that?"

"Somebody's behind all of this. And though I don't think Jordan's responsible for the worst of it, I'm sure he's got a hand in it. If you handle this right, Jordan might help guard your herd. It's as much in his interest as yours to keep rustlers out."

"So who's behind everything else?" Carl asked.

"Sonnenberg."

"How do you explain that? Van and Idalou have been friends for ages. He's helped us I don't know how many times."

"A perfect cover for trying to destroy you and pin the blame on Jordan."

Carl didn't look convinced.

"I decided a while back that Van had to learn his contempt for the law from somebody, and who better than his father?" Will said, "I still might not have figured it out if I hadn't seen Newt and Frank Sonnenberg together when I was riding back from San Angelo yesterday. Newt's Appaloosa is unmistakable, and much too fine a horse for someone like him."

"I always wondered where he got the money to buy it."

"I think Frank Sonnenberg has been paying him to drive Jordan's stock onto your land. With Newt's reputation, all he has to do is show up and cowhands ride the other way."

"Do you think Sonnenberg is behind blowing up the dam?"

"Yes."

"Why? Idalou has sworn she'll sell the place to Sonnenberg before she'll let Jordan get his hands on it."

"Frank doesn't have the money to compete with Jordan, but your ranch would give him more land than Jordan. If he can make Idalou believe Jordan is behind everything, she'll make sure Frank gets the ranch."

"And make sure I don't marry Mara."

"He intends for Van to marry Mara. It wouldn't surprise me if he'd try to discredit Jordan so that he, through Van and Mara, would have control of the whole area."

It took Carl a few minutes to mull over what Will had said. "I can believe it of Frank Sonnenberg," he said finally, "but I don't think Van would do that."

"He'll do anything his father wants."

"How do you know?"

"Let's just say he fell in love but his father made him break it off."

"Are you talking about Junie Mae?"

"I'm not naming names."

"Everybody knows they were sneaking around meeting each other for a while, but he's always been after Mara."

"You said he'd been interested in your sister."

"They're just friends."

Will decided he'd given Carl enough to think about. He needed to get back to town before Idalou started asking too many questions. He was glad she was helping in Ella's store. He had a feeling the trouble wasn't over yet, and he wanted her out of the way. As long as she didn't know where to find Carl, she would be less likely to head off by herself. Will took a swallow of his tepid coffee and threw the rest away. "Think about what I've said. In the meantime, get over to Jordan's place and remind Mara of why she fell in love with you."

Carl grinned. "Idalou has no idea how devious you are." He stood and brushed the dirt off the seat of his pants. "Why do you act dumb?"

"I don't act dumb. I'm just not in an all-fired hurry to prove I'm smart. Not sure I could do it, anyway. I've done a lot of dumb things in my time."

Right now he couldn't decide whether his plan to buy this bull was the dumbest or smartest thing he'd ever done, but he had a feeling that Idalou would be a major factor in the answer.

Idalou stared at the box on Will's desk. Six place settings of flo-blue china nestled in a bed of straw. Her eyes were so filled with tears, the colors swam and blurred before her.

"I saw them when I was in San Angelo," Will said, "and I remembered that you said your mother's set had belonged to your grandmother."

"She brought them with her when they moved from Virginia," Idalou said. "Mama said it was to remind them of what life had been like before the war."

Dozens of necessary things had been lost in the flood, but she hadn't regretted anything as much as the loss of her grandmother's china. She was surprised that Will had even remembered it. That he would understand its importance to her was incredible. That he would actually buy a set for her was unbelievable.

"I don't know what to say."

"Just tell me if you like it," Will said. "I know it can't replace the set your grandmother had, but—"

"It'll never be quite the same, but it will be just as valuable to me."

She hadn't seen nearly as much of Will since she'd moved into town as she had expected. She had felt obliged to help Ella in the store in exchange for staying in her home. Though Ella was a kind host, she was a demanding boss.

Between evenings spent in the homes of the women feeding him supper and his duties as sheriff, Will was out of the office more and more.

"You don't think he's forgotten about me, do you?" Junie Mae had asked one day when she had been unable to find Will.

"I'm sure he hasn't," Idalou had assured her, wondering if Will could have forgotten her, too. Now, looking at the china, she felt like a weasel to have doubted him. "You shouldn't have bought this," Idalou said when she looked up at Will. "I can't possibly pay you for it."

"What was Webb like?"

The question was so completely unexpected, she didn't know how to answer him. "What do you mean?"

"Is the way he acted with you the way you expect other men to act?"

Idalou had never thought of that, but she guessed it was partly true. "You think you're like Webb?"

"I don't know. That's why I asked."

"Everybody said Webb was the best-looking man

in the county. He knew he was going to take over his father's ranch someday, but he was more interested in finding tough horses to ride and having a good time."

"So he was a little like me."

She hadn't thought of Webb and Will together before. "Webb saw everything as it affected him. About the only time you've thought of yourself was when you asked for all those suppers. I still don't understand why you want to know what Webb was like."

"Any other woman would have known the china was a gift. You thought you had to pay for it, so I figured Webb wasn't the kind of man to give a person anything without expecting something in return."

She hadn't realized it, but Webb had never given her anything, not even a keepsake. Whatever he'd felt for her, it hadn't inspired him to want to give her presents. Nor, as far as she knew, to discover what she liked or what was important to her. It was becoming increasingly clear that she and Webb had been connected only by friendship and familiarity. And the scarcity of suitable companions.

"I'm not very good at accepting things from people. I find it hard to believe you would do something like this for no reason at all."

"I never said it was for no reason."

Idalou felt heat rising in her neck and flooding her cheeks, but she looked straight at Will. "What was your reason?"

"Well, I had a couple," Will said, not suffering from any apparent discomfort at her question. "I figured you had to be feeling a bit low. As necessary as clothes and pots and pans are, they are easy to replace. These dishes were something special. Isabelle would have fussed at Jake for doing something silly, but she'd have cried and kissed him anyway. I figured you couldn't be all that different."

"Did you expect me to cry and kiss you?"

Will's gaze didn't flicker. "I was willing to take that chance."

Just when she decided she knew this man, he did something to confuse her all over again. All the men she knew were pretty direct in letting a woman know they were interested in her. Instead of saying anything directly, Will had done things for her that could be attributed to his job rather than his being interested in her.

"What was your other reason?" she asked.

"I was hoping it would convince you that I like you."

Idalou swallowed. "Anyone seeing these dishes would think you like me an awful lot."

"Maybe I do, but I've never had a chance to find out. What with one thing and another, we always seem to be looking at each other from opposite sides of the horse."

"It's not like we haven't seen each other a lot."

"Not the way I want to."

Idalou's relationship with Webb hadn't prepared her for someone like Will. He didn't do what she expected. How was she to know what he really meant?

Or was she just dense? The man had paid off her loan, practically saved her life, found her a place to stay, and had now replaced a cherished set of dishes. She'd always said actions spoke louder than words. If she really believed that, then Will was practically shouting that he was serious when he said he liked her. She admitted that she'd been wrong about him in the beginning, so why was she finding it so difficult to believe he liked her? Or accept that she liked him?

Was it her niggling doubts about Junie Mae's baby,

or her fear that Will might turn his back on her when it came time for him to leave Dunmore, or just plain jealousy of Junie Mae, that undermined her confidence? He was rich, handsome, and everybody adored him. She was dirt poor, only passably attractive, and nearly everybody considered her a pain in the neck. He was respected and she was ignored. He couldn't possibly be serious about someone like her. Still, she hoped he was.

"What do you want?" she asked.

"I'd like to walk with you on an evening and not talk about the ranch or that bull. I'd like to have dinner some night when neither one of us has to worry about being anywhere else."

"All your evenings are already taken up."

"I'll free up any evening you want."

She couldn't ask for a more direct statement than that. "Your hostess of the evening would be really upset."

His grin was sly. "I could say I won't go without you."

Idalou knew she wasn't the most popular woman in Dunmore, and horning in on one of Will's suppers wouldn't help. "If people think you're paying attention to me, they'll have us engaged and practically married in no time."

Will's smile was so warm, so inviting, so genuine, Idalou didn't understand why she hadn't agreed to anything he wanted.

"I've survived this long without being married against my will. I think I can make it a while longer."

"I don't know what to do with this china," she said, aware that her tongue was running away. "I'm not used to being the object of a man's attentions, certainly not a man like you."

"Damn it!"

The explosion was so sudden, so forceful, she jumped. "I didn't mean to—"

"It's not your fault," he said, instantly regaining his composure. "I keep hoping that some day I'll find a woman who can look at me and see a normal man who's no different from anyone else. *Just once* I want a woman to look at me and not think about my face."

"It's not going to be easy."

Wealth and influence she could understand, but she'd never been utterly beautiful, and she had no idea how it affected a person. She wondered if Junie Mae felt the same way as Will, if her beauty had played a significant part in her present difficulty.

"Could you try?" Will asked. "Even if you only like me a little, can you try to see me as a man and not just a face?"

Her life had been so chaotic over the past several years, Idalou hadn't had the chance or the inclination to look at the world from anyone's perspective but her own, so it wasn't easy when she tried to see things the way Will saw them. She wasn't rich, didn't have the security of a large and loving family behind her, or have people falling over themselves to please her. She didn't know what it was like to be a man and have people automatically respect you just because you wore pants and your voice was a resonant baritone.

"You don't understand, do you?" he said. "You think I'm like a spoiled child who cries because he has so many toys he doesn't know which to play with first."

"I don't think you're spoiled. It's just that I've never thought of what it must be like to have people not bother to find out what you're really like."

But that wasn't true. People didn't know what she was like or care to find out, because she was a woman. Sometimes that made her so angry she felt like fighting. "Maybe I do," she said, a feeling of kinship beginning to grow inside her. "In fact, I think I know exactly how you feel."

"You do?"

It seemed incredible that she could give a man like Will something he hadn't been able to find anywhere else. "The situation isn't the same, but it's similar. For you, it's your looks. For me, it's being a woman."

The smile that transformed his face made his incredibly blue eyes glow from within. She ought to tell him that looking as he did right now would destroy all her efforts to ignore his appearance, but she was so glad she could make him smile that she didn't say a word.

"Let's make a promise to each other," Will said. "You'll never let my face influence anything between us, and I won't let your being female influence me." He appeared to have been stopped by some inner thought that caused him to burst out laughing. "Hell, I can't do that. If you weren't female, I wouldn't give a damn what you thought about me."

"I think we understand—"

The door to his office burst open and Carl rushed in. "Rustlers!" he said, barely able to get the words out. "They drove off half our cows."

Chapter Fourteen

"Do you have any idea who did it?" Idalou asked her brother.

"Yeah. Newt Mandrin. I recognized his horse's shoe prints."

"Are you sure?" Will asked.

"It was definitely Newt's horse. If you ask me, he left the prints intentionally. He probably thinks everybody will be too scared to go after him."

Will thought Carl was probably right. "Let's go over to the Swinging Door. I need to gather a posse."

Will's mind started spinning, and he didn't like the thoughts it was throwing out. Newt was a bully and a gunman, but Will figured he was too lazy to put together a scheme to steal cows, and not smart enough to sell them without being caught. Most important, Will didn't like the fact that Newt had made certain Carl knew who'd stolen the cows. Rustlers survived by being anonymous.

Will could come to only one conclusion. Someone else was behind this and was using Newt as a pawn.

Probably the same person who was behind the dynamiting of the dam. Will hoped it wasn't Jordan. He didn't approve of the man's ethics, but he didn't think the rancher would go this far just to get some land.

"I'm going with you," Idalou announced as they approached the Swinging Door.

"You can't," Carl said. "You lost all of your riding skirts."

"I'll split a dress down the front and back before I'll sit around waiting for you to get back, wondering what might have happened to you."

"I can take care of myself, Lou," Carl said. "You've got to stop looking over my shoulder."

"I'm not looking over your shoulder."

"You're always doing it. The only reason you haven't been plaguing me every day is because I made Will swear he wouldn't tell you where I set up camp."

Will braced for what he knew was coming next. Idalou turned on him. "You told me he didn't have a camp, that you had to run him down each day."

"Now isn't the time to hash this out," Will said. "Once we find the cows, you can have your say."

Will expected Idalou to give him a tongue lashing right then, but they'd reached the Swinging Door and Carl marched in without hesitating. Though it was just past noon, the place was bustling.

"Newt Mandrin and a bunch of rustlers hit my herd last night," Carl announced in a voice strong enough to cut through the noise of conversation, laughter, and a sad tune from the piano player. "The sheriff and I are putting together a posse to go after them."

The room fell silent. Then Jordan McGloughlin stepped forward. "Are you sure it was Newt?"

"He left his calling card," Carl said. "There's not a

man here who doesn't recognize the peculiar shoe his horse wears."

"That doesn't make any sense. Newt's never taken to rustling," Jordan said.

"It doesn't make sense that someone would blow up our dam when we've never cut off the water," Idalou pointed out, "but it happened."

Before the old tension between Idalou and Jordan could escalate, Will said, "None of this matters right now. Double-L cows have been rustled. Who will ride with me?" An ominous quiet greeted his question. "It's in everybody's interest to stop rustling before it gets a foothold," he said, turning to Jordan. "You and Sonnenberg have the most to lose."

"He's afraid of Newt." Idalou cast a scornful glance around the room. "All of them are."

"I'll ride with you," Van Sonnenberg said, stepping forward. "Dad wouldn't want me to ignore our responsibility to our neighbors."

He smiled so warmly at Idalou, Will wanted to plant a fist in the man's lying mouth and knock that smile off his deceitful face. Instead, he controlled his anger and turned to McGloughlin. "It's up to you, Jordan."

It was obvious Jordan was angry at being put in a position where it was impossible to refuse. Will was beginning to think Mara had come by her willfulness and streak of stupidity fair and square.

"Come on, Jordan," Lloyd Severns said. "If you wanted that ranch so badly, you could have paid off the loan."

Will was relieved that someone else had put the matter squarely on the table.

"That's not what's holding me back," Jordan said. "I was just trying to figure out how many men I could spare and still protect my own herd."

It was a valiant effort at recovery, but Will was certain every man in the room saw through it for the simple reason they were all afraid of being caught in a showdown with Newt Mandrin. Gradually more men volunteered. Will thought it was ironic that Van had led the way.

"Let's meet in an hour at Carl and Idalou's place," Will said. "That's central for everybody. Carl can lead the way from there."

"I'm going with you," Idalou said to her brother, "and not because I want to look over your shoulder. They're my cows as much as they are yours. If I hadn't been staying safely in town, this might not have happened."

"Nobody could expect you to stay out there in the brush," Will said.

"I wouldn't have let you," Carl added.

"It's pointless to get into an argument over what's done and can't be changed," Idalou said. "I have to tell Ella I can't go back to work in the shop this afternoon. I'll meet both of you at the livery stable. Have a horse saddled and ready for me."

"You have one determined sister," Will said to Carl as Idalou turned and marched out of the saloon.

"Don't you want to take her off my hands?" Carl's question seemed to be a mix of frustration and curiosity.

Will laughed to cover his discomfort at Carl's blunt question. "I'm not sure I'm man enough. Besides, I don't think she likes me all that much."

"She likes you a lot," Carl said, grinning and matching strides with Will. "She wouldn't get so mad at you if she didn't."

Will returned his grin. "I'm not sure I consider that a good sign."

Carl's grin disappeared. "She hasn't had much to

be happy about since our parents died. I was hoping you could do something to change that."

"You believe in getting right to the point, don't you?"

"It saves time."

"You're just like Jake. No wonder she's like Isabelle."

"Don't you love your parents?"

"I adore them, but I don't want to marry them. Would you have wanted to marry yours?"

"God, no." They turned the corner and headed down the alley toward the livery stable. "Dad was always dreaming of a way to be a bigger success, and Mom was afraid of any animal bigger than a small dog."

"Then where did your sister get her courage and her no-nonsense attitude?"

"From having to try to fix the mess our parents made and take care of me at the same time."

"Looks like she did a pretty good job."

"But it cost her Webb. I used to be unhappy about that. Now I realize you're just what she needs. You're calm, you like to think things through before you act, and you get things done. Lou respects that."

The ground was feeling a little shaky under Will's feet. "When did you turn into a matchmaker?"

"When you first asked Lou to walk with you. She was going to accept until she saw you kissing Junie Mae."

"*Junie Mae kissing me!*" Will corrected emphatically.

"Why was she kissing you? You're not two-timing my sister, are you?"

Will heaved a sigh. "First, let me point out that despite my attempts to have it otherwise, your sister has done little more than talk to me. I could be seeing half the women in Texas and you still couldn't accuse me of two-timing Idalou. Second, I'm not *seeing* Junie Mae. I accidentally became aware of a situation that has caused her great distress and I'm trying to help her. I've already explained that to your sister." They'd reached the livery stable. "Now help me pick out a suitable horse for Idalou."

"She'll have more faith in your decision than mine," Carl said.

"That would be a first."

"I'm sure they'd head for the Clear Fork canyon," Van said. "There's plenty of grass and water for a small herd."

"I'd think they'd want to sell them in San Angelo as soon as possible," Idalou said.

"Only a really stupid rustler would take your cows to San Angelo," Van argued. "Everybody knows your brand."

Will saw the logic in Van's thinking, but he was more intrigued by the fact that Van was eager to lead the search. They'd lost the trail twice, and twice Van had found it. Will was ready to bow before Van's superior knowledge of the land, but some of the other men probably knew the surroundings just as well. In light of that, Van's success seemed noteworthy.

"I think we ought to follow Van's suggestion," Will said.

"I disagree," Idalou said.

"If Van's wrong, we won't have lost much time," Will said to Idalou, hoping she could tell from the deliberate way he spoke that he had something in mind.

While several of the men in the posse argued with Van, Will took the opportunity to speak softly to Idalou. "Trust me. I'll explain later. Tell Carl, too."

While Idalou pulled Carl aside and whispered her message to him, Jordan was insisting that Van was leading them in the wrong direction.

"Van has twice found the tracks after we lost them,"

Will said when Jordan seemed ready to throw down the gauntlet. "I'm inclined to go along with him."

"We'll just be wasting time."

"We'd have wasted a lot more if Van hadn't found the trail," Will reminded him.

Jordan agreed to go along, but he continued to object. Van pulled alongside Idalou and busied himself explaining his idea all over again. Idalou listened attentively, but from time to time she cast a questioning glance over at Will. He smiled encouragingly while listening to Carl muttering.

"If the rustlers get away with this, Idalou and I will have to leave Dunmore. Then there wouldn't be anything to stop Van from marrying Mara."

Will had already considered that. It was part of the reason he found Van's actions so intriguing. Aside from his apparent friendship with Idalou, Van was a cruel, selfish man motivated entirely by self-interest. Since everyone knew he intended to marry Mara, Will found his friendship with Idalou suspect.

They hadn't ridden more than a mile when a shout up ahead told Will that Van had found more tracks. The fifty cows the rustlers had taken weren't broken to trail so they ambled in a confused jumble rather than an orderly line. That had made it hard to distinguish their trail from the footprints of cows already headed toward the water of Clear Fork. Will and Carl urged their horses forward until they were alongside Van and Idalou.

"See," Van said to Jordan, pointing to what was a clear trail. "They did come this way."

"It looks that way," Jordan admitted, "but it still doesn't make sense."

"Could be they were planning to take the herd out of the area altogether," Will said.

Less than an hour later, they were peering through a stand of cottonwood along the rim of a canyon. It wasn't a deep canyon or a wide river, but over time the Clear Fork had cut back and forth across the canyon until it was virtually flat. At this point the river was running close to the far rim, leaving a wide area of grass where the stolen cows grazed peacefully under the watchful eyes of two men with rifles stationed at opposite ends of the canyon.

"Do you think there are only two men?" Idalou asked.

Jordan studied the two sentries carefully with a pair of field glasses he'd kept since his days in the army. "Neither man is Newt," he said.

"Can I borrow your glasses for a minute?" Jordan handed the glasses to Will. Careful scrutiny of the campsite hidden in a tangle of willows and cottonwoods didn't show evidence of more than two men. Still, he had an uneasy feeling that at least one man had to have been posted on the rim of the canyon to watch for a posse.

"It seems there are only two men down there," Will said as he handed the glasses back to Jordan.

"Why didn't they post someone up here who would have seen us coming?" Idalou asked.

"Maybe the third rider has gone off for some reason."

"You mean Newt, don't you?" one of the men asked.

"You think he's hiding somewhere, waiting for us to get down in the canyon so he can pick us off?" another asked.

"He's a dead shot with a rifle," the first man said.

"So am I," Van said.

"I can handle myself when I need to," Will said.

"Let's put our heads together and come up with a plan."

Van and Idalou objected strenuously to the plan they devised.

"I found the rustlers for you," Van insisted. "I have a right to lead one of the groups down into the canyon."

"They're my cows," Idalou said. "I want to ride next to my brother."

"You and I are going to stay up here, because we're the best with a rifle," Will said to Van. "Once the rustlers realize they've got several men in front of them and riflemen aiming at their backs, they ought to give up without a fight. You need to stay up here," Will said, turning to Idalou, "because I don't want the men more concerned about protecting you than capturing the rustlers."

"Quit arguing, Lou," Carl said when Idalou started to protest. "Jordan has already refused to let you ride with him, and I agree with Will."

"You're treating me like a woman again," Idalou complained.

"I let you come along with us," Will said, "but I'm doing everything I can to keep you safe. Besides, with Van and me concentrating on keeping the two rustlers in our sights, it'll be useful to have someone watching our backs."

"He's got a point, Lou," Carl said.

"Okay. If Van will stay, I will, too," Idalou said, accepting defeat as graciously as she could. "But if eight men can't capture two rustlers without anyone getting shot, you're not the men you think you are."

Having been shaved down to size, the men headed off to find ways to get down into opposite ends of the canyon.

The next half hour passed slowly. Will had given the men what he hoped was plenty of time to find a way into the canyon and get into position. Having that much time meant the shadows of evening had begun to approach. If Newt was going to return to the camp, he could arrive at any minute, a fact Idalou had pointed out.

"That's why I need you to watch our backs," Will said.

At first Van had been furious that he'd been kept up on the rim. But he'd cooled off and spent the rest of the time talking to Idalou. Much of what he said implied that Jordan was behind Idalou's problems. If, as Will believed, Van's father was behind the recent escalation in trouble, then it would be to the Sonnenbergs' advantage to see that the blame fell on Jordan. Van was a handsome young man, as well as physically imposing. With his position as his father's only heir and his obvious charm, he would appear to be a young woman's idea of the perfect husband, but there was a cruel side to Van that Will hoped Idalou didn't overlook.

Will had a personal interest in Idalou, but it seemed that every time he tried to pursue it, something got in the way. He didn't know if Idalou was equally interested in him. But even if she didn't return his interest, he wasn't about to let her fall prey to Van Sonnenberg.

"I think everybody's in place," Idalou said, moving Jordan's glasses so she could look from one end of the canyon to the other.

"Are you ready?" Will asked Van.

"Just say the word."

Simultaneously they fired shots into the ground behind the two rustlers. The men jumped up, looking frantically for the gunman. Just about the time they realized the shots had come from the rim of the canyon, they were confronted with a posse riding down on them with guns drawn. Neither man put up a fight.

"That was quick," Idalou said.

"It was damned disappointing." Van shoved his rifle into its scabbard in disgust. "What kind of men are they?"

"Men who don't want to get killed," Will said.

"Hell, out here we hang rustlers. What difference does it make?"

"Well, nobody's hanging those men without a trial," Will said. "Anything else but a trial would be vigilante justice."

"What's wrong with that?"

"It's against the law."

"We're the law," Van insisted.

"Not as long as I'm sheriff. Let's ride down and hear what they have to say."

The rustlers were tied up by the time Will reached them.

"We didn't steal these cows," a big man with coal-black hair and a heavy beard was saying to Jordan. "We was hired to bring them here and hold them until the owner was ready to move them north."

"Who hired you?" Will asked.

"The man said his name was Saul Tombull."

"There's nobody by that name anywhere around here," Jordan said.

"What did he look like?" Will asked.

"He was a big man, over six feet, with yellow-brown hair. He was well muscled, but his clothes didn't fit real good. He cussed a lot, too."

A perfect description of Newt Mandrin.

211

"It's no use trying to throw the blame on some-body else," Van said. "We're going to hang you for the lying thieves you are."

"I'm taking you back to Dunmore," Will said to the pair. "We'll let a judge decide whether you're telling the truth."

"Why would we risk our necks for so few cows?" the man asked. "And if we was rustlers, why would we hole up here where it was easy to catch us?"

Questions Will had already asked himself. He was sure he had the right answers, but he had no way to prove his theory.

"I agree with Van," Jordan said. "You let them get away with rustling, and we'll have every two-bit thief in Texas down on us."

"They didn't get away with it, did they?" Will asked.

Van reached for the rope hanging from his saddle. "Who's with me?" he asked.

"Right beside you," Jordan replied.

Will walked to his own horse, but rather than reach for his rope, he pulled his rifle out of its holster. "I'll shoot the first man who puts a rope on either of these two," Will said.

"Not if we shoot you first," Van said.

"That ought to look real good when the judge comes around," Will said to Van. "A vigilante group kills the sheriff so they can hang two men who were denied a trial."

"We don't need a trial," Jordan said. "We found them with the cows."

"I know Van is a fool and a hothead," Will said to Jordan, "but I'd thought better of you."

"You calling me a fool?" Van shouted.

"Apparently he's hard of hearing, too," Will re-marked.

Van reached for his gun, but the hammer on Will's gun clicked ominously. They all looked stunned to see he'd drawn it with his left hand while still holding the rifle in his right.

"This is stupid," Idalou said, stepping forward. "If either one of you shoots the sheriff, you'll end up being hanged for murder." She pushed Van's hand away from his gun.

"Will is right," Carl said as he came to stand next to Will. "Besides, these are our cows. If Idalou and I are willing to let the men stand trial, the rest of you don't have anything to say about it."

Van had a lot to say, but Will kept his eye on Jordan. He could see the man's determination waver.

"Have it your way," Jordan said finally. "But if this brings a plague of rustlers down on us, it'll be your fault."

"You can't allow him to let rustlers go!" Van shouted.

"He's not letting them go," Idalou said. "He's taking them to jail to stand trial."

"You're just like every woman in Dunmore," Van raged. "You take one look at him and you'll do anything he wants."

"I'm not a woman," Carl said, "and I agree with the sheriff."

"I *am* a woman," Idalou said, squaring up to Van. "Yes, he's mighty fine-looking, but I can still think. Now put that rope up and let's go home."

"I'm staying with the cows," Carl said. "I'll bring them back in the morning."

"What if the other man comes back?"

"Are you really stupid enough to believe there is another man?" Van asked.

From the look in Idalou's eye, years of friendship were rapidly losing significance. "I'm stupid enough to believe that thieves probably tell the truth at least as often as upstanding citizens lie."

Will chuckled inwardly at the look on Jordan's face.

"You've known me for ten years," Van said. "I've helped you whenever I could. Are you saying you believe I'm lying to you?"

"This isn't a question of lying, Van. It's a question of obeying the law." She turned to Will. "I'm staying with Carl."

"You can't," Carl said immediately. "It's not safe."

"It's not safe for you to be here by yourself. Will can't stay, because he has to take the men to town. The other men have families and duties to attend to. There's nobody else to stay."

"I'll stay," Van said. "Dad doesn't need me."

That was the most logical solution, but Will could tell that Carl wasn't going to agree. "Jordan," Will said, "could I trust you to take these men to town and turn them over to Emmett or Tatum?"

"Why can't you do it?"

"It looks like I'm staying with Carl, Van, and Idalou."

Chapter Fifteen

Idalou enjoyed watching Van and Carl square off against each other. Van had the advantage of age and an innate belief that he was always right, but they were Carl's cows, and he had plenty of backbone.

"Do you still think he can't take care of himself?" Will asked Idalou after they'd watched Carl argue Van down until Van agreed to handle the herd the way Carl wanted.

"You can't blame a sister for worrying about her little brother," she said to Will. "And if you do, it's too bad, because I'm not going to apologize."

Will laughed quietly. "My sisters still worry about me, and I'm ten years older than Eden."

Will and Idalou were sitting next to the coals of the fire that had been used to cook their supper. Idalou had been shocked when Will had volunteered to make the stew.

"It's the only thing I can make," he said, "but I'm good at it."

He'd been right. Van and Carl had eaten two

helpings. They'd gone off to check on the herd and to decide on the watch schedule for the night.

Will took a long swallow of coffee and threw the rest away. "I need to walk off my supper. You care to keep me company?"

Idalou had been waiting for a chance to take Will up on his offer for a walk, but she hadn't expected it to happen in the middle of a river canyon. Or with cows for her chaperons. "I need to work out a few kinks," she said. "I've gotten a cramp sitting on the damp ground."

"Let me help you up."

Spry as a teenager, Will bounced up, took the hand she held out, and brought her to her feet. He'd held her hands many times before, but this time it was different. He wasn't pulling her out of the water, and he wasn't helping on or off her horse. He was inviting her to spend some time alone with him, and that made it *really* different.

Idalou hadn't been this excited to be with a man since Webb, but the feeling wasn't the same. She and Webb had known each other for years and had grown into a romantic relationship without really thinking about it very much. Everybody had assumed they'd get married. So had they until she started to blame his father for the trouble at the ranch and Junie Mae came to live with her aunt.

But Idalou wasn't drifting into anything this time. From the beginning, she'd fought her attraction to Will despite Carl's hard-to-believe assertions that Will was interested in her. It would have been much more logical for him to be interested in Junie Mae.

Her stomach clenched. Would she ever stop feeling jealous of Junie Mae?

"It's a little chilly down here by the river," Will said. "Do you want something on your shoulders?"

Webb would never have thought to ask her that. "I

am a bit chilly, but the blanket I brought would be too heavy."

"You can wear one of my shirts." Will pulled a tan shirt from his saddlebag. "I never travel without extras." He held it for her to slip her arms into the sleeves. "Warm enough?"

"It's perfect." The internal heat generated by his attentiveness was threatening to make her too warm. His attention felt special to her, and she liked the feeling. Van and Carl came up just as they were getting ready to leave.

"Where are you going?" Van asked.

"We're taking a walk before turning in," Will said.

"I'll come with you."

"You've got to watch the herd," Carl reminded him. "You've got first watch."

"It's not time for me to start yet."

"I'm sure you and Carl have things to talk over before he turns in," Will said.

"We sure do," Carl said, giving Will a big wink.

"Like what?" Van asked.

"I wanted to talk to you about your father investing in rebuilding our dam," Carl said.

"Why should he do that?" Van asked.

"That's what I need to explain to you. You go on," he said to Will and Idalou. "You already know what I'm going to say."

Idalou had no idea what her brother was going to say, because he hadn't mentioned it.

"Your brother is playing matchmaker," Will said as soon as they were out of earshot.

"What?"

"He thinks we ought to get married."

Idalou thought the ground was going to give away under her. She couldn't believe Carl had actually mentioned that possibility to Will.

"Did you tell him he was crazy?" she finally managed to ask.

"I've heard worse ideas."

There had to be something she was missing. They'd hardly had more than a couple of normal conversations and Will was saying being married to her wasn't a bad idea. Did he really mean that it might be a *good* idea? She didn't dare look up at him until she had a better sense of what he was thinking. As for her own mind, well, she wasn't sure she was coherent enough to think at all.

"Ever since he fell in love with Mara, Carl thinks everyone ought to be in love."

"And you don't?"

"I didn't say that." He was confusing her, when she was already having more than enough trouble knowing what to say.

"I think he's just concerned about you," Will said. "Pretty much the same way you're worried about him. He believes Webb really hurt you."

Liking Will—and she did like him—wasn't at all similar to liking Webb. First, she didn't have the same history with Will, no years of friendship that could bridge the gap to something more serious. Everything with Webb had been simple and straightforward. Everything about her experience with Will had been turned upside down when he'd paid off the loan. Anything that developed between them would be affected by their business relationship. Yet in matters of the heart, it was essential to be able to keep the lines between the two areas clear.

"It did hurt," Idalou said, "but not the way he thinks."

"What way was that?"

She wasn't sure she wanted to tell him. It made her too vulnerable, and she'd learned that being vulnerable was dangerous. Yet she wanted him to know. "Webb hurt my pride more than anything else. I wasn't in love with him. Still, no woman likes to be tossed aside for another."

"If you didn't want him, why did you care?"

Only a man would ask a question like that. "You wouldn't understand."

"It sounds a lot like *I don't want him, but no one else can have him.* Does that seem fair to you?"

"It was the way he left me, without warning, without an explanation."

"If you didn't love him, why did you care?"

Will really didn't understand, and there was nothing she could say that would enable him to see it from her viewpoint. Webb's behavior had made her feel unworthy of love, or worse, unlovable. "You don't have to be deeply in love to resent being tossed aside. It hurts even worse when you've been thinking of yourself as part of a couple, and the other woman is younger and prettier than you, has been in town less than a week, and everyone in town knows before you do."

"Junie Mae isn't prettier than you."

Maybe he'd forgotten what she looked like; it was too dark to refresh his memory. "You don't have to try to spare my feelings. I know Junie Mae is beautiful."

"Beauty comes in many forms. The face is only one of them."

"It's the most important. It's what people see every time they look at a person."

"Only in the beginning, and then only if you're not interested in looking beneath the surface. Some of the most beautiful people I know are really ugly because they've never had to develop their character, whereas even a plain woman can be pretty if she's beautiful inside."

Will was the most direct person she'd ever met. And the most unemotional. He would probably say *I love you* in the same tone of voice he'd use to order his supper. How could a woman tell if he meant what he said, or if he was just trying to make her feel better?

"You find that hard to believe, don't you?" Will asked.

"I've seen too much evidence to the contrary."

"Like the way women react when they look at me."

"That's one example."

"You don't react like that."

"No, but—"

"So why can't I be different, too?"

Men couldn't ignore Junie Mae's beauty. They simply weren't built that way. "What about me do you find more appealing than physical beauty?" she asked. This was where men always fell apart. Ask them to describe anything about a woman beyond her face or her figure, and they went blank.

"Your stubbornness."

Will grinned so broadly the shadows of evening were driven into retreat, but not even his smile could light up all the dark places in her heart. She'd never gotten over the sudden loss of both parents, having to grow up so quickly, being forced to face the world head-on with no one to guide her, being responsible for the ranch and for her younger brother. Without her stubbornness, she couldn't have survived. "Nobody likes my stubbornness, not even Carl, so you can stop laughing at me."

"I was laughing at myself." He turned her around until the moonlight was on her face. "I always avoided women as strong-minded as my mother. The joke is that you're the first woman I've ever been seriously interested in."

"I don't think I like being thought of as a joke."

"Or an irony?" Will laughed softly.

"Especially that." She tried to pull away, but he wouldn't release her.

"I don't think a complacent wife would be much fun."

"Who's talking about marriage?"

"I am."

By now she ought to be used to Will tossing off statements that would send her into shock, but this was a real ground shaker. He was rich, handsome, charming, and able to do anything a man ought to be able to do. He couldn't be seriously thinking of marrying an ordinary woman with no ranch, no family, and a difficult disposition.

"We hardly know each other. I can't even tell when you're telling me the truth." She had trouble trusting in others for fear that something would happen to take them from her. She'd had to put up a tough outer shell to hide the hurt.

"I didn't mean it like it sounds." She hated the hurt she saw in his face. "I mean I don't know you well enough to understand you. You say things—like this talk about marriage—that make no sense to me. I can't tell if you're talking about us or in the abstract."

"All you have to do is ask."

"I'm afraid."

"Why?"

"I'm not ready for either answer you'd make. And no matter what answer I gave you, I'd still have to repay you for the loan."

Now she'd landed herself in the middle of it. She didn't want him to say his interest in her was only momentary, something to while away the time until he left. She didn't want him to say it was only a matter of business. She didn't even want him to say he found her fascinating but not a woman he'd consider for a longer relationship. Yet she wasn't any better prepared to have him say he was thinking about spending the rest of his life with her.

She'd been so dazed by the turn of the conversation that she was completely unaware they'd walked well away from the campsite. Shadows from the rim of the canyon cast part of the floor into an inky blackness her gaze couldn't penetrate. At the same time, the moonlight reflecting on the sandy banks and the silver waters of the river made that part of the canyon as bright as day.

They passed cows lying down, passively chewing their cuds, their calves sprawled out beside them on the meager grass. The animals watched the humans as they passed, their heads slowly swiveling, moonlight reflected in their eyes making them glow an eerie red. The very calmness of the scene seemed to mock her inner turmoil.

"Then we won't talk about it anymore," Will said. "How are you and Junie Mae getting along?"

She wanted to talk about their relationship. She just didn't know what to say, because he'd jumped so far ahead of her, offered her so many possibilities. "We're getting along fine. She's depending on me to delay her aunt's realization that she's expecting a baby."

"Did she tell you who the father is?"

"No. She said she wants nothing to do with him. She says you're going to come up with a solution."

"I know."

He didn't sound excited about it. She tried to tell herself she wasn't jealous, that he didn't like Junie Mae the way he liked her, but she couldn't shove aside that tiny niggling doubt.

"Have you figured out what to do?"

"I have an idea. I just have to wait to see if it'll work."

She wanted to ask if he was intimately involved in the solution, but she didn't feel she had that right. She kept reminding herself that Will was the most direct person she'd ever met. If his *solution* would have any effect on their relationship, he would tell her. Only she couldn't decide exactly that their relationship was. This walk was the first time they'd spent time together as a couple. "Why did you ask me to walk with you?" she asked. "Not just tonight. Those other times, too."

Will grinned, and her knees grew weak.

"I thought that was obvious."

"We've seen each other for one reason or another every day since you arrived in Dunmore, but it's been business, not personal. I don't know—"

Without warning, she found herself in Will's arms being kissed in a way that Webb could never have managed in a million years. Her mind, overwhelmed by the implications of the kiss, shut down at once. Her body, much more resilient, responded by telling her arms to encircle his waist and her mouth to yield itself up to his lips. Once that was accomplished, her body molded itself to his, drawing heat and support from his warmth and strength.

It took about ten seconds for Idalou to realize she'd never really been kissed. She didn't know how to describe what Webb's and her lips had done together, but it wasn't vaguely related to what Will was doing with her mouth. He wasn't simply kissing her. He was exploring her, tasting her, tempting her to explore and taste him. Will's mouth and tongue were everywhere at once, leaving Idalou's head in a whirl and her heart beating a wild tattoo in her chest.

She didn't have time to question why their relationship had catapulted so far forward without warning, or to wonder whether she was ready for this unexpected change. About all she was capable of deciding was that she liked what was happening. When he finally released her, she was unable to stand on her own and clung to him.

"Does that make things any clearer?" he asked.

While Idalou battled to pull herself together enough to give him a coherent answer, she could see that Will wasn't his relaxed, calm, in-control self. Though he concealed it better, he was nearly as breathless as she. The kiss had obviously affected him more strongly than he'd expected. It made her feel good to know she was not the only one to receive an unexpected jolt. Will, the man whom every women panted after, panted after her.

"I think so," she said, "but it is a bit of a surprise. I didn't know your feelings were so . . . intense."

"You would have if you'd talked less and let me kiss you more."

That was putting it on the line. "Maybe if you'd kissed me more, I'd have talked less."

She was becoming rather fond of Will's soft chuckle. "I can guarantee that," he said.

Idalou turned and started walking back to camp. "I hope what I'm about to say isn't going to make you angry, but if I let you kiss me—"

"*When* you let me kiss you."

"*If* I let you kiss me, it'll have nothing to do with your having paid off the loan."

"I never thought your kisses could be bought. If I had, I wouldn't have kissed you. Or paid off the loan."

Idalou turned to face him. "Why did you pay it off? I mean, why did you *really* do it. If we don't find the bull, you'll end up part owner of a ranch you don't want."

Will took Idalou's hands. Putting his arms around her waist, he pulled her closer until she had to look up to see his face. "It's complicated." He sighed. "I hated seeing you and Carl so miserable. You were caught between trying to find the bull and coming up with the money to keep the bank from taking your ranch. I was certain you'd ultimately find the bull, so paying off the loan would take the pressure off."

Idalou looked up at Will, wondering if there was more he wasn't saying.

"I also wanted a chance to get to know you better, but that wasn't going to happen as long as you couldn't think about anything except the ranch and that bull. That affected everything I said or did. I wanted you to see me, and I didn't want what you saw to be colored by all this other stuff."

"And all that was important enough for you to pay off the loan?"

"Yes."

A man couldn't be much clearer than that. Now she had to figure out just how she felt about Will. She knew she liked him, she knew she wanted him to like her, but she hadn't gotten much past that. She was grateful to him for paying off the loan and pulling her out of the floodwaters, but she'd have been grateful to any man who'd done that for her. Will was talking about something bigger and more important than liking him or being grateful. He was talking about love, and frankly, that scared her. She couldn't let herself fall in love with him, knowing she could lose him just as she'd lost her parents and Webb. That was why she clung so desperately to Carl, to a ranch she didn't even like. She pulled out of his embrace.

"I was hoping you liked me, but I wasn't prepared

for anything like this," she said. "I don't know what to say."

Will reached for her hand. "Then don't say anything."

"But I ought to know my own mind."

"You've had a lot to worry about. I'm afraid it's not over. You and Carl have to be careful."

"Why?"

"I hoped things would stop when I paid off the loan, but they haven't. So far, neither of you has been hurt, but that might change. Somebody is mighty determined to get your land."

"I knew Jordan wanted my ranch," Idalou said, "but I never thought he'd blow up our dam. I should have realized that someone like Newt would take advantage of the situation to try to rustle our herd."

"I don't think it's that simple. I think Newt is a pawn. There's more than one player in this game. I just don't know how to prove it. Moreover, I don't think your ranch is all that's at stake."

"You're scaring me." Idalou had never considered that she and Carl would be in physical danger. "And making me angry. Aren't you going to tell me what you think is going on?"

"Not until I have more evidence. I don't want to wrongly accuse anyone."

"You think Frank Sonnenberg is involved, don't you?"

"Yes."

"He told me long ago that he'd match anything Jordan offered for the ranch. When I told him I didn't want to sell, he said he just didn't want to see it go to anyone else. He and Van have done everything they could to help us. Why would Frank want to drive us out?"

"Because he could gain control of the water he

needs, and get rid of Carl as a rival to Van at the same time."

Will hadn't spent many nights sleeping under the stars. Though he'd lived on a ranch since he was eight, being the youngest child meant he got the first bed available. Unlike several of his brothers, he'd never developed an appreciation for hunkering down in a bedroll with a bunch of cows for company or rocks gouging him in the back. On his list of things to avoid, waking up with dew on his face was right behind being forced out of bed in the middle of the night to watch a bunch of cows sleep. Lying awake when he should have been sound asleep was up there, too.

He glanced over at Idalou and Carl. Both were sleeping soundly, their rest undisturbed by bad dreams or a brain too full of thoughts. Easing himself out of his bedroll, he pulled on his boots, reached for his vest and hat. He could hear Van's horse approaching as he returned to camp from the first watch. Since he was already awake, he'd take Carl's turn. He was saddling his horse when Van rode up and dismounted.

"What are you doing up?" Van asked.

"I couldn't sleep, so I thought I'd exchange with Carl. How is everything?"

"So quiet I nearly fell asleep in the saddle," Van said as he stripped saddle and saddlecloth from his horse. "I told Carl we didn't need a night watch."

"It's always better to be safe," Will said, thinking of Newt and trying to puzzle out his role in this bizarre drama.

"That's what Carl said." Van tossed his bedroll on the ground and began looking for a patch of grass where he could picket his horse for the rest of the night.

Will swung into the saddle and rode out. His thoughts soon wandered from the cattle or the question of who was behind the latest attempt to drive Idalou and Carl off their ranch, to solving the riddle of his attraction to Idalou . . . and why she didn't appear to be equally attracted to him.

Always before, any woman who'd attracted his interest hadn't hesitated to return it. Yet Idalou had twice turned down his invitations to walk with him. He'd rescued her ranch from foreclosure and her from a flood, and she still looked at him with questions in her eyes. He'd kissed her, even told her he was thinking about marriage, and she'd effectively said she didn't want to hear about it. It wasn't just a blow to his ego. He was honestly confused. What did he have to do to make her believe he was serious about her?

Not until his horse lowered his head and began to drink did Will realize he'd been paying so little attention to what he was doing that his horse had waded into the shallow edge of the Clear Fork. Rustlers could have made off with half the herd and he wouldn't have known a thing. Isabelle had warned him that one day a woman would turn the tables on him. He'd joked that he was waiting for a woman like Isabelle, but he wanted a wife who was much more complacent.

His horse finished drinking, and Will guided him back up the bank to resume his circuit around the sleeping herd.

Was he seriously thinking about marriage? He hadn't thought so until the words came out of his mouth. As much as he admired and liked Idalou, he hadn't paid off the loan so she would marry him. He'd hoped she'd be more friendly toward him, but he hadn't seriously considered marriage. He didn't have a home to take a bride to. Or an acceptable means of supporting her. Under no conditions would he continue to work as a cowhand for Jake after he got married. He'd expected to have many months, maybe even years, to make the transition before the question of marriage arose.

Was he really contemplating marriage? That was hard to say when Idalou wasn't sure she liked him enough even to be stepping out with him. In some ways it might have been easier if he hadn't paid off the loan. But if she'd lost the ranch, she probably would have refused to see him altogether. She had so much pride, she probably would have felt like a charity case. Now she was probably feeling uneasy because she was beholden to Will and had no way to pay him back. Odd that fear of being *considered* a charity case might have forced her to actually *become* one. People were strange, and it looked as if he was just as bad as the rest. Paying off a loan for strangers when he wasn't sure he would get his money back was a bad sign, but being attracted to the very kind of woman he'd wanted to avoid was a clear sign of trouble ahead.

He hoped it wasn't a case of rejection making him even more determined to succeed. That was a stupid reason to pursue a relationship. It would be much easier to give up and just be a cowboy. Cows didn't give a damn about him, and he wasn't much fonder of them.

As ready as he was to get back to eating at a table and sleeping in a bed, Will would have willingly put off returning to town. Idalou had never been so friendly, had never looked at him with such admiration in her eyes. Their ride from the ranch into town had given Will hope that she was getting over whatever it was that kept her from really liking him.

The four of them had driven the cows back to Double-L range. Afterward Carl had gone back to his camp, but Van was riding into town with them.

"I'm heading straight for the Swinging Door," Van informed them when they reached the edge of town. "Are you going to join me?" he asked Will.

"I've got to check on my prisoners first."

Though that was true, Will was grateful for an excuse not to have to drink with Van. He had tried to like Van, especially after Van had behaved so well over the last two days, but he simply didn't care for the man. Nor did he trust him. Even if he hadn't suspected Van had something to do with the attacks on the Double-L ranch, knowing he had gotten Junie Mae pregnant and then refused to take responsibility for the baby convinced Will that Van was not a man of character. Being young and scared could excuse Van's initial reaction, but he'd had time to recover and step up to his responsibilities.

"I'd better go straight to the dress shop," Idalou said. "Ella probably thinks I've gotten lost."

"I doubt it," Van said. "I'm sure she knew I was in the posse to watch out for you."

Will glanced at Idalou to see how she had taken that, but she didn't appear to be aware of Van's enormous ego.

"You want to stop a minute at the jail with me?" Will asked. "I'm going to try to get some more information out of the rustlers."

"Do you think they'll say anything?" Van asked. Will thought he seemed a little uneasy.

"I don't know."

"Maybe I'll come with you."

Will had been looking forward to a few minutes alone with Idalou, but he resigned himself to waiting until a better opportunity arose. The jail wasn't an especially good setting for romance anyway.

When they turned onto Main Street, everything looked as it always did, except for Junie Mae walking up and down in front of his office. Van pulled up his horse so abruptly, it caused Idalou's horse to run into Will's.

"I'm awfully thirsty," Van said. "I think I'll have that beer first after all. If you find out anything, you can tell me when you come to the saloon."

"I wonder what made him change his mind?" Idalou asked after Van rode off.

Will forced a laugh. "I guess he's more interested in beer than in rustlers."

"I wonder why Junie Mae isn't at the shop," Idalou said. "I hope nothing has happened to Ella."

Will's suspicion was confirmed the minute his horse came to a stop in front of his office.

"My aunt found out," Junie Mae said. "She told me to leave her home."

The moment Will dismounted, she threw herself on him and burst into tears.

Chapter Sixteen

Idalou didn't like it when she saw Junie Mae throw herself at Will. She didn't like it any more when he led her inside the office and let her hang on him while she described the terrible scene that had followed on the heels of her aunt's discovery. She tried to be sympathetic, but it was hard.

"She called me a whore," Junie Mae was telling Will through her tears and hiccups. "She said I'd disgraced the family name."

"I'm sure she didn't mean everything she said."

"She did," Junie Mae insisted, crying harder. "She said women who thought that giving themselves up to a man's filthy lust was more important than their reputations ought to be forced out of respectable towns."

Idalou wanted to shake her and tell her to get ahold of herself. Carrying on like the world was about to end wasn't going to fix anything.

"What did your uncle say?" Will asked.

"What could he say," Junie Mae demanded hysterically, "that wouldn't make Aunt Ella think he approved of what I'd done?"

Will had tried to get Junie Mae to sit down, to have a drink of water, but all she did was hang onto Will and cry. He would take her arms from around his neck, dry her tears, and then she would throw herself at him again. Idalou was feeling like she was the most hard-hearted woman in Texas, but she thought if Junie Mae threw herself at Will one more time, she'd tie her to a chair herself.

"He got just as mad as Aunt Ella when I wouldn't tell them who the father was," Junie Mae said. "Then they asked if anybody else knew, and I told them you and Idalou did. She said she'd have all my things packed up and set out behind the house."

Idalou hadn't been planning to stay with Ella much longer, but now she'd probably find her own few belongings tossed out into the street, too.

Junie Mae dissolved into tears again. Before she could throw herself on Will, Idalou took her by the arm and guided her to a chair. Once she sat down, Idalou made her drink the water Will had poured and handed to her. By the time Junie Mae had drunk it all, she was in control of herself.

"What am I going to do?" she asked, turning her tear-streaked face up to Will.

Idalou thought it was particularly unkind of Mother Nature to give the most beautiful women the ability to cry without getting puffy eyes or red splotches. Despite her crying jag, Junie Mae's skin looked like peaches and cream and her clear eyes glistened through the tears.

"I'm going to move you to the hotel," Will said.

"I don't have any money."

"I'll take care of everything."

Idalou's throat closed so tightly she couldn't swallow. Why would Will do that if he wasn't the father of the baby? *For the same reason he paid off your loan*, a voice inside her head shouted back at her. The man couldn't see a woman in distress without trying to help her, but he must know that if he took care of Junie Mae while she continued to refuse to divulge the name of the father, everybody would assume he was the responsible party.

"Idalou will stay with you while I reserve a hotel room for both of you," Will said.

"I don't need a room," Idalou said. "I'm going back to the ranch." She didn't know what made her say that. She hadn't planned it.

"Everything has been washed away," Junie Mae protested. "Where will you stay? Where will you sleep?"

"Van has promised to lend me his father's tent."

"This is all my fault." Junie Mae dissolved into tears once more. "If I weren't having a baby, my aunt wouldn't have thrown me out and you'd still have a place to stay."

Idalou turned to Will, hoping he could do something to ease Junie Mae's guilt, but he was looking at her with a strange expression.

"You think that's my baby, don't you?"

Idalou was so shocked at his question, she couldn't respond right away. Then when she tried, the words got caught in her throat.

Unable to face the hurt in Will's eyes, Idalou turned to Junie Mae. "I don't think he's the father. It's my home, and I always intended to go back as soon as the ground dried." She glanced at Will, but his expression was impossible to read. She turned back to Junie Mae. "I'm not trying to scare you, but if you let Will take care of you while refusing to name the father, people are going to start to believe he's the father."

"But he's not," Junie Mae insisted.

"I've already thought of that," Will said to Idalou, "but if the people of Dunmore don't like it, they can find themselves another sheriff. I never wanted the job anyway."

His look was both understanding and accusing. It all but spoke the words, *How could you believe I'd do something like that?*

Idalou decided that being disgusted with herself was a rotten way to feel. Everything was going wrong. Worse, she was part of the problem. If she hadn't lost the bull, Will wouldn't have remained in Dunmore. If he hadn't remained in Dunmore, he wouldn't have been sheriff, wouldn't have met Junie Mae. And she wouldn't be caught between falling in love with him and trying to convince herself he wasn't the father of Junie Mae's baby.

"I'm just saying what people are going to whisper," Idalou said. "I'll do what I can to stop the rumors, but nobody listens to me after all the things I've said about Jordan."

"You can't leave me," Junie Mae said. "Everybody knows Will likes you. If you stay, nobody will believe he's the father of my baby."

Idalou knew Junie Mae was right. If she left now, she might as well point her finger at Will. "All you need to do is name the father. You don't need me."

"I can't do that," Junie Mae said. "I don't want to be connected with him in any way."

"Is he such a terrible person?"

"Yes. I'm not excusing myself, but he took advantage of my weakness to seduce me, then turned his back on me. When I told him about the baby, he swore it wasn't his, that he'd brand me a whore if I tried to pin it on him. I don't know what I would have done if Will hadn't promised to help me."

Idalou knew what she had to do. It didn't matter that she was wrestling with jealousy. It was even worse that she had doubts her head told her were unfounded while her heart said to be careful or she might get hurt. Will had stood up for her and he'd stood up for Junie Mae. He had no reason to help either one of them, but he'd put himself on the line. She could do no less.

"I'll move to the hotel with you," she told Junie Mae. "But as soon as I'm sure nobody thinks Will is the father of your baby, I'm moving to the ranch. Carl and I need to start thinking about rebuilding. I'm not running away."

"Aren't you?" Will asked.

Not running away as much as trying to figure out her life. Was she in love with Will? If so, could she live the rest of her life with even the remote possibility that he was the father of Junie Mae's child?

Was it possible for her to forget him?

No. Whatever the future might bring, she would never forget Will Haskins. She'd never met a man like him. She was certain she never would again. "So many things are tied together I don't know what I feel."

"I'll go see about the hotel," Will said.

Being left alone with Junie Mae felt awkward. There had been times when Idalou believed her life would have been perfect if Junie Mae had never come to Dunmore. Then she'd remember that she'd probably have married Webb. She knew now she had never loved Webb and he hadn't loved her.

"You hurt him," Junie Mae said to Idalou. "It was cruel of you to do that."

Idalou opened her mouth to refute Junie Mae's accusation, but no words came out.

"I told you he's not the baby's father, but you don't believe me."

"I do. I know Will would never do anything like that."

"Part of you knows it, but not all. Will could see that. It hurt him because he's in love with you."

"We haven't known each other long enough to be in love."

"It doesn't take more than a minute to fall in love with the right man." Junie Mae looked down at her hands in her lap. "I know because that's how fast it happened to me."

Will wiped his mouth with his napkin. "As always, supper was perfect," he said to Mrs. Davis, who visibly swelled with pride.

"It's nothing but ordinary fare," she protested.

"But prepared with outstanding skill."

"Delphine loves to cook."

Andy Davis's pride in his wife was easy to see, but Will wasn't sure which he was more proud of, her cooking or their children. In addition to Louise and Sarah whom Will had already met, Andy had four boys, Jack and Riley, who were old enough to help their father in the mercantile, and Bud and Corky, who had picked at each other during most of the meal when their parents' gazes were directed elsewhere. It reminded Will so much of himself and Pete growing up that he winked at them. That caused the little boys to giggle, which earned a reprimand from their mother.

Delphine rose from the table. "It's time for us to leave the sheriff and your father to their coffee," she announced.

The boys mumbled their excuses, jumped up from

the table, and disappeared, leaving Mrs. Davis and her daughters to clear the table. That would never have happened in Isabelle's house. The boys cleared the table, washed the dishes, and put everything away. If the kitchen wasn't spotless when Isabelle was ready to start the next meal, they heard about it.

"I'd like something other than coffee," Andy said. "How about you?"

"I really should be out making my rounds."

"You've got time for a little brandy. Besides, I want to talk with you."

Will had wondered how long it would be before someone *talked* to him, but he smiled and said, "A small one. I can't arrest a man for being drunk if I go around smelling of brandy."

"Nobody in Dunmore begrudges a man the right to get drunk," Andy said, pouring a deep purple liquid into two glasses. "We just don't want him to make a nuisance of himself. We're thinking about making it illegal to wear guns in town."

"That's a good idea. It'll make the job of your next sheriff much easier." Will accepted his brandy, raising the glass to his nose to test the bouquet.

Andy resumed his seat, sipped his brandy, then turned his gaze to Will. "You know, we're hoping we won't need to find another sheriff. Everybody thinks you've done a bang-up job."

"Things have been easy."

Andy laughed. "A busted dam, a rustled herd, trouble with Newt, and a stolen bull. Doesn't sound easy to me."

"I haven't found the bull."

"I expect it'll turn up eventually." Andy looked down at his brandy. "That's not what I wanted to talk with you about, though." He looked over his shoulder, but they could hear the women in the kitchen.

"You're concerned about my relationship with Junie Mae, aren't you?"

Andy glanced up quickly. "Not the way you think. I'm not about to stick my nose into what's not my business—"

"By bringing it up, you already have."

"I didn't mention Junie Mae."

"But you were going to, weren't you?"

Andy took a deep breath. "We can't have our sheriff taking care of a woman who's in the family way but hasn't got herself a husband."

"If that's all that's bothering you, you can breathe easy. I'll be happy to turn in my badge right now."

"That's not what we want," Andy said. He swallowed the rest of his brandy and got up to refill his glass. "This is damned awkward. Dammit, Jordan and Lloyd ought to be here. It was their big idea that I talk to you."

"Well, get it over with so you can sit back and enjoy your brandy."

"This isn't easy to say. I happen to have a great deal of respect for you."

"Then let me say it for you. People are upset that I'm paying for Junie Mae to stay in the hotel. Since she hasn't named the father, they feel I'm the one at fault or I wouldn't be supporting her. Everybody knows I can talk a woman out of her virtue as quick as you can castrate a bull."

"I wasn't going to say it like that," Andy said, looking deeply embarrassed.

"But that's not all, is it?" Will pushed his brandy away. "They think I'm sweet on Idalou. And as much as they like having me be sheriff, they can't have me taking up with Idalou when I've still got a ruined Junie Mae on my hands. A gentleman would take care of his embarrassment before setting his sights on his next victim."

"You make it sound so dirty," Andy said.

"What you suspect me of *is* dirty." Will leaned forward until his forearms rested on the table. "The real father wants nothing to do with the baby, and Junie Mae wants nothing to do with him. I'm trying to make permanent arrangements for her and the baby, but in the meantime, she has to have somewhere to stay. Since her aunt threw her out and no one in Dunmore has offered to take her in, it has to be the hotel."

Will paused to give himself time to rein in his temper. He had known something like this was going to happen. Andy was just putting into words what everybody else was thinking.

"You're right in thinking that I'm interested in Idalou, but she isn't sure she's interested in me. I should point out, however, that Idalou is staying in the same hotel room with Junie Mae. Do you think she'd do that if I were the father of Junie Mae's baby?"

"That's what I told Delphine," Andy said, the words escaping him as though under pressure. "No woman with Idalou's gumption would put up with that."

"Junie Mae and Idalou warned me this would happen, but I decided to go ahead anyway." He leaned back in his chair and let some of the pressure ease from him. "Twenty years ago, an incredible woman plucked me and my brother off the streets. We were only two of eleven orphans she and her husband took into their home and adopted. After what they did for me, how could I possibly turn my back on Junie Mae when the father of her child walked away and left her crying in the alley behind her aunt's store? No one in my family would do that. My brother has adopted five kids. One sister, three more." He let the last of the tension drain away and stood. "Tell Lloyd and Jordan that I'm leaving at the end of the month, with or without the bull."

"I never believed you fathered Junie Mae's baby," Andy said. "Neither does Lloyd's wife. She says no man who'd risk himself and his horse to save a little dog would ruin a woman just for the fun of it."

"It doesn't matter," Will said, even though it really did. "I was never going to be here long."

Andy got to his feet. "I wish you'd reconsider. After all, you've invested money in a ranch here now."

"That ranch belongs to Carl and Idalou. Catching the person behind their trouble is the only reason I'm still here."

"Do you have any idea who it is?"

"I'm pretty sure I know, but so far I can't prove it."

"Maybe the trouble's over. Maybe nothing else will happen."

"I wish I could believe that. I just hope I can stop it before anybody dies."

"I know why I have to go to Mara's birthday party," Idalou said to Carl, "but I don't see why you do. Don't you have any pride?"

"You've got enough for both of us," Carl said. "At least you had the good sense not to refuse to go with Will."

"I promised Junie Mae I'd stay with her as long as the rumors were flying about her and Will, but they seem to have calmed down, so I plan on moving out to the ranch in a few days."

"You've got nowhere to stay."

"Van said I can use his tent."

"I don't like him paying attention to you. You're not putting Will off, hoping Van will marry you, are you?"

"I'm not hoping either one of them will marry me."

"Will would if you'd stop thinking there's something between him and Junie Mae. No need to color up," Carl said when she felt the heat in her face. "I know you too well. You're so damned scared of being vulnerable, you'll use any excuse not to let yourself fall in love with him."

Carl had met Idalou in town so they could take a ride together. He reported that he had found the horse, the cow, and the pigs but had let them continue to run wild because he had no way to feed them. The corral still stood, but it would be at least a month before the grass recovered enough for grazing.

"I'm not scared of falling in love." Idalou's agitation was communicating itself to her horse. She patted him on the neck, hoping it would calm both of them. "You don't understand."

"You're the one who doesn't understand."

Carl's horse was becoming agitated as well. In unspoken agreement, they rode off the trail to the little patch of shade offered by a lone live oak. They dismounted and let their horses graze. Idalou walked about with short, quick strides, while Carl sank down to the ground and leaned against the tree trunk.

"A few weeks ago I asked you what you wanted," Carl told his sister. "Basically, you said you wanted a family. You didn't say you wanted this ranch."

"What I want doesn't matter. All we have is this ranch, and we owe Will a bull or a lot of money."

"You can walk away right now."

"I can't leave you with all this debt."

"Why not? I'll get the ranch. It's only right that I get the debt."

Idalou couldn't explain to Carl how or why she felt at such a disadvantage when it came to Will. Everything that had happened since he'd arrived in Dunmore had served to put her deeper and deeper in his debt. Marrying Will would cancel the monetary debt, but it would leave the question hanging in the air as to whether she'd married him *only* because she loved him. And the issue with Junie Mae just complicated things.

"I don't want the ranch," Idalou told her brother, "but the debt is as much my responsibility as yours. If we can't find that bull, then we'll have to sell the ranch to pay Will back."

"He won't care about the money."

"You may not understand it, but I simply can't marry a man I'm in debt to."

Carl got to his feet. "Come on. I have to find that damned bull."

"Why don't you do that instead of going to the dance?"

"Because I'm in love with Mara and want to marry her. She hasn't figured it out yet, but she's still in love with me."

"How do you know?"

"Will told me."

"And you believe everything he says?"

"Why not? He hasn't been wrong about anything yet."

In her mind she knew Will wasn't the father of Junie Mae's baby, but the emotional part of her wasn't completely convinced he didn't feel something for Junie Mae. She was beautiful and in love with him. Junie Mae would never argue with him or even question him. She'd work her fingers to the bone for him and think it a privilege. Why should Will be in love with a woman who'd caused him trouble from the moment he'd arrived, who'd questioned his character and his veracity, who seemed incapable of appreciating his help?

"It's not as easy as that," Idalou told her brother.

Carl had caught up their horses and brought them to the shade. "It *is* as easy as that. All you have to do is follow your heart. That's what I'm doing, and that's why I know I still love Mara and she still loves me." He helped his sister mount up. "You think too much. You have to look at everything from every possible angle." He swung into the saddle. "You think so much you don't know what you think." He nudged his horse's flanks and started toward the trail back to town. "At least stop thinking enough to enjoy the party."

Idalou made one last adjustment, then turned to Junie Mae. "Are you sure I don't look silly in this dress?"

"You look beautiful," Junie Mae said. "I can't wait to see Will's expression when he gets a look at you."

Idalou had almost refused Will's invitation because she didn't have anything to wear. She'd finally given in to Junie Mae's insistence that she borrow her best party dress.

"There's no point in it staying in the closet and you staying in the hotel," Junie Mae had said. "As fat as I'm getting, I couldn't wear it even if I was going to the party."

Junie Mae had been invited—nearly everyone in Dunmore had—but she said she had no intention of going just so people could gawk at her and gossip behind her back. Idalou had offered to stay with her, but Junie Mae had told her if she didn't accept Will's invitation, there were plenty of other women who'd be glad to take her place. So Idalou had spent the last two days altering the dress to fit her. She'd let Junie Mae fix her hair. Instead of being in a knot at the base of her neck or pulled back into a ponytail, she had allowed Junie Mae to curl it and style it so it framed her face. She'd hardly recognized herself when she looked in Junie Mae's small mirror.

"People are going to stare," Idalou said. "I've never dressed up like this before. I look strange even to myself."

"Nobody's going to think you look strange," Junie Mae assured her. "They're going to be too busy being jealous or wishing they were the man at your side."

It gave Idalou a thrill to know she looked nice. For once, she would be wearing a dress that was just as pretty as anything Mara or her mother would wear. She was even wearing some of the expensive perfume Junie Mae's aunt had given her. It felt strange to be enveloped in a cloud of scent that smelled like a spring garden.

"Maybe I should pull my hair back." Idalou stared at her reflection in the mirror, worried she might look too much unlike herself. Will had invited *her* to the dance, not the woman staring back at her from the mirror.

Junie Mae took the mirror from her and laid it face down on the dressing table. "It's perfect like it is. Trust me," she said when Idalou continued to feel unsure. "I know what men like in a woman."

All of Idalou's attention had been so consumed by the ranch, she hadn't had time to worry about making herself attractive to men. After Webb died, she'd sort of assumed she'd never marry. Will's interest in her had changed that assumption.

"Will is different," Idalou said.

Idalou smiled. "He's still a man." A very polite knock sounded at the door. "Unless I'm mistaken, your Prince Charming has arrived."

All the tension and uncertainty gathered in a ball in the pit of Idalou's stomach. What if Will didn't think she looked pretty? What if he didn't like her dress or her hair? Even though she knew she'd never looked this pretty in her life, she worried she wouldn't be pretty enough for a man as handsome as Will. She took a deep breath and opened the door.

She'd thought it was impossible for Will to look any more handsome, but he simply took her breath away. A navy-blue suit, white shirt with high pointed collar, and a tie transformed him into any woman's version of a prince.

"Who are you, and where is Idalou?" Will asked.

Before Idalou's stupefied brain could process what he'd said, Will gave a low whistle and broke into a broad smile. "Who'd have thought that a nice-looking boy like Carl could have a sister beautiful enough to make him look downright plain? You sure you want to be seen with somebody like me?"

Will wasn't the kind of man to give flowery compliments, but he did have his own way of expressing his surprise and pleasure.

"Well, you have cleaned up a bit since I saw you last, so I guess I won't be too embarrassed to be seen with you," Idalou said.

"Quit it, you two," Junie Mae said. "You'll be the most handsome couple at the party."

"Do you really think I look nice?" Idalou asked Will. "You don't think the way Junie Mae did my hair makes me look peculiar?"

"I think you look beautiful regardless of how you do your hair," Will said. "You make that dress look right smart, too."

It wasn't the way most men gave compliments, but Idalou thought she could grow used to it.

"Let's hurry. I can't wait to show everybody that the prettiest lady in Dunmore is my date for the evening."

Idalou decided she just might take Junie Mae's advice more often.

* * *

Jordan and Alma McGloughlin certainly knew how to throw a party. The interior of the ranch house blazed with lights, while the porch and portions of the yard were illuminated by more than two dozen kerosene lamps. Alma must have borrowed nearly every lamp in Dunmore. A small band of banjo, guitar, and fiddle produced a twangy, nasal music Idalou found slightly melancholy despite the upbeat rhythm.

"I've never seen such a display," she said to Will.

"A daughter turns eighteen only once. You should have seen what my family did for our younger sister this spring. We practically set the entire Hill Country ablaze. For the first time in years, everybody in the family was there."

Idalou had spent so many years feeling she carried the weight of the family alone that she couldn't imagine what it would be like to be part of a huge, supportive family. In a way, the idea frightened her. She might get lost, lose her way. At the same time, she would have the emotional, physical, and financial support of a large network of families. Dunmore had been like that when they first moved here. Then ambition for the next generation got in the way, and friendships weakened, loyalties broke down.

"Carl wouldn't let me give him a party when he turned eighteen," she told Will. "He said it was a waste of money."

"I didn't want one, either," Will said, "but I got one then, and again when I turned twenty-one."

"Welcome, Sheriff," Alma McGloughlin said with a smile that made her look ten years younger. "I'm glad you were able to persuade Idalou to come with you. We haven't seen much of her recently."

Idalou could have told Alma why that was so, but she had put rivalry and trouble out of her mind so she could enjoy the party.

"It's hard for just two people to keep a ranch going," she told Alma. "It seems we're always a day behind."

"Now that the dam is broken, you and Carl ought to sell that place and move into town. Ella says you were the best shop assistant she's ever had." Alma laughed self-consciously. "Listen to me giving advice about things that are none of my business. Come in and enjoy yourself. There's plenty of food in the house, and we're going to have dancing when it gets cooler."

Mara hurried over when her mother moved away to welcome other guests. "Thanks for coming," she said, looking at Will before turning to Idalou and asking, "Where's Carl?"

Chapter Seventeen

"He's coming later," Idalou told Mara. "He wouldn't miss the biggest party since Webb's twenty-first birthday."

"I thought he'd be with you." Mara peered anxiously over Idalou's shoulder.

"He thinks he's too old to be seen with his big sister."

Mara eyed Will in a speculative manner. "Is that why you asked the sheriff to come with you?"

"*I* asked her to come with *me*," Will said.

"It's okay for a woman to come to a party alone in Dunmore. The town's small enough that we know everybody."

Mara sounded a little jealous, but she seemed more upset about Carl's absence. Was she hoping to make one man jealous of another? That didn't seem likely, since Van was already here—he was talking to Mara's father—but Mara changed her mind so often these days, no one knew who she'd think she was in love with next.

"Are you a good dancer?" Mara asked Will.

"One of the best. What else do men with rich parents have to do with their time?" He winked at Idalou. "I've got to make sure she's good enough to keep from embarrassing me."

"I'm a very good dancer," Mara said.

"Then I look forward to dancing with you, too." He said it with so little enthusiasm, his words annoyed Mara but thrilled Idalou.

"Mama says I have to choose the man to open the dance with me." She looked up at Will, her big eyes wide and admiring. "There are only three possible choices. Carl's not here, and Van is a terrible dancer, so that leaves you."

Mara's blatant attempt to ensnare Will irritated Idalou.

"Have you thought about your father?" Will asked. "I'm sure he'd be glad to have the honor of the first dance. After all, you are his only daughter. He'll never get this chance again."

From her surprised look, it was clear Mara hadn't thought of choosing her father.

"That would also remove any possible chance of jealousy," Will added.

"What do you mean?"

"Don't be so blind." Idalou was irritated at Mara's attempt to appropriate Will as well as her inability to stop encouraging Carl and Van at the same time. "You know your father wants you to marry Van. *Everybody* knows your mother wants you to be Will's wife. You also know Carl loves you. How could choosing Will not cause jealousy?"

Mara stiffened, her voice brittle. "Van says he's not ready to settle down, and Carl has barely spoken to me in weeks. How is choosing Will going to cause jealousy in two men who don't care?"

"Look," Idalou said, softening her words, "we all

care about you in our different ways. Now, your parents have gone to a lot of trouble to throw a fabulous party. For tonight, forget about marrying anyone and have fun."

"You're the sheriff," Mara said to Will. "People won't be jealous of the sheriff."

Will looked at Idalou. She wished with all her heart he would refuse, but she knew she was being selfish.

"Ask your father," Will said. "If he refuses, then I'll open the dance with you."

"Thanks." Mara flashed a brilliant smile. "I'll ask Daddy even though he dances worse than Van. I'd better go before Mama accuses me of neglecting my other guests."

Will's willingness to help a woman in distress was an admirable trait, but Idalou was having a difficult time living with it. She'd have to learn to accept his chivalry if she was interested in a future with Will. Besides, it really was an endearing quality that could be to her advantage, too. Maybe she was having trouble with it because she wasn't sure of his feelings for her, but whose fault was that? She was the one who kept backing away.

She decided that from this moment on, she'd put all doubt out of her mind. If Will wanted to talk about marriage, she'd listen. She had a strange feeling that she would like what he had to say.

"Sorry about that," Will said. "Just another disadvantage of being sheriff."

Idalou hooked her arm in Will's. "That had nothing to do with being the sheriff and everything to do with being Will Haskins. Women can't resist you."

Will leveled a speculative glance at her. "You have managed it rather easily."

"Actually, I haven't managed it at all. I've just been too confused to know what I wanted to do."

"Do you know now?"

Idalou bit her lip. "I think I've figured most of it out."

"Will I like the answer?"

She gave Will's arm a squeeze. "I hope so."

A slow smile spread over Will's face. "I give you fair warning that I plan to test your resolution."

She returned his smile. "I give you fair warning that I'm ready. Now let's get something to eat."

People continued to arrive, some bringing food, nearly every man bringing his own whiskey bottle. Idalou was relieved to see Will turn down all drink offers. He jokingly said he had to be sober when the fights broke out. Carl arrived about fifteen minutes after Idalou and Will. He'd shaved, gotten a haircut, and put on his best suit. Except for Will, he was the best-looking man there.

Mara didn't waste a moment in hurrying over to welcome Carl. He responded coolly then came over to join Idalou and Will.

"It looks like a really big shindig," he said, glancing around.

"Mara was anxious for you to get here," Will said. "Have you two made up?"

"Not yet," Carl said. "She still gets stars in her eyes when she looks at you, and she hasn't yet had the courage to tell her father she won't marry Van. I'm taking your advice and keeping my distance, but not so far that she thinks I've lost interest in her."

Idalou looked from her brother to Will and back again. "I can't believe you two are plotting against that poor girl."

"We're not plotting," Carl said. "Things can't get back to where they were as long as she has any doubt in her mind that I'm the only man she loves. I can't fight her father's opposition and her doubts at the same time. You ought to understand that."

Idalou hoped she didn't blush.

"Did she ask you to lead her out in the first dance?" Will asked.

"Yes, but I told her she ought to ask her father."

"She asked Will, and he said the same thing."

"It's only logical," Carl said.

"Not for a woman," Idalou responded, "especially one who's confused about whom she loves."

"Then she's a lot safer with her father," Carl said and headed off toward a group of young men.

"That boy is maturing quite nicely," Will said.

It was no secret that Carl had been in love with Mara for years. When he was fifteen, he announced he was going to marry her. He'd been jealous of any time she spent with Van or any other young man. Now he was acting like a man of sophistication . . . like Will.

"I just hope he's not making a mistake. Mara is so volatile. If she thinks he's fallen out of love with her, she might marry Van to get back at him."

"Then he'd be better off without her. However, your brother's love life is not of great interest to me at the moment."

"What is?"

"You."

Will's directness never failed to knock her off her feet. In an attempt to match his boldness, she asked, "So what do you plan to do about it?"

"Dance every dance with you and steal as many kisses as I can before the party's over."

Idalou felt a little breathless. "Are you sure you're up to such an ambitious program?"

"Absolutely. Are you?"

"I am if you are."

But she wasn't sure at all. Her limited experience with Webb made her feel like a fledgling. No matter how conflicts might complicate things for her, Will always seemed to know exactly how he felt. He gave the appearance of being very relaxed, even lazy, but he'd managed to handle every situation that had come his way.

As long as she could remember, she'd had to be in control. Her struggle with Jordan and with the bank had all been for control of her life, control over the ranch, control over the changes in fortune that threatened her and Carl. She had lived with the fear that if she relaxed her vigilance for even a moment, everything would come crashing down.

Will frightened her because with him she never felt in control of anything. Not her ranch, her brother, or even her feelings. Sometimes a sense of relief—a feeling of an enormous weight being lifted off her heart—would come momentarily, but it was so brief she couldn't get a hold on it. Still, she had the sense that it was something she would like, maybe even something wonderful. She didn't understand why that should frighten her, but it did.

Yet it also drew her toward it, because on the other side was the promise of happiness such as she'd never known. She didn't trust that feeling any more than she trusted the others, but she knew that all her feelings were connected with Will. And while much about Will confused her, even more about him attracted her. She'd made the decision to find out what her true feelings for him were. In doing so, she had to risk the possibility of enormous relief, of real happiness.

She didn't know what that would be like, but she wanted to find out. She knew far more than she wanted to know about all the difficulties in life.

The next hour moved along much as Idalou had expected. People ate, laughed, and gathered in constantly changing clusters to talk about virtually everything in their lives. The women took advantage of the tables that had been set up in the house, on the porch, and in the yard. The men preferred to eat outside and standing up.

Will had brought a blanket, which he spread on the ground far enough from the house to offer a little privacy. He made sure Idalou was comfortable before he went into the house to get their food. It didn't go unnoticed that this was the reverse of what happened with other couples. Several men watched uneasily as Will made sure Idalou had everything she wanted before he sat down to join her. Women stared at Will as a matter of course, but tonight an element of longing and jealousy was added to their expressions.

"Alma tells me that the barbecue is really hot," Will said, "so be careful."

"I like it hot," she said.

"You're braver than I am. More than two chili peppers, and I'll end up at the well with my head in the bucket."

"How do you find anything to eat in the Hill Country? That's not far from San Antonio, and everything there is hot."

"My mother was brought up by an English aunt who didn't believe in feeding people food that would cause fire to come out of their ears."

Idalou watched with amusement as Will carefully removed most of the sauce from the barbecued ribs before he took a bite. "How is it?" she asked.

"Hot, but I can stand it."

She laughed when he took a swallow of water before taking a second bite. "You're a liar. Your eyes are already beginning to water."

"I don't want to look like a complete washout. You don't think a lot of me as it is."

The heat she felt had nothing to do with the barbecue

sauce. "I've had a difficult time sorting through my feelings, but I do know I like you very much. I'm sorry I didn't walk with you the first time you asked."

"If you really mean that, I'll eat these ribs with all the sauce on them."

Idalou felt the tension ease and she laughed. "Pass me the ribs and eat the chicken salad. You're supposed to have fun at a party. Not suffer for love."

She didn't know why she'd said that word. He'd never said he loved her. She'd never thought he did, but it popped out anyway. He looked as surprised as she did.

"Sorry. I don't know why I said that."

"Why? Do you think it's impossible for me to love you?"

"I hope it's not impossible for any man to love me."

"I didn't say anything about other men. I asked if you thought it was impossible for *me* to love you."

"Not impossible," she managed to say, "but not very likely."

"Why?"

"You haven't said you love me."

"Forget what I have or haven't said. You rarely listen to me anyway. Why is it unlikely that I would love you?"

"I'm hard to get along with. I have a temper, and I'm incredibly stubborn. If I don't like something, I say so and set about trying to change it. I don't like being indebted to anyone. I get really angry when I don't get what I want, I have little tolerance of people's opinions when they disagree with mine, and I don't in the least mind people being angry with me."

"All of those are admirable qualities in the right circumstances."

"I've tried to keep my brother from growing up, I

didn't trust you for the longest time, and I'm terribly jealous of the attention you give Junie Mae." There. If that didn't run him off, nothing would.

Will grinned as if he'd won a prize. "That's part of the reason I like you so much. You've tried to protect your brother because you love him very much and take seriously your responsibility to bring him up safely. You had every reason to distrust me at first. I was a stranger, I didn't want to get involved in your search for the bull, and I insisted that you stop accusing Jordan of trying to destroy you. And you wouldn't be jealous of Junie Mae if you didn't like me at least a little."

Idalou felt something very odd happening in the region of her stomach. "Any other vices you insist upon turning into virtues?" She wasn't asking for more compliments. It was a kind of backhanded way of saying she appreciated his putting a good face on things, but she wasn't buying it.

"No, but I do have one more observation. You're petrified of falling in love because it means losing control. And losing control means you're vulnerable. You've been fighting vulnerability all your life because you equate it with weakness. That's not always true. It takes a truly strong person to let herself be vulnerable, to risk hurt or pain. But happiness never comes without risk. The greater the happiness, the greater the risk, because the greater the pain of loss."

Idalou had lost her appetite. She'd promised herself that she'd open up, that she'd explore her feelings for Will, but his deft penetration of the walls she'd constructed to give her the strength to fight her battles left her feeling exposed and powerless.

Unable to face Will's gaze just yet, she looked toward the groups of people scattered about the yard. Mara was talking to Carl. She looked upset, and he looked stubborn. Both had opened their hearts, and look what had happened. Mara couldn't make up her mind whom she wanted, and Carl had to watch the woman he loved vacillate between two other men. Was this what awaited Idalou if she let down her barriers and opened her heart to love? Did she have the courage to face what she'd endured when Webb turned his back on her? She had no assurance that Will's interest would last any longer than his stay in Dunmore. Her life had been a long series of tragedies. Why should this be any different?

"That scares you, doesn't it?" Will asked.

Not knowing what to say, she nodded.

"You don't have to feel powerless. The people who love you will be more than happy to fight your battles with you."

No one ever had. Even though she'd never doubted her family's love, she'd always felt alone. She'd been the one to try to reason with her father's extravagant dreams and her mother's willingness to allow him to have his way. When the trouble at the ranch started after their deaths, she'd been driven even further into isolation. Now Will was asking her to set aside the lessons experience had taught her and trust him. She thought she had done so, but his understanding of her had made her realize she was only fooling herself. She was still running from vulnerability.

Van had joined Mara and Carl. Now Idalou was sure they were arguing. A moment later, Carl turned and stalked off. Van grabbed Mara's arm when she started to follow him. Angry, Mara turned on Van and said something before she stalked off in the opposite direction from Carl. Equally angry, Van went after her.

If this was love, why would a sane person want any part of it?

"If you're through eating, why don't we go for a walk?"

Idalou jerked her attention back to Will. Even though she'd seen him every day for weeks, her heart skipped a beat every time she looked at him. It still seemed impossible that a man could be so handsome. When she looked at him now, however, she saw a lot more than just his face.

This was a man who'd faced danger to save a small dog and a silly girl's honor, who'd faced even greater peril to pull her from the floodwaters. This was the same man who'd caused the most powerful men in town to beg him to take the sheriff's job permanently. And most incomprehensibly, he was the man who continued to be interested in her despite actions that would have caused a dozen other men to curse her name.

"You haven't eaten anything, either," she said.

His smile continued to have the power to surprise her. "I'm not hungry."

"Alma would be upset if she knew."

"Maybe one of the dogs will carry our food off when we're not looking."

That was something else about Will. No matter what happened, he always found a positive way of looking at things.

"Maybe we could find Carl," she said.

"I'll wait here."

His response surprised her because she knew he liked Carl.

"I have no right to interfere in your relationship with your brother, but as a man I can tell you that I wouldn't want my sister trailing after me when I'd had a spat with my girlfriend."

His answer irritated her. She wasn't trying to interfere. She was just worried about Carl.

"Also as a man, I find it less than flattering that the woman I'm interested in would rather be with another man, even if that man is her brother."

"That's not it at all. I'm just worried about him."

"How about after he's married? Will you want to interfere every time he and his wife have a disagreement?"

She realized that was exactly what she'd want to do. Which, of course, would be exactly the *wrong* thing to do.

"Sorry. After worrying about him from the time he was old enough to walk, I'm finding it hard to realize he's old enough to fight his own battles."

Will got to his feet and held out his hand to her. "It's about time you started thinking about yourself for a change. A little bit of selfishness is a good thing."

She didn't know if she could do that, but the thought of being able to lay aside all her worries was a great temptation. She'd never realized how tired she was of carrying the burden alone. It had colored every part of her life, destroyed her relationship with Webb, and made everyone in Dunmore wary of having anything to do with her.

When she reached up to take Will's outstretched hand, she felt that she'd reached a crossroads in her life. By taking his hand and letting him lead her away from the party, she was saying that she was relinquishing her attempts to control every part of her life. She was saying Carl was old enough to make his own decisions without her input. She was letting go of the determination to do everything without anybody's help.

But try as she might, she couldn't let go of her fear of being hurt.

"Would you have come to this party if I hadn't invited you?" Will still held her hand as they walked toward the corrals behind the ranch house.

"Probably not." Even though she knew her absence would be considered an affront, she'd intended to stay in the hotel with Junie Mae. The latter was so slim, her condition had already begun to show. Idalou hadn't even told Carl that Will's invitation had changed her mind.

"Don't you ever think of yourself first?"

"All the time."

"When? Ever since I've been here, it's been Carl or the ranch. Now it's Junie Mae. What about you? Don't you want anything for yourself?"

Jordan had planted oaks as well as junipers to form a screen between the house and the other ranch buildings. Will disturbed a meadowlark when he led Idalou through a clump of junipers. They stopped at the corral.

The contrast between her ranch and Jordan's was obvious in the secondary buildings. While she had one corral, Jordan had three. While she and Carl had a total of three horses, Jordan had a dozen in one corral alone. The bunkhouse was larger than their house had been. Looking around her, she wondered why her father had thought he could ever compete with McGloughlin and Sonnenberg.

"Of course I want things for myself," she told Will.

"What?"

When Carl had asked her that question, she'd rattled off an answer without giving it much thought. But she hadn't believed what she'd said. She couldn't conceive of a time when the ranch wouldn't be her responsibility. She didn't know a single man she would consider marrying, so children were out of the question.

Then Will had come along to change all that. Or at least make her see that the possibility of change existed.

"I want someone to love me," she said, "but that's no different from everybody else."

"True, but for some people, other things are more important than love. They'd trade it for money, security, freedom, youth, or beauty. What would you trade it for?"

She knew the answer without having to think. "If it was real love, the kind that would last until the breath left my body, I wouldn't trade it for anything."

"Do you believe that kind of love exists?"

"Yes. I saw it with my parents."

"Do you believe it's possible for you?"

Except for Carl, she wasn't sure anyone had ever loved her that deeply, not even her parents. Webb hadn't, and he was the only one who'd ever said he loved her. Looking back on it now, she believed he was just saying words that neither of them fully understood.

"I believe almost anything is possible," she said, "but that doesn't mean the odds against it aren't very high."

"Do you think you're worthy of that kind of love?"

Why did he keep asking her these probing questions? Webb had never done anything like that. He'd always been looking for things that were fun.

"Everybody is worthy of love." She turned to face him while leaning against the corral. "Some of us just find it hard to believe that anybody loves us the way you're talking about. Do you believe you're worthy of love?"

"I don't know, but I know I want it. I also know I'm willing to do a lot, give up a lot, to find it."

"What would you give up?"

"Living where I want to live. Owning my own ranch."

"Those are mighty big things to give up."

Will moved a little closer, placed his hand over hers. "I believe the kind of love I'm looking for is worth almost any sacrifice. Don't you?"

Idalou was afraid to let herself even think of the possibility of a love such as that. If she thought for one moment it was possible for her, she'd probably abandon all loyalties and responsibilities. "I don't know. It seems a lot to ask."

"Maybe I can convince you."

Chapter Eighteen

Idalou had been prepared for Will to kiss her. She *wanted* him to kiss her. She'd been waiting for it to happen again, so she didn't understand why his taking her in his arms and kissing her should seem like a totally new experience, why her mind should react with mild shock.

She felt as if he'd enveloped her, not just put his arms around her. When he pulled her against him she felt the heat of his body. Will might appear to be calm and very cool on the surface, but underneath he was like molten lava.

His lips were gentle, almost tentative in his exploration of her mouth, but each response on her part was met by an increasing intensity. Until his kisses turned hungry and demanding. More shocking was her response. She was equally hungry and demanding. Some restraint had been released, some permission had been granted.

She didn't stop to think that she was standing in the open locked in a crushing embrace with a man she had never seen until a few weeks ago. She didn't stop to think what people would say. She didn't stop to think of any consequences. Simply put, she didn't think at all. She just let herself respond.

Will broke off their kiss, pulled back until he could look into her eyes. "That wasn't so hard, was it?"

She shook her head.

"Were you thinking about the ranch?"

"No."

"About Carl?"

"No."

"Jordan, the bull, Mara, Van—"

"I wasn't thinking of anybody but you."

Will smiled. "That's what I was hoping you'd say. Now do you think you can like me more than a little bit?"

"I already do."

"Enough to let me kiss you again?"

"More than that."

"How much more?"

"Enough to want to find out if what you feel for me is more than liking."

"How are you going to do that?"

"I don't have much experience. I guess I was depending on you."

Will held her a little tighter. "You can always depend on me."

Without realizing it, she already did. All of her talk about being independent of any man, of not needing a man, was just talk apparently. She had certainly started to listen to him, even take his advice.

"I don't really know much about you," Idalou said. "I didn't need to know anything when all you wanted was to buy the bull, but now that . . ." She didn't know how to continue. She couldn't say *now that you want to marry me* because he hadn't actually asked her to marry him. Even though she liked him very much, she wasn't ready to think about anything like that.

"Now what?" Will asked.

"I don't know. That's the problem."

"Do you have to have an answer now? Can't we just like each other for the time being?"

How much time would that be? She wasn't interested in having a relationship with a man who would disappear in a few days, even a few weeks. "Why would you ask that? Have you changed your mind about your feelings for me?"

Will smiled in that way that nearly always caused her brain to disconnect. "Isabelle says I very rarely change my mind because I can't be bothered to think through any situation more than once."

"Why do you like me? I know the reasons you gave, but people don't like other people just because they're honest or do good deeds."

"I could ask why you like me."

"I'm not sure I do, not the way you mean." She turned away. "I'm trying to sort everything out, but it's not working." She looked back at him. "I do like you, and I don't mean just because you're handsome. You're kind, thoughtful, and patient."

Will looked unhappy with that assessment. "You make me sound like a preacher."

She reached out, covered the hand resting on the corral fence with her own. "I thought I was in love with Webb, but now I know I wasn't. I thought I disliked and distrusted you, but I was wrong. I'm in debt to you for saving me as well as saving my ranch."

"I don't want—"

"I know you don't want me to like you *for* those

things, but I like you because you are the kind of man who would *do* those things. But I'm having a hard time deciding if I would like you if you had never done any of those things."

"How would you know I'm the kind of man who would *do* those things if I hadn't *done* them?"

"That's my problem."

Will's laugh was so hearty, she couldn't help feeling a little hurt. "You think too much," he said. "Before Jake and Isabelle got married, they argued up and down about practically everything. She owed him for giving her orphans a home, and he owed her for taking care of him when he nearly died. She thought he was cruel and heartless, and he thought she had no idea what it took to survive in Texas, but they never let any of that get in the way of their love for each other. It was something they felt so strongly, *still* feel so strongly, nothing else mattered."

It seemed impossible that she could ever love like that. It required too much selflessness, too much giving of herself. She'd fought too long and hard to gain a certain level of independence, confidence in herself, even a degree of respect in the community. How could she give all that up?

Yet there was something about Will that wouldn't let her stop hoping she could find a reason to feel about him the way Isabelle felt about Jake. He was so . . . dependable. Every time she needed him, he seemed to appear. When she was at a loss for a way to handle a situation, he came up with a solution. Though he disagreed with her in lots of ways, he never ignored her opinions. And he liked her so much, everyone in Dunmore could see it. She didn't know why it had been so difficult for her to believe what everybody else seemed to know. Will loved her.

That had to mean he wanted to marry her. All she had to do was wait for him to say the words.

"I got a letter from Isabelle today," Will said, releasing her hands.

Idalou was thrown into confusion.

"I'd asked if she and Jake would let Junie Mae and her baby live with them for a while," Will explained. "Now that I'm moving out, they'll be sorta lonely in that big house all by themselves. Isabelle said she couldn't wait. I'll be leaving Dunmore in about a week and taking Junie Mae with me."

Idalou felt as if she'd been lifted out of a saddle and slammed against the ground. She could hardly breathe. She felt paralyzed, unable to move. She'd opened up, allowed herself to believe she could love Will, that he could love her enough to want to marry her. Now he was leaving and taking another woman with him. It was just like Webb turning his back on her all over again. How could she ever have been so stupid as to open her heart to this man? She knew he was much too handsome and sophisticated for a country girl like her. He could marry virtually any woman he wanted. Why had she believed he could want her to be his wife?

Shocked, hurt, and embarrassed, she found herself running away before she realized what she was doing. She wanted to find some dark corner where she could hide until she recovered enough to ask Carl to take her home. She heard Will call to her, but she didn't stop, didn't slow down. She wanted to get so far away he could never find her.

"Stop!"

She felt Will grab hold of her wrist. She tried to wench it out of his grasp, but he was too strong. He forced her to halt, to turn and face him.

"What's wrong? Why did you run away?"

How could he ask such a question after what he'd said? "Because I'm a fool," she threw at him. "A fool to believe that you could really love me. A fool to believe you could want to marry me. A fool to—"

Will cut off her protests by taking her in his arms and kissing her like she'd never dreamed possible. Her brain, hopelessly befuddled by two abrupt turns of events, gave up. A small voice warned her that she was behaving foolishly, but she couldn't stop herself from returning Will's kiss. She might still have doubts about his feelings for her, but right now that didn't seem to matter. She couldn't reject the comfort of his arms, the affirmation of his kiss. Foolish or not, she needed both desperately.

"Do you still think you're a fool?" Will asked when he broke off their kiss.

Idalou was too dazed and confused to know how to answer. She was running headlong toward disaster, and she couldn't do anything to stop herself. "I don't understand," she said. "One moment you say you love me, and the next you tell me you're leaving in a week and taking Junie Mae with you. I don't know where I fit in your plans, or *if* I fit in them. You haven't said—"

Shouts coming from the house shattered her chain of thought. She heard Mara's fearful voice shouting Carl's name.

"Something's wrong with Carl," Idalou said.

Will grabbed her hand and they headed for the house at a run. When they passed through the juniper thicket, she could see Van and Carl fighting in the middle of a circle of onlookers. By the time she reached the circle, some of the older men had pulled them apart.

"You're ruining Mara's birthday party," Idalou said when she reached Carl.

"*He's* ruining her party," Carl shouted, pointing at

Van. "The damned fool can't tell when he's not wanted."

"You're the one who's not wanted," Van yelled back. "You never have been."

Mara hovered between the two men, apparently undecided as to which she ought to go to first.

"Tell me what's going on," Idalou demanded of Carl. "You look a mess."

Carl's coat was half off one shoulder, his shirt was coming undone, and his tie was twisted to the side. His hair was falling in his eyes, and a bruise was forming under his left eye.

"Van has been dogging my footsteps all evening, taunting me, poking his finger in my chest, telling me Mara will never marry a penniless cowhand." He pushed Idalou away when she tried to straighten his tie. "I can dress myself," he snapped. He tucked in his shirt ignoring his tie. "I finally got fed up with it and pushed him away. That's when he hit me." He fingered the bruise under his eye. "The bastard caught me when I wasn't looking."

"Did you say something to make him angry?" Idalou asked.

"He's mad that Mara has gotten over her crush on Will and she likes me again." Carl straightened his coat. "Do I look all right?" he asked Will.

"You will as soon as you comb your hair and I straighten your tie."

Idalou didn't understand why Carl would let Will straighten his tie after he'd pushed her away.

Carl ran his fingers through his hair. "Every time Mara tries to say anything to me, Van interferes. I've kept my distance like you said," he told Will. "She's definitely been coming to me."

"It doesn't matter who's doing what," Idalou said.

"You shouldn't be getting into a fight at her party, and with Van of all people."

"Why *of all people?*" Carl asked.

"Because he's been our friend ever since we moved here. He's helped us several times when we needed it."

"I only put up with him when I thought he was interested in you," Carl said. "After Webb died, I thought you'd marry Van and I'd marry Mara and we could join all three ranches. It would have been the perfect solution."

Idalou had never thought of that. Though she appreciated Van's help and his friendship, she'd never once considered marrying him. He'd been very nice to her, but he could also be cruel and thoughtless.

"I never was going to marry Van," Idalou said. "I expect he thinks you're putting pressure on Mara to defy her father's wishes."

"I'm not putting pressure on her to do anything," Carl protested. "After the way she's behaved, the decision is up to her."

"Then stay away from Van until she decides." Idalou couldn't resist brushing some dirt off Carl's coat sleeve. She smelled alcohol. "Have you been drinking?"

Carl pulled away. "Not much, but if I had, it wouldn't be any of your business," he responded angrily. "Since Van is such a great friend, you might speak to him. He has been drinking, quite a lot from what I've seen. I'm surprised more boys don't run away from home," he said to Will before turning on his heel and walking away.

"What did he mean by that?" Idalou asked Will, her gaze following Carl until he disappeared around the corner of the house.

Will took Idalou's arm and turned her in the opposite direction. "I think he feels you're babying him."

"I'm worried about him," Idalou said, angry at both men.

"I understand, but he'll feel more comfortable if you stop showing it."

"How do you know he feels like that?"

"Because that's the way I've been feeling for the past ten years. I just didn't have the courage to say so. Instead, I learned to sit back and let everybody take care of me. They thought that was what I wanted because I didn't tell them any different."

"I can't imagine you not having the courage to do anything you wanted."

Will guided her to a spot away from the mainstream of the party. Several people eyed them as though they wanted to come over, but Will turned his back on them in a way that made it clear he wanted to be alone with Idalou.

"I used to idolize Jake." He laughed. "I suppose I still do. Pete and I used to fight over who got to sit next to him. If I could knock Pete down, I could get to Jake first. And of course I loved Isabelle. After what happened during my first eight years, I loved her attention, loved that she spoiled me. The other kids pretty much spoiled me, too." He shook his head. "I guess I was pretty rotten. But I was also unhappy. It took me a while to wise up and figure out what was wrong. Even then, I couldn't leave. After what Matt had suffered to protect me, I couldn't leave him until I knew he was safe and happy. I admire Carl for having the brains and guts to do it ten years before I did."

Idalou wanted to ask him more about his life with Jake and Isabelle, but their privacy was over for the evening. Will was a celebrity in Dunmore. And while that was more a case among the older citizens and the very young ones who came to his office every afternoon for goodies, the young men admired him for standing up to Newt and the young women admired him for his looks. Before long, so many people claimed his attention, Idalou felt like a mere accessory. This was her town and these were her friends, people she'd known for most of her life, but she might as well have been invisible for all the attention that got her.

Still, she had to admire Will for the way he handled himself. He never seemed to get impatient or irritated, regardless of the stupid things people said. Not even when Mabel Wren asked what she ought to do about her daughter's fascination with one of Jordan's cowhands.

"Take her to Fort Worth or Dallas and let her meet as many men as possible," Will said. "That way she'll be better able to judge when she's found the man who's truly right for her."

Mabel thought Will was a genius and said so. Idalou wasn't ready to declare him a genius, not even after he advised Lloyd to put as much money as possible into land.

"Once the fear of Indians is past, you won't be able to sell it fast enough."

She had to listen to several women regale him with the menu they'd planned for the evening when it was their turn to provide supper for him. She was relieved when the dancing finally started. However, that part of the evening didn't turn out as she'd expected. It appeared that every female at the party was determined to dance with Will. The women had their menfolk tap Will on the shoulder, a polite way of saying they wanted to change partners. Idalou got to dance with all the husbands and boyfriends, while Will was forced to dance with all the wives and girlfriends.

It would have been funny if it hadn't been so irritating. Idalou had come to this party with Will. She wanted to talk to Will. She wanted to dance with him. She didn't want to spend her evening with people she'd known for years and had no interest in getting to know better. She also didn't want to dance with men who stepped on her toes nearly as often as they trod upon the ground. Will was a superb dancer, a fact each of his partners was wont to announce immediately upon the end of her turn in his arms.

As one woman after another stepped in to steal Will from her, she was shocked to realize she was on the verge of tears. She excused herself to her current partner—one of Jordan's ranch hands—and hurried off the dance floor, hoping to escape notice. She'd never been so close to losing control over her feelings. She had never been the emotionally fragile type. She got angry sometimes, but her anger was controlled and directed. She could be impassioned, but that, too, was controlled and directed.

What she was feeling now was totally different. It was akin to despair, a belief that everything was hopeless, that she'd never be happy again. If Carl hadn't been so angry he'd left the party, she'd ask him to take her back to town. It seemed this wasn't the night for romance in the Ellsworth family.

"You can't stop dancing now. I've been saving the first slow dance for you."

Idalou spun around to find Will standing only inches away. "I'm sure somebody will break in," she said.

"Don't tell me you're jealous." Will's eyes danced with devilment, but turned serious when he saw she wasn't amused. "I'm not going to allow anybody to cut in. We're going to dance at least one whole dance this evening, and this is it."

Idalou was torn between risking further humiliation by going back on the dance floor and running away to protect her bruised heart. She needed time to shore up her defenses, to make herself less vulnerable, but she couldn't turn her back on the promise of love that shone from Will's eyes. She allowed him to draw her back onto the dance floor.

She had barely settled into Will's embrace when a man stepped up and tapped him on the shoulder. "No, Vernon," Will said. "Tell Dorothy this dance belongs to Idalou."

His refusal to step aside caught Vernon Hill by surprise, but he went back to his wife, who gave Idalou an angry look.

"You now have one less admirer," Idalou whispered in his ear.

"I don't care. You're the one I invited to the dance."

Idalou put all thoughts of other women out of her mind. She was determined to enjoy this dance to the fullest. She had danced with many men tonight, but not one of them could dance as well as Will. It was as though she and Will were one body moving in effortless, synchronized motion. He was too tall for her to rest her head on his shoulder, but it was just as enjoyable to lean against his chest, to feel the beat of his heart, the movement of the muscles under his skin.

She ignored the raised voices she could hear above the music of the band.

"You don't have to be jealous of Dorothy or any other woman," Will said.

"I'm not jealous," she insisted, "just irritated."

And fearful. Now that she'd opened her heart to Will, it seemed he had virtually no space for her. Yet, enclosed in Will's embrace, it was easy to imagine staying here forever. He wasn't boastful or showy, but he had a quiet strength that gave her a wonderful feeling of security. She hadn't felt that way when she'd first met him. His unflappable attitude, his calm approach to every problem, his insistence on thinking everything through before acting, had struck her as the attitude of a man who couldn't be bothered enough to care. Learning she was wrong had been a humbling but exciting discovery.

Learning that below that cool exterior burned a very strong liking for her had been stunning. Only now was she beginning to believe it might actually be true. She didn't know if she loved him, but she couldn't imagine any man who'd make a better husband.

But letting go enough to marry any man wasn't going to be easy. Feeling safe in his arms wouldn't mean much if she had to give up her independence, if she had to accept his decisions when she disagreed with him. Idalou told herself to stop staring into the future and simply enjoy the evening and being in the arms of a man who made her feel happy just to be with him.

It would be easier if the men who were shouting would stop.

"We should do this more often," Will said.

"Mara only has one birthday a year."

"I don't need to depend on birthdays or any other celebration to tell you how much I care for you," Will said. "You're a very remarkable woman."

She didn't feel remarkable. On the contrary, she felt about as unremarkable as possible.

"I never thought I'd meet anyone like you when I came to Dunmore. You know, you're the reason I took the sheriff's job."

"It doesn't matter. You and Junie Mae will be leaving soon. You won't be coming back. I know you won't. You'll want to sell the ranch. You know Carl and I don't have the money to—"

Will put his fingers over her lips. "Did anyone ever tell you you think too much?"

"Yes. Carl."

"Your brother is a very intelligent man. You ought to listen to him."

Before Will could say anything else, the sounds of a fight erupted somewhere in the distance. Before they could locate the sound, Emmett, one of Will's deputies, came rushing up.

"You'd better come, Sheriff. Van and Carl are fighting again. They've bloodied each other this time."

Most of the people had stopped dancing, some leaving the dance floor to watch the fight. Angry at Carl for being foolish enough to get into a second fight, Idalou followed Will as he pushed his way though the gathering onlookers. Two men were making only halfhearted efforts to keep Van and Carl apart. Idalou was shocked to see blood smeared over both men.

When Will waded in between the two men, others stepped forward to pull them apart. Carl and Van continued shouting and struggling to reach each other.

"They're both drunk," Emmett said. "Otherwise, they might have done some real damage."

Hair falling in their eyes, their clothes ripped and dirty, Carl and Van looked like two drunks who'd been in an all-out brawl. Blood from Carl's nose and a cut on Van's cheek had smeared their faces and fists, and there were flecks of blood on their shirts. Boots that had been glossy were covered in dirt. Neither looked liked the handsome young man he'd been at the start of the evening.

Will looked from Carl to Van. "I think jail is the best place for them to cool off. Once they're sober, I'll see if I can talk some sense into them."

"You don't have to put Carl in jail," Idalou said. "I can take care of him."

"I'm taking my son home," Frank Sonnenberg said.

"They're going to jail," Will said. "Unless Mara or her parents want to file charges for ruining the party, they'll be free to leave in the morning."

Idalou would have argued with Will, but Frank Sonnenberg beat her to it. To hear him talk, you'd think it was all Carl's fault and Van was an innocent bystander. Idalou didn't excuse Carl's participation in the fight. Fighting wasn't something Carl would normally do, especially at a party for the woman he hoped to marry.

"I'll run you out of town," Frank shouted.

"Save yourself the trouble," Will replied, not fazed by Frank's shouting or threats. "I'll be leaving soon anyway."

A murmur ran through the crowd. Idalou wasn't surprised to hear several people telling Will they hoped he would stay. What did surprise her was the feeling of desolation that settled over her. She knew he would soon be taking Junie Mae to the Hill Country, but somehow his always being close at hand when she was in trouble had caused her to begin to expect him to be there in the future. It wasn't a conscious thought, or she'd have corrected it. It was what she hoped would happen, what she *wanted* to happen.

Finally Frank Sonnenberg turned and stormed out. Will turned to Idalou.

"I have to ride into town with Emmett. Will you be okay until I can come back?"

She hadn't expected to be left behind. It was a desolate feeling. After Frank's outburst, people were looking uncomfortable. She wouldn't be surprised if they went home early.

"You don't have to hurry," Jordan told Idalou. "I'm

not letting anybody go home early just because two boys were drunk and got into a fight. Hell, I did that a few times myself. It's just one of the things that makes boys different from girls. Start worrying those fiddles, fellas," he shouted at the band. "The night is still young."

Much to Idalou's relief, the guests laughed and their mood changed immediately.

"I'm sorry about this," Will said to Mara. "I hope it doesn't ruin the party for you."

Idalou hadn't even thought of Mara or how this might affect her. She had always thought Mara was a shallow girl who enjoyed having men compete for her attention, but she'd lost color and was staring at Will as though she didn't know what he'd said. She was holding on to her father's arm as if she never wanted to let go.

"Nonsense," Jordan said. "What girl doesn't want boys to fight over her?"

"This fight was a little too serious," Will said. "Why don't you let her mother take her inside for a little while?"

"She's fine," Jordan insisted. "You've got your dancing shoes on, don't you, honey?"

Alma put her arm around her daughter's waist and turned her toward the house. Idalou had never liked Jordan, but now she added insensitivity to his sins. Alma hadn't gone far before she stopped and turned back.

"Would you like to join us, Idalou?"

Idalou was caught having to make an awkward decision with a dozen pairs of eyes staring at her. She wanted to go back to town, but she knew Will wouldn't like it and it would be rude to leave at such an awkward moment. She couldn't imagine what she would do when trapped inside for even a few minutes with Mara and her mother. Alma had never liked her son's interest in Idalou or her daughter's interest in Carl, and Idalou thought Mara was too immature and shallow for Carl. And that didn't begin to touch on the things she'd said about Alma's husband. The other alternative would have been to stay and keep pretty much out of sight until Will came back for her, but Alma's invitation took that option off the table.

"Thanks," she said. "I could use a few minutes of quiet."

"Don't stay too long," Jordan said. "The party won't be the same with the two prettiest girls missing." Jordan sounded like he'd had a little too much to drink, himself.

The women walked back to the house without speaking. Alma closed the doors, which muted the noise of the band. "Can I get you something to drink?" she asked Idalou. "I'm going to fix some sassafras tea for Mara."

"That would be fine," Idalou said.

"I'm sorry Carl's fight spoiled your party," Idalou said to Mara after her mother left.

"It's Van's fault," Mara said listlessly. "He was picking on Carl all night. Every time I tried to talk to Van, he would start in on how poor Carl was or how he was such a rotten rancher, he couldn't keep track of his own stock or keep the ranch from being sold out from under him."

"Van is jealous of Carl. He wants to marry you."

"Van doesn't want to marry me." Mara looked like she was on the verge of tears. "He just wants Daddy's ranch."

Idalou was too sure that was true to argue. "Well, that won't matter if you're still in love with Will."

"I'm not in love with Will." Mara sighed and looked a little less like she would burst into tears. "I never was. I was just infatuated because he's so handsome. I'm still in love with Carl, but he won't talk to me."

"I'm sure he will once he's certain you're no longer confused about your feelings for him, but there's not much point in talking about marriage as long as your father refuses his permission."

"Daddy won't force me to marry a man I don't like, and he's not going to keep me from marrying the man I love." Mara's expression turned hard and determined. She looked so much like her father at that moment it startled Idalou.

Despite Mara's assertion, Idalou was certain Jordan and Alma would put up a fight before they would allow her to throw herself away on a penniless cowboy like Carl.

"Your parents may not stop you from marrying Carl, but you have to face the possibility that they'll refuse to support you. You've always lived in a nice house where everything was done for you. Carl has no house to take you to. We aren't even sole owners of the ranch any longer. Even after we rebuild, there won't be anyone but you to cook, wash, clean, and take care of the livestock."

A spark of interest shone in Mara's eyes. "Does that mean you're going to marry the sheriff?"

Chapter Nineteen

Idalou hadn't expected that question. She opened her mouth to deny it, but realized she didn't want to deny it. She hadn't reached the point of believing she was in love with him, but she did know she'd never met a man she'd like to marry more than Will. Could she even say she wanted to marry him if she wasn't sure she was in love with him? "I like Will a lot, but we haven't gotten to the point of talking about marriage. We're still getting to know each other. You've known Carl almost all your life. I've known Will less than a month. Besides, things are a little awkward between us just now."

"If you mean his paying off your loan, I'd say that was proof he loved you," Mara said.

One of the joys of living in a small town was that everybody knew you and would help you if you were in trouble. The other side of the coin was that everybody knew all your business, even the parts you wished were private. "That's part of it."

"He's so gorgeous. I don't see how you *cannot* be in love with him. Everybody knows he loves you."

"He *likes* me. That's very different from love. Now tell me what you're going to do if you decide you're in love with Carl. You really hurt him when you became infatuated with Will."

"I know," Mara said, tears threatening again. "I don't know what I was thinking. Maybe I was so tired of being in love with Carl and my parents pushing me to marry Van that I turned to a man I thought everybody could like." Mara said that with such emphasis that Idalou wondered if she was trying to convince herself. "Tonight I tried to tell Carl I love him, but he wouldn't listen."

Idalou didn't know what advice to give to Mara. She knew Carl loved Mara, but Mara had hurt him badly. Just as she loved Will, but his attention to Junie Mae had hurt her badly.

She loved Will.

She'd never thought that before. Did she really love him, or was she just using the word because Mara used it? He'd shown his interest but had never said he loved her. Yet while she was waiting for him to say the words, she'd tumbled into love herself. How could she not have known? At least it explained her up-and-down emotions during the past few hours.

"You're not listening," Mara complained.

"Sorry."

"You've got to talk to Carl for me. You're his sister. He'll listen to you."

"This is something you and Carl have to settle between yourselves," Idalou said. "The less outside interference you have, the better."

That was the trouble with her and Will. One thing or another always seemed to get in the way. She'd been so distrustful, so distracted, so fearful, she hadn't been able to believe that anything this wonderful could be happening to her.

"But how can I get him to believe me?" Mara asked.

It was the same question Idalou needed to ask herself. Will had said everything but the words, and she'd continued to keep her distance from him, to shield her heart. Even when she'd finally opened up, she'd run at the first hint of heartache. Junie Mae.

"You've got to make up your mind about what you want and stick with it," Idalou said. "If it's Carl, you have to accept that your parents aren't going to be happy. It may come to the point that you have to make a choice between them and Carl. Remember, even if we find the bull and can pay off the debt, Carl has no home to take you to. Loving Carl may be the hardest thing you'll ever do."

Loving Will should have been the easiest thing Idalou had ever done, but her fear and distrust had made it nearly impossible. She had to make up her mind what she was willing to do, what she was willing to sacrifice, to love Will. It looked like the first thing she had to do was give up the ranch, but the Double-L was Carl's only inheritance. She would have to talk to him when he got out of jail. She couldn't abandon her brother, not even for love.

Much to her surprise, Idalou didn't feel an overwhelming sense of loss when she looked at what used to be her home. A couple of hard rains had washed away the mud. Already, fresh shoots of grass had sprouted in what had once been the barren area around the ranch buildings. Except for the corral and the house's foundations, nearly every sign of their ranch would be gone by next summer. She should have been devastated. Instead she felt that a burden had been lifted from her shoulders.

Immediately she was nearly crushed by guilt. She didn't understand how she could feel so uninvolved. For years the ranch had been at the center of nearly every thought. This was Carl's inheritance, yet now it was just an annoyance that clung to her despite her indifference.

"I thought about this place the whole time I was in jail," Carl said.

Will hadn't been in his office when Emmett let Carl and Van out of jail. He'd been called to investigate some rustling on one of the small ranches west of Dunmore.

"I know it looks rather hopeless now," Idalou said, "but it's not that bad. We still have the land and the cows."

"But now Will owns a big chunk of both."

She tried not to think of that because it made it harder to admit to Carl that she was in love with Will. "I'm sure he won't press us to pay him back."

"You mean he won't press *me*. He wants to marry you."

After the fight and Carl's night in jail, the trip back into town had not been a good time to discuss personal issues. Idalou understood why Will had jailed both Van and Carl, but she was still angry. Van had instigated both fights, not Carl.

"Will and Junie Mae are leaving in a week."

Carl looked surprised. "When did he tell you that?"

"Last night. He had just gotten a letter from his parents saying Junie Mae could stay with them."

"Are you still worried that it's his baby?"

"No."

Carl leveled a searching glance at her. "Are you sure?"

"Yes, but I don't like his leaving with Junie Mae."

"Then go with him."

"He hasn't asked me."

"Only because you won't give him a chance."

"I was going to give him a chance last night, but your fight put an end to that." Carl's pugnacity vanished. "I don't mean to blame you," she said. "It's my fault for being so stubborn."

Carl waved away her apology. "I don't see much point in trying to rebuild."

"Why not?" It was easy to see he was depressed, but she hadn't expected anything like this.

"You're going to marry Will. If he doesn't ask you before he leaves, he'll come back. I'm not going to marry Mara, so I won't need a ranch house."

"She still loves you. She told me so last night. Don't you still love her?"

"It doesn't make any difference unless she makes up her mind to defy her father."

He dismounted and kicked a rock, sending it rolling toward the stream. They'd been sitting astride their horses in what had been the area between the house and the bunkhouse, but the sun was growing hot so they moved to the shade of the cottonwoods that anchored the bank of the creek. The empty space felt strange, unfamiliar.

"I don't need a house to watch the herd," Carl continued. "We don't need a bunkhouse, because we don't have any hands. Come fall, I think we ought to sell the herd and put the land up for auction."

The suddenness and unexpectedness of this about-face was a shock to Idalou. She had finally accepted that she'd be relieved to be rid of the burden of the ranch, but Carl was a born cowman and he loved the

Double-L. "You can't do that. You won't have a home."

It didn't look like home anymore. It didn't even feel like it. All that was left of their house was the rocks that had been used for the foundation. Even the housing for the well had disappeared, leaving behind a hole filled with foul water.

"I'm thinking about moving away. With my experience, I ought to be able to find a job. Maybe I'll see if I can work for Will's dad."

"This is my home, too. What do you expect me to do?"

"Marry Will."

"That still doesn't mean you have to give up the ranch. You'll hate working for somebody else."

"Not as much as I'll hate seeing Mara married to Van. Do you think I could stay here after that?"

No, not any more than she could stay here if Will married Junie Mae. "Think about it before you make up your mind. The ranch is your future. I don't want you to give it up for any reason except that you don't want to be a rancher anymore."

"That's all I've ever wanted to be."

"Then don't think about selling. We'll work out something."

"Damn that bull!" Carl exclaimed. "Where in hell can it have been hiding all this time?"

"I think it's gone. Somebody stole it, or wolves got it."

"I'm going to keep looking. Will says he thinks it's still here."

It irritated her that everybody in town, right down to her own brother, accepted every word out of Will's mouth as gospel. The man wasn't infallible. "Will can't know any more about the whereabouts of that bull than you or I."

"Van told me he thought I ought to look in some of the canyons off the river."

"It's a waste of time. A calf couldn't stay alive on the little graze in one of those canyons, much less a bull."

"What else have I got to do with my time?"

Idalou felt sorry for Carl, but she didn't know what to tell him. She couldn't make up her mind about Will. He seemed more concerned about Junie Mae than about her. She couldn't trust her heart to a man who didn't put her before everyone else.

She needed to get back to town. She was still working in Ella's shop. Will refused to accept any money for the hotel room because he said they didn't charge extra for letting her share a room with Junie Mae, so she gave most of the money she earned to Carl so he wouldn't have to depend on Will for supplies. She refused to get further in debt to Will. The money she owed him was already crushing her spirit.

Will had spent three days looking for Ben Janish's cows. They'd finally caught up with the rustlers about twenty miles south of Ben's ranch. Cornered, the rustlers had pulled out sometime in the night. Ben was delighted to have his herd back, but Will was frustrated because he believed Newt Mandrin was involved in the rustling if not the instigator.

Once Ben's herd was back on his own land, all Will had wanted to do was get back to town and talk to Idalou. He'd started out the night of Mara's birthday party with hopes of convincing Idalou that he loved her and wanted her to marry him. But he'd been sidetracked before he could declare his feelings.

Now that he'd finally returned to town, gotten a good night's rest, and persuaded Idalou to drop by the sheriff's office before she went to work, Mara had to show up crying on his shoulder that Carl hadn't believed her when she told him she was still in love with him.

"Give him some time." Will had had breakfast, but no one had yet tried to overwhelm him with coffee and sweets. This morning he would really have appreciated the extra coffee. "After spending a night in jail because of you, I doubt he's very receptive just now."

"That wasn't my fault," Mara said. "It was Van's."

"Regardless of who instigated the fights, you were the reason for them. All you have to do is make up your mind which of them you love and stick with your decision."

"I have," Mara wailed. "I love Carl. I want to marry him."

Will pinched the bridge of his nose, closed his eyes momentarily. He was too old to put up with teenage tragedies first thing in the morning. "You keep thinking like that for a whole week, and I'm sure Carl will believe you."

"He does believe me, but he says it doesn't matter anymore."

Will hadn't seen Carl since he'd put him in jail, but he didn't believe the boy could have lost his mind in just three days. "Did he say why it didn't matter?"

"He said he didn't have a house, he didn't have a ranch, and come fall he probably wouldn't have a herd. He said marrying him now would be the same as marrying a pauper. He said even if my father would let me do something that stupid, he wouldn't."

At that point Mara burst into tears again immediately giving Will a headache. He never had been much of a morning person.

"What am I going to do?" Mara wailed.

Will thought honor was a fine thing, but he was reaching the conclusion that Idalou and Carl had a little too much honor for their own good. And for the good of the people who loved them.

"First of all, you're going to stop crying. Men hate it when women cry. They know they probably did something to cause it. And even when they haven't, they know they have to do something to make it stop despite having no idea where to begin. All they can think about is getting on a horse and riding away."

"That's stupid," Mara said.

"That's what Isabelle says."

"Most of the time, all we want is somebody to hold us and tell us everything will be all right."

"Isabelle says that, too."

"Then why aren't you holding me?"

"Because nothing will ever be all right again if Idalou and Carl walk in on me cuddling you."

"Carl won't care."

"If he didn't care about you, he'd have begged you to marry him so your father could support both of you."

Mara looked up, her eyes wide with indignation. "Carl would never do anything like that."

Will released a fatalistic sigh. "I know, and neither would his sister."

Mara's eyes grew wider. "Idalou refused to marry you?"

"I haven't gotten around to asking her yet, but I already know the answer as long as she owes me money."

"But it's not the same with women. They're supposed to marry men with money."

Will welcomed the sound of the office door opening because it would bring an end to this fruitless conversation. "Try telling that to Idalou," he said to Mara before turning to his visitor. "Good morning, Mrs. Truesdale. You can't know how glad I am to see you."

"I thought you might be ready for some fresh coffee," Mrs. Truesdale said. She cast a reproving glance at Mara's tear-stained cheeks. "The path of young love still proving to be thorny?" she asked.

Mara sniffed dolefully.

"The hunter who can't make up his mind which deer to shoot risks losing them all."

Will thought that was a rather inappropriate metaphor, as well as an unfeeling one, but he wasn't willing to take on more than one female at a time.

"Thank you for the coffee," he said. "I think we'll both feel better after a cup."

"I saw Junie Mae headed this way," Mrs. Truesdale said and smiled sweetly. "All you need is Idalou and you'll have every female in distress hanging on your sleeves."

Will was about to reach the conclusion that listening to Mrs. Truesdale was too high a price to pay for coffee.

"You need a wife, Sheriff. A man like you is a danger to all unmarried women."

"He's not a danger to me," Mara declared. "I love Carl."

"I'm sure he'll be thrilled to hear that . . . *again*." Mrs. Truesdale turned back to Will. "Mabel Thornton will be over with some blueberry muffins shortly. Try not to give all of them to the town brats. Mabel's daughters picked those blueberries by hand."

She spoke as if there were some other way to pick blueberries. "I'll make sure I have at least two," Will promised.

Junie Mae entered the office and came to a stop when she saw Mrs. Truesdale.

"I'm just going," the matron said sweetly. "Try not to take up all the sheriff's time. We don't want the rustlers to feel neglected."

"Don't pay her any attention," Mara said to Junie Mae after Mrs. Truesdale left. "Mama says Gladys Truesdale has the sharpest tongue in Dunmore."

"I'll come back," Junie Mae said, casting an apologetic glance at Mara. "I don't want to interrupt."

"I'm sure the sheriff hopes you will interrupt," Mara said. "I've been crying on his shoulder, and you know how much men like that."

Junie Mae smiled. "The sheriff is very good about letting us poor females cry on his shoulder." Her smile faded. "It's fortunate that at least one man cares about us."

Will had a sinking feeling that Junie Mae was about to tear up.

"A lot of men care," Mara said. "They just care about the wrong things."

Will was relieved when the door opened and Carl entered the office. He was about to direct the younger man's attention to the distressed Mara, but Carl turned to her without any help from Will.

"I want you to come outside," he said in very unloverlike tones. "I have something to show you. You come, too," he said to Will. With that, he turned and stalked out of the office.

Mara jumped to her feet and dashed after him. Though he was tempted to stay inside and let Carl and Mara settle their problems between themselves, Will paused only long enough to tell Junie Mae to have some coffee.

"That's my bull," Carl said to Will when he stepped outside. There in the street stood the long-lost creature. "I found him in one of the river canyons on her father's property." He pointed at Mara.

"I told you Jordan McGloughlin was a liar and a thief. I hope you'll believe me now."

Will didn't have to turn around to know it was Idalou speaking. He was in for it now.

"My father has always wanted your land, but he wouldn't cheat to get it," Mara declared.

"The bull had been barricaded in and was being fed," Carl shot back. "From the looks of things, he'd been moved there recently."

"If he was on our land, why didn't you find him before?" Mara asked. "Daddy gave you permission to look anywhere you wanted."

"All your father had to do was know where Carl was looking and move the bull somewhere else," Idalou pointed out.

Will didn't miss a word of the exchange, but at the moment he was more interested in the bull. He was a truly fine-looking animal, worthy of the fuss being made over him as well as of the price Will would have to pay to get him. For an animal that had had to forage for himself in the wild, he seemed remarkably calm and accepting of captivity. His presence in the street was attracting a lot of attention. Will wasn't happy when Van was one of the persons attracted.

"Where did you find him?" Van asked Carl.

"In one of the river canyons, just like you thought."

Will's attention was caught. "You told Carl where the bull was?" he asked Van.

"I was only guessing," Van said.

"I'd looked everywhere else," Carl said. "I hadn't thought of the canyons because most of them are barren." He turned an angry glance at Mara. "I never thought her father would hide him where he had to be fed and watered."

Mara looked devastated. At this point, it didn't matter whether Carl believed she still loved him. He had no reason to lie about where he'd found the bull, and every reason to believe a future with her was impossible.

"Daddy wouldn't do that," Mara said, her tears beginning to flow again. "He just wouldn't."

"Regardless of what your father might or might not have done," Will said to Mara, "it's not your fault."

"I think you ought to arrest Jordan," Van said.

With a wail, Mara threw herself on Will and began to cry with loud, gusty sobs that seemed to draw people out of their homes and shops. Will did his best to comfort Mara. Finally he cast a mute appeal to Idalou, who had watched the entire episode with a jaundiced eye.

"Come on," she said to Mara as she peeled her from Will's chest. "Let's go into the sheriff's office until you feel better. You don't want to give people any more reason to gossip about your family."

"I don't care," Mara sobbed. "My father's going to jail, and Carl won't ever believe I love him. My life is ruined."

"Just because the bull was on his land doesn't mean he's responsible for hiding him," Will said.

Idalou looked at him with shocked surprise, but it was Van who expressed what Will figured everyone must be thinking.

"Who else would have done it?" Van demanded. "Everybody knows Jordan wanted Idalou's ranch and let his cows run all over her land to breed with her bull."

"Don't forget the dam," Idalou said.

"Or the rustled herd," Carl added.

Mara wailed so loudly Idalou had to take her into the office before she collapsed.

"If he gets away with this, none of the rest of us will be safe," Van argued.

Will wasn't about to deny that someone seemed

mighty determined to drive Carl and Idalou off their land, but he couldn't make himself believe that Jordan McGloughlin was cruel or a criminal.

"Newt tried to steal the herd," one of the gathered crowd said.

"Jordan has hired Newt lots of times," Van said.

"So has your father," Will reminded him.

"I found the bull on McGloughlin land," Carl said to Will. He looked angry, as though he believed Will was trying to defend Jordan. "You can't ignore that."

"I don't intend to. I'm going to see Jordan right away."

"I'm coming with you," Carl said.

"Me, too," Van said.

Several people in the crowd indicated their intention of going as well.

"I think Carl and his sister will be enough," Will said.

"How will we know you haven't swallowed Jordan's lies?" Van demanded.

"Because my sister and I will hear every word he has to say," Carl said.

"I think you ought to arrest Jordan first," Van said. "It's plain as the nose on your face that he's guilty."

"He may be, but every man deserves a chance to speak for himself," Will said.

Van balled his hands into fists. "If you don't arrest him, I say you're as crooked as he is."

The crowd had been with Van so far, but that accusation caused a visible drawing back, accompanied by shocked protests that the sheriff wasn't crooked.

"Anytime the citizens of Dunmore are dissatisfied with the way I do my job, they can have my badge back."

Will was gratified by the volume of objections to Van's accusation, assertions of confidence in his work, and pleas for him to stay in Dunmore. It was really nice to have people look up to him, depend on him, respect him, but it was time to take his bull and go home.

"Why don't you start toward Jordan's place?" Will said to Carl. "Idalou and I will catch up with you as soon as Mara is calm enough to ride."

Most of the starch went out of Carl's anger. "This has been hard on her. She adores her father."

"How can she adore a man who's done everything but murder to get what he wants?" Van demanded.

"Because he's her father," Carl said, turning away from Van in disgust. "Tell her I'm sorry," he said to Will.

"It would be a lot better coming from you."

Carl shook his head before turning away. Will waited while the youth mounted up and headed out of town. Van continued to argue that Will ought to arrest Jordan immediately.

"I intend to see that Jordan makes reparations for everything he's done," Will said to Van, "but there's somebody else involved in this, somebody pulling strings while staying completely out of sight. I don't intend to stop until I can prove who that is."

Chapter Twenty

"I didn't blow up her dam, and I didn't pay Newt Mandrin to rustle her herd," Jordan thundered at Will before turning to Idalou. "After all the things she's accused me of doing, that would be like sticking my head in a noose."

"Not if you thought you could get away with it." Carl said.

"I didn't think I could get away with it because I never thought of doing any of those things."

"Then how do you explain that the bull was found on your land, penned up in a canyon, and provided with food and water?" Will asked.

"How do I know Carl *did* find that bull on my land?" Jordan demanded. "He could have staged the whole thing."

"Why would he do that?" Idalou asked. "All of our real trouble started when we decided to sell the bull so we could pay off the mortgage. We already had dozens of calves by him. We could have saved the best of them, sold the bull, and still upgraded our herd. You hid the bull so we'd end up losing the ranch."

"I didn't hide your bull!"

They were gathered in the main room of Jordan's house. It was a large, open space with several chairs and two couches arranged before a large fireplace in a manner to encourage social interaction rather than confrontation. Alma McGloughlin was so overwhelmed, she allowed Mara to put her arms around her to console her. Idalou had tried to comfort Mara and her mother, but they'd spurned her attempts. She guessed she could understand. After all, she and her brother were responsible for Jordan's impending disgrace.

Idalou had never really liked Jordan McGloughlin. He was a shrewd businessman who didn't mind cutting corners and throwing his weight around. Neither was he above using his children to advance his plans to become the dominant rancher in central Texas. But she did feel a twinge of sympathy now when he seemed to collapse, fold up, and turn gray in defeat. She believed he was guilty and she was determined he'd pay for what he'd done, but she knew what it was like to feel helplessly caught. He probably wouldn't be sent to prison, but this would destroy his reputation and position of influence.

"I did tell my boys to chase that bull around my range for a few days, but that's all I did." He dropped his gaze to the floor. "I didn't pen him up so Idalou and Carl would lose their ranch. I have enough money to buy up her father's mortgage. I was just waiting until Lloyd got tired of extending her credit."

"To an outside observer it would look like you got tired of waiting," Lloyd Severns said.

As the owner of the bank and the head of the committee to find the next sheriff—as well as Jordan's best friend—he had insisted upon coming when he heard about the bull.

"It was because of me." Mara had been standing back from the circle around Jordan, but now she stepped forward. "He wanted to get rid of Carl so I couldn't marry him and would have to marry Van. Well, Daddy, you did it all for nothing. I hate Van. He's mean and selfish. If I can't marry Carl, I'm not going to marry anybody."

"I'm still your father," Jordan thundered. "You'll do as I tell you."

"I don't have to listen to a man who will steal and destroy to get what he wants." Mara jumped up. "You can't ever make me do anything again." She ran from the room sobbing. Her mother cast a hopeless glance around the room before following her daughter.

"See what you've done?" Jordan said to Idalou. "None of this would have happened if it hadn't been for you and your brother."

"None of this would have happened if you hadn't been so greedy," Idalou said.

"I agree," Lloyd said. "The Ellsworth place was never going to be big enough to threaten you, Jordan."

"Are you going to arrest him now?" Carl asked Will.

"Yes," Will said, "but not for the reason you think. Is there someplace we could talk without danger of being overheard?" he asked Jordan.

They had gathered in the great room of the McGloughlin ranch house. There were no doors to close it off from the rest of the house, only archways connecting it with the other rooms.

"We could go into my office," Jordan said, "but it's mighty small for five people."

"It'll have to do," Will said.

Idalou knew Will had always been reluctant to accept the notion that Jordan was behind all the trouble, but surely he couldn't believe anything else now.

"I have no proof of what I'm about to say," Will said once they'd settled, "but I want you to think about it before you tell me I'm crazy."

"Nobody thinks you're crazy," Lloyd said.

"I've always thought Jordan was responsible for the bull being lost, but not the dam bursting or the rustling." Will looked from one face to another. "I think somebody else is involved and trying to put the blame on Jordan."

Idalou couldn't speak, his statement had taken her breath away.

"I'm aware that all the evidence seems to point to him," Will continued.

"Finding the bull on his land sure as hell does," Carl exclaimed. "Idalou tried to tell me he would do anything to get our place, but I believed Jordan when he said he wouldn't do anything illegal."

"I believe him, too," Will said.

"Why?" Idalou had finally found her tongue. "How can you possibly believe he's not guilty?"

Will's gaze focused on Idalou. "People have misjudged me all my life. When most of us look at people, we see only what's on the outside. We seldom bother to look deeper. I have to take responsibility for people misjudging me, just as Jordan now has to take responsibility for people misjudging him. He took advantage of you in little things. Even worse, he appeared to take pride in doing it. It was only natural he would be blamed when things escalated."

"Who do you think is responsible, then?" Carl asked.

"I believe Frank Sonnenberg is behind your trouble, aided and abetted by Van and Newt Mandrin."

"Van is our friend," Carl objected. "After Webb died, I thought he would ask Idalou to marry him."

"Why would Frank try to destroy us?" Idalou asked.

"He offered to buy the ranch if I wanted to sell. I would have sold it to him even if he couldn't pay as much as Jordan."

"Did you tell him that?"

"No. Why should I?"

"Let me tell you what I think," Will said. "I believe Frank Sonnenberg is eaten up with jealousy because Jordan's ranch is bigger and more successful than his. Having your land and water would give him the advantage. He probably sat back and smiled when he saw Jordan letting his cows run all over your land, but he panicked when you decided to sell the bull to keep the ranch. The only way to prevent that was to steal the bull. Jordan played right into his hands by chasing the bull onto his land. It was easy enough for Sonnenberg to have Newt find the bull, pen him up, and blame it on Jordan. Remember what Henry and Mort said about strange hoofprints? If Jordan was thought to be behind all the trouble, Sonnenberg was sure to get the ranch in the end."

"But Van let me search his ranch," Idalou said.

"Had you searched his ranch before?" Will asked.

"No."

"I think the bull was on his property the whole time, but as long as Van or his own hands were with you, he could be sure you wouldn't find anything to arouse suspicion. And by volunteering to let you search his land, he ensured that no one would think he was guilty."

Idalou found it hard to believe that Jordan wasn't responsible for everything, but she had to admit that Will's explanation was plausible.

"Frank is determined that Van will marry Mara and join all the ranches into one huge spread, but Mara is a headstrong girl and in love with Carl. Jordan is a hard businessman, but he's a doting father.

He couldn't be depended on to hold out against Mara's wishes. In that case, the best thing to do was reduce Carl to penury by destroying the dam and rustling the herd. Frank was certain Mara wouldn't marry a man without a ranch, a house, or a job."

"I can't believe all that," Carl said.

"It sounds very complicated," Lloyd said.

"Are you saying it's hard to believe that Frank would do something like this." Jordan fumed, "but it's easy to believe I did?"

"I'm saying Carl found the bull on your property and everybody knows about the bull breeding with your cows," Will said. "We don't know who blew up the dam, but we know you've hired Newt on several occasions and that he was involved in the rustling. A lot of the evidence is circumstantial, but it all points to you."

"You said you were going to arrest Jordan but not for the reasons we thought," Idalou said to Will. "What do you want to do?"

Will looked directly at Idalou. She could tell he was asking her support, asking for her to believe him. She couldn't accept that he was right about Jordan, but she did believe that Will thought he was doing the right thing. For that reason she'd listen to what he had to say.

"If, as I believe, Frank Sonnenberg is behind this, the most important part of his plan is to have Van marry Mara. If he believes Mara has defied her father and plans to marry Carl anyway, he'll have to do something to stop her."

"I intend to arrest you, Jordan, and hold you in the Dunmore jail," Will continued. "I propose that Mara run away. Just to town," Will said before Jordan could protest. "She can stay at the hotel. With Idalou, Junie Mae, and me to watch her, she ought to be safe."

"Go on," Lloyd said, though Jordan clearly didn't like the plan.

"Mara can announce, as she already has done, that she plans to defy her father and marry Carl. Now that he has the bull and can pay off his debt to me, he's not penniless any longer. And with Jordan in jail, it's possible that Mara and her mother would ask Carl to take over running the McGloughlin ranch."

"What do you expect Frank to do?" Idalou asked.

"I'm not sure. Most likely Van will ask Mara to marry him and Frank will put pressure on Jordan to force her. Whatever he decides, he has to make some move to keep Mara from marrying Carl."

"I don't like that," Jordan said. "It puts Mara in danger."

"Not as much as Carl," Idalou said.

"I'm not afraid of Frank Sonnenberg," Carl declared.

"If he's behind all of this trouble, maybe you ought to be," Lloyd said.

"Carl can move into town," Will suggested. "That way he'd be safe and could spend more time with Mara."

"I'm not ready for that," Carl said. "Besides, I can't take care of my ranch at a distance."

"You don't have to stay in town, just come in at night," Will said.

"Are you going to ask Idalou to marry you?" Carl demanded.

If Idalou thought that question would throw Will as badly as it threw her, she was mistaken. Will didn't blink. "If that's what I'm thinking, don't you think I ought to talk to Idalou first?"

Idalou held back the surge of hope. He'd practically said he wanted to marry her, but maybe Carl had forced his hand when he was still undecided.

"You've have had plenty of time to do that before now," Carl said.

"Whenever we've gotten close, there have been interruptions—your fight with Van, for example," Will said in a tone that didn't carry blame.

Now it was Carl's turn to be flustered. "Most people think Van is just spoiled and thoughtless because his mother died when he was a kid, but he's really a cruel bastard. He doesn't even like Mara, yet he's perfectly happy to marry her in order to get Jordan's ranch."

"I don't plan on dying anytime soon," Jordan said. "I'm still a relatively young man."

"Even young men have accidents," Carl said.

"We're getting away from the problem at hand," Will said. "Can we all agree on how to proceed for the next few days?"

"Your plan is okay by me, but I'm not staying in town," Carl said. "I don't relish being accepted by Jordan simply because there's no other choice."

"Nobody's saying that," Idalou said. "Besides, if you love Mara, why should Jordan's opinion make a difference?"

"For the same reason you won't let Will ask you to marry him because we owe him money. It makes me uncomfortable, and I don't like that."

"Now that you've found the bull, Idalou doesn't have that excuse any longer, does she?" Lloyd asked with what Idalou could only characterize as a sly grin.

Idalou felt heat flood her face. "We're not talking about me."

"I need to get back to town," Will said. "I'll take Jordan. Lloyd, do you mind letting Idalou and Mara ride with you? If Idalou doesn't hurry, she'll be late for work."

Idalou had disliked working in Ella's dress shop at

first, but eventually she'd come to like it. The job helped take her mind off her troubles. It also required her to interact more with the ladies of Dunmore, something she had never done but found she liked. The money she earned gave her a sense of independence and security. She didn't feel quite so vulnerable, so dependent on Will. She didn't know much about clothes, but Ella said she knew more about salesmanship than Junie Mae.

"I don't want Mara staying by herself," Jordan said.

"Either Junie Mae or I will stay with her." Idalou paused. "I hope Will is right about you," she said to Jordan. "I'd hate to think of Carl marrying the daughter of a criminal."

"I can't believe you're going along with this," Jordan replied. "You hate me so much, I was certain you'd be doing your best to have me sent to prison."

"I've disagreed with Will before and been wrong every time. This time I'm going to trust him."

"I didn't do it," Jordan said. "When I get out of this mess, I promise I'll pay you for every calf sired by your bull. Is it okay to let the sheriff decide what's a fair price?"

Idalou glanced at Will. "I think that's a perfect solution. Now I'd better go tell Mara what we have planned for her."

She also needed to find a way to be alone with Will long enough to tell him what was in her heart. She'd denied her feelings long enough, been afraid of them and the danger they posed to her self-control. That fear had ended up isolating her from everyone, including her brother. Living in town had underscored just how much she'd missed. She was determined she wasn't going to miss the chance to be with Will.

* * *

"How can I run away and defy my father when that's exactly what he wants me to do?" Mara demanded.

"He wants you to *pretend*. You intend to really do it. That makes it very different."

"It doesn't feel that way," Mara said, pouting.

Idalou hoped that Mara's bad mood was the result of Carl refusal to see her rather than a childish bout of temper. She couldn't hold it against Mara that she'd been spoiled by a rich father and an indulgent mother, but she hoped Carl would hold off on marrying her long enough to see if Mara could mature.

"Are you really going to run away?" Junie Mae asked.

Junie Mae rarely left the hotel room, so she was delighted at the aspect of having some company, and Idalou was relieved of having to feel guilty for not wanting to spend every minute of her spare time there.

"If I have to," Mara replied.

"Where will you go?" Junie Mae asked.

"Carl is going to marry me," she said.

"Carl loves you," Idalou said, "but he'll never marry you unless he's absolutely sure he's the only one you love."

"He is," Mara insisted. "I was stupid, but I'm over it now. I wouldn't marry Van if he were the last man on earth."

"I think you ought to marry the man you love," Idalou said, "but don't forget that Van is the son of a wealthy father. He can give you all the things you're used to, all the things Carl can't."

"I don't care about that," Mara declared. "I'll live in a tent and wash clothes in the creek before I'll marry anyone else."

"Junie Mae and I will leave you to unpack and rest a bit before supper," Idalou said. "Our room is next door, so you only have to bang on the wall if you need anything." Idalou left Mara in hopes that her spirits would improve after she'd had a chance to rest.

"Why is she so angry at Van?" Junie Mae asked when they were in their own room. "I thought she liked him."

"She's angry because Van started the fights with Carl. And Carl's angry because he says if Mara hadn't encouraged Van to think she liked him, he wouldn't have had any reason to start a fight. Instead of things getting better between Mara and Carl, they're getting worse. It might be better if she did marry Van. I'm sure he doesn't love her like Carl does, but being in love has only made Mara unhappy so far."

It hadn't been good for Idalou, either. It hadn't helped her stop being upset that Will seemed to put Junie Mae's welfare before hers.

"I need to tell you something," Junie Mae said, "but I'm afraid you'll think very badly of me."

Idalou reached out and grasped Junie Mae's hands. "You know I won't. We all make mistakes."

"Mine was the worst kind possible. What makes it even worse is that I was so stupid."

"You thought you loved him?"

Junie Mae nodded. "I thought he loved me, too. He said he did. For a while I thought he was the most wonderful man I'd ever met. I hadn't gotten over my parents' deaths when Webb died. I didn't love him," she hastened to tell Idalou, "but I did like him. Aunt Ella didn't understand how badly Webb's death upset me, but he said he did. He comforted me, spent hours letting me talk though all the things that frightened me, made me feel like I was the most important person in the world to him. I would have done anything for him." She looked down at her stomach. "Obviously, I did too much."

"You don't have to tell me any of this," Idalou said. "I won't judge you."

"I've already judged myself worse than anybody else can. I need to tell you why Will is helping me. I know it upsets you."

"It doesn't. Really." Inside she was roiling with doubt. She'd convinced herself that Will wasn't in love with Junie Mae and wasn't the father of her baby. She didn't want to hear anything that might resurrect her doubts.

"I don't believe you," Junie Mae said. "I know he loves you and you love him, but you've always felt that he gives me too much of his attention. He does it because he's the kindest and most considerate man I've ever met. You can't believe how lucky you are that he loves you."

Idalou was increasingly uncomfortable with this conversation.

"I know it hurt you when people were whispering that this might be Will's baby. I hope you never thought it was, but you had every right to think I should have told who the father is. I've never told anybody, not even Will, but he saw me when I told the father. Will saw him yell at me that it wasn't his baby. He saw him tell me he wanted nothing to do with me and to keep away from him. I had collapsed, was crying in the alley behind my aunt's store. Right then and there I vowed my baby would never know he had that kind of father."

"Why are you telling me all of this?" Idalou asked.

"Because I have to break my vow and tell you."

"No, you don't."

"Yes, I do, because he has the power to do great damage to an innocent woman."

"What are you talking about?"

"He wants to marry Mara. If he does, he'll destroy her life."

Idalou thought her strength would give out. "I don't believe you! Carl would never—"

"It's not Carl. He loves Mara."

"Then who—"

Junie Mae didn't have to break her vow. Idalou knew who she was talking about. "I can't believe Van would do anything like that."

"I was unhappy, scared, and very foolish," Junie Mae said. "When he offered me comfort, I couldn't turn it down, not even after I knew at what price it came. I think he liked me well enough to marry me, but not at the expense of his father's plans for him to marry Mara. Not even his own child was that important to him."

Tears had filled Junie Mae's eyes and spilled onto her cheeks. She brushed them away.

"I'm going to live with Will's parents until after my baby is born. They've offered to give me a home for as long as I need one. I'll never be able to repay Will for what he's done. That's the reason I'll be glad to keep Mara company. It's the first thing I've been able to do to repay him for his kindness."

"A lot of people owe Will a great deal for his kindness, not the least of whom is myself," Idalou said. "I'm ashamed to admit I haven't trusted him nearly as much as I should have."

"You're a strong-willed woman," Junie Mae said. "You don't like to feel that you need anyone. I'm just the opposite, which is why I got into trouble."

Being strong-willed and stubborn had gotten Idalou into trouble. Will said he liked her because of those characteristics, but it was easy to see how he could dislike her for exactly the same reasons. "It's not a bad thing to need someone," Idalou said to Junie Mae. "I suspect Will likes the fact that you need him. He once told me he's the youngest in his family, that everybody always spoiled him and did things for him. He probably hasn't had much chance to prove he can take care of someone else. I think a man likes that."

It wouldn't be so bad to let Will take care of her. She hadn't realized it until now, but she sort of liked the idea. She'd been so busy taking care of Carl and the ranch, she'd never thought of anybody taking care of her.

Until she'd met Will, she hadn't known any man she'd trust to take care of her. Webb had had a streak of immaturity, a daredevil impulse to try something just because it was dangerous. She'd always been the one to advise restraint, to make plans.

Will tended to hang back and think before deciding what to do. He made light of his success and took his responsibilities seriously. He made promises he didn't need to make, yet he always kept them. He put himself out for people, yet didn't hold their mistakes against them. He was ready to believe the best of people without being blind to the worst.

He was the finest man she had ever met, and she had done her damnedest to lose him.

"You two don't need me for this conversation," Will said to Carl and Mara.

"I want you to stay," Carl said. "I can't always figure out how to say what I mean. I might need you to help me."

That was just about the most ridiculous statement Will had ever heard. He hadn't managed to make one simple statement to Idalou—*I love you*—yet Carl thought Will could help him unravel what was going on in his teenage mind.

"I want you to stay, too," Mara said. "Carl never believes anything I say."

This was getting even better. There wasn't a man alive who could fathom how the female mind worked, especially the strong-willed, stubborn type. He hadn't been able to figure out how his mother and sisters' minds worked, and he'd been around them for twenty years. Mara was as impressionable as she was impassioned, a combustible mixture if there ever was one.

"I'll stay, but if things start getting rough, I'm running out the back door."

Will settled in a chair at his desk and waited, but neither Carl nor Mara seemed to know where to start. "Nothing's going to get decided unless one of you starts talking," he said.

"He already knows what I want to say," Mara said. "I love him and want to marry him."

"And I've already told her that she's changed her mind so many times, I don't know what to believe," Carl said.

"She's young and has been under a lot of pressure," Will pointed out.

"Like I haven't, with her father trying to ruin us."

"What about your sister blaming my father for everything that happened? Why do you think Webb broke up with her?"

"It's not going to help if you two start dragging up every problem from the past," Will said. "Concentrate on what you *really* feel now, what you *really* want."

He had the answer to both questions for himself. He just hadn't been able to coax Idalou into forgetting about the things happening around her and concentrate on what was happening *inside*.

"It's not that easy," Carl said. "Mara's supposed to pretend she'd run away from her father because he won't let her marry me, but how do I know she wants to?"

"You were there when I told Daddy I wasn't going to marry Van no matter what he did," Mara said. "They came up with this plan after that."

"She's right," Will said.

"It's not just that," Carl said. "She'll be marrying a poor man. And don't say it won't matter because your father's rich," he said when Mara started to speak. "What kind of man would I be if I let my wife's father support me?"

"I understand what you're saying and agree with you." Will could easily understand the boy's pride, his need to be able to stand on his own two feet. "But don't discount the possibility that Jordan might have a legitimate job for you. It won't be supporting you if he makes use of your skills."

"People will still think he's supporting me."

Will had seen this sudden burgeoning of tender self-esteem in his own brothers. Jake and Isabelle had been careful to nurture it. With all the trouble Carl had had, it must be even more important to establish himself as a man.

"There's something else," Carl said. "I don't want to be responsible for coming between Mara and her parents. They're the only family she's got. I think it would just about kill her mother to know she had grandchildren a short distance away that she couldn't see."

"It won't be that way," Mara said. "Mama and Daddy want me to be happy. Once they see I'm happy with you, they'll change their minds."

Will could see that Carl wasn't convinced. It wasn't hard to understand why. Will had seen nothing in Jordan or his wife to make such a change of heart likely.

"I think we ought to wait until this whole thing with Van's father is over," Carl said. "Once we know who's responsible for all the trouble, we can try to sort everything out and figure out our feelings for each other. Right now everything's too mixed up."

"I'm not mixed up," Mara insisted. "I love you. I always will."

"I love you, too," Carl said, "but I'm not ready to talk about getting married. You need to grow up more. Maybe I do, too."

Mara tried to convince Carl to change his mind, but he held firm. After he left, Mara sobbed on Will's shoulder until the front of his shirt was damp with her tears. He tried to be sympathetic, yet he couldn't help wondering why of all the women who insisted upon throwing themselves at him, one of them couldn't have been Idalou. It was probably his fault. He'd been too polite, too understanding, too willing to stand back and not put any pressure on her. And maybe he'd been a little too willing to go to the aid of any female in trouble. Isabelle had taught him to respect a woman's independence and to help any woman in need. What she hadn't taught him was that both those admirable traits could combine to work against what he really wanted.

He had a few lines of his own to untangle.

Chapter Twenty-one

Idalou hadn't managed to see Will all day. Either she was working or he was out of his office. She'd finally given up and decided to try again tomorrow.

"Are you sure you don't mind staying with Mara tonight?" she asked Junie Mae.

"I enjoy it," Junie Mae said. "We have a lot to talk about." Junie Mae looked at Mara, who was blushing. "She wants to have lots of children and wants to know what it's like to have a baby."

"My mother said the last four months were the hardest," Idalou said. Her mother hadn't wanted any more children after Carl. "Your aunt asked how you were getting along. I think she's sorry she made you move out."

"I think she really does like me and would probably learn to like the baby," Junie Mae said, "but she couldn't forgive me for not telling her who the father was."

"Do some people still think it's Will?" Mara asked.

Idalou hoped her blushes didn't give her away. She'd never truly *believed* Will had fathered Junie Mae's baby, because common sense told her the timing wasn't right. It was just jealousy that had kept her from thinking straight. And fear that if she stopped guarding her heart, she'd get hurt again.

Now she wanted Will to know she had put all of that behind her. No more doubt, no more excuses for not admitting her feelings. No more putting everything else in her life before herself. Will was the best thing that had ever happened to her, and she didn't want to lose him.

"There'll always be speculation as long as Junie Mae refuses to name the father," Idalou said, "but Will doesn't live here and Junie Mae is leaving, so I expect people will forget about it in a few months."

She stopped by Will's room, but she wasn't surprised that she got no answer when she knocked on the door. The priviledge of providing the sheriff with supper had expanded until it covered providing him with entertainment for the evening, too. Idalou had heard that Will had had to sit through adolescents singing, playing the piano, and even dancing. She hoped he was being liberally supplied with whiskey. Even Edwina Sullivan, Dunmore's legitimate star performer, was hard to take now that she was years past her prime. With Will's background, he was surely accustomed to the best theater San Antonio and Galveston had to offer.

That thought depressed her even more. She didn't know anything about San Antonio or Galveston. She probably wasn't sophisticated enough even for San Angelo, which was nothing compared to Fort Worth or Dallas, neither of which compared to San Antonio or Galveston. She couldn't imagine why Will would fall in love with anyone like her. What did he see in her? What could they have in common?

She reached her room. She lit a lamp and settled into a chair by the window. In the dark street below, lights from the saloon penetrated the darkness like long, tawny spears. Sounds of music, laughter, shouts, even subdued conversation drifting up on the soft evening air, contrasting with the heaviness that settled inside her. She'd always been weighed down by worries and troubles, but they had never seemed so terrible until Will showed her what her life could be if she would just let go of everything.

She wanted to, *she already had*, but she was afraid it was too late. She had never let herself want the kind of love he offered. She hadn't believed it existed, hadn't believed that men like Will existed.

A knock at the door caused her to jump.

"Idalou, are you in there?"

Will. She leaped to her feet, practically ran the short distance to the door, and wrenched it open. The man she saw standing before her caused her heart to swell until she could barely breathe. How could she not have realized she was in love with him days ago, maybe even weeks? Mara had been dazzled by him on first sight. Junie Mae would have married him in a flash. Nearly every female in Dunmore grew warm at the sight of him, yet she was so distrustful that she hadn't been able to see that this man was unlike any she'd ever known.

"I was hoping to talk with you before you went to bed," she said, opening the door so he could enter the room. "There are some things I need to tell you."

Will didn't move. "Maybe we ought to talk in the lobby or my office. Or we could take a walk."

"Are you afraid I'll take advantage of you?" She couldn't believe she'd asked such a question. "Come in before somebody hears our conversation and takes it all wrong."

Will hesitated a moment before entering the room and closing the door behind him. "I suppose you want to know if Sonnenberg has heard that Mara has run away to marry Carl?"

"Yes, but that's not what I wanted to talk about."

"Lloyd told him when he was in the bank this afternoon. He didn't appear to care one way or the other."

"Frank Sonnenberg is not a man to show what he's thinking. Sometimes I think even Van doesn't know what his father is thinking," Idalou said.

After what Junie Mae had told her, she was too disgusted with Van to be interested in what he might be doing or thinking. She couldn't believe she'd misjudged his character so badly. She turned away from Will, walked over to the window, then turned back to face him. He was still standing at the door looking uncomfortable. Could he have decided he didn't love her anymore and was waiting for a chance to tell her? Had she rebuffed him so many times he'd given up and just wanted to take his bull and go home? He didn't look like a man in love, only a man who was unhappy to be here.

She tried to ignore the sinking feeling in her stomach, the nausea that filled her throat. He couldn't have stopped loving her. She couldn't have waited too long. She had to have one last chance.

"Now that Carl has found the bull, you aren't in debt anymore," Will said.

She didn't want to talk about the bull. She didn't care about the ranch as long as Carl wasn't going to lose it. She didn't care whether Jordan spent one night or ten years in jail. And at the moment, she really wasn't interested in what Van or his father might be planning. She wanted to tell Will that she'd been wrong to hold back so long, that she loved him and hoped he still loved her.

"The debt will be one less thing to stand between us," Will said.

Will's words were like a barrier being torn down, pressure being released, the breaking of fear's paralyzing grip.

"I didn't mean to make it a barrier between us," she said before she could lose her nerve. "I don't know why I held back from you. I suppose I was too afraid that what we felt wasn't real and I would be hurt again."

"Did losing Webb hurt that much?"

She couldn't tell whether he was sad for her or sad because another man had apparently meant more to her than he did, but his hurt drew her away from the window toward him.

"It wasn't losing Webb that hurt so badly," she said. "It was my belief that I wasn't worthy of being loved. All the other stuff just made it worse."

Will seemed to relax, move a few inches away from the door. "Is that why you never believed I loved you?"

Loved you. He hadn't said *love* you. He'd said *loved.* Did that mean he'd fallen out of love with her, that she'd been so standoffish he'd given up and was going home?

"That and a lot of other things," she said. "But that's not true anymore. I realized I was being very unfair to you. I didn't blame you for the things that had happened to me, but I expected you to act like everybody else. I've never known anybody like you, so I didn't know what to do. I know that's not an adequate excuse, but it's all I have."

Will came closer, reached for the two hands Idalou

was twisting in front of her. He covered her hands with his before gently prying them apart. He caressed them, treating them as though they were the soft hands of some elegant woman rather than the rough hands of a woman who'd worked all her life. "What are you trying to tell me?" he asked when he looked into her eyes.

For a moment Idalou was afraid the words wouldn't come out. She swallowed to moisten her throat, to release the tension. "I'm trying to say I love you," she managed in a half whisper. "I think I have for some time. I just was too afraid to admit it."

She didn't know exactly what response she'd been expecting, but Will's lack of reaction frightened her.

"I wanted to tell you before now," she said, hoping his love hadn't died completely, "but I couldn't. I don't know why other things bothered me so much, but every time I tried to tell you, something stopped me."

"You're a proud woman, Idalou Ellsworth," Will said. "That's a good thing to be, but sometimes pride can get in the way of happiness. I'm just as much at fault as you. I watched my brother close himself off from the world because of fear. I decided I was never going to let anything have that kind of control over me. I went so far in the other direction, people thought I didn't care about anything. I just sat still and watched life go by. It took me a long time to realize I wasn't protecting myself. I was isolating myself from life, from all the things that made being alive worthwhile."

"You haven't stopped helping people," Idalou said.

"I didn't help you that first day. I had good reasons for not doing it, but I was angry at myself in spite of my reasons. I knew right then there was something different about you."

Idalou felt embarrassed. She hadn't started liking

him until a long time after that. "Why would you be attracted to anyone as rude as I was?"

"You were the first woman who didn't care about my looks. I knew right then you weren't going to be impressed by my family's money, either. I was going to have to impress you on my own. That challenged me, but it was also what I wanted. No man wants to think a woman likes him just for his looks and his money."

Idalou felt guilty that Will was giving her too much credit. "I'm no more immune to your looks than any other woman," she confessed. "I only acted the way I did because I was upset. I knew you were right, but the threat of losing the ranch had made me so angry at the world, I couldn't be fair. I didn't even want to."

Will's smile remained in check. She could tell that something was still bothering him.

"What about Junie Mae?" he asked.

Idalou looked away. "I was jealous of all the attention you gave her, the way she felt free to touch you, lean on you, cry on your shoulder. I couldn't convince myself you weren't going to turn to her just like Webb had. When neither of you would tell me who the baby's father was, I was convinced you were hiding some secret. Few things are more maddening than thinking the man you love shares a secret with another woman."

"Is everything that stood between us out of the way now?" Will asked.

"Yes."

"Then if I tell you I love you, you won't back away?"

The relief that surged through her was so enormous, she felt weak in the knees. "No. I promise I won't back away."

"Would you meet me halfway?"

"I think I can do that." She would have gone all the way on her own if necessary.

They came together, his arms around her waist, her arms around his neck. She could hardly believe how good it felt to be so close to him. He'd held her before, kissed her, but something had always stood between them, kept her from being able to concentrate on just the two of them. Things were different now. *She* was different. She could go to Will with an open and trusting heart.

She wanted love to make everything perfect, cast light into all the dark corners of her world, provide answers for all the mysteries, assure her that the future held nothing but happiness for her and everyone she loved. She was too old and too experienced to believe that could happen, but she was young enough to hope. Love had been able to transform her life, eliminate her fears. If it could do that, then everything else must be possible, too.

"You're thinking again," Will chided with a smile.

"Am I not allowed to think?"

"Isabelle assures me that a woman truly in love is beyond the reach of reason. She's not sure that a man is capable of reason even before the malady of love has descended upon him."

Idalou wanted to meet this woman who had had such a powerful influence on Will, the woman she was convinced had made him the man he'd become. "Surely she doesn't believe love is a sickness."

"She swears it's the only reason she's been able to put up with Jake for these twenty years."

"What do you think?"

"I think she loves him so much she doesn't see any faults, so she has to create some failings just to make him mortal."

Idalou wondered if it was possible that Will would

ever love her that much. She didn't think he was without fault, but he did come close to being perfect. She wasn't perfect and never would be. There was nothing remarkable about her, while he was the most remarkable man she'd ever known.

"That must be nice for Jake," Idalou said.

Will broke out laughing. "The last thing Jake wants is to be thought of as perfect. He'll do something just to make Isabelle argue with him. I used to be afraid that one of them would leave and destroy the only real home I'd ever known. I finally realized that arguing is just one of the ways they show their love."

No wonder she couldn't understand how Will could love her. She didn't understand how fighting could be a way of showing love. She'd only had her mother's slavish adoration of her father as an example. She knew she'd argue with Will if she thought he was wrong. She already had.

"Is that why you never fell out of love with me?" she asked.

"I never had a reason to fall out of love with you," Will said and kissed her nose. "You were adorable from the very beginning."

"Men don't like their wives to argue with them."

"I won't mind. It'll keep me from taking you for granted."

It was hard to think with him kissing her ears, but she had to be sure. "What if I don't agree with you?"

"We'll figure something out."

He kissed her eyes. The temptation to forget everything but Will was nearly overpowering, but she persevered. "What happens if we can't work something out?"

"Then we ask Jake or Isabelle to arbitrate." He kissed the side of her mouth. "They'll probably side with you." He kissed the side of her neck. "They'll probably advise against marrying me, but I hope you won't listen to them."

He was kissing her throat. Webb had never done anything like this. Why had she ever thought she was in love with him? Compared to Will, he faded into insignificance. "You haven't asked me to marry you."

He nuzzled her. "See? I never can get things right."

Maybe he didn't do everything by the rules, but Idalou couldn't see anything wrong with the way he did things. If he didn't stop turning her mind to mush with his kisses, she wouldn't be able to think at all.

Not that she wanted to think. It was nearly impossible to resist the temptation to turn off her mind and just let Will take her to a place where she'd be cocooned in his embrace. All her life she'd carried enormous burdens that squeezed the joy out of her, burdens that had turned her into an adult years ahead of time, burdens that had pitted her against men of greater power, that had forced her into battles she couldn't win, that had turned her into a combative woman men avoided.

"You do want me to marry you, don't you?" he asked.

"Only if you promise to let me kiss you like this every night."

Will had gotten her worked up into such a state she couldn't think, but she decided thinking was overrated. Thinking had driven Webb away. Thinking had turned her into a termagant men avoided. She made a vow to think a whole lot less in the future, and not at all when she was in Will's arms.

"Only if you let me win every argument," she said, wanting to see if his brain was in the same sorry state as hers.

His hands were taking inventory of her back. "I probably should warn you that I won't play fair. I'll search out your weaknesses and take shameless advantage of them. I'll lay siege to your strengths until I've completely undermined them."

"Are you saying you're unprincipled?"

"Completely."

"That you'll try to take advantage of me?"

"Every time I can."

"Will you feel remorse?"

"Why do it if you're going to feel sorry?"

Idalou had a feeling Will had just confessed to a woeful lack of character, but all she could think about was his kisses and her desire to kiss him back. Discussions of character could be saved for a day when it was cold, raining, and he was late to sit down to the hot dinner she'd worked hard to have ready on time. Right now it was summer, the air was warm, and she couldn't think of a single reason to complain.

Idalou didn't know how long she stood there letting Will kiss her, kissing him in return, and wondering in a vague sort of way why she had waited so long for something this wonderful.

"I'd better go."

Will's words pulled her out of the safe world she'd found in his arms.

"Why?"

"You need to rest. You have to work tomorrow."

"I don't need to go to bed just yet. Are you really tired?"

"No."

The question hung in the air between them. She knew it was up to her to make the decision. It seemed like a huge step, one far too important to be decided without a lot of thought, but this wasn't just a question of logic or what was best in the long run. It came down to what she wanted, and of that she was very sure.

"I ought to go," Will said.

"Don't."

She undid a few buttons on his shirt and slipped her hand inside. She was stunned by her brazen act but exhilarated at the same time. It wasn't just that her hand was splayed against the warm skin of the man she loved, it was the implication that her action implied.

Her lips could never have framed the words, but she was asking Will to make love to her. It was impossible to resist moving her hand across the expanse of his chest, to resist running her fingers through the soft mat of blond hair. Though she'd been around men all her life, had seen them in various stages of undress, had danced with and been held by them, she'd given very little thought to the structure and appearance of the male body. It left her at a disadvantage in knowing how to continue what she'd begun. Fortunately, Will didn't have any such problem.

With a deftness she'd someday ask how he'd acquired, he undid the buttons at the back of her blouse. The feel of his hand against the bare flesh of her back caused her to freeze. More clearly than her hand on Will's chest, Will's hand on her back brought home what she'd asked him to do. She was about to make an important commitment. She was saying she wanted to be this man's wife for the rest of her life. And she wanted him to be her husband.

It was exactly what she had been wanting for some time but hadn't been able to admit. It no longer mattered that she'd thought she had a dozen reasons to question Will's intentions, even more reasons to hold back, to doubt that she was meant to find such happiness. A life with Will was what she wanted, was *everything* she wanted, and she couldn't wait to take that first step, to make the kind of commitment that said there was no turning back.

It took only a few practiced movements for him to slip her arms out of her blouse and let it fall suspended from her waist, where it was tucked inside her skirt. Only a thin cotton chemise preserved her modesty. Yet it didn't feel like that when Will began placing kisses on her bare shoulders. It felt incredibly decadent, but she didn't care. She'd never felt so close to rapture in her life. Never had she expected that following her heart instead of her head would have such exhilarating results. She wished she'd done it sooner.

Will was laying a line of kisses from her shoulder down her arm to her elbow. His lips sent shivers racing through her body. How could she have guessed that an elbow could be so sensitive? An elbow! She'd leaned on it for years and never felt a thing, but the moment Will kissed it, it felt like the most erotic part of her body. Now he was kissing her arm all the way down to her wrist, her fingers, her open palm. A little more and she was sure she would melt where she stood.

That was what she thought until he started kissing her neck and gradually moved up to her ears. She didn't know how she could have survived so long without realizing that every part of her body could be turned into an erogenous zone. It was like discovering herself all over again, being given a new way of looking at a body she'd given very little thought to during her life. It was just there. What was there to know about it?

More than she could have ever imagined.

The sound of a soft moan drew scant attention until she realized it was her own voice she was hearing. Despite being slightly embarrassed at her vocal response, she gave herself wholeheartedly to Will's ministrations. It didn't matter that nearly everything she was experiencing was new and unexpected, even a little unnerving. It only mattered that she'd finally been able to give herself to Will, and that he loved her.

Will cupped one breast in his hand, and her nipples grew firm and sensitive to the soft cotton of her chemise rubbing against them. In a flash, all the sensitivity from the distant parts of her body converged on that single breast until she could barely endure his touch. When Will slipped her chemise off her shoulders to expose both breasts, she was certain she couldn't endure it. But that was nothing compared to the feelings that assaulted her when he gently massaged her nipples with his fingertips. The strength went out of her legs, and she sagged against him.

Will swept her up in his arms and carried her to the bed. Rather than laying her down as she expected, he sat her up, then got down on his knees to remove her shoes. The feel of his hands on her feet, her ankles, her calves as he removed her stockings caused her to tremble. When it came to Will's touch, her entire body was an erogenous zone. Next Will stood her up so he could remove her shirt and chemise. Once that was done, he laid her down on the bed.

She felt awkward lying before him stripped of her clothing while he was still fully dressed. "You, too," she said, her voice a thread, barely more than a whisper.

"I thought you'd never ask," Will said with the smile that always made her knees feel like jelly. Only this time there was something more. It was in the set of his mouth, the darkening of his eyes, the slight huskiness of his voice. He hadn't finished removing his clothes before she realized it was also in the altered shape of his body.

She moved over when Will lay down on the bed next to her. For a moment she didn't breathe, just lay there waiting to find out what he would do next. She knew what was supposed to happen, what she *wanted* to happen, but she was nervous, unsure, wondering what Will would do when he realized she had no idea what to do. She felt incapable of movement, barely capable of thought. She certainly didn't know how to move smoothly from one phase of lovemaking to another. She tensed when Will placed his hand palm down on her stomach.

"We don't have to do this if you'd rather not."

Chapter Twenty-two

Idalou was grateful to Will for leaving the decision to go any further up to her. She didn't know how he could gracefully withdraw from the present situation, but she didn't want him to leave. She was here because she wanted to be with him, to love him, to experience being loved in a way she'd never thought possible.

"I'm a little anxious, but I'm sure." She moved over to give Will more room, but he immediately moved closer to her.

"Just tell me if anything upsets you, and I'll stop."

"It's not that," she said, not wanting him to think she was getting cold feet. "It's just that I don't know what to do, don't know what to expect."

"This is supposed to be a good experience, to make you feel absolutely wonderful. If it doesn't, it's my fault."

He was tracing designs on the inside of her arm, sending more sensations spiraling through her to create havoc in her normally well-controlled body. When he moved down her side, she was caught between sucking in her breath and giggling because it tickled. Before she could ruin the mood and severely damage his ego by laughing, he moved his hand over her stomach to her breast. Leaning on his elbow, he teased first one breast, then the other, cupping it in his warm hand, rubbing her pebble-hard nipple with the tips of his fingers, squeezing it between his thumb and forefinger.

But that was nothing compared to the shocks that ricocheted through her body when he took her nipple into his mouth. She gasped and her body went rigid. She'd never felt anything so intense in her entire life. He sucked her nipple, laved it with his tongue, nipped at it with his teeth, until she thought she'd explode from the tension. She squirmed from side to side, but she couldn't escape him. She pushed against him, but that only increased the force of their contact. She clutched his head only to realize she was drawing him against her rather than pushing him away.

When he finally abandoned her tortured breasts, she didn't know whether to cry out in relief or protest. The trail of kisses he laid across her abdomen kept her from feeling abandoned. She'd never known that any part of her body could be so acutely sensitive to touch. She felt wrung out, barely having the energy to move.

Until Will's hand reached the inside of her thigh.

An electric shock surged from one end of her body to the other, reviving her so abruptly she felt dizzy. She must have gasped.

"There's nothing to be frightened of," Will said. "It won't hurt."

She didn't know right away what *it* was. But when she felt Will's fingers part her and enter, she did.

Her entire body grew rigid, waiting, anticipating, fearing . . . what?

It didn't hurt, but she felt invaded. His fingers inside her felt stimulating, slightly uncomfortable, slightly . . . "Aaaaah!"

"Did I hurt you?" Will asked, concern in his voice.

She couldn't speak, only shake her head. Will had done something, touched something, moved something, that practically made her see stars. Even her eyes watered. As he gently moved his fingers inside her, she could feel warmth grow and fill her belly. Her body seemed to relax around him, to welcome him, even draw him in. It didn't take long for the warmth to become heat and the heat to become fire. Idalou's body couldn't remain still. She moved from side to side, even rose off the bed to force Will deeper inside. Then he did that *thing* again, and she did rise off the bed.

"What are you doing ?" she managed to ask.

"Trying to give you as much pleasure as possible."

He was doing it again, making it impossible for her to think, impossible to care about anything except what he was doing to her. Her moans turned to groans which grew in volume until she was certain she would start screaming. She'd never experienced anything that gripped her with such force, that suspended her between the extremes of agony and ecstasy, that made her certain she couldn't stand it for another moment yet hoped it would never stop, that made her want to pull away at the same moment she wanted to drive Will deeper inside her. Words begging him to stop rose to her lips even though she bit her tongue to keep from uttering them. The vise tightened, twisted her insides until she couldn't breathe. She opened her mouth, but no sound came out.

Then the tension crested, broke, and she felt wave after wave of pleasure. Little by little, the tension eased until she could gasp for air, until her body could relax enough to sink into the softness of the mattress beneath her.

But before she could completely unravel the coils that encircled her, Will rose above her and slowly entered her. She was certain she couldn't contain him, but he continued to sink into her until he'd penetrated her fully. At first she was aware of little beyond the fullness, but as he moved within her, the sensations of only moments ago returned. Only this time Will's face showed that he, too, was being subjected to the exquisite torture she'd endured only moments ago. Knowing that they were experiencing it at the same time, together, joined as one, added a new dimension that was as welcome as it was unanticipated.

Everything was more beautiful, more intense, more important to her because she was sharing it with Will. *It isn't him or me. It's us.* As her body began to respond to his, rising to meet him and falling away to rise again, the familiar coils circled her body, but it was different this time. It wasn't just an amazingly intense physical experience. It was love as she'd never known it could be. Will gave to her, and she gave back to him in equal measure. The intensity of the experience affected him as strongly as it did her.

Throwing her arms around him, she clung to him, matched his kisses with her own, heard her moans an octave above the guttural sounds that were torn from his throat. When the rhythm of his movements became erratic, then culminated in one final thrust, she felt him release himself within her in a burst of warm seed. That was more than enough to send her over the edge as they floated off into ecstasy together.

Idalou woke with an unaccountable feeling of happiness filling her. She lay for several moments with her eyes closed, luxuriating in a kind of joy that was totally unfamiliar. She didn't know why she should feel this way, but she didn't care. It was too wonderful to question. But the moment she stretched and felt the soreness between her legs, everything came back with blinding vividness. Will had made love to her last night, twice, and she was naked. She reached to the other side of the bed, but her hand met only emptiness. She saw the note when she sat up and turned to look at the rumpled bed. It was short.

> *I hated to leave but thought it was best. I don't know what I'll have to do today, but save the evening for me. I promise I won't linger over supper.*
>
> Will

Idalou read the note several times before kissing it, pressing it to her bosom, and falling back against the pillows with a contented smile on her face. Will had left, but he couldn't wait to be with her again. She didn't know if she could concentrate well enough to do her work for Ella Hoffman. She'd probably give customers the wrong dresses and they'd come back to the shop angry about the mixup.

Idalou wouldn't care. She scrunched down in the bed with a smile on her face. She ought to get up and make sure Junie Mae and Mara were all right, but she didn't want to move, didn't want to shred the gossamer threads of happiness that encased her. She wanted to feel like this forever.

It was hard to believe that something as simple as being in love could make her feel so absolutely fabulous. From now on, everything in her life would be wonderful. There'd be problems, but none she and Will couldn't work out. When you loved a man as much as she loved him, nothing else was really important. His happiness was all that mattered, because she finally believed that Will loved her, and only her, as deeply as she loved him.

No more worries about the ranch or Carl. Now that they'd found the bull, Carl could rebuild or sell as he wanted. The ranch was his. She didn't want to have to think about it ever again. No more worries about whether it was Jordan or Frank who was trying to ruin them. Will had already figured everything out and laid a trap for Sonnenberg. In a few days, it would all be over and she'd leave with Will to meet his family. She'd be going to meet her future. She jumped out of bed and reached for her clothes.

She could barely wait.

Idalou knew something was wrong when Junie Mae showed up at Ella's shop. The girl hadn't seen or spoken to her aunt since the day she was told to leave the Hoffmans' house.

"What are you doing here?" Ella Hoffman asked her niece, but Junie Mae ignored her and went straight to Idalou.

"Mara is gone, and Carl has gone after her," she said

"Are you sure?" Idalou asked. "She could have gone to see her mother."

Junie Mae shook her head. "She went to meet Carl. At least that's what her note said, but Carl said he hadn't sent any note, that it must be a trap, and he was going after her." Junie Mae pulled two pieces of paper from her pocket and handed them to Idalou. "Here. Read them yourself."

The first letter was brief and printed in block letters. It said:

> *I'm sorry for everything I said. I love you and want to marry you. Meet me at our favorite tree at noon today. I can't wait for us to be man and wife. Your loving husband-to-be,*
>
> > *Carl*

The second note was equally short

> *Junie Mae,*
> *I just got the most wonderful note from Carl. He does love me and wants to marry me. I'm going to meet him at our favorite tree. Tell Idalou not to worry. I'll be back in-time for supper unless Carl wants us to elope.*
>
> > *Mara*

"She left without waking me," Junie Mae said. "I didn't see the note until Carl came asking to see Mara. His face went white when he read it. I didn't see the first note until after Carl had run out of the hotel saying he had to go after Mara as soon as he got his rifle. I went to look for Will, but he had gone out to see about some cut fences. Emmett says Will won't be back until late."

Idalou didn't know who'd written that first note, though she could guess, but she knew that someone could get killed if anything happened to Mara.

"I have to go after Carl," Idalou said to Ella. "No telling what might happen if someone's not there to stop him from going crazy."

"You should wait for the sheriff," Ella said. "Things like this are his job."

"He's already doing *his job* working for this town,"

Idalou said. "Carl is my brother. Making sure Carl's safe is my job."

"What can you do?" Ella asked. "You're just a woman."

"I've never been *just a woman*," Idalou said, "and I don't intend to start now."

But even as she left Ella's store, she had to ask herself if there really was anything she could do. She didn't know where Carl and Mara's special tree might be. They had had the run of the countryside growing up. The tree could be anywhere, but she believed it was somewhere along the creek that ran through their ranch. Because it was the only source of water year-around, it had the thickest cottonwood groves. On a hot summer day in central Texas, dense shade was a prized commodity.

"You think Van sent that note, don't you?" Junie Mae said as she walked back to the hotel with Idalou. "You think he means to kidnap Mara and force her to marry him."

Idalou wasn't certain he'd go that far, but there didn't seem to be any other reason to lure Mara into a trap.

"I'm more concerned about Carl," Idalou said. "He was still angry at Van for starting the fights and getting him thrown in jail. Kidnapping Mara could be just enough to make him do something really stupid."

"Like kill Van?"

Idalou didn't think Carl would really try to kill Van, but she couldn't be sure that Van would be equally restrained. In the heat of the moment, no telling what any of them would do. Carl was still a teenager, Van was a spoiled and irresponsible young man, and Mara was a silly girl who had no idea of the potential for tragedy she represented.

"I don't think Carl would do anything that stupid,

but you can never tell how things will turn out when two men start fighting over a woman."

"Or the ranch she will inherit."

They reached the hotel and Idalou hurried to her room. The whole time she was changing, Junie Mae tried to convince her to wait for Will, but she wouldn't. "You can tell Will anything I could," she told Junie Mae when she was ready to leave. "There's no need for me to be here as well."

"I'm worried about you," Junie Mae said.

"There's no need to worry about me. It's Carl I have to worry about."

Half an hour later as Idalou rode up to the place where their home had stood, she was surprised to see a rider in the shadow of the trees along the creek. Thinking it was Carl, she felt her heart leap, but the outline was too big. The thought had barely crossed her mind that it could be Will before she eliminated that idea, too. Will was tall and broad-shouldered, but he was also quite slim. This man was much too stocky. It wasn't Van for the same reason it wasn't Carl, Jordan was still in jail, and she really didn't know what Frank Sonnenberg's outline looked like.

"A nice lady like you shouldn't be wandering around by herself."

The voice was vaguely familiar, but she couldn't place it. Still, she didn't like the tone. There was a menacing quality as well as a sense that the man was pleased with himself. She tried to see who he was, but he remained in the shadows and the sun was directly in her eyes.

"This is my property," she said. "No one has a better right to be wandering around on it."

She was about fifty feet from the man when instinct told her to pull her horse to a halt. But instinct had kicked in too late. The man's horse burst from the shadows. The moment she realized it was Newt Mandrin, she turned her horse to ride away, but he was on her. He grabbed her horse's bridle. When she struck out at him, he lifted her out of the saddle. She struggled against him, disgusted at his touch, but he was too strong for her.

"I won't hurt you," Newt said. "I just want you as bait for the sheriff. I have a score to settle with him."

Too late, Idalou realized she should have heeded Junie Mae's advice and waited for Will. Now her insistence upon taking care of things herself had put the man she loved in danger. It was up to her to find some way to warn Will.

Will felt like letting loose a string of curses scorching enough to set Dunmore's Main Street ablaze. It was bad enough that Mara was so gullible she'd run off at the drop of a fake note from Carl. It was just plain bad luck that Carl should decide to come into town and find the note before Will could get back. But what possible excuse did Idalou have for going after them?

"She was afraid Carl would get in a fight with Van and somebody would get hurt," Junie Mae said.

Will was certain that was exactly what would happen. No man could be expected to let a rival run off with his woman without doing something about it. But if Idalou thought Carl would be grateful that she'd come running after him, she was in for a rude surprise.

"Does she know where this special tree is?" Junie Mae had done nothing but tear up and wring her hands ever since Will got back. He knew he shouldn't feel this way, but right now he was ready to swear off helping females in distress. Look at the mess it had gotten him into.

"She said it had to be one of the trees along the creek."

"Hell, that creek is ten miles long." Will opened his desk and took out his holster. Junie Mae's eyes grew wide when she saw the gun.

"She said she thought it was a really big grove of cottonwoods a couple of miles from their ranch house." Junie Mae didn't take her eyes off the gun as Will filled the chambers with bullets.

"Let's hope she's right." Will buckled his holster on and tied it down. "I won't have a chance of stopping anything if I have to spend half the afternoon searching for the right damned tree."

He walked over to the rifle rack on the wall and took down his rifle. Junie Mae drew back when he turned around.

"Are you going to shoot somebody?" she asked.

"I hope not." If this was just a matter of Van luring Mara out of the hotel so he could talk her into marrying him, Will thought he could avoid any serious trouble. If, as he believed, Frank Sonnenberg was behind this, then he needed to be ready for anything. A man who blew up dams wasn't likely to stop at much.

"Are you sure nobody but you and Idalou knows?"

"Idalou made me promise not to tell anyone but you."

Too bad Idalou hadn't stayed to tell him herself. He didn't think she'd do anything foolish, but if anybody did anything to hurt Carl, all bets were off. Emmett sauntered into the office, but he stopped when he saw Will checking his rifle.

"I need you to stay here until I get back," Will said. "Junie Mae will fill you in on what's happened. I don't want Jordan to know, because his daughter's involved, but alert Lloyd Severns and Andy Davis. Tell them to take Tatum and go out to Sonnenberg's place and wait for me there."

"Is Frank in some kind of trouble?" Emmett asked.

"I won't know until I get there. You," he said, turning to Junie Mae, "are to go back to the hotel and rest. You look worn out."

"I'm worried about Idalou."

"You let me worry about that now."

Idalou had racked her brain for the last hour trying to figure out how she could get away or how she could warn Will, but she had not come up with a single feasible idea. Newt hadn't hurt her, but he'd tied her to one of the cottonwood trees in a standing position. It was incredibly uncomfortable.

"I want to make it easy for the sheriff to see you," he'd said.

"Why? What have you got against him?"

"Lots of things." Newt settled back in the dappled shade of a willow. "You might as well relax. He won't be done with that cut fence for a while."

"You cut that fence?"

Newt chuckled. "Yeah. I ran off Alex Bowen's herd, too."

"Why?"

"Because I hate that son of a bitch!" Newt exploded. "I was hoping to get a shot at him."

"Shooting him in the back won't prove you're faster than he is," Idalou said. "I heard about what happened in the jail," she said when Newt's expression turned ugly. "You'll never get your reputation back by ambushing him. The next sheriff will just hunt you down and hang you."

"Emmett and that stupid girl lied," Newt shouted. "I was faster that day, but they just wanted to get in good with that fancy sheriff."

It hadn't taken Idalou long to figure out that Newt intended to kill Will. She had decided to play on Newt's pride in the hope of forcing him to face Will, man to man. She didn't know if Will was faster—she prayed he was—but no man was faster than a bullet fired from ambush. "Well, everybody believes them."

"They'll believe me when they see his dead body."

"They'll just think you drew first or shot him from ambush. You can be sure I'll tell them if you do." Newt glared at her with barely contained fury. She wondered if he was trying to decide whether he'd kill her or simply *how* he'd do it. "You'll need a witness," she said. "Somebody people will believe."

"It won't matter. I'll know."

She forced herself to laugh. "A reputation is worse than worthless if nobody believes it. People will laugh behind your back."

"I'll kill anybody who laughs at me."

"That still won't prove you're faster than the sheriff."

Newt got up and stomped off. Idalou's body sagged against the ropes. She didn't know what was going through his hate-filled mind, but his ego was so big it practically choked him. She just hoped it would force him to face Will in a fair fight.

But Will wouldn't have had to face Newt if she'd waited until he got back. Newt's plan had been based on knowing she wouldn't wait for help. The note to Mara was part of Sonnenberg's scheme to force her to marry Van. Newt had simply added on his plan to kidnap her so he could kill Will.

If anything happened to him, it would be her fault.

She refused to let herself believe that after having waited so long to fall in love with Will, she would lose him now. She was still trying to come up with a plan when Newt returned.

"You'll tell them," he announced.

"Tell them what?"

"That I'm faster than the sheriff, that you saw me kill him in a fair fight."

She breathed a sigh of relief, but it was only temporary. Was Will really faster than Newt? Would Newt really stick with a fair fight? What would she do if he didn't?

"I won't lie," she said. "If you try to cheat, I'll make sure everyone knows."

"I could kill you, too." Newt's face was a mask of hatred.

"You do, and every man within a hundred miles will be on your trail. No Texan will stand for killing a woman."

Newt dropped into the shade of a cottonwood.

"You blew up my dam, didn't you?" Idalou asked. "I know you ran off our cows. Did Frank Sonnenberg pay you to try to drive us off?"

Newt didn't answer, just stared down the trail as if he was waiting for Will.

"I'll bet you were the one to hide our bull in the canyon, too. What else did Frank tell you to do?"

"He didn't tell me to do nothing!" Newt exploded. "I thought of all that myself."

Idalou didn't believe him, but decided not to say that just yet. "It didn't work. We found the bull and we're still here."

"If Frank's stupid son hadn't been trying to impress you, you wouldn't be."

"What are you talking about?"

"After Van knocked up that Winslow girl, Frank didn't trust that boy to do anything right." Newt laughed. "I had to pull him off the kid, or he might have beaten him to death."

Idalou had never guessed that Frank would beat

his own son. Maybe that explained why Van was so mean. "What did Van do wrong?"

"What did he do right?" Newt said. "He helped the sheriff find the cows I ran off. He told Carl where to look for the bull."

"How did he know all that?"

"Frank used to make him ride with me. He knew about the canyon because I used it once before. I told Frank he ought to tell the boy what was going on so he wouldn't mess up anything, but Frank likes to keep everything to himself. If he'd done like I told him, there wouldn't have been any need for this stupid kidnapping." Newt suddenly grinned. "But it did give me the chance to get even with the sheriff."

They'd all played right into Frank Sonnenberg's hands, but she couldn't prove it. She couldn't prove Newt had done anything, either. Though people in Dunmore would believe anything of Newt, they wouldn't believe that Frank Sonnenberg could be so cunning and so cruel. But none of that mattered now. The important thing was getting everybody out of this alive. She just didn't see how it could be done.

When Will saw Idalou tied to the cottonwood tree, he knew they were both in big trouble. He knew immediately that Newt Mandrin figured in this somewhere, that kidnapping Idalou wasn't part of Frank Sonnenberg's plan. Newt was out for revenge, and he planned to use Idalou to get it. Hoping they hadn't seen him approach around the bend in the creek, Will pulled his horse off the trail to give himself time to think.

It looked like Newt had set him up for a confrontation using Idalou as bait to draw him into the trap. But what kind of trap? He was certain Newt planned to kill him. He'd taken away Newt's reputation as a fighter and a fast draw, which was pretty much saying he'd destroyed Newt. The only way to get his reputation back would be to beat Will in a fistfight or a gunfight. Knowing Newt, his choice would be a gunfight.

Just killing Will wouldn't be enough. He had to do it in a way that would prove he was faster with a gun. Did Newt plan to get him into a fistfight, hopefully hurt him, then force him into a gunfight? Will reached the conclusion that only a fair fight with Idalou as witness would achieve Newt's purpose. But was Newt intelligent enough to see that?

What about Idalou? Did she know what Newt was planning? Did he mean to hurt her? Even Newt had to know that harming a woman was practically a death sentence in Texas. No, this was all about revenge. Will had to make a choice: Should he ride straight ahead or should he circle around and try to come up behind Newt? Finally decided on his course of action, Will rode back onto the trail.

Chapter Twenty-three

The sun was going down, lengthening and deepening the shadows among the trees when Idalou heard the sounds of an approaching rider. Her body tensed, fearful it might be Will, fearful it wasn't. When the riderless horse appeared around the bend in the creek, her fear turned to confusion.

"Whose horse is that?" Newt had retreated to the shadows when he heard the horse approach. Seeing it was riderless, he was confused and angry.

"I'm not sure," Idalou replied.

"I think it's the sheriff's," Newt said. "Nobody else around here has a horse that good." Newt peered into the shadows of the trees that lined the creek. "Where is he?"

Idalou didn't answer because she had no answer to give. She noticed that Will's rifle wasn't in its scabbard.

"It's a trick to fetch me out of my hiding place so he can kill me," Newt said.

"The sheriff would never ambush anybody." Idalou was shocked to hear herself sounding like a woman in love. She was trying to embarrass Newt into a fair fight, not give him something to hold over Will. "He's so good he doesn't have to."

"Then why isn't he on his horse?"

"I guess he figured if you were planning to face him fair and square, you wouldn't be hiding in the shadows. You'd be out in the open, waiting for him to come to you."

"Sheriff, are you out there?" Newt shouted.

Silence.

"I'm not afraid of you."

"Then prove it," Idalou said. "Step out of the shadows."

Newt glared at her but didn't move.

"What do you want?" Will's voice was so close it startled both Newt and Idalou.

"We got a score to settle," Newt said.

"That score doesn't involve Idalou. Let her go."

"No."

A bullet smashed into the cottonwood trunk only inches from Newt's head.

"I could have killed you," Will called. "Next time I will."

Newt's eyes searched the tangle of bushes, vines, and tree trunks for Will's hiding place. Idalou couldn't find it either. Newt hesitated, then came over to Idalou and slowly untied her.

"Saddle her horse and help her mount up," Will said. "I want her well away from here so she'll be safe."

"She's my witness," Newt called back. "Nobody's going to believe I killed you in a fair fight if nobody sees it."

"I'm not leaving," Idalou called to Will. "If Newt doesn't fight fair, I intend to tell everybody in Dunmore the kind of coward he is."

"I'm not a coward!" Newt shouted.

"Then saddle Idalou's horse and let her ride out."

Idalou waited while Newt caught her horse and saddled it. She let him help her into the saddle, rode out into the sun, then turned around when she was about twenty-five yards from the creek. "I'm not leaving," she said, her eyes still searching for Will. "I'm going to make sure this is a fair fight."

"How are you going to do that?" Will asked.

Idalou's body shook with fear, but she was determined to keep her voice clear and steady. She had established a tenuous influence over Newt only because of his conceit and need to be acknowledged as the best. It was her fault that Will was in danger. She had to do everything she could to make sure he had a fair chance.

"I want both of you to step out where I can see you. No rifles, and keep your hands where I can see them," she said.

Idalou held her breath. A moment later Will stepped out from a tangle of grapevines. She nearly sobbed with relief but managed to remain calm. "I'm waiting for you, Newt."

"Can you see the sheriff?"

"Yes. Step out where I can see you."

Newt stepped just far enough clear of the trees for her to be certain he didn't have a gun in his hand. Idalou had decided that this meeting was inevitable. Acting on a decision she'd already made, Idalou rode forward.

"What are you doing?" Will's voice was sharp with worry.

"I'm going to stand in between you until you're in position. Once you're in position, I'll back away and give the signal. I'll brand anyone who draws before my signal a yellow-bellied coward."

"Move back," Will said.

She looked hard at Will. "This is the only way I can make certain no one draws until both of you are ready." She hoped he understood that she loved him, that she was sorry she'd gotten him into this mess, and that this was the only way she could figure out to help him.

"What about it, Sheriff?" Newt yelled.

"Okay," Will said.

Idalou's body tensed. "We're going to walk to the trail. I'll keep my horse between you until both of you are standing with your hands well away from your guns. When I'm satisfied you're both ready, I'll back up." Idalou's throat was so dry she had to swallow a couple of times before she could finish. "I'll count to three slowly. When I say draw . . ." She let the sentence die away. Both men knew what to do.

Keeping their eyes on Idalou and their hands out from their sides, both men sidestepped until they reached the trail. They stood perfectly still . . . waiting. Idalou knew what she had to do next, but she couldn't make her muscles move. Will was safe as long as she was between them.

"Move back," Will said to Idalou. "We're both ready."

Idalou had to force herself to give her horse the signal to back up. Her eyes went from one man to the other, to Will for fear of what might happen to him, then over to Newt for fear of what he might do.

"Back farther," Will said when Idalou stopped about a dozen feet from the trail. "Keep going," he said until she was ten yards back.

"You're wasting time," Newt said. "Your woman can't save you now."

"You can start your countdown," Will said to Idalou. "We're both ready."

Will stood still and calm, no emotion on his face. Fifty feet away, Newt was nearly dancing with anticipation.

"One."

The word was swallowed by the vastness of the space around them. It disappeared, leaving no trace, only the feeling that something really terrible was a little closer.

"Two."

Idalou didn't know why the thought occurred to her, but today was as sunny and warm, as calm and idyllic, as the day the dam broke. It seemed that Mother Nature had turned her eye away from the ugliness about to happen. Idalou wished she could do the same, but she watched the two men with near-hypnotic intensity.

"Three."

Idalou didn't know how men could move so fast. Almost before the word had left her lips, two guns were out and firing. She stared at Will, petrified of seeing him sink to the ground, blood seeping from a mortal wound.

For a moment neither man moved. Then Newt's knees buckled and he leaned to the left.

"I was faster," he said, staring at Will in shock.

"You weren't as accurate," Will answered. "You have to make sure the first shot counts."

"But I was faster," Newt repeated.

He looked down at the small hole through his vest pocket, the pocket over his heart. He sank to his knees and tumbled softly to the ground.

Carl was waiting for them when they rode into town. After Idalou finished telling her brother what Newt had tried to do, Carl went over to Will. He looked at the body of Newt Mandrin draped across his horse.

"We were stupid, weren't we?"

"You played right into their hands." Will studied Carl, paying close attention to the many signs that he'd been in a fight. "How did things go with Van?"

"It was pretty touch-and-go until Mara got tired of waiting and decided to take a hand." Carl grinned, then grimaced in pain. "Got to remember not to smile until this lip returns to only three times its normal size."

"Where is Van?"

"Emmett put him in one of the cells. I thought he'd put up a fuss, but he walked right in. Said it was better than what his father would do to him."

"Where is Mara?"

"Talking to her father in the other cell. She promised she'd tell him she was never going to marry Van." He grinned and winced again. "I figure after she hit Van over the head with a full coffeepot and kicked him in the ribs, Van will refuse to marry her no matter what either of their fathers says."

"What about you?"

Carl looked at his feet. "I don't know. I think Mara needs some time to grow up. Besides, I don't know what I'm going to do with the ranch now that you're going to marry Idalou. How about giving me a job on that new ranch of yours?"

"You thinking about leaving Dunmore?"

Carl looked up. "Only for a short while. What about you?"

Will looked to where Idalou stood talking to Junie Mae, who'd come running out of the hotel as soon as they rode into town. People had begun to come out of stores, offices, homes. Soon the street would be crowded with people wanting to know what had happened. "I'm taking Idalou and heading back to the Broken Circle, where she'll be safe. I, on the other hand, will be in mortal danger." He felt a contented smile bloom on his face. "She's promised to protect me."

"What about Van's father?"

"Newt told Idalou how Frank planned the whole thing, even trying to frame Jordan." He unpinned the sheriff's badge from his shirt. "I'm going to let Lloyd and Andy deal with him."

Epilogue

Idalou had never seen so many people in one house in all her life. No matter where she turned, there were more adults waiting to greet her, and an endless succession of children anxious to find out why their Uncle Will had been gone so long and what he was going to do with that bull.

"Don't let my family overwhelm you," said a young woman who'd introduced herself as Eden. "They just can't believe that someone finally managed to put a lasso around Will."

"Your family is so large and so *active*," Idalou said. "How do you keep your sanity?"

"I was born into this," Eden said, laughing. "I don't know anything else."

Idalou's parents had been a quiet pair, but the house had been nearly silent during the years since their death. Eden laughed again. "Leave it to Will to come home with two women. My family has always taken in orphans, but this is the first time we've taken in a child who hasn't even been born yet."

Their gazes went to where Isabelle was making sure Junie Mae was comfortable.

"It was smart of Will to find somebody for Mom to focus her energy on," Eden said. "She's not happy about Will leaving, but having a baby to prepare for has softened the blow." Eden giggled. "But not as much as your engagement."

"She's not telling you any incriminating stories about my misspent youth, is she?" Will had walked up behind Idalou and began nuzzling her ear.

"Just that you made blatant use of Junie Mae and me to blunt the family's displeasure at your moving out."

"I warned you I was underhanded." Will nuzzled her other ear.

"So you did." Idalou tilted her head to give him better access.

"If you're going to carry on like that, you'd better go outside before one of the children wants to know why you're biting Idalou's ear." Eden grinned. "If you're lucky, I can keep them away for about fifteen minutes. Don't waste any time."

"It's going to take me a little while to get used to your family," Idalou said once they had settled into a love seat Jake had built in a stand of maples.

"None of us are used to us. We all threaten to move away at least once a year."

Idalou pulled Will's arm around her and settled back into his embrace. "They all love you. I thought your brother was going to cry when you introduced me. He was so happy."

"More likely it was relief that I'm now somebody else's problem."

Idalou gave him a love tap. "Stop running yourself down. Everybody thinks you're wonderful. I do, too."

Will sat up. "If they told you that, they're boldfaced liars. If you only knew half the things they've said about me *to my face* you'd—"

Idalou put her hand over his mouth. "Why is it your family has so much trouble admitting that they love each other? Your mother is the strongest woman I've ever seen, but she doesn't hesitate to let everybody know she adores every one of you."

"She's a woman. She's supposed to—"

"Nonsense. Do you love me?"

"You know I do."

"Do you have any trouble saying it or showing it?"

Will grinned. "Not a bit."

Now it was Idalou's turn to grin. "Then you're going to practice on me until you get it right. When you get to be really good, you're going to help me teach the rest of your family."

Will kissed her on her nose. "I'm a very slow learner, but I promise to practice every day."

Idalou kissed him back. "I plan to make sure you do."

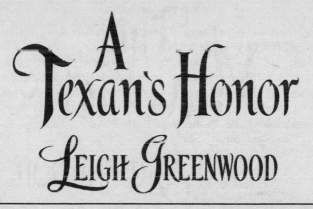

A Texan's Honor
Leigh Greenwood

Bret Nolan has never gotten used to the confines of the city. He'll always be a cowboy at heart, and his restless blood still longs for the open range. And he's on his way back to the boundless plains of Texas to escort a reluctant heiress to Boston—on his way to pick up a woman destined to be a dutiful wife. But Emily Abercrombie isn't about to just up and leave her ranch in Texas to move to an unknown city. And the more time Bret spends with the determined beauty, the more he realizes he wants to be the man in Emily's life. Now he just has to show her the true honor found in the heart of a cowboy.

The Mavericks
LEIGH GREENWOOD

Hawk and Zeke have been inseparable ever since boyhood—two loners, outsiders, as free as the wild horses they chase across the Arizona desert. So when they join up with two misplaced dancehall girls on the trail, they react about the same way as unbroken mustangs to the saddle. Kicking and bucking at every step of the way, the bachelors are gentled by soft touches and warm caresses until each finds himself riding the range with a brand-new partner.

HIRED GUN

BOBBI SMITH

Trent Marshall is a hard man. Ever since his older brother was shot down in cold blood, he's pursued justice with only his Colt .45 revolver to back him up. So when he agrees to go after a young girl abducted by Apaches, he knows he has tracking skills, years of experience, and iron determination on his side. What he doesn't anticipate is having the victim's older sister beside him every step of the way. Faith Ryan fires his blood like no other woman. As they penetrate deeper and deeper into the wilderness, Trent knows he cannot resist the primitive urge to make her his own, to take on a much more intimate role than…*Hired Gun*.

The WARRIOR TRAINER

GERRI RUSSELL

Scotia's duty is to protect the Stone of Destiny—the key to Scotland's salvation, and the reason she and the women who guarded the Stone before her had become the best warriors in the world. Yet those women had never met a man like Ian MacKinnon.

He's journeyed to her castle to learn her legendary skills so he can exact vengeance against the English. His viciousness on the battlefield stands in stark contrast to his tenderness in the bedroom. But he will soon move on, leaving Scotia to face a conflict for which she has no training: her duty to the Stone versus her desire to follow her heart.

Cornered Tigress

JADE LEE

When the white man arrives, the storm clouds make him appear an ugly baboon growling at the rain. But Little Pearl's missing master owes him money, and Little Pearl owes the Tans. They had saved her from abject poverty and disgrace, set her feet on the Taoist path. And so, barbarian or not, Captain Jonas Storm is welcome. In the alien depths of his eyes, Little Pearl sees the impossible promise of paradise. Even with the shadows growing in the Empire, Heaven is within reach—and this barbarian could take her there.
